MERCILESS

HARROW CREEK HAWKS
BOOK 1

TRACY LORRAINE

Development Editing by Pinpoint Editing

Content Editing by Rebecca at Fairest Reviews Editing Services

Proofreading by Sisters Get Lit.erary

Photography - Wander Aguiar Photography

Model - Aaron G

Have faith. Everything will work out as it's meant to in the end.

AUTHOR NOTE

Dear reader,

Merciless is the first book in the Harrow Creek Hawks series. It is a dark captive why choose romance. This means our lucky lady gets to enjoy three guys and doesn't have to choose.

If you're not okay with that, or any of the warnings below, you might want to pass this one by!

Dub con, non con, rape and coerced sex (not on page, but implied from past), bullying, violence, child sexual abuse (in flashbacks), murder (on page), captivity, knife play, breath play, sociopathy, physical abuse, forced body modifications, confinement, kidnapping, mutilation, nightmares, PTSD, detainment, obsession, narcissism, verbal abuse, forced masturbation, torture, blackmail, slut shaming, scars, sibling loss, infertility, Loss of the ability to conceive via trauma.

If, like me, you're now internally screaming *give it to me*, after reading that, then let's go.

Enjoy the ride!
T xo

PROLOGUE
ALANA

Five years ago...

With my heart in my throat and my entire body trembling with fear, I stuff as much as I can into my bag.

A couple of shirts, a spare pair of pants, and some underwear. My movements are robotic and methodical. My only focus is getting out of this prison while I have the chance.

Stopping at my desk, I grab my diary, the only sentimental thing I own, and I slide it into the back of my backpack, ensuring it's tucked safely at the bottom.

Every second of my life up until this point is written inside my beloved diaries. This is just the latest in a pile of them that I've stashed somewhere safe, in the hope of them only ever being retrieved by me one day. They're an extension of me. And that isn't something I'm willing to leave behind to be read and ridiculed by those who have done their best to break me.

I refuse to give them the satisfaction of seeing me suffer

at their hands any longer and I'm certainly not letting *them* into my head.

There's nothing left for me here. Only pain. My only reason for staying here has been ripped away.

They think I'm just going to sit back and take it. But she's out there somewhere. Suffering. And I'm the only one she's got to fight for her.

Shoving my arms into my black hoodie, I cover my head with the hood, tucking my hair inside.

I want to vanish. I want to slip into the shadows and leave this hellhole of a town with my head held high, knowing that they didn't win.

They tried. They really did. But they didn't break me.

Not really.

My body might be battered; my sanity in shreds. But I'm still here, I'm still standing, and like fuck are they going to take anything else from me.

Throwing my bag onto my back, I move toward the door. Cracking it open, I listen, but the house is wrapped in silence, just like I knew it would be.

I overheard him earlier, planning his night out.

I also know exactly how it's going to go.

He's going to go to the Hawks clubhouse and get fucked up. Smack around a few of the club whores, who seem so intent on having their lives ruined by these twisted motherfuckers, before he stumbles back here looking for me. And if I'm really un-fucking-lucky, he'll bring some friends.

My stomach knots at the prospect. Acid burning within, as bile threatens to make an appearance as my injuries from the last time I was forced to endure them ache all over again.

With my grip on my backpack so tight my knuckles are white, I make my way through the only house I've ever known.

It might be in darkness, but I see it all. Every item that can be used as a weapon, every placed object that can hurt.

I barely remember any happy times here. They're few and far between.

The only good thing in the past few years was her.

But she's gone now, and all I can do is hope that she's found something better, not just different flavors of the same men who only want one thing.

I cry out as pain explodes up my shin, before clapping my hand over my mouth.

Glancing down, I find the coffee table shoved aside. Maybe I don't know this place as well as I thought I did.

But I don't stop to look; instead, I continue hobbling forward with my eyes locked on the backdoor.

A door that leads to freedom.

My salvation.

Spotting a couple of dollars abandoned on the kitchen counter, I stuff them into my pocket. It's not much, and it certainly won't get me very far. I just have to hope that my determination will make up for my lack of resources.

A sob rips from my throat the second I wrap my fingers around the handle and pull it open.

A rush of cool night air dances over my face and down my neck, making me shiver.

But it's not enough to stop me. Nothing will be.

Deep down, I knew this day would come.

I did my best to protect her, but my best isn't—and never has been—good enough.

I'm at the mercy of the men who think they can control our lives, who use us as puppets, as slaves, as whores.

But I'm done answering to my so-called master.

I'm done with all of it.

Tonight is the first night of the rest of my life.

I'm going to walk out of this house and then straight out of this town.

I have no idea what I'm going to find on the other side. This has been my home since the day I was born. My knowledge of what lies on the other side is courtesy of television and books.

The only thing I do know is that it can't be as bad as here.

Nothing and nowhere in the world can be as bad as Harrow Creek.

As I step out into the night, every inch of my body is trembling.

The thought of all of this being a trap hits me out of nowhere.

I'm hardly ever left completely alone. There's usually someone 'protecting' me.

Protecting me. What a fucking joke.

What if *he's* waiting for me outside. Testing me to see whether I'll do as I'm told and stay in the house like the perfect little lap dog he's trained me to be. Or whether I'll defy him.

Fear swirls in my stomach, bile burning up my throat. He likes playing games. They all do. I know that all too well. What if this is another?

I pause, second-guessing myself.

But in the end, I refuse to let my fears overrule my chance.

Keeping to the shadows, I creep around the side of the house.

I'm on full alert, listening. Waiting to see if there are men out here.

But there's nothing. No noises other than the wind in the trees.

I put one trembling foot in front of the other as I race

across the yard and out the gate, waiting for the inevitable. But it never comes.

With every step I take, my breathing comes a little easier and my muscles begin to relax. Only so much though, because there is still a very long way to go.

Every rumble of an engine, hoot of an owl, or snap of a twig startles me as I vanish in the cover of darkness and follow the road signs out of town. I've been walking for hours, praying that my legs would move faster, eat up more distance between me and the house I left behind.

He's going to know I've left soon.

He's going to come looking.

He can't find me. I have to make sure of that.

I don't have a phone, a map or anything useful.

I don't even have any money, save those few stolen dollars.

But it's going to work. I'm going to make it happen, even if I spend the rest of my life begging, stealing, and borrowing.

I'm stronger than the men who run this town. I can do this.

My body trembles with fear, exhaustion, and hunger, but I forge on.

The sight of the 'You're Leaving Harrow Creek' sign illuminated ahead makes my heart beat wildly and my stomach flip with excitement.

I'm going to do this. I'm going to defy all the odds and get out.

Without looking back, I emerge from the darkness and pick up speed.

Once I get to the other side of that sign, everything is going to be easier.

Everything is going to get better.

Everything is—

My steps falter when headlights ahead get brighter, lighting me up like a fucking homing beacon.

I swallow nervously, tugging my bag up higher on my shoulders, and will my legs to just keep going. I lower my head, hiding from the driver.

But this is me, and my luck just isn't that good.

The car slows, and I immediately take off running in the opposite direction and into the trees.

Darkness engulfs me once more as I stumble over thick tree roots and rocks.

The bang of a car door slamming startles me, and I pinch my lips closed before a scream of terror can rip from my throat.

Just keep running. Just keep running.

Your life isn't going to be worth living if they catch you.

White noise fills my ears as I run. My bag slows me down, especially when it gets caught on a branch, but I refuse to abandon it.

I can't.

Just when I begin to think I might have outrun the man in the car, my bag is yanked backward. I scream as an arm wraps around my waist, restraining me while a large, hot hand covers my mouth.

"Nice try, Doll," a deep, deadly voice whispers in my ear.

Ice-cold fear rushes through my veins as I fight to drag the air I need through my nose.

I was so close. So fucking close.

"You've got a lot of dangerous men out looking for you." I whimper, only vaguely relieved that the voice isn't that of my father. Or worse, his boss. "You've no idea how lucky you are that I'm the one who found you."

1

ALANA

Present...

I sit with my thighs against my chest and my arms wrapped around them, attempting to fight the cold as I stare at the wall ahead of me. It's the only thing I've done since being locked up a few hours ago.

There's nothing in this prison cell besides a hard cot, a toilet and a sink.

That's it.

The complete opposite from the home comforts I've had for the past five years, and a harsh bump back down to Earth. What I've had these past few years was a dream, a fantasy. I was stupid to allow myself to believe it could be my future. My reality.

This... This is more the kind of life I'm used to.

My bullshit life has once again been reduced to being held captive by a man.

No. This time it's not just a man.

The devil himself.

Reid Harris is a man most people will never have the misfortune of meeting in their lives.

But for anyone unlucky enough to be born in Harrow Creek, or unfortunate enough to find themselves here, then the risk of running into him, of having their life tainted by him, or his father, is strong.

And I'm one of the unlucky ones. Because not only was I born here, but I was born into a life of abuse and corruption that's so entwined with Reid and his father, Victor, that I stand no chance of escaping it.

I've tried. Fucking hell, have I tried.

But just like their pets, the Hawks keep a very tight leash on their most valuable assets. And for a reason I can't fathom, I'm one of them.

Five years ago, I nearly made it.

I was so close to freedom, I could almost taste it.

But then *he* had to drive past me. He couldn't have just ignored the order that had been put out when my father discovered I'd gone missing and continued on his way.

He had to stop. He had to chase me. He had to... *rescue* me.

To a point, he did.

My life from the moment he caught me changed significantly.

I was no longer a toy for men to play with. I was no longer scared to fall asleep at night or equally as terrified to wake up the next morning to a horrific cycle of abuse continuing. I had a home for the first time in years where there was laughter, happiness, and dare I say it... love.

But one thing never changed.

I was still at the mercy of a man. Albeit, this time, the man was kinder, softer, gentler.

It was weird.

I should have been relieved.

I mean, I was relieved.

But also, I felt like I was missing something.

Something I couldn't put my finger on, but it was there —or not—all the same.

He gave me everything I could want.

He fed me food I never knew existed. He bought me anything I wanted. He encouraged me to continue with school and helped me to graduate. He promised to keep me safe, and he made the ultimate sacrifice to ensure that happened. Something I haven't quite gotten my head around to this day. But equally, something I've been incredibly grateful for because he changed everything for me.

He gave me everything I could have possibly wanted. Everything apart from him.

He promised himself to me. He gave his life in return for keeping me safe.

Yet he never gave me his body.

And after the life I'd lived, I craved it.

I wanted his touch, his kiss. His everything.

I got the soft side of him. But I knew there was so much more to the man who allowed me to restart my life.

He was a brutal, vicious, bloodthirsty killer, just like the rest of them.

So why wouldn't he unleash that beast on me?

Am I so irrevocably broken that even a man with that much blood on his hands can't bear to touch me?

Am I that poisonous? That tainted?

A heavy sigh passes my lips as I rest my brow against my knees.

I know the answers to those questions.

I have for years.

It doesn't make them any easier to swallow, though.

My breath catches when there's a loud bang on the

other side of my door and my heart jumps into my throat, my pulse picking up speed with the thought of my captor swinging my door open and coming for me.

He might have tried scaring all my secrets out of me at first, but he's been weirdly quiet ever since. His only brand of torture so far seems to be the arctic temperature making my teeth chatter loudly.

Being here isn't a surprise, not really.

I knew what I was getting myself into the day I agreed to be Victor Harris's little bitch.

If it weren't him who got bored of me and finally put an end to my pitiful life, then it was going to be his eldest, most sinister, and twisted son.

The guy is a fucking legend on the streets of Harrow Creek.

The infamous son of their beloved Hawk leader. The heir, the future boss.

The merciless killer who stops at nothing to get exactly what he wants.

And right now, he wants intel from me.

Well... I might look like a dumb blonde who lets men do whatever they want to her, but beneath the façade, there's a lot more. And Reid Harris is about to learn that I'm not the easy target he probably has me marked as.

I've survived twenty-one years on this Earth, and every single day I've been surrounded by Hawks. Some might be more deadly and terrifying than others. But I've learned a thing or two about how they work and what they want.

And I have prided myself on being the very opposite. I don't bend to their will and follow their demands at the drop of the hat. I refuse to worship them like the kings they think they are. Unless the job calls for me to get on my knees and beg for mercy, in which case I'll make an exception for the sake of my life.

I haven't survived all this time to give up now.

If I wanted to end it all, I could have a long time ago.

Maybe I should have. After I lost Kristie, maybe I should have put myself out of my misery.

It sure would have saved a lot of pain and suffering.

But it hasn't all been bad, a little voice pipes up.

My mind takes me back to better times. To running around the backyard with my little sister. To laughter and happiness. To drinking and smoking with my husband, enjoying having a real friend for the first time in my life.

But my door never opens.

No visitor appears.

I know what he's doing.

The devil wearing nothing but his ripped muscles and a pair of dangerously low-hanging gray sweatpants and a few blood splatters is letting me sweat it out.

He wants me weak, vulnerable, and desperate.

He should know better though. I'm more than used to this.

The solitude, the loneliness, the hunger, the cold.

They're all welcome friends.

The past few years might have been a little more comfortable, but that doesn't mean I've forgotten how to survive when times get tough.

It's how I know I'm going to make it through whatever Reid Harris throws at me. Unless it's one of those knives I've already seen in his cabinet of torture devices beyond the reinforced locked door I'm stuck behind.

One of those bad boys might just take me down.

I guess if it's my time, then there really is no better way to go to hell than to be condemned by the devil himself.

A wicked smirk curls my lips.

Yeah, maybe my stay here won't be so bad.

I mean, hell, things have certainly been worse than they are right now.

I've no idea how much time passes. I've no idea if it's day or night when I open my eyes again.

The bright spotlights in the ceiling of my cell still shine down on me from above, and it's still as cold as it was before I fell asleep.

The only difference is that my stomach is growling, desperate for some food, and my need for the bathroom means I'm going to have to give the toilet in the corner a whirl.

Could be worse. It could be a bucket.

Been there before.

I do my thing and wash my hands in the tiny sink before bending down and drinking the cold water straight from the faucet.

I've no idea if it's fresh, but it's all I've got. And I have no intention of giving that asshole an easy way out by dying of dehydration before we get to have any more fun.

He's coming for me. I know he is. He's just... waiting. Biding his time.

He wants me weak and vulnerable, so I cave to his will and answer his questions.

But it won't happen.

He can hurt me, punish me, abuse me.

I won't spill my secrets.

There is only one person in this world who's ever protected me. And I will not thank them by putting their life in danger, by putting them directly in the line of enemy fire.

I owe him more than that.

Hell, I owe him everything.

Well, maybe not everything. If he'd let me go that night... that would have been everything.

I walk around the cell, dragging my fingertips over the rough gray walls, my eyes everywhere looking for... anything.

But there's nothing. I'm stuck in a gray box with no means of escape and nothing to do other than dwell on all the mistakes and bad decisions that landed me here.

I didn't want to do it.

I didn't want to be playing anyone, especially not Kane Legend, one of the Hawks best foot soldiers.

He might not believe it right now, but I actually like him.

He thinks I'm nothing more than a cheap, lying whore, mind you. Which is totally justified. But it's also not true.

We're a lot alike, the two of us.

Both Harrow Creek kids, born and raised. We've been fucked over by life, although in very different ways. But because he was born with a dick between his legs, he was invited into the Hawks, the gang that rules this town with an iron fist. Victor found a way to harness Kane's anger. Add the fact that Kane is a close friend of both Reid and his younger brother Devin, and he had a fast-track ticket to becoming Hawks' royalty.

He didn't want it though.

He's spent the past year or so trying to escape this life and his entanglement to the Hawks. Something I know all about.

But every time he gets close, he gets reeled back in at the command of Victor fucking Harris.

And over the past eighteen months, the responsibility of keeping him tied to this life has fallen on me.

Victor stupidly thought I could be the one to convince Kane to stay.

It was never going to work. Kane Legend has the promise of a better life. Hell, he could be one of the few who gets out of Harrow Creek and actually makes a life for himself. A life in the NFL, if all goes well. I may know shit about football, but he's good. Really good.

I was barely a blip on Kane's radar. He thought I was the job. He just had no idea that he was the one really being played.

All of us are nothing but puppets in this game.

A game that Victor Harris holds the rule book to.

If he says jump, everyone beneath him, even his eldest devil child, is expected to ask how high.

It's wrong. But it's the way it is. Has been for years. And what is a blonde bimbo like me supposed to do about it?

I sigh, falling back on the bed, a sense of defeat and disappointment settling over me. Resting my hands on my stomach, I twist my wedding ring around my finger as I think about the man who gave it to me.

As soon as he realizes I'm not home. He'll be searching for me.

It might have already happened.

I haven't been getting very far on the outside, but I'm going to achieve fuck all in here.

There are only two things I want in life.

I want to know the truth about my sister, to find her if that's even a possibility after all these years.

And I want to see Victor fucking Harris die. Right in front of my very own eyes, I want to see the life drain out of his.

Somehow, I'll get out of here, and somehow, I'll make both happen.

His time here is quickly running out, all I need to do is

figure out a way to ensure it doesn't come back and bite me, or my husband, in the ass, and I'll pull that fucking trigger myself.

Each minute that passes as I sit here with my arms wrapped around my middle feels like an hour. Every time the purple of my Panthers jersey catches my eye, I cringe at what I did tonight. The lies I told in order to protect the man I love, to get the justice I deserve.

I've lost all track of time, and with nothing else to do but wait, I relax and stare up at the ceiling, trying to focus on better times, instead of my tragic reality.

Eventually, though, the temptation to come and play with his new pet gets the better of Reid. The heavy lock on my door disengages, making me jump and shift into the corner as if I'm scared of him. I might try and put on a good show, but he's Reid Harris, anyone in their right mind would be a little hesitant about being the object of his attention.

I manage to pull my legs up to my chest before he throws the door open and his large, toned, and deadly body steps into the doorway.

He's not even in the room, but already, the space feels smaller.

He glares at me. Silently trying to intimidate me. But he's going to need to try harder than that.

"I knew you wouldn't be able to stay away for long," I taunt, my words and the strength behind them at odds with my body language.

But he doesn't bite. Not yet at least.

2

REID

I sit back on the couch and lift the glass to my lips, savoring the smoothness of the whiskey with my eyes locked on the screen.

I want to say that I'm watching her every move, discovering her weaknesses, figuring out what the easiest way to break her is going to be.

But seeing as all she's doing is lying on the cot staring up at the ceiling, that would be a lie.

Instead, I'm just staring at her. Wondering what she's thinking, if she's regretting everything she's done that's led her to this point. Or... is she silently celebrating.

What she did was fucking stupid. The lies she told so easily proven false.

Was it all a game to land her in here? To put her in front of me in a way she never has been before?

I know who she is.

Every motherfucker in Harrow Creek knows who she is.

Her father is one of my father's most trusted men.

And her husband...

My grip on the glass in my hand tightens as I think about the smug fucking cunt that is her husband.

The whole thing is fucked up in a way no one has been able to figure out. But then I guess most relationships are like that.

What I know of the two of them all leads me down the same path... it's a game.

Alana Murray is playing a fucking game.

It's what she does. Entitled, little Harrow Creek princess trying to wrap the big bad gangsters around her little finger.

Well, if she thinks that shit is happening under my roof then she's got another thing coming.

I've no idea what wicked schemes are floating around in her head; she's welcome to imagine whatever outcome she likes.

But there will only be one ending. And it won't be her still standing at the end.

She's chosen the wrong man to go up against this time.

I will show no mercy, and I will get her secrets. No matter how much it hurts.

The corner of my mouth twitches when I sense someone behind me.

He might try to be all stealthy in his attempt to surprise me, but he hasn't succeeded once in the ten years he's been trying. I'm not sure why he still bothers. Pigheaded stubbornness, I guess.

Unfortunately, this time, I don't get to point out the fact that I'm aware he's standing behind me. The scene playing out on the screen in front of us is too intriguing for him to stay quiet.

"You got a new pet?" JD, my roommate and best friend

asks, forgetting about his shitty stealth-like skills and marching into the room like he owns the place.

"Something like that," I mutter, tipping the glass up and swallowing the contents.

"Who is it?" he asks, as he refills my glass with the bottle in the middle of the coffee table and knocks it back without so much as a wince.

"Do you fucking mind?" I grunt.

"No, not really," he replies with a smirk before he flops down on the other end of the couch.

His eyes lift as he studies the screen a little closer.

I remain silent. He knows the current occupant of that cell as well as I do.

"Wait," he says, sitting forward as recognition hits. "Is that—"

"Yep," I confirm.

Not bothering with the glass this time, I lean forward and swipe the bottle, lifting it to my lips.

"What the fuck did she do?" he asks, resting back once more and spreading his thighs wide as he watches her.

"Tried convincing Kane she was pregnant with his kid," I say flatly. Aside from my brothers, Kane is my closest friend, most trusted Hawk. There is only one reason I can think she'd fuck with him... surely she's trying to get to me. Where the hell else did she think that lie would land her?

"The fuck?" he mutters in disbelief.

"Exactly. What fucking game is she playing?"

"Mav know?" he asks, mentioning Alana's husband and making my fists curl.

"Fuck that prick."

"I know their relationship is fucked up. But claiming to be preggers with someone else's spawn can't be good for any marriage. And a fucking brother too. That shit ain't cool, man."

"That ain't a marriage," I scoff. I've no idea what it is, but it ain't a fucking marriage.

"Nah, you see the way he looks at her, man."

"Doesn't fucking touch her though, does he?" I scoff.

Ripping his gaze from the TV, the side of my face burns with his attention.

"Just spit it out if you want to say something," I hiss.

Holding his hands up in defense, he turns back to the screen.

"So she's not pregnant?" he asks, disregarding whatever he was just thinking.

"No, she's not," I confirm.

"So why—"

"That's what I want to know."

"So go ask her."

"I did. She wasn't very forthcoming. Hence..." I gesture toward her current predicament.

"Where's Legend?"

"Gone to get his girl before this bitch ruins what they've found."

"Fucking pussy," JD mutters lightly, thinking of our loved-up friend.

Kane's been in love with Scarlet Hunter for as long as I can remember. It's a real shame he wasn't as aware of the situation and instead of grabbing it by the balls, he spent the past few years fucking everything up.

Right now, he's got a second chance, and the opportunity of a new life away from us and all this shit. Although that does rely on my father standing by his word to let him walk away. And that motherfucker is about as trustworthy as a pedophile in a kids' home.

Sitting forward, I thread my fingers through my hair.

"What you thinking?"

"Other than she's playing us? Not a lot."

"Would she though? Has she got it in her?"

I consider his question for a while.

"What if we've all significantly underestimated her?"

"You think she's some underworld mastermind?" he asks doubtfully.

I shrug. Unable to get my thoughts together in regard to all this.

"Mav is a lot of things, but he's not fucking stupid. He wouldn't have been manipulated into marrying her, especially without the benefit of her pussy."

Silence falls between us.

"He knows she's been fucking Kane, right?"

"Dunno. I don't believe it's common knowledge."

"She fucking anyone else?"

"Dunno," I repeat.

"So why the fuck are we sitting up here watching her stare at the ceiling when we could be down there getting the information out of her?" He rubs his hands together as an excited smirk appears on his lips. "Having a little fun." His brows wiggle.

"We?" I ask simply.

"Fuck, yeah. You know we're the dirty duo. We'll drag her secrets out of her one way or another."

"No," I bark, pushing to my feet before I turn and glare at my best friend. "She's mine. This is personal."

"Something you're not telling me, bro?" JD teases.

"Alana? Really?"

He chuckles. "If it involves fucking Mav over, I wouldn't put anything past you."

"I ain't going anywhere near his wife."

"Nor is he," JD quips before I storm around the couch. I think she's been waiting long enough.

It's time to turn the heat up and get the answers I need. I'd hate for her to think I'm going soft.

I glance down at myself as I move down the hallway, tracking the splatters of blood that cover my bare chest.

I'd hoped that allowing her to listen to another one of my guests begging for mercy might have given her a push to make this easy and blurt out her secrets.

But fuck. I'm glad it didn't.

I do love a challenge. And something tells me that Alana is going to push me right to the edge of my sanity.

It's been a while since someone really made me work for it.

Cracking my knuckles, I pause as I spot her purse on the dresser in the hallway, where Kane dumped it after he dragged her ass in here.

Undoing the clasp, I dig around inside until I find her cell.

I wake it up, and am unsurprised to discover seven missed calls from her husband.

"Nice try, asshole," I mutter, shoving the thing in my pocket.

If I can't hack into it later, I know a guy who can.

Pulling open the heavy door that leads to the basement, a rush of adrenaline shoots through my veins.

I love my house.

No, I fucking love my house.

I spent all my childhood gazing up at this dark, mysterious, and imposing building that looks over almost every inch of Harrow Creek.

At twelve years old, I told myself that one day I would own it. That I would restore it and bring it back to its former glory. That JD and I would move our asses in and embark on our future of ruling the town below with an iron fist, yet being fairer than my cunt of a father.

Part of that dream has come true.

I have the house. The world's most annoying and messy

roommate, and if all my work pays off, it shouldn't be too long until I get control of the town.

Victor Harris's days are numbered. And I have every intention of being the one who finally pulls the plug on his reign and his life.

And it will be a sweet as fuck day when that happens.

What I don't need is a certain blonde getting in the way and stealing my attention from where it should be.

Hunger stirs within me as I descend the stairs to my most favorite part of this house.

The basement used to be this old, cold damp wine cellar, but since I took ownership of this supposedly haunted house, it's been fully transformed.

Yes, it's still cold and damp. But while the old wine cellar entrance and stairs are still accessible from the kitchen, there is a new secret doorway and a whole new extension that only a few know exists. It's now outfitted to be one of the most secure prisons in the state. Hell, the country. No motherfucker is getting out of here unless they're personally escorted or in a body bag. So far, only the latter has happened.

The chill in the air makes my skin prickle as I hit the bottom and make my way past the securely locked doors.

Everyone who is down here, for one reason or another, deserves their place in my cells. Some more than others, but I don't like to discriminate, so they all get similar treatment.

Some even enjoy their time here. Like I said, they deserve their place, which means they deserve their punishment. They fucking well know it too.

It's late, long past midnight. Some are probably sleeping. If I wasn't so enthralled with watching Alana upstairs, I might have checked on my other guests. But right now, they don't interest me. It's not like they're going anywhere. They'll still be waiting when I get bored of playing with my new, little pet.

The sound of the locks disengaging vibrates through the concrete floor beneath me and the excitement that flutters inside me only intensifies.

I could look through the peepholes and into all of these rooms before I enter. But where's the fun in that?

Knowing what I'm about to walk into is fucking boring. Anyone who knows me knows I like to be kept on my toes. I fucking love walking into unknown situations. It's one of the things that really gets my blood pumping.

Although, this time, I have a pretty good idea about what I'm going to find because I spent an embarrassing amount of time upstairs watching her do absolutely nothing. She might have taken a few minutes to check the place out but that's all the excitement I got.

Oh, that and watching her pee. Not exactly the things a captor's dreams are made of. Or maybe it is. Who the fuck am I to judge?

But throwing the door open, I find things are improving slightly.

While her face might remain as impassive as it was when I questioned her earlier, her body tells a slightly different story.

She's backed into the corner with her arms wrapped around her legs, as if she's trying to hold herself together.

So which is it?

Is she the confident hardass she tried to convince me of earlier by refusing to give me anything? Or is she the weak, terrified little woman her newly-taken position would make me believe?

If my thoughts upstairs about her reasons for being here are right, then I'd go with the former.

The rest is all an act.

Although, if I find out that I'm right and she and Mav are playing some sick and twisted game to try and bring me down, then she has every right to be fucking terrified.

Him too.

I've been waiting for fucking years to have it out with him.

He's been a thorn in my side since I was old enough to know his name.

He might be older, but he's never going to have the power I have. And he fucking hates it.

He wants my position. My gang.

It's never going to fucking happen, though.

He can send his little bitch in to do his dirty work all he likes. Neither of them will ever get what they want from me.

Lifting her chin, she lets her eyes drop down my body, blatantly checking me out.

"I knew you wouldn't be able to stay away for long," she taunts.

"Is that why you're sitting there shamelessly showing me your panties?" I ask, without breaking our eye contact, to look at the small strip of lace that covers her cunt.

She really needs to reconsider if she thinks she's going to be able to manipulate me that easily.

I couldn't give a fuck if she's got a pussy or a dick. She fucked with one of my closest friends.

As far as I'm concerned, she's the enemy right now, and only one of us holds the power.

"Whoops," she whispers innocently as she releases her legs and presses her feet to the floor.

The air crackles as she saunters over. Her sweet, floral perfume fills my nose, and I swear it goes straight to my dick.

Holding my eyes, she moves closer until the heat of her body hits my chest.

Her head tilts to the side before she asks, "Was there something you wanted, Big Man?"

"Something I wanted?" I reply dryly. "I'm not the one locked up in a basement with no promise of ever seeing the light of day again, Pet."

"That's where we disagree."

I startle when her knuckles brush the skin beneath my belly button.

The fucking audacity of this bitch.

My fists curl with my need to physically stop her from touching me. But my need to appear unaffected by her touch is stronger.

"I can't figure out if you're really this stupid or just playing a very clever game."

Her lips twitch at my statement.

"I guess that's something you'll need to figure out."

"Seems like I have a whole lot of things to get out of you."

Her smirk grows.

"Looks like we might have some fun ahead of us, Big Man."

Faster than I can comprehend, her hand drops, and she squeezes me through the soft fabric of my sweats.

Unlucky for her, though, my self-restraint is strong and my body reveals nothing.

She can try as hard as she likes. Only one of us will crack here.

"You know, all it's going to take is the truth."

"I'm more than aware of what you want from me. Doesn't mean I'm willing to give anything up, though."

"Fair enough," I mutter, watching as she sits back on the bed, looking entirely too comfortable for my liking.

"This place is pretty sweet you've got down here," she says, completely unfazed by the whole situation.

"The fact you know it exists doesn't put you in a very good position. I've killed for less."

"Maybe so. You won't kill me, though," she says confidently.

"Is that right?"

She stares down at her nails as if this conversation is boring the shit out of her.

"It is. Before long, I'll be walking back up those stairs into the loving arms of my husband."

I can't help but snort.

"Maybe I'll go with stupid after all. He won't be coming for you. Not when he finds out what you've been doing."

"You're assuming he doesn't know." She finally looks up after picking at a bit of skin on her finger.

"I'm happy to test the theory and find out. It hasn't just been Kane you've been fucking, has it?"

She shrugs. Fucking shrugs.

I knew this woman was going to be a royal pain in my ass. But her complete lack of concern or fear is throwing me off balance.

I've had men twice my size cowering. Yet, this slim, five-foot-five, blonde-haired woman apparently couldn't care less that I've tortured and killed more men than the number of years I've lived.

Who the fuck is she?

"Why Kane, Alana? I got it last year. He was working and you needed... a real man to help you out every now and then. But now? He's out. He's got a new life. Why the fuck are you still going after him?"

Another fucking shrug. That move makes my eye twitch.

"He's a good fuck. Why wouldn't I?"

"No wonder your own husband refuses to go anywhere near you. You really are nothing but a whore."

"Judge me all you like," she says, cutting me a look that I'm sure would affect anyone else. "But you don't know me. You only see what I want you to see."

3

ALANA

His heated stare burns into the side of my face as I force myself to keep my eyes down. I fear that if he were to look into them right now, he'd see the pain his words have caused instead of my usual bright blue eyes.

I don't want him to think he's affecting me in any way.

Everyone else might cower and worship the ground he walks on. But I won't be falling in line.

That's the thing when you no longer care. It makes everything so much easier.

He can hurt me, punish me, torture me.

What's it really going to achieve?

He isn't the one I want to hurt, but if I have to suffer his wrath to get what I want, the justice I deserve after years of torment and abuse, then so be it.

"I don't judge, Pet. I base my opinions on cold, hard facts. Now, if you want to point one out that proves my opinion of you wrong, feel free."

I keep my mouth closed.

"Exactly as I thought."

Finally, he takes a step forward and moves into the cell. I swear he replaces the air as he does it. His manly scent is almost overwhelming as he comes to stand beside me, looming over the low cot and hoping to intimidate me.

"Here's how this is going to go."

At his words, and his assumption that I'm going to fall in line, I stare blankly up at him. Cataloguing his features. His rich chocolate eyes that hold the promise of more pain than I can endure. The fullness of his lips and the faint old scar on the underside of his jaw that's mostly hidden by two-day-old scruff.

"I'm going to ask you a series of questions, and you're going to answer them honestly."

I raise a brow at him in question.

"I already know your medical records, Alana."

My entire body tenses at his confession.

I knew he knew something. That much was obvious when he took that phone call down here earlier.

I expected him to launch into whatever he'd learned from the person on the other end of the line. But he didn't say a word. All he did was tease me with that fucking switchblade that glinted temptingly under the harsh electric lights above our heads.

Naïvely, I assumed that maybe the phone call had nothing to do with me. After all, I'm not the only person he has to deal with. As second-in-command of the Hawks and Victor's personal torturing machine, there have to be plenty of others who probably deserve a spot in that chair in the middle of his torture chamber.

But clearly, I was right to be suspicious.

"I know you're not pregnant. I know you can't get pregnant." The words hit me right in the chest. But I fight it, continuing to hold his eyes, desperately keeping a tight hold on my well-constructed walls.

Do not let him see his words touch any broken part of you.

"Ellis find all that out, did he?" I ask, mentioning one of his younger brothers. The computer geek to be more specific.

From what I've heard, if you need intel on someone, then Ellis can get it.

Honestly, I expected them to do exactly this.

Self-destruction at its finest.

I'm sure a psychologist would have a fucking wet dream with all my lifetime trauma shit.

"Where I get my intel from isn't a concern of yours. All that matters is whether it's correct. And I can see in your eyes that this is."

"Fuck you," I hiss, hating that he's pressing on one of my few weak points.

"Oh, that hurts, doesn't it, Pet?"

He kneels down, pressing his knee to the hard surface of my bed, and leans in close.

Too fucking close.

I want to lean back to escape him, but I refuse to show any kind of weakness.

But as the heat of his body rushes across my skin, I can't help the urge to do the opposite and move closer.

And it only gets stronger when I suck in a breath. It's laced with his scent. It makes my mouth water. It's entirely too tempting, seeing as the man kneeling before me is nothing but a monster.

"Keep your secrets," he drawls, his warm breath rushing over my skin, making goose bumps erupt. "Lock them up as tight as you can, if you wish. But don't think they'll stay that way forever.

"I have ways of making people talk. Ways that would keep you up at night. Ways that always produce results."

"There's always one exception to the rule."

"That there is. But I can assure you, you're not going to be it. I've no idea what's going on here, but Kane is one of my closest, most loyal men. You go up against him, you go up against all of us. And I'm sure I don't need to tell you that you don't want the wrath of the Harris brothers. One of us is bad. But all of us. That's the thing nightmares are made of right there, Pet."

"Do what you want. What I've done and the reasons why are none of your business."

His eyes darken dangerously.

"Oh, Pet. That's where you are so very wrong. Right now, you are locked up in the basement of my house, with every chance you'll never see above those stairs again. Everything about this situation is my motherfucking business.

"Didn't you get the memo? I own this town. Every single inch of land and every single cunt that walks on it.

"You. Your pathetic excuse for a husband. Anyone else you might be working with. All of you belong to me."

"Victor," I spit. "We all belong to Victor. You're nothing. Just his little puppet who runs around doing his dirty work. The only person anyone answers to in this town is him."

It's bullshit. Everyone is fucking terrified of Reid Harris, but equally, they're all desperate to see him take over and rule our town better than his corrupt old man ever has.

It might be hard to believe while I'm locked up in his basement, but Reid has a hell of a lot more morals than his father.

That asshole will do anything, sell anything, and kill anyone if it makes him a few bucks.

Reid isn't about the money or the fame.

There's more to him than that. Something that Mav refuses to see or accept. But it's something I haven't been able to deny after spending so much time with Kane over the past eighteen months.

Reid wasn't wrong earlier when he said Kane and him are tight. I learned more about my husband's mortal enemy in just a few dates than I ever thought I would.

I hoped that by accepting the job Victor lined up for me that I might be able to get some solid evidence behind Mav's hatred of Reid. But I never did.

All I managed to do was add even more reasons to the already very long list of reasons as to why I loathe Victor Harris.

"Think what you like, Pet." Pushing from my cot, he stands to his full height again, gazing down with an unreadable expression on his face. "Is there anything you need?" he asks, confusing the shit out of me.

"Uh... yeah, I'm starv—"

I slam my lips shut the second his laughter rings out around the room.

"Right," I mutter. "And here I was thinking you had a humane bone in your body. Silly me."

"Don't worry, I won't let you starve. I need you alive for all the fun things I have planned."

Before I get a chance to argue, he's gone. The ominous slam of the heavy door echoes through the air, leaving me alone once again.

Sliding down the bed, I wrap my arms around myself once more and close my eyes.

Everything Reid just warned me about is true.

He's going to use every tool at his disposal—literally—to force my secrets from my lips.

I knew that going into this job, and I sure as shit know it now.

I can't help but wonder if deep down, really, really deep down, the broken and scared little girl wants me to confess. Wants me to finally spill all the atrocities of her past, of the abuse, the pain, the suffering she endured long before she was old enough to understand it.

Emotion burns up the back of my throat, making my nose itch and my eyes water as I think of that little girl.

Looking back now, it's hard to believe we're the same person. Back then, I was so naïve, so innocent. It didn't take long for it all to shatter to pieces.

After Mom left, all I wanted to do was look after my little sister. Protect her in a way only a big sister can. I just had no idea what I'd have to endure to try and keep that innocent glint in her eyes and a smile on her lips.

I'd have gladly continued too if she hadn't been ripped away from me. I'd do anything to protect her, just like I'd do anything to have her back.

Just an hour. A day. Anything to get the chance to tell her how much I love her. To let her know that I never forgot her. Never stopped fighting for her.

Reaching up, I grab the length of my hair and begin braiding the end like she used to. It only makes the lump clogging my throat grow until I can barely suck in a breath.

No sounds leave my lips as my tears finally slip from the corners of my eyes, running down my temples and soaking into my hair.

Silently, I cry for everything I've lost. For everything I've been forced to walk away from. For the man who cared enough to swear his life to protect me but doesn't care enough to give all of himself to me.

I lie there until my hair is soaked with tears and my eyes are sore. I hate myself for it. I hate being so weak and so easily broken down by my past.

What I need to do right now is focus. I need to focus on

the job at hand and figure out a way to get out of here. If that's even a possibility.

I mean, I'm still alive, so there's a chance, right?

I could already be dead and thrown into Reid's furnace, or chopped up into tiny pieces and fed to a pen full of hungry pigs. Or whatever other creative ways he has to dispose of a body unnoticed. I bet he's got a whole load of tricks up his sleeves. His body count is large enough to suggest he can be creative when he wants to be.

I guess it helps that the majority of people who fall victim to his deadly ways are scumbags who deserve it. Something I do not have in common with them. I might be broken, tarnished, and poisoned by my past. But I am not a bad person.

Despite what Kane, Letty, Reid, and anyone else might think. Deep down, I'm just a broken little girl desperate for freedom, for love, and for acceptance. Not because anyone feels sorry for me.

At some point, I cry myself to sleep, but my reality never leaves. Not really. Instead of drifting off into a peaceful slumber, I fall headfirst into one of my darkest, most terrifying nightmares. I wake numerous times over the next few hours screaming in fear, my body dripping in a cold sweat.

But no one comes. Not that I expected them to.

You did this to yourself, you stupid bitch.

Time to deal with the consequences.

4

MAVERICK

"Hi, you've reached Alana. I'm too busy to talk to you right now. Leave a message, and if you're lucky, I might call you back."

"ARGH," I roar, barely controlling my need to launch my cell across the room. "Where the fuck are you?"

Concern for my wife rushes through my veins.

Sure, it's not the first time she's been late coming home. She's nothing if not a loose cannon at the best of times. But it's almost sunrise and she is not here.

My heart pounds as I pace back and forth through our living room.

Our home isn't much. A cabin in the woods on the edge of Harrow Creek. I bought it not long after she came into my life to give her some peace, and most importantly, distance.

I've known Alana all my life. Our fathers have always been good friends, which meant that as kids, we spent time together. I preferred her to the others. To Reid Harris and his brothers, who arrogantly spent their time ensuring I was aware that in terms of Harrow Creek royalty, they'd always be above me.

I didn't need the fucking reminder. I knew the pecking order. But I also knew whose orders I needed to follow, and it wasn't theirs.

All my life, I've been looked down on by them, despite the fact I'm older than them and experienced everything first.

Everything about life as a Hawk.

I'm pretty sure I was born with a hawk inked onto my back. From as early as I can remember, it was all my father talked about. He was so proud to have had a son who could follow in his footsteps. And then when Reid arrived a few years later, Dad and Victor got this great idea in their heads that we could be the next generation of them. Working side by side to continue their twisted legacy.

Just one problem though. Neither of us can stand the other.

He's an entitled, twisted douchebag. And fuck knows what he thinks of me. It ain't good, whatever it is. We've spent all our lives butting heads and throwing punches and barbed insults at each other.

But Alana. The girl with the beautiful light blue eyes and a soft smile that can light up a room... I was enthralled with her from a very young age.

While I felt like I was stuck in the dark, having every single one of my puppet strings pulled by Dad and Victor, she was this free spirit who was yet to be tainted by the world.

If only I knew the truth...

But it just goes to show that you never know what's going on behind closed doors. And as a child, and then a young adult, I had no fucking clue what Alana's life was really like.

The night her father put the call out that she'd run away, I was in the middle of a job. But the fear of Victor's wrath wasn't enough to stop me from doing an about-turn and abandoning it. Fuck the stupid Hawk who decided to make use of the goods he was selling. If I was lucky, he'd OD on the shit. And if not, then he'd still be around tomorrow. Someone who's stealing the product and getting away with it would be an idiot to give it up.

And thank fuck I did because no sooner had I driven back into Harrow Creek did I find a slim figure trying to escape.

I couldn't believe my luck. I was terrified that her father, or worse, Victor, would have been the one to pick her up.

By the time I was an adult, the façade about her life had been more than shattered.

She wasn't a girl who caught my attention more than she should, seeing as she was a kid and I was a man. She was a girl who was suffering.

I was also no longer naïve to the kinds of activities my father and his friends embarked on.

What they did. How they treated women, young women, turned my stomach. And I was determined to somehow do something about it. I had no idea how, but the second I saw her spot me and run, I knew it needed to start with her.

I didn't know the depth of her secrets, her abuse, but I knew she needed me. And I had every intention, for once, to be the hero.

Even if she didn't want me to be.

Lifting my cell again, I wake it up and hit call.

Maybe this time will be the time she answers.

But just like all the others, it goes to voicemail.

Combing my fingers through my hair, I stare out at the

beginning of the sunrise, trying to come up with where she might be.

But I really only have one answer.

She's gone.

After five years, has she finally completed the journey I stopped her from taking? I might have prevented her from going that night, but that didn't mean I took away her dream.

Honestly, I expected her to go the second I gave her some freedom—which, admittedly, took longer than it probably should have.

I wasn't stupid. I knew she'd run from one prison and stumbled straight into another. But how else was I meant to protect her?

She was sixteen. A kid. She should have been at school; she should have been thinking about graduating and what she was going to do with the rest of her life. Not plotting how to run away from the years of abuse she'd suffered through at the hands of her tormentors.

I did everything I could think of to give her a chance at having a future. I figured that once she turned eighteen, I would give her the option of leaving. I'd give her the money she needed and whatever escape route she needed.

But I couldn't do it.

I couldn't let her go.

So I did the opposite; I tied her to me in a way that ensured she'd always be mine. I gave her my ring and my name. Both the ultimate protection from the men of this town.

Unable to sit around waiting for the front door to open or my cell to ring, I grab my wallet from the kitchen counter and take off.

Ignoring my car, I swing my leg over my bike and start the engine.

The vibrations rumble through me, settling a little bit of my unease as I back out of the drive and take off.

Dawn is probably the best time of day in Harrow Creek. The demons that walk the streets in the darkness disappear back into their caves and the orange glow of the sun almost makes it look like a half-decent place to live. Almost.

The streets are mostly deserted, apart from a few drunks who are still stumbling around, trying to remember where they live, if anywhere. There's the odd street cleaner out, trying their best to make the place look respectable, but I can't help thinking that it's too little too late.

It's not just the drug ring that Victor controls in this town. He literally owns Harrow Creek. Every policeman, politician, and councillor are corrupt and on his payroll. If he wanted this place to look like a town the inhabitants could be proud of then all he'd have to do is snap his fingers.

But as it is, he seems to thrive on breeding the scumbags who will line his pockets by buying his drugs and using his women.

It could be so much more than it is. So much better.

We're surrounded by growing towns like Rosewood and Maddison, yet we seem to be going backward. The crime and violence getting worse with every day that passes.

I know I'm partly to blame for some of it. I'm ranked pretty high in the gang that rules these streets. Some of the blood that stains them has my name all over it.

But what am I meant to do?

I was born here. Brought up with no other option but to become a Hawk and follow in my father's footsteps. I don't like to think what might have become of me if I didn't follow that path. Hell, I probably wouldn't be here to tell the tale.

I scour the alleyways and darkened shop entrances for any sight of my wife, but I find nothing.

Pulling up at one of our worst trailer parks, I kill the engine and climb out.

I check my cell again, but just like I already knew, there's nothing from her. Opening the tracker app, it still shows the same. At home.

Trying to keep a lid on my frustration, I make my way through the dilapidated homes, searching the groups of kids who are mostly huddled around fires, in varying states of consciousness. I want to say that they're letting go because it's Saturday night. But honestly, most of these delinquents wouldn't know what day it was if it slapped them in the face.

The few that are still sober enough to notice me jerk their chins in greeting. A couple even grunt a few words, but the second they discover I'm not here for a social visit, they soon go back to their bullshit lives.

I make my way to the second to last trailer on the main strip and push the door open.

"Mavwick," a little voice calls before she races my way with her arms out wide. My lips spread in a wide smile as my heart tumbles in my chest.

"Hey, trouble. What are you doing awake?" I ask, lifting the dark-haired little cherub up and making her giggle.

She's the best thing this town has to offer. It kills me that she's forced to grow up here, experiencing the worst that life has to offer.

"The sun is up, so I am up," she announces, before her exhausted looking grandmother shuffles into the room.

I study her closely, noting the extra lines on her face and the dark shadows under her eyes. She's too old to be running around after a wild toddler, but she won't have it any other way.

I get it. I do. I just wish she'd let me help more.

"The blackout blind I brought is working well then?" I quip.

"As good as a chocolate teapot," Sheila mutters, making a beeline for the coffee pot. "Coffee? You look like you need one."

I smile grimly at her in agreement, before putting Daisy down and letting her run toward her toys.

"Come and play with me, Mavwick," she shouts, way louder than necessary for this time in the morning.

"I will," I promise. "I just need to talk to Grams first."

She stares up at me from her spot on the floor beside her toybox, her argument on the tip of her tongue, but she knows better than to complain.

"What's going on?" Sheila asks once Daisy is distracted and chattering away to her dolls.

"Alana has vanished," I confess quietly.

"Maverick," Sheila chastises.

"I don't need a lecture," I mutter. "I just need to know if you've heard anything."

Her hands still, and she sucks in a breath before she turns her eyes on me.

"Maverick, don't you think that I'd have called you if I heard anything?"

I stare back at her, trying to pretend I'm not intimidated by a seventy-something-year-old woman. But hell, this old-school Creeker just has some kind of aura about her that can bring even the baddest gangster to his knees—metaphorically and literally, I'm sure.

"Yeah, I know," I say, rubbing the back of my neck.

"I warned you that this would happen. Free spirits aren't meant to be tied down, Maverick Murray."

"She wouldn't just run. Not without—"

"Telling you?

"Don't be naïve, boy. If she wanted out, the last thing she would do is tell you. She knows too well that you'd drag her straight back, kicking and screaming. Maybe this is for the best."

"No," I argue.

I know what she's saying is true. It's the first option I came up with when she never returned home yesterday.

But I don't want to believe it.

I won't believe it.

What we have. It might be unconventional, but it works for us. Or at least it does to a point.

I thought she was happy-ish.

I thought—

"Mav," Sheila sighs. "You need to face facts. She never wanted to be here. You should have let her go five years ago. You're holding her back, and in return, she's doing exactly the same to you. Let her go. Let her be free."

"Mavwick," Daisy finally complains.

With a sad smile at Sheila, who turns her attention back to the coffee machine, I walk over and lower my ass to the floor, refusing to believe that this is it for us.

Alana might have been mine for five years, but I can't help feeling like we've barely even started our lives together.

5

ALANA

By the time there's a noise on the other side of the door the next morning, my stomach is growling loudly and my entire body is trembling due to the cold.

I've no idea at what point in the night—I assume it was the night—that that motherfucker turned the air conditioning up, but he did. Every time I woke up, terrorized by the images haunting my dreams, the temperature had dropped. Though it didn't stop me from being soaked through with sweat.

I'm weak, both physically and mentally. The last thing I need is to face Reid Harris. But no matter how beaten down I might be, there's no fucking way I'm going to break because of a bad night's sleep.

He's going to have to try a hell of a lot harder if he wants any kind of information out of me.

The locks disengaging rock through my body as I push myself to my feet and roll my shoulders back to look stronger than I feel.

I might not have the privilege of a mirror in here, but I don't need it to know I'm a mess.

My clothes are still damp with sweat. My long blonde hair is like a bird's nest around my head, from the amount of tossing and turning I did last night, and I can only imagine how my face must look. I probably have makeup everywhere it shouldn't be, that's if there's any left.

The door swings open, revealing a freshly showered Reid Harris. His hair is still damp, his shirt clinging to his torso, giving me almost as good a view as when he was shirtless the last time he graced me with his presence. And he smells insane.

Damn him.

Running my eyes down his dark-fitted, ripped jeans, I go right down to his booted feet before making my way back up.

Well, at least one of us looks presentable this morning.

And from the satisfied yet terrifying smirk I find playing on his lips when I finally get back up to his face, I think he's happy with his findings too. Only for a very different reason.

"Good morning, Pet. I hope you're ready to have some fun."

"Do what you want. I find it hard to believe you've got any chance of making my life worse."

It's not entirely true. I do have something good in my life right now. Someone who I hope is out there wondering why I never returned home last night.

My and Mav's relationship might be... unconventional. But he's everything to me. My best friend. And I hate the thought of him freaking out over my disappearance.

Something that I'm sure Reid gives very few fucks about.

He scoffs. "We'll see. I want answers from you, Pet. And I'm not going to stop until I get them."

I hiss when he reaches out and wraps his giant paw around my upper arm and hauls me across my cell and out of the door.

I get a couple of seconds to look at the other locked doors that line the long hallway before I'm thrown toward the chair I was in last night.

Only this time, he doesn't trust me to sit and remain here because, no sooner have I righted myself, does he begin wrapping tight, rough rope around my left wrist, binding me to the arm of the chair.

"I'm not stupid enough to try running," I hiss, watching him work with such precision that I should probably be impressed.

Once he's happy my arm isn't going to slip free, he ties it in some kind of fancy-ass knot.

"Didn't have you down as the Boy Scout type. Thought you'd have been too busy setting bugs on fire and gutting soft fluffy bunnies."

His eyes shoot to mine, and without saying a word, he confirms my suspicions.

"I've never hurt a bunny. I tend to stick to things like raccoons and beavers."

"Oh, because that's so much better," I mutter as he starts working on my second wrist.

"Why? Did you know someone who had a pet beaver?" I can't help but smirk. "Don't answer that," he mutters after realizing what he said.

Dropping to his knees before me, he works on my ankles.

The second his hand connects with my leg, a bolt of electricity shoots through me.

And fuck if he doesn't notice it as well.

"Don't be flattered. It's been a while," I hiss.

"A whore like you? I find that hard to believe."

This time when his fingers brush down my calf, his actions are calculated and designed to weaken my resolve.

What Reid seems to be forgetting in this whole game between us is that I'm just as skilled as he is when it comes to manipulating people.

You don't spend your entire life around twisted cunts like I have and not learn a thing or two about how to make people—mainly men—bend to your will.

It's why Victor plucked me right out of my happy—although utterly unsatisfied—life with Mav and offered me the job he did.

Unlike almost everyone else I've ever met, he saw my worth. Although, I really fucking wish he hadn't.

As Reid secures my ankle to the unmoving chair, I shift as if I'm uncomfortable and shamelessly spread my thighs.

His head is at the perfect height and like the predictable male that he is, his eyes lift—albeit briefly—and lock on my lace-covered pussy.

Every man's kryptonite.

Well, almost every man. Other than my husband, I'm yet to come across one I've been unable to manipulate with a few promises of getting a taste.

"Nice try," Reid murmurs as he ties off my first ankle then moves to the other.

"What?" I ask innocently.

"You do know who I am, right?" He growls, the roughness of his deep voice rolling through me like a wave. Giving me feelings that I really should not be having right now. Although, I can't say I'm surprised. I've always been a little twisted where sex is concerned.

A product of my upbringing, I guess.

A laugh tumbles from my lips. "You think there's anyone in this town who doesn't know who you are?"

He doesn't respond. He doesn't need to. I know I've just well and truly stroked his twisted ego.

"There," he says, pushing to his feet and taking a large step back to admire his handiwork.

"I'm glad you're proud of yourself. You really are your father's son, aren't you? Sick bastard," I spit.

It's not until the hint of a smirk twitches at his lips that I realize what I just said.

Lock it down, Alana.

Just because he has a pretty face and a hot body, doesn't mean you need to lose your head.

"I suggest we start over," Reid says, walking behind me so I've no chance of seeing what he's doing.

The room is almost as bare as my cell. The walls and floor are gray, although splatters are staining the paint out here. It doesn't take a genius to work out what that is. The only furniture I can see are a lonely chair tucked into the corner and cupboards that I already know hold rows and rows of tools, all designed to torture and maim people.

A shudder rips down my spine.

I wonder how many lives Reid has ended here in his underground torture chamber?

Or I guess the more important question might be... how long do I have until that number increases by one and I'm finally put out of my misery?

He crashes around with something before the most incredible scent fills my nose. My mouth waters and this time, it's not for the monster who's tied me to this damn chair. Instead, when he walks back around in front of me, it's the steaming mug of coffee in his hand.

Lifting it to his lips, he takes a sip. Sighing in contentment as he gets his fix.

Asshole.

"Did you want some?" he asks as if it isn't abundantly clear that I fucking well do.

I've been locked down here for hours with nothing but the faucet and tepid water that I'm not entirely sure won't kill me to keep me going. Of course I want his fucking coffee.

I hold his hard stare, not willing to ask him nicely like I know he wants.

"No?" he asks, his brows shooting up. "Fine by me."

When he takes another sip, an involuntary whimper spills from my lips.

"Sure I can't tempt you?" he offers again.

He's being too nice. There has to be a catch.

I want to say that he hasn't poisoned it seeing as he's happily drinking it. But there is no way he's just offering it up.

Moving closer, he waves the mug under my mouth.

"Please," I whimper, hating myself for being so weak.

His face remains impassive, but I swear his eyes smile.

Asshole.

To my shock, he presses the mug to my lips and tips it up.

Greedily, I open my mouth, ready for a rush of rich coffee. But the second the liquid touches my skin, it burns.

I shriek as it covers my lips and fills my mouth.

Reid predicts my next move, though, and jumps out of the way before I can spray him with the nuclear liquid gold.

"What the fuck is wrong with you," I bark when he rests back against the wall and sips his coffee.

Shrugging one shoulder, he states, "I like it hot."

"I like it hot. That is not hot. It's fucking nuclear."

"You should have savored it. You won't be getting any more if you're going to waste it like that."

I sneer at him as he stands there enjoying his coffee, as if we were sitting at a table having a nice breakfast together.

I knew this man was fucked up. That's not news to anyone in the Creek. But this is even fucking weirder than I was expecting.

"Is this it? I'm meant just to sit here and watch you drink coffee?" I hiss.

"Nope. I'm hoping you're going to start talking."

"Then you're going to be waiting a long time."

No more words pass his lips as he continues to drink his lava. But his eyes never stray from mine. Not for a single second.

It's unnerving as fuck. I don't think I've ever held eye contact with anyone for so long. But, like hell am I going to back down and look away.

He might think I'm going to be an easy target, but he's about to learn a lot about me. And it won't be my secrets.

I've no idea how much time passes, but it's long enough to make me wish I rolled off my cot bed and used the bathroom before he barged in.

I don't bother asking for a bathroom break, though. Something tells me it won't be permitted.

"I've got all day. All week actually. I've cleared my diary, especially for you."

"I'm honored. Truly. I think you might have wasted your time, though."

He lifts a brow in question.

"Why did you tell Kane you were pregnant with his kid, Alana?"

I keep my lips pressed together.

"You knew you were going to be found out. If you didn't end up here with us snooping through your medical records, then we'd have noticed when you didn't start growing a bump, don't you think?"

My teeth grind so hard I'm sure I'm about to crack one as he talks about what they have discovered about me.

"Here's the thing, Pet," he says, pushing from the wall and disappearing behind me again.

There's a rush of running water as I assume he rinses his mug out before his deep voice fills the space again.

"You're not stupid. You might try to look it. Let all the old, horny bastards think you're some kind of damsel in distress who needs saving. But that's all an act, isn't it?"

I jump the second something hits the top of my head, but thanks to my tight bindings, I barely move as a drop of water runs down my scalp.

"What the fuck?" I ask, but the question goes unanswered.

"You knew that by telling that lie, you'd end up here. The thing I can't quite figure out is... did you want to be here, tortured by me? Is that some fucked-up kink you've got going on? I know your husband doesn't exactly take care of your needs, so has his lack of touch left you craving something dark and twisted? No, that can't be it, can it? We both know you've been having your needs catered to by Kane. And others, I assume."

He studies me as he paces back and forth.

"Either that, or you decided your time was up and that you'd hand your life over to me.

"I can't lie. I'm more than happy either way. I don't think it'll surprise you to hear that both torture and murder are quite high up on my skills list."

6

REID

She glares right back at me, showing very little sign of weakness as another drop of cold water lands on her head.

It's tame, and I'm dying to drag out something a little more creative to make her talk, but also, I want to enjoy this.

It's not often I get to play with such a beautiful victim. They're usually ugly, overweight, shitty gangsters. Or more so, wannabe gangsters.

And if she's going to be as strong-willed as I expect, then these next few days, maybe even weeks, if I'm really lucky, are going to be a lot of fun.

A shiver rips through her as the water droplet runs over her skin.

"So?" I prompt when she doesn't respond to my assumptions about why she landed herself here.

But all she does is glare.

That look. Fuck me, that look makes my cock hard.

The need to break her is all-consuming.

She doesn't think I'll manage it. She thinks that she's stronger than me, smarter than me.

She's wrong.

The only thing she's got on her side is her beauty. She knows it too.

That's why she pulled that move earlier while I was binding her legs. But if she thinks she'll crack my resolve with one flash of her pussy, then she's got another thing coming.

She could put on the best fucking strip show in the world and it wouldn't be enough.

"Let's recap what we know, shall we?" I start when she makes it more than obvious that I'm going to be the only one talking right now.

That's fine. I'm happy to fill the silence for a while. Make her think she might win in this battle of wills that will only end one way.

"Kane has been keeping you entertained because you're a bored, lonely, under-loved housewife.

"What exactly is wrong with your husband, Alana? Gay? Impotent?"

Her eyes narrow at my guesses.

"Should have been a woman?"

Her right eyebrow twitches in anger.

"Or does he have better standards? Did he marry you thinking you were young and innocent and then discover that you're nothing but a filthy whore?"

Another twitch.

Oh, I'm hitting a soft spot.

"So Kane keeps you entertained. That's his job. But then you turn up out of the blue when Kane is doing everything in his power to start his life over and announce that you're pregnant.

"It's bullshit, obviously. Pretty sure everything that falls from your pouty lips is. Because you've been hurt so badly in the past that you're unable to conceive."

I might be a cold-hearted bastard with few morals and more blood on my hands than I'd ever confess to, but even the thought of what she might have been through makes me wince.

I'm all for hurting those who deserve it. I fucking thrive on it, in fact.

But innocent kids.

Nah, I fucking draw the line there.

As far as I know, Mav married Alana when she was barely eighteen.

I didn't know much about her prior to her being Mrs. Murray. She was homeschooled while her sister attended Harrow Creek Middle School.

I never asked why. Didn't give a fuck. I was too busy ruling that fucking place with JD at my side and my brothers and Kane, following close behind.

Our dads might have been tight. But I didn't have time to worry about some girl who never seemed to leave their house.

Although things are starting to add up. And I don't like the fucking figure I'm coming out with.

It won't stop me from doing what I'm doing though.

This only ends one way, and it's not because I feel fucking sorry for her.

"He brings you here because he trusts you about as much as I do right now.

"And here we are.

"Your so-called husband is blowing up your cell like he cares about your well-being, and you're here with me. My pet."

She blows out a breath, her cheeks puffing out as if my little trip down memory lane is boring the fuck out of her.

"Still nothing to say?"

Her eyes hold mine, her lips remaining locked together.

Tucking my hand into my pocket, I pull her cell out.

That makes her react.

Her eyes widen in interest.

"How many times do you think he's called?" I ask. "How many voicemails? Texts?"

Still, silence as another drip falls.

They're getting faster, her hair beginning to darken as it soaks through.

"From what I've heard. He spent all night running around town searching for you. Fucking pussy.

"He didn't get very far. There are only a handful of people who know where you are. And all of their loyalties are with me.

"So tell me, Pet. If he can't bear to touch you, why does he care so much about the fact you never came home last night? Wasn't the kitchen floor scrubbed, or..."

Nothing.

"Fine," I say, pushing from the wall and walking around her. Her eyes follow my every movement until I'm out of her line of vision. "But you will talk."

Without warning, I turn the faucet for the showerhead that sits right above her chair. Ice-cold water rains down on her, soaking her through in an instant.

Her shriek of shock rips through the air and I can't help but smirk as she discovers who holds the upper hand here.

Cracking my knuckles, I walk around in front of her, the cool spray of the shower hitting me. The water is chilled especially for guests.

"I'd think about your vow of silence very seriously if I were you."

Without another word, I turn my back on her and march past all the other doors and up the stairs.

The occupants of a couple of those rooms probably deserve a visit. But much like my pet, they can wait a little longer.

None of them are going anywhere.

The second I pull the heavy door open, voices hit my ears.

Combing my fingers through my hair, I make my way to see who's decided to turn up for a visit instead of going to class like they fucking should be.

I find JD at the coffee machine, making Devin and Ezra coffees.

"Don't you have anything fucking better to do?" I bark, turning all their eyes on me.

"Bro, you look pissed," Devin happily points out.

"She not squealing?" Ez asks.

I'm not surprised they know who I've got downstairs. I called Ellis for help with her medical records. He and his twin share everything. Aside from intelligence. Ellis seemed to get Ez's share of that.

"Delayed gratification is real, man," Devin teases.

"I'll get every last drop from her lying lips. Don't you worry. I'm just warming her up." Or cooling her down, as the case may be.

"You know I'd gladly help," JD offers, passing me a coffee, which I immediately lift to my lips and sip, pointedly ignoring his offer again.

"Looks like big brother wants Alana all to himself," Devin teases.

"She's his type," Ezra adds. "Can't say I'm surprised."

"Lying whore isn't my type."

"So gag her and fuck her from behind. Easy," Ez says, rubbing his palms together like a douchebag. "Wrap that long blonde hair around your fist and—"

"How the fuck you ever get laid is beyond me," JD mutters, making his way to the couch and falling into it.

"Why the fuck are you two here anyway? You should have your head stuck in books."

Ezra snorts. "Oh yeah, that's what we do at college."

"Supplies are out, man. Where the fuck are our shipments?" Devin demands fiercely. "We've got Victor on our asses about how much we're shifting, yet we've got no product to fucking shift. Care to fucking explain?"

A few years ago, I wasn't sure if Devin was going to have what it takes to make it in this world. He was a soft-as-shit kid. But as his balls dropped, his confidence and attitude grew and he soon morphed into the irritating motherfucker that's standing before me demanding answers right now.

He wasn't destined to be a college student. Ezra either. But our father's insatiable need for control and money saw them accepted to Maddison Kings University, despite their shortcomings, and the fact they both barely graduated high school. But Victor Harris's reach knows no bounds. And that was proven when he helped get Kane, not only accepted at MKU, but also walked straight onto the football team as their starting wide receiver.

It was dodgy as fuck. Everyone knew it. But one thing about our father, he knows what he's doing. He crosses his t's and dots his i's, ensuring no evidence of any corruption is left behind. Of course, no one would ever dare question him. Not unless they want to end up in an early grave. And by grave I mean their incinerated ashes dumped in a swamp.

"No, I don't," I say, remembering that Dev asked a question.

"Dude, this can't fucking carry on. We can only hold off

Victor for so long. We fuck this up and we won't initiate to become senior members."

"You've nothing to worry about."

"But—"

"I said," I seethe. "You've nothing to worry about. Victor can't touch you, your future is safe."

"Who the fuck do you think you are all of a sudden? The boss?"

"I will be," I state.

"What are you playing at?" Ez asks.

"Nothing that you need to worry about. You'll have product for the weekend. I'll text you when it's ready. Just go to class and do your fucking jobs. Leave the rest to me."

"And what happens the next time he sends someone in to bug our place, huh? Or when he sends one of his men in to beat the truth out of us."

"Ellis is checking for bugs daily. If he plants something, you'll catch it. And even better, how about you don't talk about shit there," I suggest like a smug prick. Seems fucking obvious to me, but I'm not exactly talking to the brains of the operation here. I fucking love my brothers something fierce. But they all have their skills. And thinking isn't Devin or Ez's. "And if he sends anyone, the only men who should be walking away are you three. You've been trained better than his men. Fucking show it."

They mutter something in agreement, but I'm done with this conversation.

"Can you fuck off to where you're meant to be now and stop drinking my coffee?"

"Bro, you need to get fucking laid. You're like a bear with a sore head," Ezra scoffs.

"You've got a girl downstairs who's good for it. I bet she'd even beg if you asked nicely. I've heard she—"

"Out," I demand, pointing toward the door. "We've all got jobs to do. How about we fucking do them."

Silence falls as they abandon their mugs in the kitchen and disappear from sight. A few seconds later, the front door slams, leaving me and JD alone.

"They're right, you know. You're in a bitch of a mood, considering you've got a new pet. How is she, anyway?"

"Wet," I mutter, dumping my own mug in the sink and turning to pull the refrigerator open.

"Kinky. I like it."

"Shut the fuck up," I bark, pulling eggs and bacon out as my stomach growls. "Go do your rounds. But you so much as fucking touch her and I'll cut them off," I warn.

He salutes me like the prick he is before backing out of the room.

"I'll have mine sunny-side up. Thanks, man."

Before I can tell him where to go, he's gone, the sound of a slamming door echoing behind him.

I trust JD with my life. But I also know how his mind works and the second he sees Alana tied up down there sopping wet, it's going to go straight into the gutter.

7

ALANA

My teeth chatter and I'm pretty sure my bones are shivering.

I've been cold a few times in my life. It was one of my father's favorite punishments to lock me in a dark, freezing cold shed so that I could think about my actions and bad decisions, while he was up in the house with Kristie.

Fuck, I used to be so scared.

As far as I knew, he never touched her, never said a bad word in her company. But just like his temper, I knew that could switch at any moment.

The only thing I wanted back then was to protect her. And if I fucked up, I ended up locked away, unable to do anything should he turn on her.

I've never been more terrified in my life.

They could do whatever they wanted to me. I'd endure it so long as they kept their filthy hands off my little sister.

She was too innocent, too pure, too perfect to be tainted by them.

She was going to be something, do something important. I was sure of it.

I just had to help give her the opportunity. Hell knows that no one else was going to do it.

Mom was gone. Dad was...

A violent shiver rips down my spine as the torrent of rain continues.

My skin is so cold that each drop of water that hits is like a needle piercing me. Although, the thought of the warm blood that would spill after makes me wish it were.

My clothes are soaked through, I'm sure making me even colder.

Fighting is futile. I did for a few minutes after that prick walked out but quickly gave up.

I tugged and twisted both my arms and legs hoping to myself. But none of my bindings so much as loosened. Instead, the rope just ripped into my skin.

At least with the amount of water raining down on me, no one ever has to know that I pissed myself in his chair while I wait for him to take pity on me and come back. That can be my little secret.

Each second sitting here feels like an hour. The only noises are the running water and my teeth clanking together. They're annoying the shit out of me, but I can't stop them. I am that fucking cold.

I've no idea how much time has passed when there's a loud bang in the direction that Reid disappeared. It's probably fruitless, but a small amount of hope seeps into my veins that this might be over.

In the grand scheme of things, a cold-water shower is tame as fuck for the likes of Reid Harris.

I'm not stupid enough to believe this is how he gets his prisoners to squeal. He's capable of so much more.

This is just the beginning. He's easing me in. Warming

me up, metaphorically at least. And he's enjoying every goddamn minute of it.

Footsteps approach and I open my eyes. They instantly fill with water, making everything blur. But I know it isn't Reid. The aura is totally wrong.

It's the other occupant of this house. Reid's right-hand man. Julian Dempsey. Or JD, as he prefers.

I blink away the water, forcing myself to focus.

Wearing a pair of dark sweats and a wifebeater, he has his thick tattooed arms crossed over his chest and is resting against the wall as he studies me.

"You know, when Reid told me that you were down here wet and waiting for him, this wasn't exactly what I had in mind. Kinda disappointed, not gonna lie."

"Get fucked," I hiss, water spraying from my lips as I speak.

"That sounds like a fantastic idea," he mutters to himself, before pushing from the wall and moving closer to get a better view.

Just out of the spray of the water, he drops to his haunches.

"You fucked up, little dove," he states simply.

"Dove?" I hiss. Reid calling me his pet is bad enough. I don't need to be called after a fucking bird as well.

"Yeah. White hair. Fragile. Locked up in a cage waiting for its owner to free it."

My teeth grind as he explains his thought process.

"Birds have feathers," I point out. "And I'm not fucking fragile."

He smirks as his eyes roam over every inch of my body.

The way he studies me, I might as well be naked.

It's unnerving. It's... thrilling.

For just a moment, the bone-chilling coldness of the

water is forgotten as I soak up the warmth in his gaze, the heat of his obvious desire.

Unlike Reid, JD gives things away. And right now, all kinds of filthy things are flickering behind those stunning blue eyes.

Things that make my blood heat and my core tighten.

I've heard the rumors about his skills. The club whores all like to share notes on the Hawks they've been lucky enough to spend time with. And let's just say, this man fucking loves giving head. His tongue isn't his only good feature, if the gossip is to be believed either. What he's rocking beneath those sweats is pretty fucking fierce too, apparently.

Of course, it might all be bullshit and bragging rights.

It's not likely I'll get a chance to test the theories out while I'm stuck down here.

I'm sure it's not part of Reid's torture plan for me to let JD eat me until I can't take any more and scream my secrets in exchange for relief.

Although, I could think of worse ways for it to happen.

"They sure do, Dove." Wiping his thumb across his bottom lip, he checks me out again.

"See something you like?" I bark, already pissed off with whatever game he's playing.

"You know," he mutters, pushing to his full height again. "I do. You're looking hot and I think we could have a lot of fun together."

"Right," I scoff. "Because I'm a whore?"

His jaw pops.

"You think that just because I've been fucking Kane that I'll happily climb you like a tree too? I mean, you're a Hawk, after all. That's what all the girls around here want, right?"

"I've never had any complaints," he states proudly.

"Of course you haven't. They're all too desperate to please, that's why."

His chest compresses as a puff of air rushes past his lips.

"Oh my God." I laugh, forcing a smile onto my frozen face. "You really rate yourself that highly, don't you? Fucking hell, that's hilarious."

"Shut the fuck up, Dove."

"Make me," I hiss.

A smirk curls at his lips, making a dimple appear on his cheek.

"I'm not sure you're in any position to be making suggestions like that," he says, stalking closer, not giving two shits about the fact the water begins soaking his shirt and sweats. "Seeing as you're still sitting here, I assume that Reid did a good job of these knots." His fingers brush the rope that's wrapped around my wrist, ensuring I don't move an inch.

"He knows I've got a thing for rope play. Anyone would think he bound you up and left you here as a gift. Motherfucker did forget my last birthday. He does owe me."

The second his fingers leave the rope and connect with the painfully cold skin of my arm, I jerk violently in the chair.

"Whoa, Dove. Not scared of little ol' me, are you?"

My eyes narrow, and my teeth grind as he walks his fingers up my arm.

"Look at these pretty goose bumps."

"I'm fucking freezing, asshole. You want to do something nice for me, turn it the fuck off."

He chuckles, sending a waft of clean minty air over me. It only reminds me that my breath must smell the opposite.

"Ah, no can do, little dove. I can only break so many of the boss's rules before he starts dishing out punishments."

I want to keep my mouth shut, but my curiosity gets the better of me.

"How many have you broken already?" I ask, my voice all breathy and needy.

"Nice try, Dove. It'll take more than that to sweet talk me," he murmurs, his eyes still roaming over my body.

"If you're not going to help me then you might as well fuck back off where you came from," I sneer.

He might be pretty, even more so now that his shirt is soaked, showcasing every muscle of his chest and abs. But if he won't be of use to me, then he may as well not be here.

"You're hot when you're angry. Did you know that?"

I raise a brow.

"Try pretending you're not interested in what I could offer you all you like, we both know it's bullshit."

"Are you always this full of yourself?"

His responding laugh confirms my question.

"Your nipples are hard, Dove."

"I'm freezing my tits off. This water is ice-cold, if you hadn't noticed."

"It's not the reason they're hard, though, is it?"

"Why did you come down here?" I ask, changing the subject.

"Got a job to do."

"I'm assuming that's not to torment me?" I guess.

"Pretty sure I'm not meant to be anywhere near you, little dove. But I have never been very good at following the rules."

He steps forward and stands with his feet wide between mine, forcing my knees farther apart.

The little bit of heat where our skin touches rushes through me, a whimper of relief almost spills from my lips, but I manage to catch it before it escapes.

"Why doesn't that surprise me," I mutter, staring up into his eyes.

They're so incredibly blue. It's like staring into the ocean on a perfect summer's day.

I always wondered what it might be like to be swallowed up by that mass of water. Right now, I think I might be getting a taste of what that's like.

"It didn't need to end here," he says, reaching either side of my head and resting his hands against the backrest, bringing our faces in line.

His minty breath washes over my face again and I try not to breathe on him.

I tell myself it's not because I don't want to put him off, but I know it's a big fat lie.

He leans closer. So close I start to wonder if he will stop or just swoop in for a kiss.

"You could have made a different decision, little dove."

"Easy for you to say. You've no idea what my life is like and why I make the decisions I do."

"How about you try to help me understand," he suggests, his eyes bouncing between mine. "We could help. You need people killed? Done. Your husband needs punishment for clearly being blind to what belongs to him? Easy. Name it, and it's yours."

"That's a risky offer for a girl who's possibly only days away from death."

"Days?" he balks. "You're not really rating the big man's skills, huh?"

"He's enjoying this too much to end it quickly."

"Is that right?"

"If he wanted me dead, I'd already be done," I state firmly, lifting my chin confidently.

He falls silent, his eyes locked on mine before he pushes from the chair and stands again.

Lifting his arm, he pushes his sopping wet hair back from his brow, his eyes dropping down my body to where he's spread my legs.

"You've got some balls, I'll give you that."

"I'm a Creek girl, JD. And I'm more than just a whore. Or a pet. Or a toy. The men of this town can kiss my ass for all I care."

"Interesting," he muses before a bang comes from behind him and footsteps pound our way. "Oh, looks like our time is up, little dove. I'm already looking forward to next time."

"Bite me," I hiss, his eyes widening in delight.

"Promise?" He winks before Reid appears behind him.

Reid's eyes are blazing with anger, his lips pressed into a thin line.

"What the fuck are you doing?" he barks, forcefully shoving JD away from me.

"Getting to know our new pet, Boss," JD teases as he shoots me a cheeky glance.

"Our? I don't remember inviting you to play with her."

"When do I ever ask for an invite?"

A deep growl rumbles in Reid's throat before he takes a warning step toward his best friend.

"If you're going to go at it, could you take your shirts off first and really give me a show?" I ask, making both of their faces snap in my direction. JD's brightens with amusement while Reid's darkens angrily.

"Go and do what you came down here to do," Reid demands before he walks around me and thankfully turns the torrent of water off.

I want to cry out with relief as the air around me instantly warms, but I swallow it down.

Thanks to JD's distraction techniques, the effects of the

cold have been forgotten a little, making it look like I was coping better than I really was.

"I like your suggestion, Dove," JD says, walking toward the doorway that leads to the cells. "But I think I'd much rather roll around in the puddles topless with you."

"JD," Reid snaps, making the man in question salute and finally disappear.

The showerhead above me continues to drip, making me shudder every time a drop makes contact.

Reid doesn't say anything, but his presence behind me is imposing.

His eyes are on me, my skin tingles with his attention, but no words are said.

In fact, I don't hear anything from him and the next noise that hits my ears is a painful scream from down the hallway that makes my stomach knot painfully.

8
—
JD

I've got a wide smirk on my face as I push the door open to the cell farthest from where Alana sits strapped to her chair.

The basement is silent as I slip inside, although any thoughts of the sexy woman bound and soaking wet back there are ripped away the second the stench of the room hits my nose.

The man sees my shock and tries to make the most of it by rushing toward me. But the thing about being locked up in either a bright or pitch-black room for days on end with limited food means his reactions are just a tad sluggish.

I'm ready for him long before he gets to me, lifting my arm from my side and cracking him in the face.

He screams like a little bitch as his nose explodes, spraying blood everywhere.

"Was there something you wanted?" I seethe, cracking my knuckles, more than ready to land another blow on the cunt if he wants to try again.

"Fuck you," he spits.

Honestly, I've no idea who this motherfucker is or what

he's done. I stopped asking questions about Reid's intentions a long time ago. I just trust that he deserves his place down here and to be treated like the scum of the Earth he is.

I take a step forward, and his confidence withers and dies as he scrambles back into the corner next to his shitty toilet.

Fucking thing needs to be incinerated after the mess he's made in it.

Besides his bed and the sink, it's the only thing in the room. How the fuck he keeps missing is beyond me.

"If you didn't want feeding today, you should have just said, asshole," I sneer. "Not that you need it."

I regret the fact that I'm not wearing boots the second my foot lifts from the floor, but I don't let it stop me as I plow it into his gut, making him grunt in pain.

"I've seen pigs live in less shit than you," I mutter, before fleeing the room in favor of some fresher air.

"Everything alright?" Reid calls the second I slam the door shut and lock the cocksucker back inside.

Needing that shower, or better, a bottle of bleach to clean up with, I march back toward Reid and his pet.

Alana's eyes widen when she takes in the blood sprays across my wifebeater.

The moment she realizes she reacted, she locks it back down.

But I'm not ready for her to give up on me yet, so I reach behind me and pull my tank from my body then shove my sweats from my hips, leaving me in my tight black boxers.

"What the fuck are you doing?"

"Shower please, Boss."

Alana is so focused on my body that she doesn't register my demand. That soon changes when the water once again rains down on her.

The scream that rips from her throat makes Reid grin like a demon, knowing she can't see him.

Stepping closer, I keep my eyes locked on hers, while Reid's warning stare burns into the side of my face.

"You look like you're waiting for something down there, little dove. If you ask nicely, I've been known to give a killer lap dance."

I don't need to look up to know that Reid is grinding his teeth over my suggestion.

Usually, he wouldn't give a fuck.

Hell, prior to yesterday when his little pet arrived, I wouldn't have thought that making that suggestion to Alana would stir anything inside him.

But something has rocked him.

It makes me even more curious about what's been happening down here and why we have her locked up for the foreseeable future.

Last night, Reid was pretty sure she was playing us. And while it's certainly a possibility, I'm finding it hard to believe.

Sure, she's feisty, sassy, and beautiful. She's got all the requirements to pull the wool over most men's eyes. But she's not stupid.

She's lived this life of violence, corruption and death just as much as we have. She's just seen it from a different angle.

She knows being down here is the closest thing she's probably ever going to get to a death wish.

So why is she here? And why is she refusing to talk?

"I think that's probably something I can live without. Doesn't look like you're hiding all that much down there anyway."

Unable to contain his amusement at that, Reid snorts, although he tries—and fails—to cover it up with a cough.

"Oh, did you want in on the action, Big Man?" she taunts. "Maybe JD could show you what he's made of."

"You've got real fascination with that, haven't you, Dove?"

"Dove?" Reid echoes.

"Apparently, I'm this delicate little innocent bird you've got locked up down here," Alana teases. "Think that means you need to treat me with care and a gentle touch."

Reid scoffs, clearly not impressed with my nickname, while I continue rubbing the blood from my body right in front of her eyes.

"Reid doesn't do gentle. I, however—"

"Enough," Reid barks.

"C-careful, B-big Man," she stutters, the cold starting to get to her again. "Y-you sound awfully j-jealous."

Suddenly the water cuts out and she sighs with relief.

"Go and find some clothes. Those motherfuckers need food."

"Me too," Alana says with a seductive smirk as I step away from her.

"You'll eat when I say you eat," Reid barks.

"Is he always this pissy?" Alana asks, making me laugh while I shake the water from my hair.

"You haven't seen anything yet."

"Brilliant," she mutters.

"I'll see you later, yeah?" I say as I move toward the hallway.

Reid's impatience to get her alone again has him on the verge of snapping. I might like to toy with him every chance I get, but I also know when to rein it in.

"I'll be here."

"It's a date."

I disappear before Reid can react and dart up the stairs,

leaving wet footprints behind me. He'll fucking love me for that.

They continue down the hallway, up the stairs, and into my bedroom.

Kicking the door closed, I march straight into my bathroom and turn my real shower on.

I might have washed the blood from my body, but that cunt's smell is still stuck in my nose. If only Alana's sweet scent was enough to wipe it out.

Shoving my boxers from my hips, I kick them in the direction of the laundry basket and step under the warm spray.

My skin erupts in goose bumps as I think about how much she wants this right now.

I bet she'd probably do just about anything for a warm shower and a set of dry clothes.

Just like I'd have done quite a lot of things to make the most of her tied to that chair, while we were alone down there.

Fuck, Ezra might have taunted Reid with the fact that Alana is every bit his type. But as best friends, we have very similar tastes. And fuck if Alana with her long blonde hair, blue eyes, and sinful curves, isn't it.

Yeah, she's married. Not usually the kind of woman I make a play for. Hawks' wives are off-limits unless an agreement has been made. Which most do because they don't give a shit about anyone but themselves. I might be able to take every motherfucker in this town, but that doesn't mean I want to just for the sake of a half-decent fuck with his whore.

Which, let's be honest, most of them are.

Alana wasn't wrong with what she said downstairs about the kind of women who hang around the clubhouse hoping to hook up with a Hawk.

They want an easy lay, some alcohol, and a free hit or two if they're lucky. That is the extent of their pointless lives.

I want more than that.

I always have. Not that I've ever had a taste of anything better.

I've been forced to move around from place to place my entire life. This place is one of the only homes I've ever known, despite living in more houses than I can remember now.

All of them, especially the bad ones, have blurred into one big clusterfuck of painful memories and experiences.

Alana's different though. She's nothing like the club whores we're used to. She doesn't have stars in her eyes when she looks at us. She doesn't think we're special because of the positions we hold.

She's never been one to hang around the clubhouse all hours of the night in the hopes of a high or an easy way out. Hell, she's hardly ever there. I can't help but think it's the last place in the world she wants to be.

Mav's the same. He might be Razor's son, but that doesn't mean he lives his life like his father. Not any more, that is.

He and Alana have a private life. He works, does his duty to the Hawks and then he disappears. Goes home I assume to what... not fuck his wife.

Why the hell wouldn't he? She's smoking.

She literally has his ring on her finger and he won't touch her.

What the actual fuck?

I'd be all over that if she were walking around town wearing my ring and using my last name.

Not that I want a wife or that kind of life, of course.

I fucking love being free and single. I don't want anyone

keeping tabs on how late I stay out or how much I drink. It's bad enough I have Reid following my ass around the house, pointing out what a messy fucker I am.

I love living here with him. It's what we spent all our teenage years planning.

We can do exactly what we want, and have complete freedom.

The manor house is no secret. You can see it sitting high up on its hill from almost every single place in Harrow Creek. The main town sits in a valley and we both look over it like motherfucking kings.

I can't lie, though. There is something appealing about the thought of having a woman here to come home to. And I don't mean in the chauvinistic way of doing the washing and cleaning or any of that shit.

The image of crashing onto the couch with a woman, our limbs tangled together as we rip at each other's clothes, desperate to have each other, fills my mind. And before I know what I'm doing, my fingers are wrapped around my shaft and I'm stroking myself as I think about having a certain blonde ride me right where Reid could walk in and catch us at any point.

It sure wouldn't be the first time he's seen something along those lines. Hell, the two of us are about as close as two straight guys can get. We've got into all sorts of shit together over the years.

But seeing his reaction to her since she's been locked up downstairs makes me wonder just how he'd react.

He seems to have staked some fucked-up claim on her, despite the fact he's probably down there torturing her right now.

The thought of him doing exactly that makes my jealousy soar, but fuck if my hand also doesn't pick up its pace.

The thought of watching him bring her to ruin is way more tempting than I think it should be.

Fuck. I bet she's so beautiful when she falls apart.

"Oh shit." I groan as my release slams into me and I spill my seed all over the shower floor.

My muscles relax, but only a little bit, as my fantasy continues playing out in my mind.

Might need to up my stealth skills when I go back down, see if I can catch him up to something he shouldn't be.

"What are you doing?" I snap when Reid continues to silently linger behind me like some weird little gremlin.

If only he was a little ugly thing. JD too. It might make all this easier.

I'm not a stranger to fucked-up relationships and unconventional desires and fantasies. Not only have I experienced and enjoyed things that would terrify most people, but I've already read a lot of it too in an attempt to sate my twisted cravings.

That's probably why I'm not overly freaked out being bound and at the mercy of the monster behind me.

There isn't much he can do that hasn't already been done or that I haven't fantasized about happening.

He doesn't answer, just continues to linger.

"Fine. Be like that. But is there any chance of getting something to eat? Been down here quite a while now, in case you hadn't noticed, I think I deserve something."

He scoffs, letting me know he's listening.

"I'm not sure what's on Tripadvisor about this place, but

I can't say I'm going to be giving it five stars. Cold shower, lukewarm, possibly bacteria-infested drinking water. No food."

"It's not a fucking hotel, Pet."

"Still better than some of the shitholes in the Creek. And the view has been pretty good. You got a gym in this mansion?"

"Of course." He grunts, obviously intrigued enough by my line of questioning to go along with me.

"You might want to start putting in a couple of extra hours in a day. I hate to break it to you, Big Man, but JD has you beat in the body department." It's lies. Total fucking lies, but I figure it might hit a sore spot. I bet those two are hella competitive and I'm more than happy to feed into it. "His definition. Mouthwatering."

Silence.

"Got nothing to say about that, Big Man?"

"I know what you're doing, Pet."

"If that were true, I wouldn't still be tied up here now, would I? You'd have all your precious answers and you'd have either decided to send me back to my husband or I'd be dead.

"I think it's more than clear to both of us that you have no idea what I'm doing."

His shoes thump against the concrete floor and I suck in a bated breath.

It all rushes out of my lungs when he finally steps in front of me.

Why are all the worst ones the prettiest?

Wait, no. Reid Harris isn't pretty.

Breathtaking is more like it.

He's dangerously good-looking. But unlike JD, who owns his looks and knows exactly the power he holds over women—and probably a good few men alike—Reid relies on pure fear to get what he wants. However, he's quickly discovering that it's not working all that well on me.

"Looks are important to you, aren't they?" he asks as he paces back and forth in front of me, rubbing his hands together like he's scheming something wicked.

"You've got to use everything you have to your advantage, don't you think? Take you, for example, you're scary to some people, so you ensure you turn it up to one hundred when the time suits. JD... I'm pretty sure he could flirt the panties off almost every woman on the planet. Bet he's used that to ensure you get what you need a time or two. Devin and Ezra too. Their skills definitely lie in their moves and not their brains."

He stills, glaring me dead in the eyes.

"And I have plenty of experience that tells me that my looks get me the things I want."

"Like Kane. Or your husband."

I chuckle.

"Sure, if you want."

"What is it all the men fall for? Your pouty lips? The eyes? Or is it the long blonde hair they can wrap around their fist while fucking you like a dirty whore."

"Careful. I'll start thinking you're imagining doing just that if you're going to be that specific."

"I think we'll start there. It'll be the least painful."

I'm about to question him when he marches toward his cupboard full of torture devices.

The second he reveals a pair of scissors, my mouth runs dry.

The steel glints in the harsh lights above me as he turns to face me with a sinister grin on his face.

Of all the painful, traumatic things he could do to me, how has he stumbled across the one thing that's going to hurt more than almost anything else?

"I love your pretty hair, Lana. Promise me you'll never cut it."

Kristie's voice rings out so loudly in my ears as he closes the space between us that I'd think she was standing right next to me if I didn't know better.

She's gone, Alana. You don't need to keep those stupid childhood promises.

I swallow thickly, desperately trying to get it together.

It's hair.

It's only hair.

Only hair.

I hold his eyes, praying that I'm able to keep a lid on my raging emotions.

"Didn't realize you moonlighted as a stylist. But now you mention it, my dead ends do need a little t-trim." My voice cracks right at the end and I mentally kick myself to losing control.

He sees it too. The corners of his eyes crinkle in amusement.

"I think my skills are the least of your worries right now. You'll be lucky to walk away from this with a bad haircut. You're more likely to have a slit throat."

"You're all talk and no action, Big Man."

Before I've even finished that sentence, he's on me, his fingers wrapped around the sopping length of my hair, wrenching my head back painfully.

"You really don't need to worry about me following through on my threats, Pet. I deliver every single fucking time."

The sound of metal on metal hits my ears as he opens the scissors. His grip on my hair tightens until my eyes water and I'm pretty sure he's going to pull it clean out instead of cutting it off.

But then, just when the pain shooting down my neck begins to get too much... Relief.

He cuts clean through the entire thickness of my hair in one go.

I want to stay strong. I fight it until I'm alone in my cell once again, but the pain is too much.

It's like losing my sister all over again.

My scream of despair fills the silence before the scissors clatter to the side and Reid's giant form steps before me.

"No, please," I cry when he threads his fingers into my hair and drags my head back again. But this time, he looms over me. The heat of his body warms mine, but it's little relief after what he just did.

"Why did you do it, Alana? What fucking games are you playing?" He roars in my face.

"I'm not playing anything," I cry. "It might be hard for you to believe, but I don't actually have time for your petty gang bullshit, but some of us don't have a fucking choice."

His grip tightens, and my tears finally spill free.

His chest heaves as his breath races over my face.

"Talk, Alana. Why did you lie? Why are you trying to fuck up Kane's chance at a new life?"

"I'm not. Victor is," I blurt before I realize I've even opened my mouth.

He releases me in a heartbeat and steps away.

His fingers thread through his own hair before he roars, "Motherfucker," so loudly, the chair beneath me vibrates.

Tears continue to stream down my cheeks as my new short hair falls around my neck.

My lips part to say something, although I have no idea what, when a figure suddenly emerges in the long hallway.

"What the hell have you done?" JD barks, his eyes locked on me.

"Untie her, put her back in her cell," Reid demands before he takes off.

"What the fuck did you say to him?" JD asks as we both watch the barely-restrained bull practically run down the hallway.

I don't answer. What's the point?

I've already said too much.

I promised myself. Fucking promised myself to keep my secrets locked up, but the second he found a soft spot, there I go spilling everything I was desperate to keep concealed.

Lowering my gaze, I stare down at my lap, letting my hair fall around me. Although it's no longer a curtain I can hide behind when things get hard.

A sob rips free as I stare through my tears at my hacked-off locks.

"Oh shit." JD gasps. "It's okay, Dove. Sit still, I'll cut you free."

Sit still? Is he having a fucking laugh?

I've done nothing but sit still since the moment that asshole tied me up here.

I don't look up as JD rummages around, I assume for a suitable knife, not a machete or whatever else Reid has to terrify his inmates.

My eyes widen when he drops to his knees before me and holds up a vicious-looking serrated blade.

"I'm not going to hurt you."

"Do you always do what Reid tells you? I know you always follow him around like a lost puppy, but I didn't realize you were his little bitch."

"Careful, Dove. I don't need to cut you free. I could just leave you here," he mutters.

"And defy orders?"

His stare burns into the top of my head, and finally, I cave.

The second I look up, my blue eyes lock on his and I swear they swallow me whole.

"You're trouble, little dove."

Our eyes hold for a couple of seconds more before he drops his in favor of cutting the rope.

He starts with my right wrist, sawing through the rough rope until the final strands snap, releasing me.

I whimper as I lift my sore arm, my muscles aching from how long they've been locked in the same position.

My wrist is red and raw from the unforgiving rope and I cradle it against my damp chest as he sets to work on the second one.

"Ow, fuck," I hiss when the blade slips and cuts into my wrist.

"Shit. I'm sorry," he says regretfully as he hops up and rushes behind me.

He returns a couple of seconds later with some tissue that he presses to the cut that's dripping blood on the floor. I guess it's only right that some of mine is added to the stains.

"Crap, that's really bleeding," he says, pulling the tissue away to inspect it.

"Just cut me free," I demand.

"Shit. Yeah."

A little more hesitantly than before, he works his way through. The second I'm free, I lift my wrist from the armrest and hold it up to stop the blood flow.

He watches me as I cradle it to my chest with regret glittering in his eyes.

"Don't pretend you care," I snap.

"Dove, I—"

"Don't. Just finish the job and lock me back up again."

He wants to argue, I can see it on every inch of his face. But he won't. Despite my teasing, he knows better than to defy Reid Harris's order. Being the psycho's best friend might come with some perks, but he can only push things so far.

With a sigh, he lowers down and begins cutting the bindings around my ankles.

"And be careful. If Reid wishes for me to bleed to death then something tells me that he'll want to cause it himself."

"Fucking control freak," JD mutters.

If the situation were different, I might laugh. But as it is, I'm shutting down faster than I want to confess to.

All I want is to crawl onto the cot in my room, curl up in a ball and retreat to that place inside myself I discovered when I was little and experienced some of the worst days of my life.

In short and thankfully pain-free minutes, both of my ankles are released.

The second he moves back, I push to my feet.

I wobble violently as my body fights to comply, after sitting still and in one position for so long, but I refuse help, slapping his hand away when he reaches out to steady me.

"I can see myself to my cell. Just lock me inside and walk away."

"Dove," he warns, but I've no interest in hearing what he might have to say.

I'm done. So fucking done.

My clothes are still wet and cold. I'm exhausted, both physically and emotionally, and my wrists and ankles burn like fuck.

But it's the pain in my chest that I'm suffering with the most.

I'm sorry, Kristie.

I'm so fucking sorry.

10

ALANA

I don't bother trying to close the door once I'm back in the safety of my cell. It looks heavy as shit, and I don't have the energy to even attempt it.

Instead, with my bleeding wrist still cradled to my chest, I crawl onto the cot bed and curl into the fetal position as my tears continue.

Shivers rip through my body. Not only am I still damp, but the air-conditioning is high as fuck in here, making my clothes feel like ice wrapped around my body.

Honestly, if I had the energy, I'd probably take them off.

But as it is, I just lie here listening to the sound of my pounding heart and erratic breathing, waiting for the door to slam closed, signalling my safety.

Once I'm alone. Truly alone, then I can break.

I'm so up in my own head that I don't hear footsteps, or sense that someone else has joined me.

"Dove," he whispers as a warm hand lands on my upper arm.

My heart jumps into my throat and I scream like a banshee before jumping up as fast as I can.

"Whoa," JD soothes, holding his hands up in defense, "I'm not going to hurt you."

"Get out," I demand weakly.

But, unsurprisingly, he just stands there staring at me.

I cringe, only able to predict what a state I look and how awful my hair is.

"I don't want or need you here, JD. Go follow your leader like a good little puppy and see if he has a bone or something to keep you entertained."

"You're a real bitch, you know that?"

I shrug. What the fuck is there to say in response to that.

Yeah, I'm being a bitch, but is it any surprise?

He's one of two men who has me locked up like some kind of criminal.

Yes, I lied. Yes, I've been dishonest and unfaithful. But it wasn't by choice, or because I thought it would be fun.

I didn't have any other option.

It was either follow orders or watch someone I love suffer. And I've already experienced too much of that in my lifetime.

Or worse...

"Sit back down, I'm going to clean up that cut," he says, his voice losing its bite from the last comment.

"It's fine," I mumble, happily lowering my aching body back to the cot.

It's hard and uncomfortable. But while it might not be a luxurious bed in some fancy five-star hotel, at least it's not that solid, unforgiving chair out there.

"No, it's not. I'm sorry for hurting you."

He says the words with such conviction that I can't help but laugh.

"What's so funny?" he asks, sounding a little offended by my reaction.

"Have you looked in a mirror lately? You're a Hawk. You hurt people for fun."

"If they deserve it. I don't go around doing it for shits and giggles," he confesses, opening a first aid box at his feet.

"I'm locked up down here, you think I don't deserve it," I scoff.

He pauses before he looks over at me.

"Your actions say you do, but there's something in your eyes that tells an entirely different story."

"Maybe I'm just a good actress," I counter as he puts a couple of antiseptic wipes between us and a decent-sized bandage.

"Dove, if you're that good, you deserve to be in Hollywood, not rotting down here in the Creek."

"One can dream, right," I mutter.

"Where would you go?" he asks absently, ripping open a wipe before gently pulling my hand toward him and removing the tissue from the cut.

"Hawaii. I'd spend my days on the beach, in the ocean, and drinking out of pineapples and coconuts," I answer without thought.

"Sounds like a dream."

"Yep. When reality sucks, you've got to have something. Ow," I hiss.

"Sorry."

"What about you? If you could be anywhere else in the world, where would you be?"

"The mountains."

"You'd leave the ocean behind?"

"For a log cabin, an open fire, and total tranquillity? Yeah, I would."

"Then you clearly haven't experienced the ocean properly."

"Maybe not."

"Ever been surfing?" I ask.

"No, you?"

I shake my head.

I used to spend hours watching those who do, though. To the point, I felt like I knew every move, how to catch every wave, and exactly how I'd look on top of that board.

But it's just like everything else in my life. A fantasy. A dream.

"You should," he says, grabbing the bandage and gently placing it over the cut.

"Sure. I'll put it on tomorrow's agenda, shall I?"

He chuckles. "I'm sure Reid would be down for getting you in a bikini, Dove."

"Well, he can fuck off. You might be happy following orders, but I'm not his puppet."

"What did you say to him to make him do this?" JD asks, lifting his hand and tucking my short hair behind my ear.

"The truth," I confess.

"Which was?"

I don't answer, and JD doesn't prompt me for the longest time.

The silence stretches on, and I start to think that's it. That he'll tidy up and walk out.

But then his warm fingers connect with my jaw, and before I know what's happening, I'm facing him, his bright blue eyes boring into my watery, emotional ones.

"Little dove," he whispers. "I can't help you if you don't let me."

I gasp, but the shock of his words isn't enough to make me answer. I'm not sure anything ever will be.

There's only one man I trust in this godforsaken place, and he isn't staring back at me, asking me to open up to him. Instead, I'm staring back at one of two men who know exactly where I am and who isn't about to sneak me out because he feels sorry for me.

JD might be playing the nice guy right now, but I can't forget that he's one of them.

He's a Hawk.

Reid Harris's best friend.

I know exactly where his loyalties lie. And they aren't with me.

"Who said I wanted help?" I scoff. "Reid is right. I knew exactly what I was doing. I knew I'd end up here, or worse. Time to face the music."

His lips part to say something, but he swallows back the words before they spill free.

Releasing my jaw, he takes my uninjured hand instead and studies my wrist. His thumb brushes over my tattoo as he reads the words, but he doesn't comment on it.

Warmth spreads up my arm as he holds me. The urge to jump onto his lap and demand he wrap his arms around me until I'm warm is almost too much to deny. But thankfully, I manage to keep a lid on such a ridiculous request.

"This looks sore."

"It's fine," I argue, trying to rip my hand from his grip.

But he doesn't let me go. He holds me tight as he reaches for some cream in the first aid kit. He undoes the lid with his teeth before spitting it free and squirting a blob on my wrist.

I watch silently as he works, gently massaging the cool cream into my red, angry welts.

"JD," I whisper when he moves to the other, being extra careful of my wound.

His touch feels too good.

Warmth rushes up my arm as tingles erupt south of my stomach.

I swallow the whimper that wants to fall from my lips as he continues massaging my skin. His fingertips soothing my sore, exhausted muscles, forcing me to relax for the first time since I was hauled down here.

Fuck, he's good.

I roll my neck as I think about the magic he could work there. The image of me stripping down and lying before him fills my mind, making my temperature finally heat up.

I almost can't fight my smirk as I consider what Reid's reaction would be if he caught us.

I'm meant to be in hell down here, not allowing JD's hands to show me a little bit of heaven.

I bite my lip when he releases my wrist to stop me from crying out in protest, but the second he reaches for my leg and squirts more cool cream on my ankle, my protests die.

"Lie back," he encourages, his electric blue eyes holding mine, leaving zero room for argument.

My weak body complies, my frail arms trembling as I shuffle down until I'm flat on my back with one of my legs in his grip, the other resting across his lap.

His focus locks on where he's working for a few seconds before he lifts his head, his gaze leisurely wandering up my leg.

His eyes widen the moment he notices just how high my skirt has risen with my movement, but I don't do anything to hide from him.

"Damn, Dove." He growls, his eyes locked on my lace panties.

My heart pounds as I wonder how far I can push him and if it would make an ounce of difference.

Fuck making a difference. Those few minutes of pleasure would be worth it.

As his fingers gently circle my tender, marked skin, I shift my hips a little and lift my leg higher up his thigh.

My chest heaves and my temperature soars as his teasing touch continues.

"Do all your prisoners get this kind of treatment?" I ask, my voice a breathy whisper. I want to say it's all fake, but I'd be lying.

He chuckles. "They're all ugly assholes. Not my type."

"Blondes more your thing, huh?"

He clears his throat. "Something like that, yeah."

"From what I've heard, you're not discriminative of hair color, body type, or age."

He chuckles.

"Sometimes we've just got to do what we've got to do. I'm sure you understand that."

I swallow thickly.

More than he could possibly understand.

Our eyes hold as my chest heaves and my boiling blood continues to pump through my veins.

His touch is meant to be innocent. He hasn't moved from my ankle, but from how damp my panties are, you'd never believe it.

I really am nothing but a shameless whore who'll do anything for a man's touch and attention.

Releasing my foot, he gathers up the other one and gives it the same gentle treatment.

"You shouldn't be doing this," I warn him quietly. "If Reid comes back then—"

"I'll deal with the consequences, Dove. He's not all that scary, really."

"If you say so," I whisper.

"Maybe you should be the one stopping it," he counters, my foot so high that his breath races over my skin as he works. Goose bumps erupt and a shudder of desire rips down my spine.

"Maybe I should. But much like you, I don't tend to follow the rules."

Pulling my knee up, I slide my foot over JD's thigh until I find exactly what I was expecting.

"Dove," he warns when I rub the hardness hiding beneath his sweats.

"Sorry," I whisper. "Cramp."

He laughs, making his entire body shake with amusement.

"You're trouble."

"So are you," I counter.

His eyes shutter as I continue teasing him.

I close mine, focusing on his hardness against my foot, trying to imagine how thick and long he is.

My mouth waters as I picture discovering the truth with my tongue.

Whore, a little voice screams. But I slam it down.

I'm locked up with nothing else to do. What's wrong with having a little fun where I can find it?

It's stupid. He's barely touching me, and yet, it's like he's everywhere. His manly scent overpowers the antiseptic cream, and the heat of his fingers makes every inch of my skin tingle with awareness.

"Fuck, you're sexy," he murmurs, making my eyes spring open.

I'm pretty sure there are only a handful of days when I've looked worse than I do right now, but the way his eyes burn with desire, I can't help but believe him.

"Julian," I breathe when his hands begin to slide higher.

My nipples pebble, pressing against the lace of my bra and the jersey I'm wearing, begging to be freed.

I rub him harder, faster, hoping to break through whatever is holding him back.

"Fuck, Dove. Don't do that."

Lifting my uninjured arm from the bed, I walk my fingers up my stomach, making JD's eyes widen with interest before I cup one of my breasts.

"Oh God." I moan, but the pleasure only lasts a few seconds before JD's cell's ringtone cuts through the air and shatters the tension.

"Fuck," he barks, lowering my other foot to join the other on his lap before digging his cell from his pocket. "Fucking asshole."

Tipping his face to the ceiling, he sucks in a breath through clenched teeth before slipping from beneath me and getting to his feet.

"Yeah," he snaps into the phone.

There's a deep voice on the other end, and whatever he says makes JD's jaw lock up tight.

"You're a cunt," he snaps, before hanging up and dropping his cell back into the pocket of his sweats, making the fabric pull tight across his already more than obvious erection.

He swallows thickly as he holds my eyes for a beat, but they soon drop lower.

"Shit," he hisses before shoving his hand into his sweats to rearrange himself.

"Tease," I mutter, when he obviously squeezes himself to find some relief.

"Rain check?"

I shake my head. "Run along, little puppy, your master has called."

His brows pinch as irritation darkens his eyes.

"This isn't over."

Turning his back on me, he stalks toward the door.

"Wait," I cry before my brain catches up with my lips.

He pauses with his hand on the door, ready to slam it closed, locking me inside.

"I'm starving. Please can I have something to eat?"

"I'll see what I can do. Anything else?"

I pause, and he takes it as a no, pulling the door closed.

"A notebook."

"A notebook? If you want to write Mav love letters, then I'm pretty sure you'll be shit out of luck."

"I'm not writing to anyone. I just... please?" I ask weakly before he finally slams the door, leaving me alone. And horny.

"ARGH," I scream, kicking out my tired legs like a toddler having a tantrum.

Not my finest moment. But I really don't give a fuck.

11

REID

I stand with my palm resting on my desk staring at the screen in disbelief as JD massages Alana's fucking ankles.

He had one rule.

Don't fucking touch her.

And what does he do?

Fucking touches her.

I want to be pissed off that he defied me. But honestly, I knew he would. I'd probably be disappointed if he didn't. What really pisses me off is the way she's melting for him.

He's barely doing anything and she's practically a puddle of need on that cot.

I tell myself to let it go. If he turns her into a needy little whore who's desperate for his cock then maybe he'll manage to get more out of her than I have.

Hell knows she's fighting hard against my techniques this far.

Although I must admit, I wasn't expecting the hair thing to touch such a nerve.

I expected her to care. Most girls with long hair would,

but after everything I've thrown at her so far, I wasn't expecting that to be the thing that broke her.

Watching her tears, though. Fuck me. She looked beautiful. The only thing that would make it better would be if she were choking on my cock at the same time.

Don't go there.

Ignoring JD and the way she's rubbing her foot against his junk, I focus on her.

She probably thinks she looks like a hot mess right now. But she's wrong.

There's a reason why he's probably as hard as nails under her foot.

I know I fucking well would be.

Jesus. I'm fucking jealous of him getting his cock rubbed by her foot. What is wrong with me? It's like I've reverted back to being a horny twelve-year-old boy, hoping for a hand job at the back of class.

Grabbing my cell from the side, I grip it so hard I worry it's about to shatter in my hand as I wait for a sign I know is coming to get him the fuck out of there.

I love the fucking man, but fuck me, is he a dog. Given half a chance, he won't stop. If we want her secrets, we need her desperate. Right on the edge, whether it's out of fear, exhaustion, or desire. That's when she'll spill.

The second her fingers begin walking up her stomach, dragging her jersey up, exposing more skin in the process, I know it's time.

And I'm only proved right as the call connects at the exact moment she cups her breast.

Fucking hell. She's as bad as him.

No wonder she agreed to be my father's whore.

I watch the screen with a smirk as JD drops her exactly like I knew he would at my demand. The slight pout on her lips makes it worth it.

"Sorry, Pet. No more fun for you today."

The second he slams and locks the door, I turn the monitor off and leave my room.

My footsteps pound down the stairs as the door to the basement in the hallway slams closed.

I don't need to look up to know he's glaring up at me. He's too fucking predictable for his own good.

"The fuck, man?" he barks.

"We need to go," I say, shoulder-checking him as I pass to find my wallet in the kitchen.

"Go where?" he asks, following me, also like I knew he would.

"Clubhouse. Victor wants to discuss something."

"Oh?"

"Don't be dumb, JD. That bitch is working for him," I hiss.

"Victor? She's working for fucking Victor?"

"Apparently."

"Mav wouldn't allow that," JD states, pissing me off more than he already has.

"How the fuck would you know what Mav wouldn't allow of his whore of a wife?"

He shrugs. "I dunno. Assuming, I guess."

"Fuck me. One fucking rub of your dick and she's got you whipped up like a fucking pussy. Get your head in the game, man."

"It is," he snaps back, his jaw locked tight.

"Whatever. We need to go."

"What does he want?" JD asks, trailing behind me.

"Probably to see if we've seen his little bitch."

"And what the hell are you gonna say if he does."

"The truth. That I couldn't give a fuck about Alana or what she's done."

His laughter bounces off the walls as I walk toward the front door.

It hits my last fucking nerve.

I spin around faster than he can compute and have him backed up against the wall with my forearm against his throat.

"You had one thing to do, JD. One. You know exactly what I'd do to any other motherfucker who disrespected me like that."

His smirk grows.

"Fuck off, Harris. You knew exactly what I was gonna do down there after getting a warning not to touch her. You wouldn't have planted the seed if you didn't want me to try and break her. Not my fault you took the wrong course of action with your big bad scary gangster routine. Haven't I told you before? It's the gentle touch that gets results."

Like a patronizing little prick, he pats my cheek.

"Cunt," I hiss, shoving away from him.

"Guilty. Just like you, motherfucker. What was that?" he asks, not hearing the curses I mutter under my breath.

"Fuck off."

"You're just pissed because you know I'm going to get the intel before you. How about we make it really worth our while?" he suggests.

I don't respond, instead focusing on climbing into my car, but he continues the second he's in my passenger seat. "I bet I can break her with gentle touches and sweet words long before you can scare the truth out of her."

"You seriously want to make a bet out of this?" I ask as I spin my Charger around in front of the house and press my foot to the gas, sending stones shooting up behind us as we take off.

"Sure, why not. It's about time we had some fun. Shit's

been hella serious recently. And in case you hadn't noticed, you're stressed as fuck."

"Then maybe I should be the one trying to convince her to talk with my dick," I mutter.

He barks out a laugh. "Yeah, maybe. You won't though, and we both know it."

"What the fuck is that meant to mean?" I growl, irritation rolling through me at his assumption.

"You had her strapped to a fucking chair for hours and you never laid a finger on her. You ain't gonna fuck her, even though you want to."

"She's Mav's wife." I grunt. "Brothers' wives are off-limits."

"Even more reason to, don't you think?"

"No. I don't think. I don't want anything that belongs to him."

"He still calling her cell?" he asks, changing the subject slightly.

"Yeah."

"So safe to say that he's not in on this then if he's freaking the fuck out."

My grip on the wheel tightens as the gates that hide the entrance to my castle slide open, revealing the road on the other side.

I want to agree, but I don't trust that sly motherfucker.

It could easily be an act. Just like their marriage.

"Only time will tell," I state, taking a sharp left that will lead us into the pits of hell, where my father chooses to rule his empire.

He still has the house we all grew up in, but he's hardly ever there. Instead, Hannah, our youngest brother's mom, is in that house alone, while Victor fucks whatever whore he wants at the club.

Fuck knows why she still sticks around. Victor can't be

bothered with her, and Gray is gone. She hasn't really got much to hang around for. It's not like any of us need her.

We might have a better relationship with her than we used to, but she's not exactly a mother to us. We had one of those, a really fucking good one who didn't deserve to be replaced.

She was way too good for a cunt like Victor. She should have gotten so much more out of life than what that prick gave her. Aside from us of course. Her boys were everything to her. She just hated what we were ultimately going to be.

Younger versions of him.

Our lives were always going to revolve around the Hawks. It's in our blood. I'm pretty sure if we turned our backs on it then we'd have found a bullet lodged in said back as we tried to flee.

It's a relief that we all chose this life, to embrace our heritage, our birthrights. Although it doesn't mean that the four of us aren't always looking over our shoulders, waiting for the other shoe to drop.

While we might have followed in our father's footsteps, we're not exactly singing from the same song sheet with how he runs his territory.

As usual, cars and bikes are everywhere when we pull up into the old warehouse. Back in the day it used to be some old clothing factory. But that was before the Hawks turned this up-and-coming town into the down-and-out place it currently is.

Now the biggest warehouse is our clubhouse, consisting of a massive bar and lounge area, along with apartments for the members to crash in and offices where the higher-ranking members make all the fucked-up decisions. And not forgetting the playground out the back where we take our enemies to 'play.'

"Game face on, man," I command.

"I appreciate the warning, but I'm more than competent at lying through my teeth when required."

I glance over at him, feeling like the shittiest friend in the world. For all intents and purposes, JD is my brother. We're as close, if not closer, than me and Dev.

He appeared in Harrow Creek Elementary one day and was told to come and sit next to me, and that was it. We've been inseparable ever since.

For a long time, I didn't really know him. He wanted to hang out and be friends, that was more than obvious, but he was also terrified of letting anyone close.

I get it now; I know his story and where he came from. But back then I didn't understand it. Why he never spoke about his parents or any siblings, when my family was such a huge part of my life.

"Shit. I know, man. Sorry." JD is probably one of the only people in the world who will ever hear me apologize for being an asshole. I don't give a shit about many others to bother making the effort.

"S'all good. Shall we do this?"

I nod and push my door open.

With my mask firmly in place, we walk into the clubhouse side by side.

Almost every set of eyes in the main communal area turn our way as we enter, but I don't look at a single one of them.

Most of them are our junior members, who prefer hanging out here pretending to be gangsters than living whatever bullshit lives they're trying to drown out with booze, drugs, pussy, and violence.

Some are young and naïve—many still in high school—but others are just assholes who've never initiated but can't give up the life or the status of being even loosely affiliated with us.

Music booms, and in only a few seconds, the chatter and laughter that filled the air before we walked in returns as we head toward the stairs.

Silently, we make our way up. We don't need words; I already know exactly what JD is thinking.

"This better be quick," he mutters as we approach Victor's office door. "Got something pretty waiting for me at home."

"You're an asshole," I hiss.

"That's why you love me."

"Irritating motherfucker," I mumble.

Knocking once, I shove the door open. He isn't getting any more warning or pleasantries from us.

12

MAVERICK

Beneath the table, my hands curl into fists as Reid and JD walk into Victor's office as if they own the place.

Reid might be the heir to all this, but Victor is still very much living and breathing. And from what I can figure out, it's going to take some serious work to change that, unless luck is on our side and he suddenly drops dead.

That motherfucker, unfortunately, has just as many allies as he does enemies, and they'll protect him until their last dying breath.

Anyone stupid enough to attempt to take down Victor 'Vicious' Harris has a death wish. And while many of us might hate him, we choose our lives over ruining his.

I know what he does to people he's supposed to like, so I hate to think what he'd do if one of us were to turn our backs on him and try to bring down his reign of terror over this town.

"You're late," Victor barks, his eyes locked on his prick of a son as he saunters in and pulls a chair out. Dad sits on one side of him, Kurt, Alana's father on the other. Both of their expressions are blank as they wait impatiently. Reid's best friend follows suit until the two of them are sitting there like everything is right in their fucked-up worlds.

"Didn't realize we were on a deadline. You should have said."

Victor's lips press into a thin line, but he doesn't respond.

"So, what's going on? We've got shit to do."

"Alana has disappeared." My chest contracts at the cold, detached tone of his voice.

My eyes dart to Kurt but there isn't a flicker of concern in his dark, demonic eyes.

They don't give a shit that my wife is missing. Victor might have reluctantly agreed to hold a meeting, but he made it more than clear that he wasn't interested in my domestic issues.

Not sure he'd have the same opinion if his woman disappeared.

Although, he's Victor Harris. He probably wouldn't even notice.

Hannah is nothing but a toy to him to use as he sees fit. Which, seeing as he spends most of his time here, isn't very often.

Lucky her.

"And?" Reid asks, crossing his arms over his chest. There isn't a flicker of concern, of anything, on his face.

"She's gone," I bark, my irritation levels rising.

There aren't many things in this life that really get my blood boiling, but Alana is one of them.

"Yeah, I got that from the word disappeared," Reid snarls.

I'm on my feet, my chair on the floor behind me before I realize the red haze has descended.

"Mav," Dad barks, demanding I stand down.

This rivalry between me and Reid has been going on all our lives. When we were kids, it turned bloody more times than I can remember. I'm pretty sure it was how we both honed our fighting skills. But it's been a few years since we've caused each other any real damage.

After the past twenty-four hours though, I'm more than fucking ready for it.

"She didn't come home Saturday night, and I can't find a trace of her," I force out through gritted teeth, instead of doing what I really want and throwing a few punches in his smug fucking face.

"And this requires a meeting, why? I didn't call one the last time I lost an odd sock."

My teeth grind so hard I've no idea how one doesn't crack.

"She's my wife."

"Is she, though?" JD counters.

"Yes."

"We'll keep an eye out for your stray, Mav. But can I suggest that you try and keep better care of the things that belong to you?" Reid pushes to his feet. "Are we done here? Or has someone lost a pet fucking hamster as well that we need to hear about?"

"We need to talk," Victor says, holding his eldest son's eyes. "Give us all a minute, will you."

"That's it?" I balk. "She's fucking vanished and you're going to do nothing about it?"

"Pussy comes and goes, Mav. Probably for the best you get used to it," Victor states coldly.

"She's not just some pussy, though. Is she?" I bellow, ripping my eyes from Victor's, levelling Alana's cunt of a father with a glare that most would shy away from. Not that prick, though. He's as cold and corrupt and as the man he's sitting next to.

I wasn't expecting him to care about Alana's disappearance. He hasn't cared about her well-being since the day she was born. All he wanted her for was entertainment. Sick fuck.

The day I get to pull the trigger and put that motherfucker in the ground can't come soon enough.

Both of them. All of them. Every asshole in this room can follow right behind for all I care. Then I'm going to take my wife's hand and we're going to walk out of this shithole once and for all and start over somewhere new. Somewhere no one knows us, where we can be the people we were meant to be before the toxicity of our lives dug its claws in and dripped poison through our veins.

I'm addicted to seeing her smile, the lightness in her blue eyes in the moments where she lets go and forgets about our reality, her past. It's everything.

I want to give her everything she deserves and start over. Together.

I've given her everything I've been able to up until now. Everything I'm willing to while we're still surrounded by her past. Every night she has terrors and I wake up to her screaming. Every single night those motherfuckers pull her back into their clutches and punish her. They're still in control of her life and I fucking hate it.

She deserves so much more.

I'm not worthy of giving it to her, though. Not really. I might not be as bad as the men of her past, but I'm not fucking good either. I've got more blood on my hands than she knows about, and I'm guilty of so much more.

I'd do it every fucking day if I could banish everything that haunts her. And if it comes to it, I'll make the ultimate sacrifice if it means she gets to leave it all behind.

Unless it's too late and she's already found her escape.

The thought of her leaving me rips through my chest.

The reality of her giving up on me hurts more than I ever thought it would.

She wouldn't just walk away. Not after everything. It's too easy.

I hold on to that little voice with both hands.

Someone knows something. They have to.

Yes, women might vanish in plain sight almost daily in a place like the Creek, but not Alana. Not the wife of one of the highest-ranking Hawks.

Just like I'm not stupid enough to put a bullet in Victor, they shouldn't be stupid enough to take what belongs to me.

I want to shout, and demand answers from her father, for all the things he put her through. But what's the point? He's never shown an ounce of remorse in the past, why should I expect him to care now?

A pair of hands forcefully shove me forward and when I glance back, I find my father glaring at me.

JD holds the door open, allowing us to slip out, followed by Alana's father.

"He's right, you know. You really should have put her on a shorter leash if you wanted to keep her in check. We all know that whores like Alana don't stick around long," JD taunts.

I surge forward with my fists clenched ready to land a blow or two that I hope will help to expel some of the restless energy that's buzzing through my veins.

But I don't get close enough to even throw the punch I crave because Dad's solid arm darts out, stopping me.

"She's not a whore," I seethe. "She's nothing like the girls downstairs. She's not selling her cunt for whatever she can get."

"Are you sure about that?" JD asks, his signature smirk fully in place on his lips.

"I know my wife."

"So well it seems that she vanished and you've no idea where she's gone."

My teeth grind and my nostrils flare as I glare at him.

"Do you even know where she went before disappearing?" he asks.

"Of course," I lie.

The way his smile grows tells me that he can see right through my bullshit.

"She's really done a number on you, hasn't she, Mav? Have you checked your bank accounts since she vanished to see if she left you with anything?"

"She's not a thief," I argue.

Alana has never stolen from me. Hell, for the first few years she was with me, she point-blank refused to accept even the cheapest of things from me, stating that I didn't owe her anything.

She was right. I didn't.

The person who did was still searching for her. He should have been the one to give her everything she needed. But I was quickly learning that the only thing he ever did was take things away.

Her innocence, her self-esteem, her self-worth, her childhood.

I wanted to show her that not all men were monsters. That they didn't only see one thing when they looked at her.

I wanted to be better. To be worthy, despite my position with the Hawks.

And more than anything, with every day that passed and the more I learned about the life she'd been living, I wanted revenge.

I hated my father for the way he chose to live his life and the people he hurt in the process. I hated him for the things he did that I was meant to just go along with. I hate the person he tried to make me.

A little version of him.

Being with Alana allowed me to be the person I wanted to be.

Behind closed doors, where no one was watching or expecting anything of me, I could attempt to repent for my sins and do something good.

I thought it was enough. I thought I'd given her the life she needed. Well almost.

There's something I've always held back. Something I've refused to allow either of us to indulge in. Because if I did... I'd be as bad as them.

I refuse to stoop to their level and give her any reason to think that the only reason I took her home that night was because I had any other intentions than protecting her.

"I dunno," JD mutters, reminding me that we were in the middle of something. "She certainly seems to have stolen something from you. Your fucking balls, maybe?" He laughs.

"Come on, let's go and get a drink," Kurt, Alana's dad, says, as if nothing is wrong in the fucking world.

"You're not serious?" I blurt, unable to keep the words in.

"Deadly."

He takes off and is halfway down the stairs before I speak again.

"Last time she vanished, you had every single Hawk on the roster out looking for her."

"Yeah, and look how that ended." He growls, reminding me of the fallout when the truth about what I did that night was exposed.

I wasn't stupid. I knew hiding her away and keeping her safe would come with a price.

I was willing to pay it too as long as she was safe.

And pay, I did. In ways I don't ever want her to know about.

With my arms wrapped around my middle, I curl up in a ball, willing the sharp pains in my empty stomach to abate.

But unsurprisingly, it does very little to help.

I really thought JD was going to come back and bring me food. The notebook might have been a bit of an ask, but I really thought he was going to feed me.

Stupid, stupid, naïve little Alana. Always seeing the good that doesn't exist in people and being taken in by a pretty face.

Just when I think I'm winning, another man comes along and kicks me where it hurts the most, proving to me that none of them can be trusted.

Not a single one.

By the time the door lock rattles, I'm beyond empty. Not only does my stomach feel like it's eating itself, but my chest aches and my eyes burn from the number of tears I've shed.

The door swings open and I keep my back to whoever has finally turned up to check on me. I tell myself that I don't care about anything they might have finally brought or anything they have to say.

But then that scent hits me.

A scent I can't ignore.

My mouth waters and my stomach rumbles so loudly I'm pretty sure it bounces off the walls.

A deep, cocky chuckle hits my ears, but I don't care.

Everything I told myself about men and their inability to follow through on anything flies straight out the window.

Flipping over, I barely see which asshole has invited himself into my cell. My focus is solely on the bag in his hand.

"I didn't know what you wanted so I just got—"

The second he's close enough, I snatch the bag from his hands and set it on my lap.

Ripping into it, I breathe in deeply, letting the greasy addictive scent of burger and fries flow through my nose.

Stuffing my hand inside, I grab a load of fries and lift them to my mouth.

I don't give a shit how I look. I just need to eat.

"Oh my God." I groan around the mouthful of crisp, salty goodness.

JD chuckles again, his attention burning the side of my face. But I don't look over. I can't. My focus is fully locked on the double cheeseburger I pull out of the box.

I'm pretty sure it's the best burger I've ever tasted. The moan of pleasure as I chew is nothing but obscene.

"You really like the meat, huh?" JD deadpans as I practically inhale the entire thing.

"Shut the fuck up," I mutter, diving back into the bag to find what other delights he might have got me. "Jesus, did you order one of everything on the menu?" I ask, appreciating just how big this bag is and how much food is inside.

"Not quite. Like I said, I wasn't sure what you liked. And," he says, reaching for the bag that I'm unwilling to let go, "some of it is for me."

"Hey," I complain, clutching the bag to my chest like it's my lifeline.

"Just one burger?" he asks, giving me his best pouty face.

"Don't tell me that actually works with girls." I snort.

"I don't usually have to beg for food," he reasons.

"No, but from what I've heard, you have to offer up anything you can to convince them to suck your cock."

"Ouch, Dove. That hurts."

"Not denying it though, I notice."

"Little dove, the only begging that happens around me is them desperate for my cock."

"Sure, it is. Here," I say, handing over one of the boxes.

"Filet-O-Fish?" He balks, glaring down at it in disgust. "Out of all the things in that bag, you give me this?"

"I don't like it."

"Nor do I," he counters.

"Yeah, well, you're not locked in a cell still wearing yesterday's clothes, having had your hair cut off and a bandage on your wrist, where some asshole tried to amputate your hand."

"Whoa, I was trying to be nice. The knife slipped."

"Sure, it did," I mutter, diving in for the box of Chicken McNuggets.

I glance at him after throwing an entire nugget into my mouth and instantly feel bad. He genuinely looks gutted about hurting me.

"Does it still hurt?" he asks.

"Everything hurts. And I stink. And my hair is probably a fucking disaster. I understand why there are no mirrors in here."

"That's more so you don't decide that death is better than being Reid's pet and slash up your wrists with the glass."

"I haven't survived this long to bleed out in here for that cunt to find me. What?" I ask when he stares at me in disbelief.

"Nothing."

I raise a brow.

"You're stronger than you look, huh?"

"I guess you'll find out if my stay here continues."

"All you've got to do is answer Reid's questions honestly," he says like it's the simplest thing in the world.

"Yeah, that's not going to happen."

"You're working for Victor," JD states, letting me know that he's been talking to Reid.

"What I do is none of your business. Neither of you."

"I'd have fully agreed until you ended up down here."

"It's probably a good thing that I don't care what you think then, isn't it?"

Throwing the McNugget box on the floor, I dive in for more.

"Does Mav know you're working for Vic?" JD asks as I pull out a McChicken Sandwich and flip the box open.

I should probably stop before I make myself sick. But I'm still too hungry. And something tells me that Reid is clueless about this, and I need to make the most of the opportunity while I have it.

I shoot JD a glare.

"I'll take that as a no then," he mutters, reaching for a couple of fries, which I allow. "So that leads me to believe that he either has something over you, or you're trying to get something out of him."

"Think what you like, I'm not talking because you

brought me a bag full of McDonald's. It'll take more than that to get my secrets."

"I just saw him," JD says, making my head spin.

"Who? Victor?" I ask, my blood turning to ice just thinking about the twisted cunt.

"Well, yeah. But I was talking about Mav."

"Oh," falls from my lips as I fight to lock down how I really feel. "How was he?" I ask, hopefully nonchalantly.

"Honestly?"

"Well, I'm not sitting here hoping you're going to lie to me," I scoff.

"He's a mess."

All the air rushes from my lungs as he delivers those three words. He might as well have swung a bat and struck me across the back.

"He called a meeting because he can't find you, or any trace of where you disappeared to. Victor, Razor, and your dad couldn't have looked less concerned about it."

A bitter laugh falls from my lips.

"I'm shocked."

"Well, if you really are working for Victor, I'd have expected him to be a little concerned."

"That would mean he'd have to explain why he's suddenly so interested in me."

"So no one knows you've been working for him." It isn't a question. It doesn't need to be.

"Even the most corrupt have limits with who they associate."

JD's eyes widen.

"What? You think he wanted me on his payroll?" Not that the cunt actually pays me, of course.

The reason I didn't have a choice but to agree to his demands had nothing to do with money.

JD studies me and I internally cringe.

Without saying much, I'm giving things away. And I'm quickly learning that JD is much more astute than most would believe him to be. Something tells me that there might just be more to this cheeky playboy than meets the eye.

"Did you want a shower?" he asks, changing the subject and giving me whiplash.

I look down at the half-eaten burger in my hand, realizing I can't stomach any more.

"A shower?" I echo. "Why?"

His smirk widens. "Well, generally people shower to get clean. But I guess some do other things." He leans closer, to whisper in my ear, "Like get off."

A needy whimper passes my lips before I manage to catch it as the memory of his hands on me earlier floods my mind.

"You ever done that?" he rasps, his warm breath rushing down my neck, making my nipples pebble.

"Done what?" I ask innocently.

"Nice try. I know you're not that sweet and innocent. I've heard some of the things you've got up to with Legend."

"I didn't have him pegged as a gossip," I state, my heart rate increasing.

If JD and Reid know all about what I was up to with Kane, then it could so easily get back to Mav.

The others Vic had me spend time with weren't as tight to the Hawks' inner circle. They were safer. But Kane... He was always going to be the one to unravel this whole thing.

But would he even care? A little voice mutters in the back of my head.

JD said that Mav's a mess trying to find me. But is that just his need to be my big brother taking over again?

I appreciate his support more than I could ever express. But at the same time, it's frustrating as fuck.

Mav isn't my big brother. Nor have I ever wanted him to be.

I might have been only sixteen when he rescued me, but I'd experienced more than most adults by the time Mav took me in and gave me a real home.

My body knew what it wanted, and my head was fully on board too. It's a shame he wasn't in the same place. And never has been.

I did everything I could think of. Tried to tempt him in any way I could. But he never cracked. I'd seen him with girls before we started our life together, so I know he isn't gay.

So why was I never good enough?

"So?" JD asks, his brows wiggling.

"What do you think?" I snap.

With my husband not putting out, I was forced to do the job myself. Safe to say, I've got a very good imagination and I've long learned all the things I like, and how to get myself off faster than I once thought possible.

His smile grows.

"I think I'm going to need evidence."

"And I think you're a pig," I mutter, shoving the bag on my bed and climbing to my feet.

Despite having food, the room still spins and my legs tremble.

I guess it'll take a little longer to get my strength back up.

"You okay?" JD asks, his large, hot hand landing on my waist to steady me.

"Yeah. Which way is the shower?"

Taking my hand, he tugs me toward the door.

"I'm capable of just following, you know," I hiss.

"Humor me."

"You must be going through a dry spell if holding hands is making you happy right now."

"Who said we're stopping at holding hands," he counters, shooting a wicked look over his shoulder.

"I am," I state, continuing to be towed along until I'm standing in the middle of a bathroom behind a door I didn't know existed on the other side of Reid's interrogation room.

"Go on then," JD encourages, a little too close, seeing as he's suggesting I get naked and step into the shower on the other side of the room.

"I don't need a spectator."

"Then you don't need a shower badly enough," he counters.

"You're kidding?" I ask, spinning around to face him with my hands on my hips.

I desperately want to clean up, but I'm not sure I want it enough to be watched.

"Nope. Your choice."

Crossing his thick arms over his chest, he stares at me. Daring me to cower.

He really needs to learn... I'm not the kind of girl anyone can easily intimidate.

Alana glares right back, waiting for me to tell her that I'm joking.

I'm not.

If Reid knew I was offering this to her, he'd have my balls in that vise we just passed.

I dare not leave her to her own devices. Fuck knows what she might do.

And yeah... I totally want to watch.

Call me a perv or whatever. I don't care.

"Just think how nice that warm water will feel rushing over your skin," I say, letting my eyes drop down her body as if she's already standing naked before me.

"Fine," she hisses, her hand going to the button around her waist. "I've nothing to hide."

Her skirt falls to her ankles, leaving her in Kane's Panthers jersey and her tiny black underwear.

I'm not really all that into football, but right now, I could be convinced to change my mind if she were to walk around like that with my name on her back.

Dempsey 01. Has a nice ring to it.

Would piss Reid the fuck off too.

My cell burns in my pocket with my need to find somewhere to order it.

Extra small so it hugs her curves and lets me know the second her nipples get hard beneath.

Visions of fucking her from behind, my hand twisted in her hair, my name on her back as I thrust inside her fill my mind.

Goddamn, it's good.

"You okay?" Alana asks with a smirk.

"G-great. You?"

Her eyes drop to my waist, but I don't follow. I already know what's happening down there.

"We don't have all day, Dove. He could be back any moment. And trust me when I say that neither of us needs him to catch us right now."

"Oh, JD, are you being a naughty boy and breaking the rules again?" she teases, dragging the jersey up and exposing her toned stomach.

One thing is for sure, this girl knows how to work out.

My mouth runs dry as she peels it from her body, leaving her standing before me in her lingerie.

"I see you were planning on the night with Kane playing out differently," I mutter.

"Maybe. Maybe not."

I chuckle.

"Maybe I always wanted to be stuck down here as yours and Reid's little plaything."

"Now that conjures up an image I can't ignore, little dove."

Turning her back on me, I watch as she unhooks her bra and lets it fall to the ground before she tucks her thumbs into her panties and pushes those from her body too.

Fuck me, this was the best idea I've ever had.

She moves slowly toward the shower, her hips sway and her toned ass clenches before reaching in and turning the dial.

I watch her in silence as she waits for the water to warm, and just before she steps inside, she looks over her shoulder.

"I didn't get the impression Reid was very good at sharing his toys."

"He has his moments," I muse as she steps under the spray.

The moan that rips from her throat as the warm water rushes over her skin is downright filthy.

Unfolding my arms, I grip my dick through my sweats and squeeze.

"What else happened at your little meeting, JD?" She shoots over her shoulder as she reaches for the shower gel and begins rubbing it over her curves.

"Not much. Mav got shot down for caring and Victor kicked us out to talk to his golden child alone."

"Careful, you sound a little jealous there, JD."

"Of having a father like Victor. I don't think so," I scoff.

"So you got kicked out. Did he say anything?"

I laugh. "You really think that because you got naked and showed me your ass, I'm going to tell you everything I know. I was starting to think you were smart, Dove."

"What is this, tit for tat?"

"I guess you could call it that, yeah. You want something from me, you're going to need to give me something in return."

"What if you don't have anything?" she asks, squirting some shampoo into her hand before soaping up her new, shorter locks.

"I guess that's a risk you'll have to take," I counter as I

push from the wall and move closer. My pull to her is too much to deny.

Resting my ass back against the counter opposite her, I curl my fingers around the top in the hope it'll stop me from reaching for her.

"Does he suspect you and Reid have anything to do with me disappearing?" she asks.

"Nah, he's fucking clueless." I laugh. "Almost feel sorry for the poor, miserable fuck. You really have him wrapped around your little finger, don't you?"

A growl of frustration rumbles deep in her chest.

"It's weird because I only ever thought men lost their heads to women after getting inside their cunts. But Mav seems to be an exception to the rule. Unless you've been lying." She stills but doesn't say anything. "Maybe the whole 'her husband doesn't treat her right' line is nothing but bullshit so those men you've been keeping entertained feel good about themselves when they fill the hole. Pun intended."

Silence.

"What's wrong, little dove? Cat got your tongue all of a sudden?"

"Mav's a good man," she says quietly.

"I guess that depends on who you ask. The bodies he's put in the ground over the years would probably say otherwise."

"Is he still out looking for me?"

"What do you think?" I mutter, my eyes locked on her ass.

"I think he's smarter than both of you put together. I think he'll figure it out and come after me."

"If he does then he's not as smart as you think. Coming here would be akin to a death wish for him."

"So just let me go." She tips her face toward the spray, letting the soap bubbles rush down over her curves.

Fuck, I wish I could see the front.

"Not going to happen, Dove. That ring on your finger might make you think you belong to Mav. But you're ours now.

"You. Belong. To. Us."

"Wrong," she states, before finally spinning around and giving me exactly what I need.

And ho-ly fuck.

No wonder this woman has Hawks all across town on their knees for her.

She's a fucking goddess.

Her fingers massage her scalp, making her round tits bounce lightly. Her rosy nipples are hard, her chest heaving —probably with anger, but I'm happy to lie to myself right now. The dip of her waist and the flare of her hips are the kinds of things you usually only see in your dreams. But right now, it's standing in front of me.

"No conditioner?" she asks, checking the bottles on the shelves.

"Reid isn't overly concerned with the moisture content of his prisoner's hair."

"Surprised he cares about their cleanliness," she mutters, reaching for the shower gel again.

"Trust me, torturing someone who smells like a garbage truck and who's shit his pants for a week isn't fun for anyone."

"I guess every job has its hardships," she quips as she lifts both her hands to her breasts.

All the air rushes from my lungs as I watch her.

"What else did he say, JD?" she demands.

"H-he said..." I stutter like a sex-starved fool. "That you're not a whore or a thief."

"Why would he think I was a thief?"

"Because I suggested he check his bank account to see if you've run away with his fortune."

"He'd never believe I'd do something like that."

"Then he trusts you more than he should."

"Is that what you think of me?" she inquires, continuing to put on a show for me.

"Right now, I'm not sure I'm capable of thinking," I confess.

"What's the plan here, JD? Keep me locked up, torture my secrets out of me, get off on driving me crazy, and then what? Hand me back once you're bored of me?"

"I don't know the plan."

"Oh, that's right, I'm talking to the puppet, not the master."

My teeth grind at her words, but I can't deny they're true.

Reid beats to the tune of his own drum. I just follow the music.

The only thing I do know though, is that this isn't about Alana, not really. It's about Victor.

And if she's been working with him, then she's just as much of a target as he is.

"Mav won't stop," she assures me. "He won't forget about me."

"You sure about that?"

"Yes," she states confidently.

"Why did he take you in, Dove? Why did he marry you and not fuck you?"

She stares at me, the answers to my questions dancing right on the tip of her tongue.

"You can tell me, little dove. I'm not here to hurt you. But we need to know what we're dealing with."

"What you're dealing with is me. The whore that Victor

has been pimping out for whatever reason he sees fit. Mav has nothing to do with this."

Her words, the way she describes herself, lights a fire inside me.

"No. This has everything to do with him," I bark, pushing from the counter and closing in on her.

Her eyes widen as I stop just before getting sprayed with water.

"You want him to fuck you, don't you? Is that what all of this is about? Desperate little housewife doing something stupid to get her husband's attention?"

"No," she argues. "That's not what— What are you doing?" she cries when I step closer and reach behind her for the showerhead.

"But you are desperate, right?"

"Julian." She moans when I hold the showerhead right in front of her nipple. Both of them harden as I tease her. "Oh God, this shouldn't feel this good." She gasps as I switch to the other side.

"Dirty whore," I whisper in her ear, ensuring my breath rushes over her neck.

"Is this what you want from him? You want him to see you as the beautiful, sexy woman that you are? You want him to take one look at your curves and drop to his knees to worship you?"

Her breathing becomes erratic, her chest heaving, making her tits even more tempting.

My mouth waters to dip low and suck her nipple into my mouth. But I don't.

I'm not going to touch her.

That's exactly what she wants.

"Yes," she whimpers.

"You've tried tempting him, haven't you?"

"Yes."

"I bet you walk around looking like a dirty little whore to catch his eye."

"Worked for you, didn't it?" she whispers breathlessly.

"Clearly, Mav and I are very different. He has the self-restraint of a rock and I—

"Have none?" she guesses. "Reid has told you to keep your hands off me, hasn't he?"

My lips part, but no words spill from them.

"That's why you're letting the shower do the job you're desperate to. You really are his little bitch, aren't you?"

I chuckle. "You know nothing, little dove. You've no idea the thoughts that are spinning through my head right now."

"I can make a good guess. Holy shit." She gasps as I suddenly drop the showerhead lower.

"Be a good little whore and open your legs for me," I demand.

Really, it's not necessary, I've hit the spot already and we both know it. I just want to see how compliant and desperate she really is.

I left her high and dry earlier.

Has she been thinking about where it could have gone since the moment my cell rang and I dropped her like a rock?

It takes her a second, but her feet finally shuffle apart.

"Good girl," I praise, making her whimper.

Her hips roll as I hold the showerhead steady. Her palm slaps against the tiles as her body begins to tremble with her incoming release.

"That good, little dove?" I ask, my voice rough with my own desire.

It would be so easy to spin her around, bend her over and take exactly what we both want.

But that isn't going to get me what I need.

I need her desperate, needy, craving my touch.

I'm going to prove that motherfucker wrong.

You can get way more results with desire than you can fear.

I've got this bet in the bag.

It's just a shame Alana's orgasm isn't such a sure thing.

15

ALANA

My head falls back as my release surges forward.
"Oh God. Yes. Yes," I cry.

My muscles lock up and I stop breathing, ready for the delicious crash I'm right on the edge of.

But it never comes.

The second before orgasmic bliss, the pressure on my clit vanishes, and the heat of the man standing before me disappears.

"What the—"

"Come on, time's up," JD says, making my head spin as he throws a small, dirty towel at me. I let it drop to the floor and stare at it with my top lip peeled back in disgust. "Feel free to stay naked for what I have planned next. It'll make it much more enjoyable for me."

"Glad to see you're not in denial about enjoying what you just did to me," I hiss. Deciding that the towel is the lesser of two evils, I bend down to pick it up.

"I think there's more than enough evidence to prove just how much I enjoyed it. My only regret is that I didn't film it to make use of later." Something flashes in his eyes, but it's gone before I can even attempt to decipher it.

"Pig."

He shrugs. "It was hot. Sue me."

"Suing you is the least of what I want to do after that stunt."

He chuckles as I march out of the bathroom with the towel around me.

I don't know why I bother, half of my ass is still on full display and it comes nowhere near to meeting at the front.

"You're an asshole."

"Oh, Dove. You've no idea. Sit," he demands, sneaking up on me and tugging me into the damn chair I've spent too many hours sitting in today.

"I swear to God, JD. If you tie me to this thing and leave me here for Reid, I'm going to—"

"You're going to what, little dove?" I glare at him as he steps in front of me. "I think Reid would fucking love it if he came down here to find you naked and bound to this chair.

"I've got to warn you though, he's a bit of a selfish lover and he'll probably get himself off and leave you even more desperate than you are now."

The thought of Reid pleasuring himself in front of me, coming all over me just to prove his point about who is in charge here makes my thighs clench.

"Oh, you like that, don't you, Dove?"

"Fuck off," I hiss, although it does nothing to disprove his point.

"That's why you're here, isn't it? You want to make Mav jealous, all the while being a dirty little whore who is desperate for us both.

"Maybe I should get Reid to pick up Devin and Ez on the way too. You know they'd be down for the party."

I keep my mouth shut as the picture he paints plays out

in my mind. Although, honestly, I couldn't give a crap about Reid's little brothers.

They're hot, sure. All the Harris brothers were gifted with the good-looking gene. It's just a shame they also got the sick and twisted ones from their father as well.

"Keep those pouty lips closed all you like, little dove. I can see it in your eyes." He leans close, so close his lips brush my ear. "I can smell it in your arousal."

I clamp my thighs together and he laughs.

"One day, Dove. I'm going to strap you to this chair and I'm going to do exactly what I want to you, and you'll have no say.

"I'll bind you up, blindfold and gag you and there will be nothing you can do about it."

I hate myself for the needy whimper that erupts from my throat.

"Or better yet. Did you know that Reid has hooks installed above your head and others in the floor?

"Can you imagine what it might be like being tied up and totally at our mercy? I could be at the front," he says, reaching out to tug the towel away from my body—not that it was hiding much anyway, "and I could finally go to town on these tits." He glances up at me. "They're fucking fabulous, by the way." He winks at me before looking back down.

"I know how badly you want me to suck on them, Dove. It's written all over you. They're sensitive too, aren't they? You reckon I could make you come from them alone?"

Lifting my chin, I refuse to dignify that question with an answer.

Anyway, he already knows. He saw it just now in the shower.

"Then I could drop to my knees and feast on your cunt

until you're screaming for mercy, desperate for me to let you come."

Whimper.

"And all the while, Reid could be behind you. He is rather fond of anal. He could have his tongue on you at the same time."

Whimper.

"Would you like that, Dove? What about if we both filled you at the same time? Have you ever done that before?"

I shake my head from side to side. Not to deny his question but to try and shake the image his words are conjuring up from my head.

"You're going to be dreaming about that tonight, aren't you?"

I fucking hope so. It'll be a hell of a lot more pleasurable than my usual nightmares.

"Sorry, I got a little distracted there, where were we?" he asks himself, before standing to full height and giving me yet another look at how much he wants everything he just described.

"It's funny how you call me a whore for being turned on and yet there you stand with your boner loud and proud."

"Oh, little dove," he muses as he pushes his hand into his sweats. "I never claimed to be anything else. I fucking love women, and sex. I have no shame in admitting that. And sharing you with Reid, while you're totally at our mercy. Fuck, yeah, that gets me hot."

"Asshole," I hiss as he continues walking away from me and pulls open Reid's torture cupboard.

I want to ask what he's searching for, but I keep my lips locked tight.

He's JD, not Reid. His torture seems to come in a very

different form to the twisted demon who roams these halls. Although, honestly, I'm not sure which one is worse.

"Ah-ha," he says before spinning back around.

My eyes widen at the things in his hand.

"What are you—"

"Don't you trust me?" he asks with a wicked glint in his eye.

"Is that a trick question?"

He laughs before pocketing a comb and expertly spinning the scissors around his finger and stepping in closer behind me.

The comb gently brushes against my scalp as he works through the knots left behind from the lack of conditioner.

"You need your roots done," he muses.

"No shit."

"You should let it grow out. I bet you're hot as a brunette."

"No," I state simply.

"Fair enough. You know, Reid didn't do half a bad job here."

"I don't believe that for a second; he just hacked straight across," I mutter as he makes use of the comb, pulling sections out straight and trimming the ends. "Although I'm worried you're about to make a bad job even worse."

"Have faith."

"Easy for you to say, you're not sitting here naked after being let out of your cell."

"I can get naked if it'll help. I can't promise you won't start begging the second you get a look at my cock though."

"As if," I mutter.

"I'll remind you of that when it happens."

"There's desperate and then there's desperate. I'm not that far gone yet."

I gasp the second his knuckles brush across my shoulder, proving my words to be nothing but bullshit.

"So I see." I don't need to turn around to know he's smiling.

"Just get on with it and lock me back up."

"So ungrateful," he mutters, continuing to work.

As the seconds tick by, I almost forget where I am as he works his way through my locks.

Each tug of my hair reminds me of all the things he teased me with earlier, the images he painted still playing out in my mind.

I bet they work well together.

Reid's rough and brutal touch and JD's gentle teases and precise touches.

"All done," he announces all too soon.

"Thank you... I think."

"There isn't a mirror down here so it doesn't really matter what I've done."

"I'll be walking out soon enough."

"You sound awfully confident about that seeing as you're refusing to talk."

"Nothing to say."

Pushing to my feet, I leave the towel behind and walk toward the hallway that leads to my cell.

"I would say thanks, but I'm not sure I'm all that grateful."

His eyes burn into my back as I put as much sway into my hips as I can manage.

"At least one of us enjoyed ourselves." His deep, growling voice continues to vibrate down the hallway as I slip into my room, getting a waft of fast food in the process.

But despite how hungry I was earlier, it now smells anything but appealing.

Grabbing the bag, I throw it out in the hallway and kick

the door closed, knowing that he'll come and lock me in at some point, and I fall down on my bed naked.

He's seen it all now, might as well use it to my advantage where I can.

It only takes two minutes for him to follow me and poke his head inside.

"Just so you know, there's a huge part of me that doesn't want to give you these," he says, placing my clothes on the end of the bed. "This though," he says, lifting my thong up in front of his face. "This is mine. And I know just what I'm going to do with it."

"Eat your heart out. We both know that you're going to be wishing you were down here eating something else."

Shamelessly, I part my thighs, letting him see exactly what he's going to be missing out on.

His breath catches when he spots something he didn't discover earlier.

"You're pierced."

"Yep. Shame you're never going to test it out, huh?"

I watch with a smirk as he sucks his bottom lip into his mouth and bites down on it as he stares at my vertical hood piercing.

"Reid know you got that?" he asks.

"I haven't sat him down and shown him it, if that's what you're getting at," I snark.

"Mav?"

I smile at him. "I guess that's just something you'll never know."

"Doesn't matter. He hasn't experienced it like I'm going to."

"Awfully presumptuous of you," I sneer, closing my legs once more.

"Or naïve of you to think it's not going to happen.

There's only one reason your cunt is wet right now, and we both know it's because of me."

"Actually," I argue. "It's because of you promising me that Reid is an anal man. Really gets my engine revving."

"You're a shit liar, Dove."

"Am I?"

He shakes his head, scrubbing his hand that's got my panties twisted around his fingers against his rough jaw.

"Enjoy your night, little dove. I know I will," he says with a wink, backing up toward my door with my panties against his nose. "Don't do anything I wouldn't do."

The slam of the door jolts through me, ending right at my clit.

"Fuck," I hiss, blowing out a long breath and closing my eyes.

But I don't relax. Every single muscle in my body is locked up tight, desire pulsing through my veins.

I need to fight it. I should be stronger, but fuck, the temptation to slide my hand down my body and finish what JD has started twice today is too much to deny.

16

REID

Being questioned by my father never puts me in a very good mood. But not knowing what JD was doing back at the mansion made it all the worse.

My cell was burning red hot in my pocket. If I were somewhere else, anywhere fucking else, I could have looked. I could have pulled up the live feed and seen what he was doing.

And the second I'm alone in my car, that's exactly what I do.

My heart jumps into my throat when I pull up the feed of her cell and find it empty.

"What the fuck have you done?" I seethe, clicking out of it and finding the one for the main room. "MOTHERFUCKER," I bellow into the confines of my car when the image of her sitting naked in my fucking chair appears before me.

I barely notice what he's doing. My eyes are glued to her body. Her tits, her curves, her flawless skin.

I had her bound to that thing only hours ago. Why

didn't I strip her naked first? She'd have looked so fucking perfect.

Because you wouldn't have been able to resist.

I've no idea what it is, but twenty-four hours in my cell and this woman is driving me crazier than any other I've ever met.

She's married. One of my father's whores.

I shouldn't be looking fucking twice.

But I can't help myself.

Movement over my shoulder drags my eyes from her and I find my douchebag of a best friend with a pair of scissors in his hand, tidying up the mess I made of her hair.

I want to say I'm surprised, but I'm not.

JD might not be as dark and fucked up as me, but he can deliver pain and punishment without much of a second thought. There's also another side of him, a caring side that I don't possess. And right now, that side of him has overtaken everything.

Putting my cell into its holder, I start the engine and gun the gas, desperate to get home before this goes too far.

He works meticulously, fixing her hair. Knowing him, he's making it better than it was before I touched it.

By the time I pull up at the house, he has her back in her cell.

She's lying in her cot, still fucking naked, but he's standing right in the way of the camera, blocking my view.

Bet he's fucking doing it on purpose too.

I'm torn between sitting in my car and seeing what he does next and storming down there to drag him out to put an end to it all.

Only a few seconds later though, I discover my interruption isn't needed because JD walks out of her cell, leaving her naked and alone.

Sucking in a deep breath, I grab my cell and throw the car door open, storming toward the house.

"What the fuck?" I bark the second I enter to find him emerging from the basement.

JD holds his hands up in defense. "I didn't touch her."

Dropping my eyes down his body, I take in the tent in his sweats.

"And apparently, she didn't touch you either," I deadpan.

"Fuck off," he grunts. "Some of us don't have the self-control of a fucking robot. She's hot. Fucking sue me."

He throws his hands up and marches toward the stairs.

"Where are you going?" I demand.

"To enjoy the show. I suggest you do the same. Take the edge off a bit."

"The show?" I ask.

"Bro, you might fool everyone else. But I can see through your bullshit." He smirks. "You've been watching me; I know you have. Which means you know exactly how I left her. Desperate as fuck." He takes off, walking up the stairs backward and he sinks his hand into his sweats. "So as I said. Enjoy the show."

The second he vanishes from my sight, I pull my cell from my pocket and open the video.

"Fuck me." I groan when I find he's right.

"Thank me later," the asshole calls down before his bedroom door slams closed.

With my eyes locked on the screen, I take the stairs two at a time, and in only seconds, I close myself into my own room.

Grabbing my AirPods, I turn the volume of the feed up and fall back on my bed.

"Yes," she hisses, her back arches and her hips roll as she twists and pulls both of her nipples.

I've no idea if she's aware of the cameras yet. I can only assume she isn't. Something tells me she isn't. If she knew, there is no way she'd willingly give us this kind of show.

With her eyes tightly closed, she squeezes her breasts, biting down on her bottom lip.

This is wrong. So fucking wrong. But no matter how much I tell myself to close it down and walk away, I can't.

She's got me in a fucking chokehold, and she has no idea.

She plays with her tits for a few more seconds before her hand slides down her toned stomach.

I might be imagining it, but I'm pretty sure a hoot of celebration comes from down the hall.

Fuck. I need to stop.

JD is a few doors down with his dick in his hand, getting off to this.

I should kill the feed and stop us both from watching. Give her some privacy.

But then her fingers collide with her clit and her moan of pleasure bounces off the walls of her cell, echoing in my ears, and all decent thoughts fly straight out the window.

My cock aches, my body burns as fire races through my veins. But I don't move. I don't do anything but watch as she expertly brings herself to ruin.

Her fingers alternate between rubbing her clit and plunging inside her. She moans and mewls, but thankfully, she doesn't gasp anyone's name.

"Oh God. Yes. Yes," she cries as her release surges forward.

My cell trembles in my hand with my restraint. My dick is painful behind my pants, but I refuse to do anything about it.

I'm stronger than this. I will not bow down to her

beauty. It's what she wants. Even if she did know this film was running, all she's doing is trying to make us weak.

She knows full well that if she can make us want her badly enough, then she'll effectively have us wrapped around her little finger.

It's what she's done to Mav.

I bet he's been walking around with blue fucking balls for years.

I smirk at the thought of that epic torture. Nothing less than he deserves.

What if it's not him that refuses to sleep with her, but the other way around.

What if she doesn't allow it, and instead, does everything she can to make his life hell? If it's the case then from just these few minutes alone, I know she's damn good at it.

What if Victor didn't choose to employ her? What if she orchestrated the whole thing?

She certainly has the power to bring that cunt to his knees. Anyone with a pussy does until he gets bored.

I loop right back around to my first suspicion when I locked her up downstairs.

What if she's playing all of us for her own gain?

"Julian," she cries as she finally falls.

"Fucking asshole," I seethe through gritted teeth.

I imagine him in his room fist pumping the air, knowing I just watched the same thing. I can see his smug, winning grin almost as clearly as if he was standing right in front of me.

Alana falls limp on her bed, her legs spread wide, showing us both every—

Holy fuck. Is that...

"Jesus Christ." I moan, scrubbing my hand down my face as I stare at the piercing glinting in the light.

A smirk pulls at my lips as ideas begin swirling around my head.

But before I can even think about implementing them, I open the app that controls the house and find the air conditioning. With very little concern, I turn it up to high, blasting all the cells in the basement with ice-cold air.

It's a risk. She might put two and two together and realize what I just watched. Although, chances are that she's so blissed she won't even notice.

I stare at her lying there with her chest heaving, her nipples hard and her legs splayed for a few more minutes before I can't take it any longer.

Dragging my hoodie over my head, I toe off my boots and shove my pants to the floor before replacing them with a t-shirt, shorts, and sneakers.

Shutting down the feed, I pocket my cell and head out of my room in favor of the gym.

The second I'm inside, I find a playlist with the angriest, deepest bass I can and hit play.

No sooner have I stepped onto the treadmill, do I have the speed as high as I can keep up with hoping to outrun everything watching her ignited in me.

In only minutes, my heart is pounding for a whole new reason and sweat covers my body, making my shirt stick to my back. My muscles burn, but I push harder and harder, forcing the memory of her to the back of my mind where it belongs.

I've no idea how long I run for, my legs tell me it's a long fucking time, while my head tells me that it's nowhere near enough when movement behind me makes my steps falter and I go flying off the back of the treadmill.

JD roars with laughter as I crash into the wall behind me and collapse to the floor in an exhausted heap. My muscles quiver and my head spins as I gasp to catch my breath. It's exactly what I needed. Well, not the ending.

"Can you shut the fuck up," I bark as JD continues to howl with laughter.

"Bro, that was fucking epic." He roars. Tears leak from his eyes as he rests his hands on his knees and tries to catch his breath.

Fucking moron.

"I'm glad I amuse you," I state flatly, finally getting to my feet and smoothing my shirt down my chest. "Are you here to work out or just to piss me off?" I glance down at his fresh sweats and bare feet.

"You wanted it, didn't you?" he asks like a smug prick.

"If you're not here to work, fuck off and make dinner or do something useful."

"I need to go and feed the rodents. I haven't given them anything all day."

"You've given one of them something," I mutter under my breath.

"Didn't touch her though, did I, Boss?" he mocks. "And from your tone, I'd be tempted to say that you haven't touched anything either. You know, a good orgasm would fix that mood right up."

I glare at him in the mirror as I move toward the weight bench and lie down.

"Thanks for that insight. Now will you fuck off? I'm busy."

"Busy thinking about Alana's pussy," he mutters. "Did you see the piercing? Fucking hot. I bet it makes it so sensitive."

"Are you fucking done?"

"Yep, all over her panties. It was good. Could have been better, though."

"JD," I bellow, my patience all but gone as I shove the barbell from its holder.

So much for the run to take the edge off.

"I'm going. I'm going. Just remember that you have me to thank the next time you go down there."

"Why's that exactly?" I ask, my arms trembling with the weight that was already loaded.

"Because I stole her underwear. You can borrow it if you want."

"Get out," I roar, dropping the barbell and almost crushing my chest in the process.

Fucking JD.

Fucking Alana.

Lifting the bar back into place, I sit up and comb my fingers through my hair.

I had a plan. It was all going fucking smoothly and then she turns and throws everything into chaos.

How does one little blonde woman cause so much fucking drama while locked in one tiny room?

17

ALANA

The heat from my release soon disappeared, right along with the high as my reality returned and I found myself alone in my gray cell.

My clothes might have dried by the time I pulled them on, but I was missing my panties and my bra. I remember JD holding the lace thong in front of his nose and inhaling. It really shouldn't have been as hot as it was. But then that's JD in a nutshell. Nothing about him or this situation should be turning me on. But it is.

It only confirms what I already know. I'm fucked up and broken beyond belief.

I should be terrified. Crying in the corner and begging to be released, not lying back on my bed getting myself off to fantasies about two men tying me up and doing a whole host of unholy things to me.

I might have been freezing, my entire body shivering again, but my exhaustion soon dragged me under. I'd hoped that maybe JD would be right and I'd spend all night having filthy dreams about all the things he described to me. Maybe I did. But the only dreams I remember were nightmares.

I might have been bound and totally at the mercy of two men. But it wasn't JD and Reid who stepped out of the shadows to punish me but two older, eviler men, who had a hand in ruining my life all those years ago.

I thought running from them would help. I even believed that being with Mav would provide me with the relief I was so desperate for. But while they might not have been anywhere near me, for the first few years at least. They never left. As soon as the sun set and I closed my eyes, there they were. Taunting me, torturing me, hurting me.

The opening of my heavy door drags me out of my fitful sleep. And despite how wrong it is, when Reid steps into my space, relief floods me that it's not *them*.

The same DNA might run through his veins. But he is not his father.

Vicious, corrupt, dangerous, and a whole host of other things.

But he is *not* his father.

I stare up into his eyes, trying to read anything in them. But it's impossible. They're closed off and dark.

He could just as easily be about to ask me to dance with him as he is about to murder me. Okay, so maybe the former might be a bit of a reach.

"Pet," he greets with a nod.

"Master," I tease. My lips twitch into a smirk when I get the smallest flicker of a reaction.

"Great. Shall we?" he asks, gesturing to the open door behind him.

"I'd love to." I smirk, getting to my feet and making a show of running my fingers through my now dry and freshly cut hair.

I might hate it because of how it happened, but I can't deny that it feels nice, even without the conditioner my bleached hair usually craves.

He doesn't move, forcing me to step around him, and go ahead.

Assuming he's not about to lead me to the stairs and to freedom, I turn toward his torture chamber with plenty of sass in my step.

"Do you want to explain why I found JD with your underwear last night?" he asks as I lower myself to the chair and cross my legs.

If I weren't already incredibly aware that I'm going commando, then I really am the second that question falls from his lips.

"Not really." I smile sweetly at him as he stops in the doorway and crosses his inked arms over his chest.

"So you didn't take them off to seduce him then?"

"What if I did?" I ask. "Maybe I gave him a full show, stripped down to nothing and let him see what he's never going to get."

Reid's jaw ticks as he studies me, letting me know that I'm getting to him.

"Did you want that too? It'll be quicker, seeing as he's stolen a layer, but I'm up for it you are. I'm nothing but a whore anyway, so I may as well make use of the goods God gave me."

Uncrossing my legs, I spread my knees. But he doesn't take the bait.

"I can't be as easily played as JD, Pet. It would do you well to remember that."

"Nor can I," I counter. "Oh, how was your meeting with Daddy yesterday? Did he have anything interesting to say?"

He clenches his jaw.

I wince. "Was I not meant to know about that? Whoops. Naughty JD. I hope you're going to punish him like you are me. Feel free to throw him into my cell. I think we could have some fun."

He smirks at me before pushing from the wall and walking behind me. Seeing as I'm not bound to the chair this time, I'm able to twist around and watch him as he starts the coffee machine.

"Latte for me, please," I order, making him snort in amusement.

While his coffee grinds, he reaches into a cupboard and pulls out a glass, which he fills with water and passes over.

"You've already proven that all you do with my coffee is waste it," he mutters.

"Maybe I wouldn't if you didn't try to singe my lips off with it."

"Not my fault you can't take the heat."

I shake my head at him.

The temptation to throw it at him is strong, but my need to relieve my dry throat is stronger.

"So what's the plan then, Big Man? More cold showers? Waterboarding? Maybe you're going to do a one-eighty and turn up the heat today with fire."

His eyes twitch as does my mouth. My overconfident word vomit has always been a flaw that's got me into more trouble than necessary with the men of this town when I'm backed into a corner.

"Why are you still talking?"

"Because I can." Probably not the smartest thing I've ever said because the next thing I know, he's walking toward me with a dirty rag.

His smirk is wicked and full of dark intentions.

My thighs clench as he moves closer, the threat of something delicious sparkling in his eyes.

I gasp as the rag is pressed against my lips, but me being me, I refuse to make this easy for him.

"Pet," he growls, irritated by my disobedience.

Get used to it, baby. It's going to take a lot to beat it out of me.

I smirk, my eyes crinkling with amusement, while his continues to grow darker.

Our battle of wills stretches out, neither of us willing to crack.

I see the second his patience runs out. His left eye twitches a beat before the fabric loosens, but I only get a beat of relief before his hand wraps around my throat.

I gasp in shock, my lips parting, and he makes the most of my surprise by tightening the rag across my mouth and quickly tying it behind my head.

"Asshole," I hiss, although I doubt he can make the word out.

His smirk of satisfaction only grows.

"You won't win here, Pet."

I want to point out that he won't get any of the answers he wants out of me while I'm gagged, but obviously, I can't, so I simply glare.

"I think I like you better silent," he taunts.

He studies me for a few seconds before he pulls rope from his back pocket and embarks on tying me to the chair again.

"I hate you," I scream behind the rag.

I've no idea if understands me, but his grin grows and his eyes darken nonetheless.

The fact I've still got a fresh wound on my wrist doesn't stop him from tying me up as tight as he did yesterday.

And this time, when I spread my legs, just to be a bitch, he doesn't try to look away.

"Pretty," he mutters, staring right at my pussy. "Shame it's probably bitter as fuck."

I growl as he continues to stare, and fuck if my body doesn't react to his attention.

He notices too.

"Nothing but a cheap and easy whore," he mutters before pushing to his feet.

Without giving me a second glance, he walks away. But he doesn't go too far because the sound of a door opening and a guy crying out fills the air.

Oh my God, I mutter to myself when Reid emerges dragging a dirty, skinny guy behind him. His hands and ankles are bound with the same rope that ties me to the chair, but it's clearly been there a while because it's dark, dirty, and disgusting. I dread to think about the state of the skin beneath it. Although, if the blood that's running down his arms is anything to go by, I'd say it's not pretty.

I watch in horror, acid churning in my stomach, as Reid hoists the man up and hangs him from one of the hooks JD taunted me with last night.

My eyes widen as I take in the state of the man. He's so skinny I can see all his ribs. His underwear hangs from his hip bones and his legs are stick thin.

Safe to say, he's been here a while. And I'd hazard a guess that he did something pretty bad for it to have gone on this long.

He's silent as Reid stands back and watches, his eyes tracking the cuts and bruises that litter the man's body.

"Tommy here tried stealing from me," Reid explains as if that excuses the state of this man. "He was a cocky asshole about it as well. Thought he was going to get away with it."

Reid paces back and forth as the man swings from side to side.

"It's been a while since we played, hasn't it, Tommy?"

The man whimpers, clearly in pain.

"What should it be?" Reid muses as he walks over to his cupboard of toys and scans the offerings.

Eventually, he reaches for something, and when he steps back, he has a baton in his hand.

Fear rips down my spine, despite the fact that he's not about to turn it on me. Or at least, I assume he's not.

Ripping my eyes from Reid, I stare up at the man hanging from the ceiling and I find him watching me.

Bile races up my throat and I fight to force it back down.

I refuse to show Reid any weakness.

"Pretty, isn't she?" Reid taunts.

The guy's throat ripples as he swallows, but he doesn't say anything. His eyes also never leave me.

"She's a whore." His description of me makes my teeth grind, or they would if they could meet. "A good one, from what I hear. Lets men do anything to her. Isn't that right, Pet?" I growl at him, which makes him chuckle like a maniac.

He's enjoying this way too much.

"You'd like that, wouldn't you, Tommy?"

Silence.

"Don't be shy, Tommy. She loves it when men want her. Do you want her?"

A low, rattly moan rumbles in his throat before he nods.

The next thing I know, Reid lunges toward him and smacks his baton across the man's ribs.

My stomach clenches and I slam my eyes closed, unable to watch.

There's a chilling crack before a blood-curdling scream rips from the man's throat.

But Reid doesn't stop there.

Just that one response is enough for him to turn feral, and he batters the already barely-conscious man until he's hanging limp from his bindings.

Blood runs down his body, dripping from his feet and onto the gray concrete floor beneath.

My heart pounds in every inch of my body as I stare wide-eyed at Reid. His chest heaves with exertion, his arms lie limply at his sides, the baton barely in his grip. But his attention on the man never wavers.

Despite knowing it's going to happen, a shriek rips from my throat when it slips, crashing to the floor.

He turns to me, his eyes wide as if he's forgotten he had a spectator.

18

ALANA

Tears continue to fall, soaking into the fabric that's wrapped around my face as Reid clenches his fists and moves toward me.

Fear rips down my spine, making my heart pound harder.

I might not know him very well, but his reputation precedes him, and right now, I believe every single story I've heard about him.

His eyes are dark, wild. The need to hurt, maim, and kill radiates from him in waves.

He looks... he looks deranged. His need for pain, for violence, has been unleashed, and he's about to turn it on me.

"My little pet," he muses darkly, making my stomach knot in anticipation. "You just can't help yourself, can you?"

My chest heaves as I fight to drag in the air I need through my nose.

Silently, I beg him not to touch me, but I can see from the threat in his dark eyes that it's not going to be enough.

"One look and you make all the men want you. Even

him." He scoffs, shooting a glance at the unconscious man hanging only a few feet away. "He can barely muster the energy to breathe and yet, he wants you."

I shake my head, refusing to accept his words. Words I've heard before.

"That's what you do, isn't it, Pet? You know you're beautiful, that your body is sinful, and you use it against every man you meet. Flash them your smile, or a look at that pretty gem in your cunt and they drop to their knees and give you whatever you want.

"Is that why Victor is so enthralled with you?"

The mention of his father touching me makes my body tremble violently.

"What are you trying to get out of him, Pet?"

I shake my head harder.

"It's something. He might be powerful, wealthy, and have control of this entire town, but something tells me that you're prowling around him for something other than to be his next wife.

"And then there's me. You put yourself here.

"Was Daddy not putting out? Although I must be honest, I find that hard to believe. Pretty sure there isn't a cunt in this town he hasn't fucked."

"No. No," I try to scream, but it comes out muffled and indecipherable.

I whimper when his hand reaches out and wraps around my throat, squeezing just enough to reduce my air.

My eyes burn, the tears coming faster as he looms over me and stares right into my eyes, as if he'll find all the answers written inside them.

"You want power, Pet? Money? Status?" I shake my head violently as his grip on my throat tightens.

He leans closer, his scent filling my nose.

"I hate to break it to you, Pet. But you're not going to get any of them."

I whimper, my traitorous body sagging when he moves closer and licks up my cheek, collecting my salty tears and stealing them for himself.

"So pretty when you cry. But I bet you've heard that a time or two before, huh?"

With our eyes locked, he releases my throat and takes a step back.

His gaze is predatory yet full of hunger.

He might taunt me with being a whore and making men bend to my will, but he's not immune. Either that or beating that guy half to death got him hard.

"Oh, Pet." He chuckles. "Look at you staring at my dick like it's your next meal. You think this is for you?" he asks, grabbing his junk. "Silly, silly little Alana."

He moves, walking behind me, making every single one of my senses come to life.

My skin tingles and my blood heats as I wait for him to do something.

I don't care what it is. Something. Anything.

Make it hurt. Make me scream. Just... don't make me wait.

I crane my neck, desperate to see what he's doing behind me, but he's out of sight.

Keeping my eyes on the wall ahead, I suck in deep calming breaths in an attempt to slow my racing heart. I refuse to look at the other man to see if he's still alive or not.

I put him out of my mind as I focus on myself.

Reid's not going to beat me. Hell, he might not even hurt me. He just wants to torment me.

And he's stumbled across the perfect way to do it.

Digging up the most painful parts of my existence and rubbing them in my face.

I am not a whore. I don't sell my body for money.

When it's not being stolen from me, I'm forced to hand it over in favor of my life. Or the life of someone I love.

It is a very different thing.

Finally, after what feels like some of the longest minutes of my life, he moves.

The creak of his cupboard opening makes me wince right down to my toes before I jump with every bang and crash as he pulls out whatever tools he needs to do whatever it is his twisted little brain is imagining right now.

The implements clatter against the counter behind me and I jump, making him chuckle darkly.

"Nervous, Pet?"

I refuse to give him any kind of answer. Although, I'm not stupid. He can practically taste my fear right now. It's what's turning him on.

He moves closer, his boots squeaking against the floor.

The second his fingers grasp the knot at the back of my head, I almost sigh in relief.

It gets even harder to contain when he undoes it and the fabric falls from my mouth.

Flexing my jaw, I lick my dry lips, but the relief is short-lived because the only place the fabric moves is up.

"No," I scream as he ties the drool-soaked, dirty rag back around my head, only this time, it covers my eyes.

I thrash my head from side to side in the hope of stopping him, but it's futile. He's stronger than me, and I hate to say it, more determined.

I don't want this. I don't want to be at his mercy.

Keep lying to yourself, Alana. It'll make all this better.

"You don't get a choice here, Pet. The moment you lied to Kane, you lost your free will. You handed your life and your body to me.

"I didn't have a choice," I spit.

"Not good enough."

The blindfold is tied tightly behind my head before his hands drop, leaving me cold.

"Now what? Your other playmate isn't much fun now that he's unconscious. I can hardly listen to him scream as you torture him more," I taunt, my mouth running away with me again.

"Plenty more where he came from."

"Twisted fuck," I scoff.

I might not be able to see him, but something tells me that he's grinning like a demon.

With my vision cut off, I focus on my hearing. But there's nothing but breathing.

A painful rattle comes from Tommy and a smoother, shallower sound comes from the monster who's watching me. Mine is heaving as a war of emotions, ranging from fear right through to lust, collide inside me.

My body burns and my skin tingles with awareness.

"I hope you're getting a kick out of watching me do nothing," I hiss. "It's not exactly the show I'd have expected you to enjoy."

"Don't worry, you're about to be perfectly good entertainment for me."

The heat of his body burns into me as he looms closer and my mouth runs dry.

"Look at you," he muses. "You're practically begging for me."

"No."

"Your chest is heaving, your nipples are hard and we both know that you're wet, you dirty whore."

"Get fucked," I bark.

He chuckles.

"Now, now, that isn't what you really want, is it?"

My teeth grind, but I refuse to respond as his breath rushes over my face and down my neck.

Goose bumps erupt, and my nipples harden even more.

Damn JD for stealing my bra and making it even more obvious.

"Oh my God." I moan loudly when he suddenly cups both of my breasts.

My head falls back as the warmth of his hands on me rushes straight to my clit.

"What are you—" He pinches my nipples, making me cry out.

"Whore." He growls.

Then he's gone and before I can catch myself, I cry out again, missing his touch.

That longing soon vanishes though when my shirt is dragged up and the cool air of the room rushes over my skin.

"Reid." I moan, aware that he's staring at my bare chest.

"JD was right. Not all of you is toxic."

"Asshole," I hiss.

"I can understand why men fall under your spell, Pet."

He moves behind me before something wraps around my shoulders, tying me back to the chair and ensuring my shirt can't fall over me. It leaves me unable to move even an inch.

What the fuck is he doing?

There's a clank of something metal before the heat of his hand surrounds one of my breasts.

"Oh God." I groan, but then there's coldness against my nipple. "What the hell is that?" I snap.

He chuckles.

"Your clit tells me that you're a bit of a masochist, Pet. I want to test that theory."

"Fuck you."

"No thanks. I've no idea where you've been."

"Oh, that's original."

"Sit still."

"Asshole," I snap.

He knows as well as I do that I can't move.

"Ready?" he asks.

I don't answer, but apparently, he doesn't actually give a shit because not even a second later, whatever is on my nipple tightens and then turns into a burning pain.

"MOTHERFUCKER," I roar as the burn only intensifies.

The pinching releases and there's tugging.

"What the fuck did you just do?" I ask, although I'm pretty sure I have a good idea.

"More?"

"You mean I have a choice?"

He chuckles. "No more than Tommy did before my baton broke his ribs," he mutters before moving to the other side and repeating his previous actions.

I expect the pain this time, and instead of screaming like a little bitch, I grit my teeth and bear it. Although I'm pretty sure I don't breathe until he steps back.

"Are you just standing there admiring your handiwork, you creep."

"It looks good," he confesses.

"I'm glad you approve. Can I go now?"

Before he gets to answer, there is a loud bang somewhere in the distance and then footsteps running down the stairs.

"Oh shit, bro. What did you do?" JD gasps.

Every inch of me wants to curl in on myself, but I force my shoulders wider and hold my head high.

"Fuck. That's hot."

Both their eyes on me makes my skin burn.

"Help me get this motherfucker back into his cell, yeah?" Reid asks.

"What about me?" I demand.

"What about you? Right now, we're enjoying the view too much to really care, Dove."

"Fuck you."

"Hmm, now there's an idea. I assume you haven't forgotten that scene I painted for you yesterday. Such a shame to see this cunt is making use of one of the ceiling hooks I promised you, huh?"

"What scene?" Reid asks.

JD laughs. "Oh, bro. It was epic. I'm not sure you could handle it though. Ow," JD hisses when I assume Reid punches him.

The minutes drag on as the two of them work in silence to get Tommy back in his cell. All the while, I've no choice but to sit there with my jersey tucked up and my burning tits on display.

They burn like a motherfucker. But I guess I'd better get used to it because I don't think it's going to be fading anytime soon.

My teeth grind.

It would be easy to think they've disappeared. But I know they're still here. I can feel their stares burning into my skin.

"You're a pair of creeps standing there in silence staring at my tits. I hope you know that," I fume. "Take a photo if you love them that much."

Silence.

"Fucking weirdos," I mutter with a huff. "I bet you're over there jerking off together, aren't you? You claim to think I'm a filthy whore, but neither of you are unaffected. I've seen the evidence with my own eyes. Felt it even."

"Reid tries his hardest to cover it, but you were

practically begging for it earlier. Torture and tits really got you going, huh, Big Man?"

JD snorts a laugh, confirming what I already know. They're really fucking close.

"Give me one reason why I shouldn't turn the shower on again and leave you here. Try and drown that smart mouth right out of you."

"I don't have one. And even if I did, it's not like you'd listen anyway. So what's it going to be, boys?"

19

JD

"Can I trust you to sort her out and not get too excited?" Reid asks, although his eyes don't leave Alana's tits.

"Haven't you heard, Big Man? JD loves breaking all the rules. I wouldn't trust him if I were you," Alana taunts.

I glance back at Reid just in time to see his jaw pop with irritation. She's getting to him. The harder he pushes, the feistier she gets, and he has no idea what to do with it.

"You're trouble, Dove," I murmur, pushing from the counter Reid and I are resting against, while she sits here under our burning stare.

As afternoon activities go, it's a pretty fucking good one. And, I have to admit, Reid has done a killer job on her nipples.

Fuck. My mouth waters just thinking about sucking those bad boys into my mouth and teasing her until she's squirming.

She was sensitive when I was using the showerhead on them yesterday. They're going to be even more so now. Once they stop hurting, of course.

Walking around in front of her, I study his handiwork close up.

"You sneaky motherfucker," I mutter, taking in the pink diamonds in the barbells that match the one in her clit. "Zoomed right on in there, didn't you?"

I catch the smug prick shrug out of the corner of my eye.

"You're in charge. I got shit to do."

"Really?" I ask with a shit-eating grin.

"You know the rules," he says, before giving Alana one last look before marching down the hallway and up the stairs.

"And then there were two," I murmur, taking my time to log every inch of her tied up before me.

"Yeah, and you can free me now."

"Can I?" I ask, reaching out and brushing my thumb over her full bottom lip. She startles at my touch, but she doesn't pull away. "But what if I had other plans?"

"Depends what they are, I guess," she teases as my thumb traces the line of her jaw. She tries to jerk away, pretending my touch burns. But it's all an act.

"You know what he did here, right?" I ask, my eyes shamelessly dropping to her chest.

"I have a good idea, yeah. And if I find out he's done them wonky, I'll be taking that needle to his balls," she seethes.

"Careful, little dove. He would probably love that."

"Fucking hell, he's already full of metal, isn't he?" she mutters, making me smirk.

"If you're trying to sound uninterested, you're failing. Just so you know."

"I have no interest in any part of Reid Harris's body, pierced or not."

"Sure, you don't."

Her lips purse in frustration, but she doesn't bother correcting her lie.

Leaning forward, I rest my hands on either side of the chair and let my loose-fitting tank brush over her chest.

She gasps as the soft cotton grazes her sore nipples.

"JD," she warns as my lips brush the shell of her ear.

"What's up, little dove? Didn't you want untying?"

"You're an asshole."

"Been called worse."

Reaching for the knot, I loosen it and slip the dirty fabric from her face.

She blinks as the bright light from above burns into her eyes before she looks down at herself.

A small gasp passes her lips as she takes in Reid's handiwork.

"Hot, right?"

Her tongue sneaks out, licking her lips as she takes in her new jewelry.

"They're pink," she comments.

"Your color."

"Hmm," she muses.

"Wanna see mine?" I offer, making her eyes jump to mine.

"Already have. You stripped in front of me yesterday, remember."

"How could I forget? I wasn't talking about my nipples though, little dove."

Her eyes widen before the bright blue of her irises darken with understanding.

"Oh?" she asks. She was too focused on Reid's dick that she didn't consider mine.

Reaching behind me, I drag my tank off and throw it to the side.

Just like her, both my nipples are pierced, but it's not those she focuses on as my hands drop to my waistband.

"This had better be good," she warns, making me smirk.

"Have you been disappointed yet?"

"Is that a serious question? You've left me hanging twice in as many days."

"Didn't stop you last night though, did it?"

Her eyes narrow as I tuck my thumbs into my sweats.

"Perving through the peephole again, JD?"

"Nah, little dove, I can do so much better than that."

It might be a dick-ish move, but I quickly shove my pants down before she can really think about what I mean, fully distracting her from the conversation at hand.

"Is that it?" she balks, although her attention on my dick doesn't lessen.

"Oh no," I murmur, wrapping my fingers around my shaft and lifting it up. "That's not it."

"Oh fuck." She gasps, attempting to lean closer. "That's—"

"Hot, right? Been told it feels fucking fantastic too. Each and every step of this ladder can take you to heaven, baby."

"That line really get girls to jump on?" she asks skeptically.

"Nah, they're no longer listening to what I'm saying."

"Probably for the best, you do talk a lot of shit."

"You don't seem to have an issue with my mouth."

"Could find a better use for it," she counters.

"Oh, I'm sure. Don't forget those rules, though," I say, beginning to stroke myself.

"Julian, are you seriously—"

I groan as I squeeze the base of my dick.

"Do you know how fucking hard I came last night thinking of you down here finishing yourself off?" I ask.

No doubt Reid is upstairs watching us right now, but I can't find it in me to care. He's probably as hard as I am after what he's done to her today. Motherfucker is probably jealous that I'm man enough to own my desire; whereas, he keeps running from his. Literally.

My lips twitch as I think about him flying off the end of that treadmill last night. Fucking pussy.

"Oh really?" she asks, her eyes locked on my dick.

"Fuck, yeah. Can't stop thinking about it either. Your fingers and that naughty little piercing. So bad, Dove. So fucking bad."

She grins like a devilish sinner as I continue.

"The second you slammed the door, I had my hand between my thighs," she muses. "I was so wet."

"Fuck, yeah. You were. You were gagging for it." I groan, working myself harder.

She might be mostly unable to move, but it doesn't stop her from spreading her thighs, letting me catch sight of her hidden gem.

"Fuck, Dove. Do you have any idea how badly I want to get on my knees right now and tug on that little diamond with my teeth?"

"I have a good idea. You won't though."

"Fuck."

Fuck, she's right too.

As hot as that might be. I know I can't.

Not yet.

I need her begging. Her entire body trembling with need. Her pretty, pouty lips spilling all her dark and dirty secrets before I can even consider getting a taste of her.

"You'll do it again, won't you? I'll set you free, leave you in your cell and you'll spread those thighs and go to town rubbing one out.

"Will you be watching?"

"Damn fucking straight, I will."

"What about Reid?"

"Fuck him." I grunt, my release surging forward.

With my pants around my knees, I shuffle closer to her. My grip on my dick like a fucking vise. But it's not enough. Nowhere fucking near enough.

But I know it's as good as it's gonna get.

"But it was him," she whispers.

"What was him?" I force out, my orgasm right there. "Fuck. I'm gonna come all over these delicious tits, Dove. And you're gonna watch as I mark you. Shit. Fuck." I groan as my dick jerks in my hand, pleasure saturating my body.

"When I got off last night. It was Reid I was imagining with his cock deep inside me."

"Motherfucker," I bellow, doing exactly what I just described and unloading all over her porcelain skin. And because I'm a fucking gentleman, I don't get any on her nipples. None of us want those bad boys infected. The sooner I get access, the fucking better.

"Oh, sorry. Did you think I was imagining you when I was making myself come last night? Sorry, to disappoint, but it was his name I moaned when I came, not yours."

I smirk as I step back and reach for my sweats, knowing full well that she's lying.

"Sure, it was."

"Are we done here? Can you clean me up and let me free?"

I stare at her for a beat. "Dunno. You look pretty perfect exactly how you are right now."

"JD," she warns.

"Okay, fine. I'll clean you up."

With my sweats back in place, I close in on her again and swipe my fingers through my cum on the swell of her tits and hold it up in front of her lips.

She holds my eyes, silently warning me to fuck off, but I don't miss the twitch of her lips.

She wants to be a good girl and please me. I can see her need to submit in her hungry blue eyes.

Moving closer, I paint her lips with my cum, loving the way they glisten under the bright spotlights above.

"Taste me, little dove. Lick those tempting lips."

Her eyes narrow as she holds her ground.

"You owe me for lying."

"I didn't lie," she blurts, unable to keep her mouth shut.

"Oh, no?" I mutter, swiping another load of cum from her chest and repeating my previous actions, recoating her lips. "I think the name on your lips as you fell last night was mine. And I don't think you moaned it. I think you screamed it while your fingers were deep inside your cunt, the other hand on these incredible tits."

"You wish." The second her lips part, I plunge two fingers deep into her mouth.

"Suck, little dove," I demand.

She defies me for a few seconds, but then her tongue laps at my digits, cleaning them up before sucking hard, making my dick swell again.

"Fuck me, Dove. I'm gonna need those lips wrapped around my cock sometime soon."

"We'll see," she mutters, the second I pull my fingers free.

"Yeah," I agree. "We will. And your view will be from the floor on your knees."

"Don't think that's allowed."

"Reid told me not to touch you. If you're sucking my dick, I don't have to touch you."

"Semantics."

Walking around her, I find the knot on the rope that's holding her shoulders in place and release it before I start working on the bindings holding her wrists and ankles to the chair.

Her relief is palpable, but she doesn't say a word. Unfortunately, she does tug her jersey down, covering herself up. Although she hisses as she does so, letting me know how sore she is.

"Go sit on your bed. I'm going to get some salt water for your nipples."

"I'm fine, thank you."

"Let me look after you, little dove. I can assure you, the last thing you want is for those to get infected."

"Maybe the prick who forced them on me should have thought about that before he shoved a needle through my skin then."

"It'll have all been sanitized. Reid might be reckless, but he's safe."

"I'll believe it when I see it."

Pushing from the seat, she stumbles toward the hallway, and I stand there frozen until she slips into her room.

"Fuck." I groan, squeezing my semi.

I'm entirely too enthralled with our latest prisoner.

It's either going to be fucking epic. Or a massive fucking disaster.

I'm kinda excited to find out which way it's going to go.

20

ALANA

JD does as he's told, despite my arguments to try and stop him.

He turns back up in my cell with a glass of cloudy water then he demands I lower my fucking nipples into it.

I've met men who are into some kinky shit, but this is up there with a bit too fucking weird for my liking.

He's hard throughout the whole head-spinning situation. And I can't say that I'm all that much better off. I can still vividly remember him jizzing all over my tits like he owned me. And I can still taste him on my tongue.

Needless to say, I was ready for him to up the ante, despite the fact I knew he wouldn't.

He'd been given his orders and that was that.

And by the time he leaves, having only done his job, my body is buzzing with need.

But this time, I fight it.

My skin tingles with awareness. From the comments he made earlier, I know he was watching me. And I know he's doing it right now. Watching and waiting for me to put on a show.

It isn't going to happen. I wasn't going to give him the satisfaction.

Instead, I curl up on my side, giving the door my back. My tits burn like a motherfucker, but I like the pain.

It's been one of the constant things in my life all these years that helps me to remember that I'm alive.

I had forgotten how addictive it was when I first went to live with Mav. But it's just like riding a bike.

I want to look at them. Inspect Reid's handiwork up close, but that has to wait. They've already stolen enough from me recently.

I am locking that shit down.

The room is as cold as ever, but still, it doesn't stop me from falling into a fitful sleep.

"Looks like you were waiting for us tonight," the deep voice praises, making all the hairs on my body stand on end and bile rush up my throat.

Squeezing my eyes closed, I fight to lock my emotions down.

They love it when I fight. When I scream, kick, punch, and cry. Sick bastards.

I continue cleaning up the kitchen, trying my best to ignore their burning stares.

It's hot. Really fucking hot, hence why I'm not exactly wearing a lot. But I wasn't expecting them back yet.

Dad's usually gone a few hours before he returns and comes searching for me.

My stomach turns over.

"Looks like she's ready to party," another deeper, more terrifying voice says.

Fear licks down my spine. My skin erupts with goose bumps, but it's not the good kind. Nowhere near.

Disgust rolls through me.

"Turn around, Alana. Let us get a better look at you."

Pausing my cleaning, I suck in a deep breath.

They weren't meant to be here yet. I wasn't meant to look like this.

Or were you?

I desperately want to hang my head in shame. These men, and the others, have all stolen pieces of me that I know I'll never get back. They've morphed me into their little plaything, and my subconscious is theirs to control. They're in my head, and they know it too.

Squaring my shoulders, I finally turn around.

Defying them isn't worth it.

I've tried it before and I've got the scars to prove it.

"Well, damn. It looks like she dressed up for us tonight, boys."

My skin is slick with sweat from cleaning and my tank is nowhere near thick enough to hide anything. It's old and ratty and full of holes.

Exactly as he likes...

And my booty shorts don't exactly cover much.

"Come over here, Alana. Come sit on Daddy's knee."

I wake with a start, vomit burning the back of my throat and I scramble off the bed and rush toward the toilet, heaving into the bowl. I was only thirteen. A child. I should have been out playing with my friends, doing homework. Not being forced to endure that kind of abuse and pain.

Leave me alone, I silently scream. Begging for mercy.

It's been years since they touched me. Since they irrevocably broke me in every way possible.

I retch until there is nothing left, desperately trying to expel the memories of their touch, their words, their pain, their everything.

Pain grips my stomach as I curl up on the cold, hard floor and hug my legs to my chest.

Mav might have taken me away from hell. But I never left. Not really. Those monsters imprinted themselves on my soul, and even when their deaths finally come, I know they'll still live on through me.

I'll never forget them. Ever.

It's why it doesn't matter what happens to me down here. Reid can do his worst. It still won't be as bad as the memories I'm forced to live with daily.

I don't cry, but that doesn't mean my cheeks aren't soaked.

I hate shedding tears over them. They don't deserve it.

All they deserve now are painful deaths.

It'll happen. Somehow, I will find a way to make it happen.

Mav and I were working on a plan. Discovering all their secrets, ready to bring them to their knees. Shame them, just like they have me, before finally giving them the kind of ending they deserve.

I want it to be painful and bloody and I want it to haunt them long after they turn up in hell.

But like always, Victor storms in and ruins everything.

Now I'm locked down here useless, and Mav is out there running around Harrow Creek trying to find me.

It's pointless. If Reid doesn't want me found, then I won't be.

Mav might as well give up. I may as well be dead.

After long, painful minutes, I finally wipe my cheeks with the backs of my hands and walk over to the sink to attempt to freshen my mouth with the tepid water from the faucet.

Feeling, and I'm sure looking, like shit, I fall back down onto my bed.

My entire body trembles with lingering fear and disgust from that nightmare. Yet my stomach is empty and growling once again, making me regret tossing those extra burgers out yesterday.

I glance at my wrists and I'm amazed to find that this time, they're not red and angry. They're... almost normal.

I didn't even fight.

That motherfucker stuck two needles through my nipples and I didn't fucking fight.

What the fuck is wrong with me?

I'm so lost in my own head that a shriek of fright spills from my lips when my locks disengage, and the door flies open.

Reid stands there in the doorway, looking larger than life. Totally unfazed by what's happening in this basement.

Looking at him, you'd never know he almost beat a man to death down here a few hours ago. The blood he'd covered himself in has been long washed down the drain.

"Let's go," he says quietly. "You've got a visitor."

My heart jumps into my throat and hope rushes through my veins.

Has he found me? Is Mav here to rescue me? It's wishful thinking, but I can't help but hold onto the hope with both hands.

I push to my feet and stumble forward, desperate to look into my husband's dark eyes.

The warmth of Reid's hand radiates from where he presses it against my lower back to steady me. It's probably the nicest thing he's done since I was thrown down here. It makes my head spin.

"I gave my new pet a makeover. What do you think?" he asks as we emerge from my cell.

I look up, more than ready to throw myself into Mav's arms and never let go.

My heart drops when I find the angry, yet intrigued eyes of Kane Legend.

Fuck.

"Yeah, I think I might have missed my calling in life," Reid says, shoving me forward until I have little choice but to sit in the damn chair again.

Kane's stare doesn't leave me, and I can't help but wonder what he sees in my eyes.

My pain? My rough and jagged broken bits?

The truth?

"No, no. I think you're exactly where you should be," Kane says, amusement laced through his tone as he looks between the two of us then around at Reid's torture chamber.

To my utter shock, and proving just how fucking awful I look, Reid pours and hands me a glass of water.

It's ice-cold and exactly what I need. Although, mouthwash would probably be more effective right now.

Kane studies me as I sip it, praying it doesn't upset my empty stomach and force me to puke all over his feet.

I'm pretty sure I've already tried to ruin his life enough recently.

Eventually, though, the silence and Kane's rapt attention on me gets too much for Reid.

"Come on, Pet. Don't keep my boy waiting. Tell him exactly what you told me."

I think back briefly to the confessions I've made and I look Kane dead in the eyes, hoping that along with the exhaustion and pain he can also see my apology.

"H-he made me," I whisper, the weight of my confession pressing down on my shoulders.

"He? Who's he?" Kane growls, his voice low and deadly.

Many in the Creek might be scared of Kane. Hell, I have been a little cautious a time or two. The man has a fucking temper on him. But right now, he's the least of my worries.

"V-Victor," I stutter, hating that I stumble over his name when the image of my nightmare comes back to me.

The water in my stomach turns to acid, burning me from the inside out.

"He made you tell me that you were pregnant?"

I nod. What else is there to say?

I lied. He caught me. I'm now stuck down here with the devil and his best friend, who's trying to kill me with nothing but unfiltered desire.

"Why?"

"He wants to keep you," I explain as if it's not obvious.

Kane made an agreement with Victor Harris a couple of years ago that he'd walk free and attend college on a football scholarship if he was offered one.

Victor agreed and then did what he could to help Kane succeed.

It was weird. Beyond weird.

No one walks away from Victor Harris and the Hawks and gets away with it. Especially someone as high up as Kane.

But he made it sound possible, and who are we to question the oh mighty Victor Harris?

He doesn't react to my words. There's not so much of a flicker of emotion on his face.

I guess he learned that trick from the devil standing just over my shoulder. His presence is oppressive and unavoidable.

"He wanted you to fall for me," I continue, when no one else says anything. "To come back to this life and forget about college."

One moment Kane is standing, the next he's collapsed

into the only other chair in the room and drops his head into his hands.

Guilt rips through me as I watch him fail to deal with the shit he's been dealt and the hand I've had in it.

Long, painful minutes pass as he fights to accept the words I've said.

I didn't want to hurt him.

But I also didn't have a choice.

Do what Victor says, or hurt the one person who's ever cared about me.

I gasp the second he jumps to his feet, but that's nothing compared to the shriek that rips up my throat when Kane picks up the chair and throws it against the wall with a roar that echoes off the bare, concrete walls around us.

"Why, Alana? Why did you do it?" He rumbles, getting right in my face. Spittle covers my skin as his eyes blaze with fury.

"Because I didn't have a choice," I cry, my own heart pounding against my ribs as we glare at each other.

"Didn't your husband have something to say about it? About you being sent to fuck me?" he sneers, making me rear back.

"I told you, we don't—"

"Why, Alana? Why doesn't your husband want to fuck you?" His eyes drop to my body and I swallow thickly.

He knows exactly what's beneath his Panthers jersey I'm still wearing from Saturday night. We've been together more than enough times over the past eighteen months for him to be familiar with every single inch of me.

Despite being clothed, I'm pretty sure I've never felt more exposed in my entire life.

But I refuse to cower. Instead, I hold my head high and try to look as strong and as in control as I can.

It works because his eyes lift to Reid's, narrowing in suspicion, only seconds later.

But the silent demon says nothing.

"Because he won't," I sneer. "It doesn't matter. The less you know, the better."

"What the fuck does that even mean?" Kane demands.

"It means that I'm as much as a fucking puppet as you are, Kane. I don't fucking want this," I say, throwing my hands out. A move which I regret the second the fabric of the jersey brushes over my nipples. "I never fucking wanted this," I cry.

"You married in. You didn't have to be a part of this."

"Didn't I?" I scoff.

"What are we missing?" Kane asks before looking up at Reid, as if he's going to start filling in the blanks.

"It doesn't matter. Not knowing is safer," I plead.

He takes a step back, his eyes burning into me again.

"Your medical records true?" he asks, making my blood run cold.

"Yes. I can't... I can't have—" My voice cracks, and this time, I'm unable to stay strong and my gaze drops.

I hate that I'm weak. I hate that they're beating me down. But I only have so much strength to give.

"I need you to tell Letty," he says, his voice softening the second her name rolls off his tongue. "Because you are going to apologize to her, and you are going to tell her the truth."

"Okay," I agree, thinking about his girl. Scarlet Hunter is... well, she's beautiful, smart, funny. And not only that, she was lucky enough to get out of the Creek before it swallowed her and her siblings' lives whole like it has ours.

Shock covers Kane's face when I glance back up at him and I hate it. Does he really think I'm this cold-hearted monster who doesn't care?

Don't answer that.

"Believe it or not, Kane. I never actually wanted to hurt you, or her."

"I'll believe it when I see it," he snaps, before turning his back on me and stalking away. Just before he disappears, he declares, "We need to talk," over his shoulder.

"I'll be right up."

The slamming of the door at the top of the stairs echoes through the silence.

"You know, you could have apologized," Reid mutters.

"Yeah, and you could be nicer. We don't always get what we want, do we?" I hiss as he wraps his giant hand around my upper arm and hauls me out of the chair.

"Is what you said true?" he demands.

"Yes," I admit honestly.

"So all of this is Victor, and not you and Mav playing games?"

I can't help but laugh.

"Jesus, are you really that insecure that you think we'd scheme up something like this to try and knock you from your pedestal? You really think a lot of yourself, huh? Believe it or not, not everyone's lives revolve around you."

He stutters over a response, making me want to fist-pump the air for tripping him up.

"I will find out the truth. Every last bit of it."

"Oh, I'm looking forward to it," I sneer as he throws me in my cell and slams the door before I crash onto the bed.

"Control freak," I scream, despite the fact I know he can't hear me.

21

MAVERICK

I lie on my bed staring at the photograph on my nightstand of me and Alana the day we said our vows.

It's been three years.

It's nothing really. But when I look back, all I can see is how young she looks.

She'd just turned eighteen.

I told myself that I was going to set her free on her birthday, but that was five days prior to this photograph.

I couldn't do it. And thankfully, she didn't make me.

"So, what now?" Alana asks, staring at me over the top of the flickering candle on the birthday cake I bought her to celebrate today.

She's been with me for almost two years. She's such a huge part of my life. The best part of my life and I don't think she has any clue.

She thinks I rescued her that night. But she has no idea that really, she saved me.

She's given me so much in our time together. So much laughter and light. Things I so desperately needed yet didn't feel like I was ever going to experience again.

"Now..." I force out through the massive lump in my throat, "I guess you've got a decision to make."

She studies me, her eyes bouncing between mine.

"A decision?" she asks hesitantly.

I swallow nervously and rest my forearms on the table. "I... uh... I..."

"You're scaring me. Are you kicking me out?" she asks, her eyes wide with fear.

"What? No. I'd never do that. I love having you here," I say in a rush.

She doesn't believe me. Even after all this time, she still thinks it's a hardship for me to have her here.

Yes, it's painful. It makes me crave things I shouldn't want. But there isn't anyone else I want to be sharing this house with.

Hell, I bought it for her. A place for her to have peace and tranquillity. A place she could heal and attempt to rebuild her life.

She's only told me the basics of why she was running that night. But the basics are more than enough.

"So what have I got to decide?" she asks innocently.

"Blow out your candle first. I don't want cake with wax on it." I smirk.

"Oh, I'm sharing, am I?" she teases, her wide smile that I love spreading across her face.

"Yeah, Doll. We're sharing."

As we hold each other's eyes, something crackles between us. Something I've been trying to ignore for two years now.

I keep telling myself that I need to be better.

Alana has spent her life surrounded by men who only want her for one thing. I'm determined to be the opposite. Prove to her that it's not her body I'm interested in but who she is. She makes it really damn hard though. Pun intended.

Especially when she makes it more than obvious what she wants from me.

She's eighteen now.

I could be a selfish asshole and break the one rule I set for myself.

Or I could put her first, a place she deserves to be, and treat her right.

Leaning forward, she holds her hair back as she purses her lips, closes her eyes, and blows.

Fuck me, she's so beautiful.

"Did you make a wish?" *I ask, forcing my gaze to lift from her lips.*

I bet they're so fucking sweet.

"Sure did," *she says with a coy smile playing on those kissable lips.*

It takes her a second but then she remembers that we were having a serious conversation and her face falls.

"Go on then. What's this big decision?"

"I made myself a promise the day I put you in my car and drove you back into town," *I confess.*

"To protect me?"

"Yes, that was part of it. The other part was when to let you go," *I say, unable to look her in the eyes as I deliver the words.*

"L-let me go," *she whispers quietly.*

Silence falls between us as she thinks about what I mean.

"No," *she gasps, standing so fast her chair topples over behind her,* "no, Mav. No."

"Doll, I can't keep you hidden here for the rest of your life."

"So don't. I'm a big girl now. I can handle myself."

"It's not you that I'm worried about."

Her shoulders fall with my words.

"If they want something then they'll do whatever it takes to get it. Your father wants revenge, and you can bet your ass he's going to take it."

"So what do you suggest?"

I swallow nervously. "You leave. You name the place and I'll make sure you get there safely with no trail."

"Or?" She hisses, clearly not liking that suggestion very much.

"Or..." I hesitate, not really wanting to say the words.

"Mav." She warns impatiently.

"Or I make you mine in a way they'll appreciate and keep their hands off you."

All the air rushes from her lungs.

"Make me yours?" she breathes. "Like..."

"Marry me," I blurt like a fool, as I get to my feet and round the table to get closer to her. "They might be sick assholes, but a wife is only shared with her husband's permission. And they won't be fucking getting that."

Her lips open and close like a goldfish, but no words spill free for the longest time.

"B-be... be your wife?"

I shrug. "It's stupid I know but—"

"Yes," she cries.

"What?"

"Yes. I'll marry you. I'll be your wife."

"Alana. Doll. You're going to need to think about this. It's a huge commit—"

"I don't care, Mav. Yes, I want to leave. I want to get out of his hellhole more than I can explain. But I'm not going until we find the answers we need. And to do that, you need me here. We need to work together. And if us being married helps with all of that, then I'm in. All fucking in, Mav."

She slides her hands up my chest, wraps them around my neck, and crushes her body to mine.

My hands land on her waist, ready to gently push her back, but before I do, her lips press against mine in the sweetest kiss I've ever received.

My blood boils and my body screams at me to do something. To take what I've been craving from her for almost two fucking years.

My fingers grip her hips tighter, pulling her up against me, losing myself in the softness of her body.

I'm about to do it when a voice screams in my head, she'll think you're using her. She needs you to be better than this.

"I'm sorry," I whisper, doing what I should have done sooner and forcing her to take a step back.

Her expression is wrecked as she stares up at me in disbelief.

"You have four days to change your mind," I tell her before walking out of the room and soon after, the house.

"Stupid motherfucker." I grunt as I stare at myself in the photograph.

Even now, I know I did the right thing.

I wanted to shatter the opinion Alana had about men. I wanted to prove to her that her past experiences weren't the kind of things that all men wanted.

She begged me, and pleaded for more. But I stood strong.

I wanted her for her, not for her body. Okay, yeah, I wanted that too. But I watched her cry herself to sleep at night, and listened to her scream when she should have been snoozing peacefully only minutes later. I listened to the few things she dared confess.

She was so young. So innocent. So perfect.

How could they have done that to her? Treated something so precious, so beautiful so badly.

She was so broken. Especially in those first few years. All I wanted to do was fix her. Show her how beautiful she was, and show her that she could be respected instead of tarnished.

She was everything to me.

Hell, she still is.

"Where are you?" I whisper into our empty house.

Closing my eyes, I send up a silent prayer, hoping that if there is something, someone, up there, they might just fucking answer me for once.

Tell me you haven't run away. That you haven't left me. Give me some kind of sign and I'll fight harder than I ever have to get you back. I'll give you everything you want, just walk back through that door and straight into my arms.

But nothing happens. There is no noise, no door slamming, no footsteps.

"FUCK," I roar, flipping onto my back. Staring up at the ceiling.

I don't know how to fix this.

I don't know how to rescue her, protect her.

But what if she has run and she no longer needs you?

Needing to ignore my subconscious, I grab my cell and open up my camera roll, finding hundreds upon hundreds of photos of my wife.

Many she knows I took, but there are so many more that she's no idea about.

I've almost deleted them so many times. Hating myself for my weakness.

Every time I look at them, I begin to question my morals.

Am I just as bad as them?

I stop scrolling when a photo of her sunbathing outside in a bikini catches my eye.

It was three years ago. The summer she graduated high school—not that she went. We had an incredibly hot summer and she spent her whole time in the yard, wearing practically nothing, as she studied and finished her assignments to get her credits.

She didn't think she was going to be able to achieve it. She hadn't spent a day in a classroom in years, thanks to her father deciding she would no longer attend.

I had faith in her though. She was always incredibly smart and wise beyond her years. She just needed the chance to be able to harness it, to focus on it.

And she nailed it.

I tried to convince her to do an online college course, but she was adamant that I wasn't paying for it after everything I'd already done.

I also suspected it was because she had every intention of running the moment she could. Another reason I was keen for her to do it. The more reasons I had to keep her here, the better.

I was trying to do what was best for her, but, deep down, there was always this selfish asshole screaming at me to do anything I could to keep her.

Anything but what she really wanted...

The more my eyes rake over her skin and the more I think about her and how incredible she is, the more my body heats.

It's wrong. So fucking wrong, but it's the only way I've been able to survive these past five years.

Did I think that day I wrapped her in my arms in the shadows of the woods on the edge of town that I was officially saying goodbye to my sex life?

No, not for one second.

It's been worth it. Mostly.

Watching her find the incredible person who was hiding deep beneath the fear has been a privilege I never want to lose sight of.

And if holding back on my needs ensures she's able to

heal and become the person she was always meant to be then, hey, I'm pretty sure it's worth it.

I've always got my right hand and my imagination, right?

I groan as my cock hardens, but I don't reach for it. Instead, I keep my eyes focused on my wife.

She's the only woman I'm interested in. Even if I didn't make a promise to be faithful to her that day in the courthouse, I still wouldn't have been with anyone else.

No one interests me.

No one makes me as hot, or angry, or frustrated, or as happy as she does.

She's one of a kind. And I can only hope that one day she sees herself as I see her.

She won't admit it, but I know she thinks her past makes her weak.

But really, it's done the opposite.

She's so strong. So incredible.

She's a survivor.

All she needs are answers and some closure and she'll be able to start over and fully embrace the amazing woman she truly is.

And if I'm lucky, I'll get the chance to see it.

I hate myself for needing her as fiercely as they did. No matter how many times I tell myself that it's different, the voice in my head disagrees.

She's too young. You shouldn't look twice.

But she's no longer a child. She's a woman. A stunning one.

My wife.

I know I'll never be the man she wants or needs. I'm just the man who inserted himself in her life.

It doesn't mean I don't love her with everything I am though.

With a sigh, I push myself to my feet and pad through to the bathroom to shower and set about spending another day searching for any sign of my missing wife.

Someone in this town knows something. And I'm not going to stop until I find out what it is.

"What's that?" Alana asks after I've let myself into her cell, balancing a tray on one hand.

It's been two days since Reid decided to pierce her, and I've been down here three times a day, making sure they're healing nicely.

It's torture at its finest. Getting to see her bare and touch her, but get nothing in return.

She's been tempting me, teasing me, showing off everything she knows I want, but I'm being a good boy and doing as I'm told. Mostly.

"Gifts," I say with a wide smile.

"Aw, you shouldn't have," she says, sitting up and bringing her knees to her chest. It's not an innocent move, she's fully aware of what she's flashing me. And while I might not take the bait, I appreciate the fuck out of it all the same.

"Well, you know me. I do like to spoil you."

"Bullshit," she scoffs.

"Now, now. I let you have a shower."

"Oh, yeah, how could I forget that epic show of kindness

before you left me here high and dry? Or how you jizzed all over my tits before once again leaving me frustrated."

"I just want you begging, Dove. Gets me hard as fuck."

"Get fucked. I'm not begging either of you for anything," she warns, her eyes narrowed in anger.

"So you don't want these homemade cookies or the notebook you asked for then?" Taking a step back, ready to steal the plate of cookies for myself.

She tries to look uninterested, but I see the spark in her eyes as she glares at me.

"Cool, I'll just go then and eat these bad boys myself."

I'm almost out of the door when she cracks.

"JD, wait," she calls and I grin like I've just won the fucking lottery.

Spinning around, I pin her with an amused look.

"Alright, you don't need to be so fucking smug about it."

Walking over, I drop down beside her and place the tray on the floor.

I expect her to make a grab for a cookie. Hell knows I did the second I marched into the kitchen, stealing one when it was red hot from the oven.

The world might think that Reid is this scary monster, but really, he's nothing but a big ol' soft teddy bear who bakes the world's best cookies.

But instead of snatching one up, all she does is look at me out of the corner of her eye.

"What?" I ask, not understanding the issue.

"I know I stink. I won't be offended if you want to stand on the other side of the room."

I can't help but laugh.

"It's not funny. I'm gross."

"If you say so."

She mutters something under her breath before finally

reaching for a cookie and taking a bite. "Ohmygodwhomadethese?" she asks, the words blending together as she chews.

"Reid."

"Fuck off," she gasps after swallowing.

"Okay, but I'm taking them with me," I say, reaching for the plate.

"NO," she screams as if I'd just told her that I was kidnapping her firstborn. Her tiny hand wraps around my forearm.

"How about a deal?" I offer.

"A deal?" she echoes, her brows lifted in suspicion.

"Let me shower with you, and I'll only eat half."

Her chin drops.

"You can watch me in the shower and only eat one." I narrow my eyes at her. "We both know you've got more upstairs."

Pushing to my feet, I hold my hand out for her.

She slides her palm against mine, allowing me to pull her to her feet thinking that I've accepted her terms.

Tugging her arm sharply, I pull her into my body and press my other hand against her lower back, keeping her pinned against me.

Dropping my lips to her ear, I whisper, "Let me shower with you and you can have all the cookies..." She gasps happily, before I add, "As long as I can eat yours."

Her body sags against mine, giving away what she really wants.

"JD," she breathes.

"I know you've been down here getting yourself off to thoughts of me doing exactly that. Let me prove that your imagination has nothing on my skills."

Sliding my hand down to her ass, I squeeze hard enough

to make her moan before hooking her leg around my waist, opening her up for me.

"I-I'm pretty sure that's against the rules," she whispers, her breath catching as I roll my hips against her.

"When the boss is away..." I tease.

She pulls back and looks me dead in the eye.

"He's left you in charge?" she asks suspiciously.

"You know I'm the man for the job, little dove."

She studies me for a few seconds.

"I have conditions."

I can't help but laugh.

Of course cookies, a shower, and the promise of the best head she's ever had isn't enough. Oh, and not forgetting the notebook and pen I stole for her out of Reid's office.

"Go on," I encourage, curious as to what else she wants.

"If we're showering, I want it done properly. I want conditioner for my hair, a razor and a toothbrush. And clean clothes"

I study her, trying to read in her eyes if she's playing me.

Aside from wanting food, a shower, and quite clearly sex from the number of times I've watched her get herself off in the last few days, she seems entirely too happy to be down here. Much happier than the rest of our residents.

So what gives?

Surely, she can't *want* to be down here.

I smile at her, having already expected all of this.

"Done. Let's go."

With her hand still locked in mine, I drag her out of her cell. Although there is no reluctance on her part, she happily skips along behind me, still munching on her cookie.

I flip the lock the second we're in the bathroom. Not

that it'll do much good. If Reid appears and wants in then a flimsy lock won't stop him.

My stomach knots in excitement at the thought of being caught.

He wants her; I know he does. It's why he keeps warning me off.

He also wants to win. But fuck that.

I know I'm right. Alana reacts better to care than she does fear.

Without missing a beat, I reach behind my head to pull my tank off before folding it and placing it on the vanity. I have plans for that later. Really fucking good plans.

"I thought you were desperate for a shower, Dove," I say, pausing with my thumbs tucked into the waistband of my sweats as she does nothing but stare.

"I-I am," she stutters.

"Then you need to get naked."

Ripping her eyes from me, albeit reluctantly, she walks to the vanity. "Teeth first."

"Bottom cupboard," I instruct, watching as she bends over and grabs what she needs.

The second the fresh minty toothpaste floods her mouth, her eyes shutter.

"Jesus, that shouldn't be so hot," I mutter, unable to stop myself.

"Sogood," she mumbles around the toothbrush.

Walking behind her, she keeps her eyes on me as I lean into the shower and turn it on.

"It's like you don't trust me, little dove," I say, finally shoving my sweats from my hips.

Her eyes drop, but I'm right behind her, and she can't see anything.

"I don't," she confesses, pulling the toothbrush from her

mouth and dropping it into the sink. "All of this. It's too easy. You're giving me too much."

My hand darts up, my fingers twisting in her short blonde locks, dragging her back into me and twisting her head so I can look into her eyes.

"Maybe I have an ulterior motive, Dove."

"From what I can feel against my ass, I'd say you do."

She grinds back against me.

"Fuck. You've no idea."

"Pretty sure I do," she murmurs.

"Oh yeah, I forget that my dove is a needy little whore."

"JD," she screams as I twist us around and march her into the shower, pressing her against the tiles.

Her breathing is erratic as the water soaks through her clothes.

"Please," she whimpers.

"You're going to need to beg for it, little dove. As you just pointed out, I gave you this much too easily. You want my dick, you're going to have to work for it."

She groans as I press her harder against the wall.

"You're already wet for me, aren't you?"

She doesn't answer.

"Now isn't the time to be shy. It's much too late for that."

Releasing her hair, I keep her pinned in place with my hips and slide my palms down her body.

She trembles violently and then gasps when my hands slip beneath her shirt and slide up her belly.

"Needy little whore, aren't you, Dove?"

"Oh God," she whimpers when I cup her heavy breasts, being careful of her new piercings.

"You've been down here thinking about me, haven't you? Every time you slide your fingers down your stomach and sink them into your pussy, you're imagining it's my cock, aren't you?"

"Julian." She moans, making my dick ache.

It's been too fucking long since I saw any action that wasn't self-delivered. Sure, I could have turned up at the clubhouse and had almost any woman there on their knees for me in seconds.

But I didn't want them.

My dick has been firmly on Team Alana since I saw her on the screen upstairs the night Reid threw her down here.

Teasing her has been fun. Coming over her tits was fucking epic. Watching her get herself off and cry out my name, mind-blowing—especially because it's driving Reid to the brink of insanity. But. It. Is. Not. Enough.

"I could lift your skirt and part your thighs right now and you'd be ready for me, wouldn't you?"

My mouth waters as I think about sliding into her slick pussy.

"No," she cries, not answering my question, but mourning the loss of my hands as I release her breasts.

Curling my fingers around the hem of her soaked jersey, I peel it up her body.

She hisses when I pass her nipples.

"Sensitive?" I ask, my lips brushing her ear as I do.

"A little," she lies.

"Can't wait to suck on them. To drive you crazy with just those alone."

She lifts her arms, allowing me to rid her of her top easily.

It lands on the floor with a wet slap.

"Please," she whimpers, getting closer and closer to the desperate whore that I want.

I squeeze her breasts again before sliding my hands down her toned stomach and undoing her skirt.

In seconds, it lands on the floor at her ankles, leaving her naked for me.

"Kick it away," I demand roughly before my lips find her neck.

"Oh God." She gasps as I kiss a trail down to her shoulder.

"You're so sexy, Dove," I mutter as my hands begin to wander.

I've been imagining for days just how soft her body would be. Massaging her wrists and ankles was the biggest tease ever.

Gripping her hips, I drag her ass back, grinding myself against her.

"Julian, please."

"Fuck, that sounds good."

She gasps when I suddenly spin her around, pressing her back against the tiles, holding her in place with my hand around her throat.

"Damn, little Dove," I murmur. "Look at you."

Her chest heaves, making the diamonds in her new piercings sparkle in the light. Her waist dips in, her hips flare, and that spot between her legs draws me in.

Fuck. I want it.

I want it so bad.

The temptation to drop to my knees and feast on her is strong. But she's going to need to work harder.

I want her so desperate for it—for me—she can barely stand it.

Ripping my eyes back up, I find hers. But she isn't looking at me. Not this part of me anyway. Her gaze is firmly locked on my hard cock.

"You really want my dick, don't you, Dove?"

The second her tongue sneaks out to lick her lips, I almost lose the tenuous grip I have on my restraint.

"Soon," I promise her. "I'll let you choke on my dick very, very soon."

Reaching out, I grab one of the new bottles I stocked this shower with and squeeze a generous amount of cherry shower gel into my hands.

The sweet scent explodes through the air and it's enough to drag Alana's eyes up.

"What—" Her words are cut off as she looks at the shelf.

"You can thank me later," I tell her before cupping her breasts again with my soapy hands.

I watch her expression as I run my hands over every inch of her body, soaping her up and washing away the last few days of her being stuck in that cell.

23

ALANA

My head falls back as the warmth of the water and JD's giant hands rush over my body.

I've pretty much been cold since Reid slammed the door to my cell on Saturday night. And while I might not know exactly how many days ago that was, I know that aside from my previous shower with JD's burning stare, I've been cold ever since.

It has to have been a few days now.

No one has said any more about Mav and what he's doing, but something tells me that he hasn't given up.

He'll still be out there looking for me, trying to find any hint about where I went.

My heart aches every time I think about him going home alone. Doing the things that we used to do together without me.

Margarita Monday. Taco Tuesday. I'm pretty sure both of those have passed.

"W-what day is it?" I blurt.

JD's hands pause at my question.

His eyes meet mine, searching for something I already know he won't find before he leans in.

My breath catches as I wait for him to kiss me, but it never comes. Instead, his lips brush across my jaw, sending a violent shudder of desire through me before his hot breath rushes down my neck, making my entire body taut with need.

"Thursday," he whispers, his voice rough with desire. "Why? Did you have plans?"

I shake my head slowly.

Other than being forced to work for Victor, my life revolved around Mav before I was locked up in here.

He encouraged me to apply to college when it was looking likely I'd graduate from high school, but I refused, aware that the only person who would be paying for it was him. He'd already done enough, spent enough. I wasn't accepting anything else. But without college, I had nothing. I wanted to do something, but my employment options in the Creek were slim pickings. I wanted something for me, something of my own, and working in a store dealing with the shoplifting and violence this town breeds wasn't it.

Mav assured me that I didn't need to bring any money into the house, and while that made me feel useless as fuck, I was grateful. I promised myself that one way or another, I'd repay him for everything he's given me. I just had to hope the right thing would come along at the right time. And while I waited, I made sure the house was perfect in every way possible. I cleaned, tidied up, did the washing and all the usual stuff, but I also began refurbishing furniture and turning my hand to fixing things. It was fun, giving something old and boring a new lease on life.

"Good, because I do," JD says, dragging me from my memories. "And they all involve hearing you scream my name in person."

"In pers— Oh God." I moan when he sucks on the sensitive patch of skin behind my ear. "Yes, please."

"So fucking hot when you beg, Dove."

He kisses down my neck and to my collarbone before his lips lift from my body. My nipples harden and ache in the most delicious way. He knows it too, because his eyes are locked on them when he pulls back.

"Beautiful," he murmurs. "I can't wait to play."

His eyes raise from my chest and lock on mine.

I've been with more men than I'd be willing to count in my life. I've endured much, much more than most other young women, but the way he looks at me. I've only experienced that once before and it makes my heart ache in the best kind of way.

"Do it," I whisper, completely overwhelmed by the moment and everything I can read in JD's eyes.

"No, little dove," he states fiercely. "Not until I'm happy with how they're healing."

"Bet it wouldn't stop Reid," I scoff, making him chuckle.

"Wouldn't it? Why do you think it's me down here right now and not him?"

"Because he's gone out and you have the self-control of a flea?" I offer, his smile widening even more.

"Because I can admit what I want and take it like a man."

I let my eyes roll down his body, lingering on his dick.

I might not be able to see his piercings from this angle, but knowing they're there makes my mouth water.

Before I get a chance to do anything other than just stare, he moves.

His knees hit the floor as his hands skim over my hips and down my thighs.

"W-what are you—"

"Hand me the razor."

I gaze down at him, blinking away the water that's running into my eyes.

"Dove. Razor," he demands when I don't move.

Unable to do anything but what he says, I reach for it and pass it down with a trembling hand.

"What are you doing?" I whisper, utterly enthralled as he lifts one of my feet from the floor and rests it on his thigh. He rubs a whole load of shower gel on my leg. Heat blooms from his touch as my body sags against the wall, my eyes glued on his hands. Once he's happy I'm prepped, he reaches for the razor, but just before it touches my skin, he pauses and looks up. For long agonizing minutes, he just stares at my pussy.

My clit throbs, desperate for his touch, but it never comes. Instead, his eyes climb up my body before locking on mine.

His are electric and full of wicked ideas that I'm totally on board with.

These past few days have been torturous. I expected pain down here; I expected to hurt. But I never could have imagined this—him—the first time I was locked in my cell.

"J-JD?" I whisper, my brows pinched together.

He blinks, dragging himself out of his daze before looking down again and slowly dragging the razor up my thigh.

Tingles erupt beneath the innocent object, all of them rushing to my clit, making the process so much more arousing.

"Such a shame," he muses, his hand pausing as he glances up at me quickly.

As his eyes drop back down my body, his gaze lingers on my waxed vagina.

"No need. Already taken care of," I say, reading his thoughts.

"Damn. Maybe next time."

He goes back to my legs, working meticulously to ensure he has every hair.

"You really mean that, don't you?"

"I never joke about pussy, Dove."

Once he's happy, he places my foot back on the ground and taps my other foot.

He covers my skin in gel, right up to my hip, and sets to work.

"You're doing a lot of touching for someone who isn't allowed to do so."

"You're doing a lot of whimpering for someone who isn't meant to be enjoying this," he counters.

"Who said I shouldn't be enjoying watching you on your knees for me."

"You're a prisoner, little dove. Everything should be torture."

"In that case, you're really killing me with kindness right now."

"How many times have you imagined Mav doing something like this?" he asks absently as he continues working.

"You're assuming this isn't a daily thing for us."

His eyes shoot up in warning.

"Okay fine," I huff in irritation. "So I imagine something similar daily at least."

"I find it hard to believe that you didn't snap his self-control long before now," he tells me.

"Maybe he's just not as big of a whore as you."

JD barks out a laugh, not the least bit offended by my comment.

"Not what I remember from back in the day. Mav was as bad as the rest of us. What changed?"

Tears flood my eyes as I think about all the times he's turned me down over the years. It's never a blatant no; instead, he's become the master of diversion. Changing the subject, suddenly needing to go out or make a phone call.

"Did it? I can only tell you what didn't happen under our roof. I've no idea what he did elsewhere," I confess, my cheeks heating the second the words roll off my tongue.

"You're kidding?" JD asks.

I shrug. "Why would I be? He has needs and I wasn't fulfilling them. He had to be getting his kicks elsewhere, right?"

"Like you were?" I tense at his question and immediately try to remove my leg from his grip, but his fingers lock around my ankle like a vise.

"JD," I growl, still trying to free my leg.

"Dove," he counters, his eyes lifting from the razor to mine. The second we collide my mouth runs away with itself.

"I didn't sleep with anyone else by choice. The only man I wanted was him."

"So why do it?"

My teeth grind. "You don't need me to tell you what a manipulative bastard Victor is, you're more than aware."

He studies me for a beat. "So he has something over you?" he surmises, but when he doesn't get any kind of reaction out of me, he tries again. "No, that's not right. You don't care enough to protect your name. He has something over someone you care about. Someone you love."

I fight to keep my expression neutral, but Mav is my soft spot. Victor knows it and JD is on the brink of discovering it.

Shit. Shit.

"Victor has something over Mav, and you are doing whatever it takes to keep it quiet."

"Please," I whisper, shaking my head in an attempt to squash his assumption as tears burn red hot behind my eyes.

"If that's true, Dove. You keeping your lips shut and extending your stay down here doesn't put your husband in a very good position, does it?"

Fear snakes down my spine, my blood turning to ice.

"They all know you're missing. How long until Victor needs his whore to take care of a job? How long until he pulls out the big guns to ensure you crawl your ass back to protect your husband?"

"He won't," I state. I want it to come out strong, but it's anything but.

JD laughs, but there's no happiness in it. Only pain. A pain I'm more than familiar with.

"Don't be naïve, little dove. Victor will do whatever it takes to get the job done."

"He won't risk losing one of his best men," I say, my voice a little more stable this time. "Without me to bend to his will, he won't throw Mav under a bus."

"Are you sure about that, little dove? Victor barely cares about his own sons, he won't spare a second thought for Razor's."

My chest heaves as I consider his words.

"Then free me and things can just go back to how they were."

JD's eyes flare with anger and... possessiveness? "And let those men touch what's ours?"

"No, I'm not—"

"Not happening, Dove. Reid wants answers from you, and until he gets them, you're going nowhere. And while you might care about your husband's well-being, Reid certainly doesn't.

"Your previous life is over, Alana. And only you can choose how the next one starts."

With those ominous words hanging in the air between us, he finally moves my leg, although he doesn't put my foot back on the floor. Instead, he lifts it and spreads me wide, his eyes locked on my core.

"Such a pretty pussy, little dove," he murmurs, licking his lips.

Desire rolls through me, the tease of his lips, his tongue, his touch, it's too much, and I roll my hips invitingly.

"Please," I whimper.

"I guess you do need a reward for what you told me."

Oh God.

My body wobbles, balancing on one leg with nothing to steady me.

He leans forward, and I close my eyes and suck in a deep breath, but... nothing happens.

My leg is dropped and when I open my eyes again, he's standing in front of me with a smirk playing on his lips.

"Asshole," I hiss.

"Aw, little dove. Are you feeling frustrated?"

"I hate you," I seethe.

"No, you don't. Want me to prove it?"

"Not really," I mutter as he reaches for another bottle on the shelf.

Holding his palm out, I watch as he squeezes a generous amount of purple shampoo onto it before rubbing them together. I guess his hair knowledge isn't limited to cutting.

"Turn around," he demands, his voice so fucking deadly that I've no choice but to follow orders.

"Oh God." I pant when his fingers slide into my wet locks.

His deep growl fills the air before he says, "See. You actually love me."

Gathering all my hair up, he ensures every inch is coated and then rubbed clean before the pressure he's applying increases and he begins massaging my head just like the pros.

"Holy shit, Julian." I gasp.

My legs tremble, barely able to hold me up as he works his magic. My nipples are so hard that they hurt with my new piercings.

"Turn back around," he demands, leaving little room for argument.

Doing as I'm told, I twist to face him.

My breath catches when my eyes find his. His pupils are so dilated, they've practically swallowed the blue.

"JD," I whisper.

"Head back," he states, continuing with his job.

Once the suds are gone and the water's running clear, he reaches for the conditioner and repeats his previous actions, only this time, it's face-to-face.

Every time he moves, his fingers are hitting the sweet spots of my scalp, his chest brushes my nipples, and his hard cock grazes my hip.

It's foreplay at its finest. The perfect tease to what could follow. Only, I already know it's not going to come—no matter how much we both want it to.

Once he's happy that he's driven me to the brink of insanity, he rinses my hair and then turns the shower off.

"No," I complain, nowhere near ready to lose the warmth of the water or his proximity.

"Trust me, I think you'll like what I have in mind next," he teases.

I watch him go, my body yearning for him to return and continue what he's started.

But he never does; instead, he marches naked across the room and grabs a towel.

Making the most of my attention, he scrubs at his hair, giving me a few more seconds to check out his incredible ink-covered body before he turns my way. His dick stands proud, thick, hard, and desperate.

My mouth waters as I imagine what it might be like to drop to my knees and crawl to him. To open my lips and take him into my mouth. I've experienced piercings before. Kane most recently. But I've never had the pleasure of a Jacob's ladder, and I'm dying to experience it.

But before my fantasy has a chance of becoming reality, he stretches the towel out and wraps it around his waist. Hiding his best asset.

Such a waste.

"Come here," he says, holding a giant fluffy towel out. It's the total opposite of the one I was forced to use the last time I was in here, and I soon find my legs moving without instruction from my brain.

Stepping into him, he wraps it around me, then uses another to squeeze the water from my hair.

He combs it before grabbing a bottle of moisturizer. But instead of flipping the cap and getting started, he just holds it and grabs my hand to tug me out of the bathroom.

"What are you doing?"

"We'll do this back in your room."

"My room?" I deadpan. "I'm not staying in a hotel."

"You have a bed and get fed," he argues.

"Barely," I mutter, the thought of those cookies that are waiting for me makes my stomach growl loudly.

"Point taken. I'll try and sneak more out for you."

"Why are you being so nice?" I ask.

"Because you're hot. And I like spending time with

you," he confesses, making my stomach flutter with happiness.

For the briefest moment, his words give me hope. But then I remember exactly where we are. He's playing a game.

And damn him, it's working, because I've already let more slip than I wanted to.

24

ALANA

I notice the difference the second we step foot in my cell.

It's warm.

Warmer than out in Reid's torture chamber, and warmer than it's been the whole time I've been locked in here.

"What did you do?"

He chuckles. "What do you think? Turned the temperature up a little."

"Does Reid know?" I ask, allowing JD to guide me to the bed.

"Contrary to popular belief, I'm not actually his little bitch. Yes, he might have more power than me and be able to call rank, but we're a team."

"Sure, you are. Correct me if I'm wrong, but you said something earlier about needing to hurry before he came back. He doesn't know you're allowing all this and we both know it."

He spins me around and grips the back of my neck.

"Do we?" he asks darkly. "For all you know, he's sitting

up there watching everything we're doing right now." My breath catches in my throat when he leans in, his lip brushing my ear. "And if he is, you can bet your ass that he's hard as fuck."

I gasp as he tugs the towel that's wrapped around me before discarding it on the floor, leaving me naked for him again.

"There are cameras in here?" I ask, realization slamming into me.

Shame burns up my neck, making my cheeks flame bright red as some of their previous words come back to me.

Why didn't I figure that out earlier?

"Hear you scream my name in person."

"Oh my God. You've been watching me. Listening to me." It's not a question. It doesn't need to be.

It's fact.

"Have we?" he asks, a naughty glint in his eye as his brow quirks in amusement.

Ripping my eyes from his, I look around the cell I've been locked in for days. But just like every other time I've studied it, I find no evidence of cameras.

But they're here. I know they are.

Sliding his hand around to the front of my throat, he brushes his thumb over the line of my jaw.

"You're mesmerizing, little dove. Can't get enough of you."

"Knowing you're watching me is creepy, not hot, JD," I snap.

"Oh, so your pussy isn't wet thinking about us with our dicks in our hands watching you?"

Whatever he sees in my expression gives him the answer he was looking for.

"Exactly. You're soaked just thinking about it. Go lie down, little dove. We're not done yet."

I take a hesitant step back.

"Is he watching right now?" I ask, looking around again and hating that they have me on edge.

I couldn't give a fuck about them watching me get off. But my nightmares. I know I talk during them. Mav's told me some of the things I call out. If they were to hear them...

Shame threatens to burn me whole as I lower my ass to the cot and lie back.

I'm so lost in my head, I don't notice JD leave the room or return with his beloved cup of salt water for my nipples.

"The fuck?" I bark when the cool water hits my skin and runs over the side of my breast. "You couldn't have warmed it?" I ask, watching as he squeezes a cotton ball over my sore nipple, bathing it.

"I did," he assures me. "Not my fault your body is hotter. I wonder why that is, little dove."

I glare at him, but all it does is make him smirk.

"No, you're not," I accuse, watching amusement dance in his eyes as he teases me.

"I'm not. I do like getting a reaction out of you."

"I can think of better ways than salt water to my nipples."

"Me too," he mutters, his eyes never leaving my tits as his tongue sneaks out to wet his bottom lip.

He takes his time, making sure my piercings are okay. As if he hasn't spent most of the last thirty minutes inspecting them closely before he abandons the salt water in favor of the moisturizer.

"Your skin is dry," he tells me.

"I wonder why. I'm living in an air-conditioned box."

He smirks but doesn't respond as he flips the lid and squeezes some lotion out.

Rubbing his hands together to warm it up, he places both of them on my arm and begins massaging it in.

I fight to stay rigid and not allow his touch to affect me, but it's pointless.

When he gets to my shoulder, he stands from the floor and straddles my waist to get a better angle. He hits one certain spot and a filthy moan rips from my throat.

He might still have the towel wrapped around his waist, but he's naked beneath and his hard, hot length rests against my stomach, tempting me with what I could have.

"Arms above your head," he demands, after working his way down my other arm.

I hesitate but do as I'm told, while my heart thrashes in my chest.

"Good girl," he praises, only making my core tighten and the desire that's coursing through my system that much more potent.

He leans over me, his face dipping to mine, but I don't get carried away this time. I already know he isn't going to kiss me. If he wanted to, he would have done so by now.

Instead, his lips brush my cheek.

"Do you think he's up there watching, wishing he were me right now?" he whispers, his hot breath rushing over my skin.

"JD," I warn.

"I bet he's hard as fuck."

There's a clank of metal, but I don't think anything of it. I'm too lost to his scent, his warmth, his words.

"You reckon he's caved yet and pulled it out?"

Another clank.

"He wants you so bad, but he won't let himself have you. Not while you're lying to him."

"'Let himself?' That's assuming I'd let him."

JD laughs darkly. "Seeking permission for anything isn't exactly how Reid rolls, Dove. When he decides he wants something, you can bet your ass that he'll get it, no matter what."

"There's always an exception to the rule," I counter.

"Why are you doing all this, little dove?" he asks, changing tactics. "You're married to a man who doesn't want you. Working for a man who whores you out to whoever he wants. Why haven't you left and started over? Why are you still here?"

For revenge.

For her.

The words are right on the tip of my tongue, but I refuse to let them free.

I can't tell them about mine and Mav's plans for Victor. I can't tell anyone.

Reid's loyalty will be to his father, and if he thinks we're a threat, he will take both of us out.

At least you'd be together, a little voice says.

I keep my lips locked up tight.

"You've already confessed to protecting Mav from whatever Victor has over him. But what do you have over Mav, little dove? Why is he faithful to you?"

I shake my head.

Nothing. I have nothing over him.

I don't tell JD that, though. He'd never understand.

Hell, most days, I don't understand why Mav couldn't let me go like he said he would.

Maybe I should have gone. Cut him free and left my past behind. But the thought of walking away from him after everything he'd done for me felt wrong. Shadows filled his eyes every time he so much as thought about me leaving. It would have killed me, knowing I'd put them there permanently. So when he offered a lasting solution to keep me safe while we continued to plot our revenge, I jumped at the chance.

Twisting my wedding ring around my finger, I cast my mind back to the day we said our vows.

It was selfish. I knew that at the time, and I still know it now. It's never been enough to sever our tie, though.

"Come on, little dove. I can make life so much easier for you if you just tell me." His teeth nip my ear, and I yelp in shock, but no words appear. I swallow every single one down.

"Okay, you asked for it," he murmurs ominously before something hard and cold wraps around both of my wrists.

I lift them, and look up, trying to see what he's done, but they barely move.

"JD," I squeal as he crawls down my body and climbs to his feet. "What are you doing?"

His hands wrap around my ankles, pulling me down the bed until my arms are straight and I can't move.

"Now, where were we?" he asks, grabbing the abandoned bottle of moisturizer and squirting more out.

He starts on my right foot, making my eyes roll back in my head and my back arch as he presses his thumbs into my arch.

"That good, little dove?"

"Oh God. More."

"Whatever you want. We've got all the time in the world. You're certainly not going anywhere."

"Assh-hole." I want to shout and chastise him for tying me up, but it comes out as a moan.

He works up both legs, leaving me as relaxed as I am tense. My muscles are like jelly from his magic fingers, but my blood is at its boiling point.

My clit throbs so hard I can barely stand it, and I'm so wet I'm pretty sure I'm creating a puddle on the cot.

"Please, JD," I whimper as he spreads my legs wide and places my feet to the cold floor.

I'm totally exposed to him, and the cunt on the other end of the camera, I'm sure. But I don't care.

"I need to get off. Please, JD."

"Fucking love it when you beg, little dove. Tell me something. Give me something so I can reward you."

Slowly, so fucking slowly, he walks his fingers up my trembling thighs as he blows a stream of air over my pussy.

My hips jerk, desperate for more, but there is no more.

I cry out in frustration.

"Not fun, is it? Someone holding out on you."

"I love him," I blurt, beyond frustrated.

He blows another stream of air over me as a reward.

My hips jump up, desperate for more.

"I don't have anything over him. Just love."

"He has no idea you're Victor's whore, does he?"

"No," I cry. "It would kill him if he knew the truth."

"Why?"

I shake my head, refusing to dive any deeper into our lives.

"I should probably feel bad about doing this to another man's wife, but right now, I really don't give a flying fuck," he explains before lying down between my thighs, my pussy right in front of his face.

"Oh God, yes," I cry, desperate for that first touch of his tongue against my desperate skin. "JD. Please, please."

He leans forward, his hot breath washing over me. I'm a millisecond from relief when a deep voice booms through the room.

"Stop."

25

REID

I stand in the hallway outside her room, listening to her moan and beg for more.

I'm hard as fucking steel, and I know for a fact that JD is too.

I've watched almost every second of them down here together. I saw them shower, him on his fucking knees for her, and then him leading her back to her room and laying her out like an offering.

Cunt knew I was watching. And while he might have been teasing her relentlessly to get answers, he was torturing me right alongside her.

I shouldn't want her. She's married to a man I can't stand, and working for one I hate more than anything else in this world.

But I can't get her out of my fucking head.

And despite the fact I haven't uttered a single word to my best friend, he knows.

He always fucking knows.

This little show he's been putting on down here has been as much for himself as it has been for me.

I keep my eyes locked on my phone screen, watching them on the other side of the wall, waiting for the moment he's going to take it too far, but it turns out his words are all I need to register the point of no return.

"I should probably feel bad about doing this to another man's wife, but right now, I really don't give a flying fuck," JD explains, his voice rough with desire.

"Oh God, yes," she cries, like the desperate little whore she is. And fuck if it doesn't make my dick jerk. "JD. Please, please."

Dropping my cell into my pocket, I press my hand to the heavy door and force it open, and step inside.

I find him kneeling in front of her, his face right in front of her cunt, ready to have himself an early dinner.

Something hot and uncomfortable explodes inside me that makes my hands shake, and my demand for them to stop tumbles from my throat without warning.

Both of their eyes snap to mine in surprise. But honestly, neither of them can be as shocked as me.

I never act without thinking. Ever.

Everything I do is always well-thought-out and meticulously planned.

"You have got to be shitting me," Alana cries, her angry eyes narrowed on mine.

"JD. Get up," I bark, my fists curling at my sides.

Pushing to his knees, he looks between the two of us as we glare at each other.

Fuck, she looks incredible lying there with her chest heaving and her legs spread wide.

"Oh no," she warns, ripping her eyes from mine to focus on JD. "You're not leaving me like this. No fucking way."

"Shame you're not in charge here, Pet," I mutter, folding my arms across my chest as I lean against the doorframe and hoping I look way more chilled out than I actually feel.

Thankfully, Alana is too frustrated to notice my reaction to her. JD, though, that motherfucker can read every single one of my thoughts as if they're written all over my face.

"Don't fucking touch her," I bark when his hand lifts, testing me.

"I fucking hate you," Alana screams, thrashing against her bindings.

"I'll try not to lose sleep over it," I tell her with a smirk.

"JD, please," she begs shamelessly when he gets to his feet and secures his towel. Not that it really fucking matters, he's tenting that motherfucker like a pro. "JULIAN," she screams like a banshee when he marches toward me and slips out of the cell, as if she's not laid out before him, offering herself up on a platter. "I'm going to kill you. Both of you."

"What are you doing?" I ask as I follow him down the hallway and find him standing at my tool cupboard, studying the contents.

"You been listening?" he asks, reaching out and grabbing a dagger. "Stupid question. Of course you have. It's why you're so fucking pissed off right now."

When he spins around, he has a shit-eating grin spread across his face.

"Anyway, you've heard her confessions. I'm this close to getting everything out of her," he says, holding his fingers a centimeter apart like an arrogant dick. "And winning our little wager. You want to watch me finish the job?"

"With a knife?" I ask. "I thought I was the one trying to scare the truth out of her."

He chuckles, shaking his head at me like I'm an idiot.

"Don't worry, bro. I'm going to follow orders." He winks before taking back off toward her cell.

I follow and love the way her eyes widen when she clocks the dagger hanging from his fingers.

"What are you doing?" she asks, lifting her feet from the floor.

"Don't move them." He growls fiercely. She stops immediately, her eyes widening at his tone.

She might not have experienced the dark side of JD during her stay down here. He's certainly been playing the good cop while I'm the bad, but she'd be naïve to think that side of him doesn't exist.

He's as dark and twisted as they come. He might have the cheeky smile and crack a few bad jokes, but that doesn't mean he can't cause a bloodbath and then crawl into bed only minutes later and get a full night's sleep as if nothing happened.

Some might even say he's worse than me because he hides it so well.

I know I'm a scary motherfucker. I wear my scowl and warning sign like a fucking label. JD doesn't. You won't even notice him slit your throat because he's too busy charming the pants off you.

Dangerous. Really fucking dangerous.

She watches him as he drops to his knees at the end of her bed again and stares down at her cunt.

"You seen how wet she is, bro?" JD asks me.

Of course I fucking have. And despite being desperate to look again, I keep my eyes locked on her face, hoping like hell I'm pulling off the impassive, almost bored expression I'm aiming for.

"She's a whore. Of course she's wet."

She whimpers.

"How many men has my father had you fuck exactly, Pet?"

She wants to close her eyes and hide from the question, but she's too stubborn for that.

"Kane, obviously. But five others? Ten? Twenty?"

Her lips press together.

"And why did you need to entertain them? Were they just bored of their wives? Imagined trying out a younger model to reminisce about their youth?"

Her lips twitch as if she wants to answer, but they don't part.

I shoot a look at JD and he moves, twisting the dagger around and swiping the handle through her folds.

She jolts at the contact, her gaze switching to what he's doing between her legs.

"Oh God."

"You want more?" I ask, loving the way her hips roll as she seeks more. "Then you answer my questions."

"Please," she begs.

"How many men, Pet? How big of a whore are you?"

"I-I didn't count."

Giving up on not watching, my eyes focus on her cunt just as JD pushes the end of the handle inside her.

"Fuck." She gasps.

"Look at you," JD muses, his fingers gripping the blade as he teases her. "Desperate little whore, aren't you, Dove?"

"Please," she begs.

"Why did you fuck them, Alana?"

"M-many reasons."

"Like?" I ask.

"Take their phones. Wallets. Plant drugs on them. Anything."

"Why?"

"JD," she screams when he pushes the handle deeper inside her.

"Alana, focus," I demand.

She squeezes her eyes closed before opening them and focusing on me.

"I-I don't know. I never a-asked."

"But you knew about Kane."

"He w-was different."

"Do you have names?"

Her lips slam shut.

"You want him to finish you. You answer my questions," I tell her firmly.

She nods as JD slowly fucks her, pushing the whole handle inside her this time as he holds the blade between his fingers.

"Some. I have some names."

"And you'll give them to us?"

She nods. "Yes, yes. Please," she begs, tears spilling from the corners of her eyes as her frustration gets the better of her. "Oh my God."

"Why did you do it, Alana? Why did you agree?" I heard what she said to JD earlier, but there's more to the story. There has to be.

"To protect Mav."

"Why?"

"Because he's my husband," she screams, her release getting closer and closer.

"But he won't touch you. Why would you agree to be Victor's whore for a man who won't touch you."

"He's protecting me," she sobs, thrashing against her bindings.

"Why?"

"Because I'm fucked up," she cries.

She squirms, right on the edge of her release, one more move and JD will shove her right over the edge.

He looks over at me. A silent understanding passes between us. It's the kind of connection that only grows with a lifetime of friendship.

There is no one on this Earth who knows me as well as JD, and I'm more than happy with that.

"So why did he marry you?" I ask after a few seconds of nothing but her heaving breaths and moans of desperation.

"To... to protect me," she repeats.

"You were eighteen, what did you need protecting from?"

Her entire body locks up tight. At first, I think JD's fucked up and let her fall, but I quickly realize he hasn't when her expression hardens into her standard 'get-fucked' scowl.

"I'll give you one more chance to tell us, Pet."

"I don't owe you anything," she spits. Her body is flushed with sweat, her chest heaving and her toes curled onto the concrete floor.

"No, you don't. You'll give us what we want eventually though. JD," I instruct.

"No, please. Please," she begs when he pulls the handle from her body.

"Ow, fuck," he hisses as he cuts his palm on the blade.

"Really?" I deadpan.

"Well, maybe if you didn't sharpen them within an inch of their lives then it wouldn't have happened," he barks back, as if this is my fucking fault.

Crawling over her, he straddles her waist, holding his bleeding palm up in front of her face.

"What?" she hisses.

"Tit for tat, little dove."

He lifts the dagger handle to his lips and sucks it into his mouth.

All the air rushes from my lungs as I watch his eyes roll back as he savors her taste.

Fucking asshole.

"So fucking sweet," he murmurs once he pulls it free with a pop. "Your turn."

Unsurprisingly, she just lifts her chin in defiance, refusing point-blank to return the favor.

JD's not having that though and no sooner has the knife clattered to the floor does he wrap his non-injured hand around her throat, making her lips part in shock.

She tries to fight, but she's no match for the handcuffs and his weight and in only seconds, his hand is in her mouth, forcing her to taste his blood.

It really shouldn't be as fucking hot as it is.

"You're a cunt," she spits the second he pulls his hand free.

"Fucking hot though, right? Nothing like a good old-fashioned blood ritual to get the juices flowing."

"Get the fuck off me," she shouts, attempting to buck him off.

He makes a show of pinning her in place before he climbs off and walks toward her hands.

"JD," she warns, predicting, like I am, where this is going.

In a heartbeat, he has the knife back in his hand and is dragging the tip across her palm.

She howls as blood bubbles to the surface, but JD doesn't waste it. Instead, he leans forward and licks it up.

She screams again, thrashing around on the bed.

"I think my pet is a bit of a painslut," I mutter, rubbing the scruff on my jaw as images of all the fun we could have with her play out in my mind.

"Get fucked. I don't want anything from either of you."

"Did you want to try convincing us of that when your juices are dripping from Reid's knife?"

"Get the fuck out of my cell," she bellows, her voice echoing off the walls.

"Why did he marry you, little dove? What are we missing?" JD tries again. But unlike everything else he's managed to achieve this afternoon, he gets nothing but a scathing look.

"Come on," I say. "A few hours tied to the bed, lying in her own wet patch might make her change her mind."

JD gathers up the bowl of salt water and the moisturizer, and less than a minute later, I'm closing the door and locking her inside as she curses us out in as many creative ways as she can muster.

"Fuck me, that was hot, right?" JD says, turning to me with a wicked smile on his lips.

Lifting my hand, I point to his mouth. "You've got a little blood."

"Jealous?"

"Get fucked, man," I bark before turning toward the stairs. "Meet me in the ring in five."

"Oh no," he taunts as I walk away. "Not jealous at all. I can promise you though," he continues when I make no attempt to respond, "hitting me won't make it better."

I leave the basement to the sound of his smug fucking laughter.

The only thing that cheers me up is knowing that he can't possibly deal with that raging boner in only five minutes, and he knows it's not worth the pain of being late.

26

ALANA

I t didn't take long for the temperature in my cell to plummet once more. It seemed my relief and special treatment was long over.

I knew it wasn't going to last. Looking back now, I just wish I appreciated it more while I had it.

Shivers rip through my bare body as I lie here with my arms still above my head, tied to the bed.

I rub my thighs together, but I've long forgotten about trying to get myself off after JD, once again, left me high and dry.

I was right there. Right fucking there and then he pulled that knife from my body, leaving me dangling with one foot right over the edge.

One day, I'm going to get him back for this shit.

I'm going to suck his cock so fucking good, and then right before he falls, I'm going to punch him in the balls and see how he likes the epic fall from grace.

He wasn't wrong though. It was hot as fuck.

And the blood thing... the second I licked his palm and

the copper taste flooded my mouth, I almost came. So fucking hot.

I've no idea if my cut is still bleeding; he did the cuffs so tight that both of my hands are numb. For all I know, I'm bleeding out all over the floor.

Although, if they are up there watching me on a screen somewhere then I'd like to think that they'd probably notice and wouldn't actually let me die.

That would be too easy.

"I hope you're enjoying this," I shout, wishing I could do something to really piss them off.

Despite the cold, my hunger, my anger, and my dead arms, I somehow manage to drift off to sleep.

I've lost all concept of time down here. I could sleep for twenty minutes, or twenty hours, and I'd have no idea.

I wake with a start, the threat of one of my regular nightmares is enough to drag me from the darkness. Not that the reality is much better.

I wriggle, hoping to loosen the pressure on my arms, but it's pointless.

I open my eyes and part my lips, ready to shout for the two assholes who think this whole thing is funny as fuck, but I don't get a chance to form any words because a high-pitched scream rips from my throat when I find a figure watching me from the doorway.

JD stands there with his hands deep in his pockets, his face swollen from a recent beating and dark bruising forming on his ribs.

"Can't say you didn't deserve it."

"What, this?" he asks, gently dragging his palm up his abs and to his ribs. "It's nothing. You should see the other guy."

"Really?" I deadpan.

"I'm not just a pretty face, little dove."

"Could have fooled me," I mutter. "Are you here to finish the job you started or what?"

"Reid wants answers."

"And I want to go home. But we can't all get what we want, it seems," I snark.

"Dove," he warns.

"It's my life, JD. My marriage. It has fuck all to do with Reid fucking Harris. Why Mav married me, why he was protecting me, isn't for public knowledge."

He doesn't say anything. Instead, he just pushes from the doorway and prowls toward me.

His eyes leisurely work their way up my body.

I fight against reacting, but my temperature soars nonetheless.

"Haven't you already had your fill?" I snap.

"Oh, Dove. You've no idea."

When he's done, he drops to his knees by the head of my bed and, thankfully, reaches for the cuffs.

"He doesn't want your secrets to be public knowledge. He wants to know that whatever they are, aren't going to be used against him."

"They're nothing to do with him, how could I use my secrets against him? It's not like he was one of the men who —" I slam my lips shut with a gasp. And obviously, JD notices.

He releases both my wrists and holds one of them hostage, massaging my numb limbs.

I want to pull it away, refuse his touch and comfort, but I can't.

It's too good. The warmth of his fingers is too much.

"He isn't one of the men who, what, little dove? What happened to you?"

I shake my head, refusing to give him anymore.

"I need to use the bathroom," I whisper, finally pulling my hand from his grasp.

Every inch of me aches as I crawl from the cot and get to my feet.

Ignoring his presence, I step toward the toilet.

"Here," he says, getting closer, "I brought this for you to wear."

Fabric covers my head for a beat before it falls around me.

Looking down, I find one of JD's wife beaters. Not exactly the warmest thing he could offer up, seeing as they like to keep this cell like a fridge, but whatever. It's better than nothing. And, I won't admit it to him, but it smells like heaven.

"Thank you," I whisper before continuing to the toilet.

His attention burns into me as I pee, but I'm long past caring. He's seen worse. What's a little pee between captive and captor anyway?

I finish up and wash my hands before walking toward him.

I don't stop until I'm standing right in front of him. The warmth from his skin burns into me, but I ignore it as I glare up into his bright blue eyes.

"I hate you, Julian Dempsey. I suggest you turn around and walk straight back out that door. I don't want or need you here. Go and find another toy to play with."

I walk away before he has a chance to respond, grabbing the pen and notepad he got for me, I lower myself to the cot, fold my legs beneath me and open it.

"Is it still Thursday?" I ask, hating that maybe I do actually need him.

"No. It's Friday."

"Great," I mutter, pulling the cap off the pen and writing the date at the top of the page.

"Shit, I didn't realize it was a school day," he teases.

My body tenses, but I don't give him any other kind of reaction.

"Okay, so I'll just go then, shall I?"

Silence.

"Okay, well... enjoy."

He's slow to leave, but if he thinks he's getting anything else out of me then he can think again. I might be grateful for his shirt, but that's about it.

The second the door slams and the locks engage, I start writing.

Dear Diary,

It's been a week since I've been able to get my thoughts out.

A week where I've needed to vent more than I have in a very long time.

I fucked up.

I knew I had, and I knew things were going to get worse for me because of it. But I couldn't see any other way.

I was selfish to stay here.

When he asked me to marry him on my eighteenth birthday, I should have turned him down and walked away.

It was what I always dreamed about. Turning my back on Harrow Creek and all the monsters who lived there.

But I'd discovered that one of them was anything but a monster.

From that very first day, despite my best intentions, I started falling in love with him.

I was broken. So incredibly broken beyond repair. I still am. But he saw something within me, something he thought he could save, and he did everything he could to fix me.

It's just a shame it'll never be enough.

Violent tremors rack through my body as I hug my bag to my chest and squeeze my eyes closed. The rumble of the engine vibrates through me as I fight to keep myself together.

I was so close. So fucking close.

But just like everything else in my life, it's been ruined by a man.

It could be worse, though.

It could have been one of them.

As much as I hate to admit it, Mav isn't one of them. He's been nothing but sweet to me in the times we spent together growing up. But I don't know who he is anymore. He's a man now, not a boy. He's a Hawk. And for all I know, he's forgotten all about that sweet little boy he used to be and turned into a monster just like the rest of them.

"I'm not going to hurt you, Alana. It's okay."

I don't say a word. What's the point?

I've been lied to so many times in my life, that at this point, it's easier to believe that everything that comes out of a man's mouth is bullshit.

For all I know, he's telling me everything I want to hear, while driving me toward the devil.

A terrified sob spills from my lips as I consider what my father is going to do to me after this.

He won't kill me. But I'll wish he did.

"I'm going to keep you safe, Doll. I promise you that."

"W-why?" I stutter.

"Why?" he asks, his voice much stronger, more powerful and determined than mine. "Because you deserve it."

I shake my head, unable to believe him.

"If you really want to do that, drive me out of town and leave me at a bus stop somewhere. I'll disappear and you'll never see me again."

"I can't," he states firmly.

"Why not? No one wants me here."

"That's a lie and we both know it. They want you here, and no matter where you go, they will find you." *My blood turns to ice. He's right. I know he is, but it doesn't stop me from dreaming.*

"Where are you taking me?" I whimper.

"Home."

A shudder rips through me, my grip on my bag tightening.

"H-home. N-no... y-y-you can't."

All the air rushes out of my lungs when the warmth of his large hand rests against mine.

I'm used to a man's touch repulsing me. But the need to vomit up the bile burning in my stomach never comes, and my skin doesn't prickle with discomfort.

Instead, I relax. Instantly.

"I promise you, Alana. I'm going to look after you. No one is going to touch you ever again."

"T-touch me?" I whisper.

He's silent for a few seconds and when I look up, I catch his throat work on a thick swallow.

"I know, Alana. And I hate that it's taken me this long to do anything about it."

"You know." The words are barely a whisper as shame burns through me.

"I'm sorry, Doll. I'm really fucking sorry."

Despite the fact none of this is his fault in any way, for the first time in my life, I actually believe words that come from a man's mouth.

"If I could have done something sooner, I would. I need you to believe that."

Releasing my vise-like grip on my bag, I rest my other hand on top of his, sandwiching it between mine.

"I believe you."

"You have every right not to trust me, I understand that. But I'm going to prove to you that you can. I'm on your side."

A sob rips from my throat. They're words I never thought I'd hear, but ones I've been dreaming about for so long.

Kristie always made it easier. We never talked about what I was being forced to endure; she was too young and I did everything I could think of to protect her from it. But her presence, her smile, her laughter, her friendship, it helped.

Without her, there's nothing. No reprieve, no happiness, no joy.

We drive in silence for the longest time as I repeat his words over and over in my head, trying to convince myself not to believe them. But I do. Despite my head telling me not to trust him, my gut and my heart say otherwise.

It's not until we're pulling down the street to his house that my fear takes over.

"Y-your dad?" I ask, hating that he can feel my hands trembling.

"MOTHERFUCKER," he bellows, making me shriek in

fright and curl in on myself as he repeatedly slams his hand down on the wheel. "Shit. Fuck. I'm sorry, I'm sorry," he says in a rush when he realizes the result of his outburst. "I'll kill him for this, Alana. I'll kill all of them. I fucking promise you that."

His body vibrates with anger, but unlike what I usually experience, it's not directed at me.

"No one is ever going to touch you again, okay?" he says softer, just about managing to rein in his fury.

I nod, unable to do anything but agree.

"Dad is never at this house. He lives with Shelly and the kids. I'll make sure he doesn't show up or find you."

Ripping my eyes from his, I stare up at the house.

It's old and run-down just like the one I ran from not so long ago, but it's not as scary. A monster might own it, but if Mav is right then... it might be safe.

"Come on, let's get you inside."

He kills the engine and throws his door open, but despite wanting to follow and agreeing that I'll probably be safer inside if half the town is out looking for me, I can't move.

"Fucking hell," he mutters when he pulls my door open and stares down at me.

I've no idea what he sees. Honestly, I'm glad I can't see the same thing.

I'm weak, pathetic, and terrified. Everything I don't want to be.

But this is what they've done. They've broken me down until there's barely anything left.

I'm no longer a person, only a shell.

He leans in, and before I know what's happening, his addictive, manly scent fills my nose before his warmth surrounds me.

He lifts me into his chest as if I weigh nothing.

"Hold tight, Doll," he whispers, before carrying me into

the house, making a point of securing every single lock and bolt on the front door.

He walks me through to a living room. It's seen better days, but it's more luxurious than anything I've ever experienced.

Dropping to his haunches, he studies me closely. I've no idea what he can read in my eyes. I hate to think.

"What do you need, Alana? Name it and it's yours."

27

MAVERICK

She shakes her head as tears continue to coat her cheeks.

I hate seeing her so weak, so terrified.

But other than going out there on a suicide mission with a gun and as many bullets as possible, I've no idea how to fix this.

"Food?" I blurt. *I'm so out of my comfort zone here, but I'm determined to prove to her that I'm trustworthy and can keep her safe.* "Are you hungry? I can cook or order something in."

She shakes her head, although I'm not sure I believe her. I just carried her from the car. There's nothing to her. She has to be starving.

"Drink? Water? Soda?"

But instead of answering, a sob breaks free.

"You can't do this," she whispers, her voice fractured with emotion.

"I can. I am."

"They'll kill you." She whimpers. "Because of me, they'll kill you."

I shake my head. "No, they won't. I won't let them. Just like I won't let them anywhere near you ever again."

Her sobs get louder. I wish I knew if they were from fear, or relief, or what.

I hesitate, my fists clenching with indecision.

My instinct says to hold her, but my brain screams for me not to.

The house I grew up in sits on the nicer side of Harrow Creek. The nicer side... what a fucking joke. The road outside is quiet, our neighbors are far enough away not to see anything, but still, my need to protect her takes over.

"Don't move, okay? I'm going to double-check all the doors and windows and close the curtains."

She nods, sucking in shaky breaths as I move toward the sliding door leading to the backyard.

I keep one eye on her as I move through the room, before slipping out and meticulously checking every way a person could enter the house.

When I return, it's with a plate of cookies and a glass of milk.

I know she's sixteen. She's not a child, not after everything she's endured. But cookies and milk are good at any age. Right?

Fucking hell.

Her eyes track every single one of my movements as I get closer. It's as if I'm a lion and she's my prey.

Placing the plate on the couch cushion beside her, I pass her the glass before lowering my ass on the coffee table.

She takes a sip and swallows tentatively. I've no idea what she's checking for, but it makes my stomach knot regardless.

Happy with how it tastes, she tips the glass and swallows it all down as if she hasn't had anything to drink all day.

"More?" I ask, the second she pulls it from her lips.

Her dark, haunted eyes meet mine and my heart sinks.

The happy little girl I remember from years gone by is long gone.

"It's okay. You can have as much as you like. No restrictions," I explain, hating that I have to say such words.

She nods, and I rush to get her another glass. Anything that might help push some of those shadows aside.

When I get back, she's staring down at the plate of cookies as if they're going to bite her.

"Go on," I encourage. "There are more in the kitchen if you want them."

Turning to look at me, her lips twitch with the slightest hint of a smile.

"I can eat them? All of them?"

"As many as you want?" I promise.

Her hand trembles as she reaches for one, but the second she gets a taste, all her hesitation flies out the window.

I sit and watch her demolish the entire plate of cookies with more fervor and excitement than I've seen grown-ass men eat pussy.

"Good?" I ask with a smirk, loving how much she's enjoying something so simple.

"Sogood," she mumbles with a mouthful.

Finally, my shoulders relax for the first time since I got the message earlier that she'd disappeared.

I have no fucking clue what I'm going to do with her. I've made her promises in the past thirty minutes that I know I can't deliver. But whatever happens from here on out, I will keep her safe and I will never let any of those motherfuckers who've hurt her in the past anywhere near her again.

I don't care what I have to sacrifice in the process. She deserves to have someone in her corner, fighting for her, giving her the life she should have been enjoying for sixteen years.

*I will bring back the light in her eyes, I will see her smile
and laugh. I will give her her life back, even if I have to give
mine in exchange.*

"Would you like me to run you a bath? I don't have any
clothes that will fit you, but they will be clean. We can go out
and burn those if you like?" I ask, assuming that she'll want
everything that reminds her of anything prior to this moment
gone.

She nods.

"While you're in the bath, I'll order you some things and
make some plans."

"Maverick," she whispers, the sound making my heart
clench in a way I'm not sure I've ever felt before. "You don't
have to do this."

"I do, Alana."

"**H**ey, man. How are you doing?" Brody says as he
slides into the booth I'm sitting in at the back of
The Nest, a dive bar in the middle of town.

It's a fucking wreck, but other than the clubhouse, it's
the best place to drink and hook up.

In a few hours, there will be girls up on the bar top,
wearing very little and encouraging all the dirty old men to
spend every cent they have in the hopes of spending ten
minutes in the bathroom with one of them. There will be a
band playing, usually a couple of high school kids who have
yet to realize that Harrow Creek doesn't breed successful
musicians or anyone who's likely to get out and make
something of their lives. We breed gangsters, dealers,
druggies and hookers. That's pretty much the limit.

Got to give it to them for trying, though. Shame no
fucker is going to be listening, no matter how good they are.

I jerk my chin at the barman, silently ordering two beers before I turn my eyes on my old school friend.

Brody and I were tight growing up, but we've drifted apart over the past few years. We took different paths after graduating from Harrow Creek High, although we've been drawn back together just like everyone else in this town.

While I was the son of the high-ranking Hawk with the promise of following in his footsteps, Brody came from conservative parents who ended up here by accident and thought everything could be fixed with better laws and policing.

So while I was being trained to be a mini-me of my father, his parents were brainwashing him into believing that he could make a difference if he became a cop.

Such wishful thinking.

Here we are only a handful of years later, and while Brody might wear the badge, he's as bent as every other cop in this town.

There isn't a single one who isn't under Victor's control. You either get in line or find yourself hanging from the trees in the woods I caught Alana running through all those years ago.

I shake my head. It's all he needs to see to know how I'm doing.

"Shit, man," he says, rubbing the back of his neck as the barman delivers our beers. "Seriously, no sign of her?"

"Nothing. The only thing missing is her purse. I can't pinpoint what she was wearing besides her sneakers."

"And nothing on her tracker?"

I shake my head, swallowing several mouthfuls of the watered-down shitty beer that Otis thinks he can get away with. Well, I mean, he does. It's mid-afternoon on a Friday, and this place is already almost full.

"I've run another search on her," he says. "Nothing."

"Fuck. She can't just have fucking disappeared, man."

He looks at me with sympathetic eyes. I know what he thinks. It's what everyone thinks.

My little housewife got bored and ran off into the sunset to find a better life.

Hell, I couldn't really blame her if she has. But I know she hasn't.

She had too many reasons to stick around here and get the revenge and the answers she craves.

"Yeah, well. She has. And I need to fucking find her."

"Her old man is most likely to have intel," he muses.

"That motherfucker hasn't cared about her a day in her life. He's unlikely to start now."

"Where's her mother? Has she gone running to her like her sister did?"

A bitter laugh almost spills from my lips at his innocent question.

For such a corrupt and toxic place, every fucker seems to believe all the bullshit they're told. It should be obvious that anything that sounds nice, like a little girl going to live with her happy mother, is too good to be true.

Kristie didn't go to start a new life in California like Kurt told everyone. But no fucker has questioned it.

Anger burns through me as I think about Alana, Kristie, and all the other kids that have come and gone in this town and whose hellish lives have been overlooked and ignored because of people's ignorance and selfishness.

"She's not with her mother."

"I know you don't want to hear it, bro. But she's Alana Murray. There might be some stupid motherfuckers in this town, but none of them are dumb enough to hurt her."

"Someone is." I growl, my voice barely audible over the rumbles of conversation floating in the air. "And, somehow, I will find out who that is."

Grabbing my drink, I drain the contents before climbing out of the booth.

If Brody doesn't have anything useful for me then I'm wasting time sitting here shooting the shit.

My wife needs me, of that I'm sure. I just need someone, anyone, to point me in the right fucking direction.

There's a crowd of kids around my bike when I storm through the bar doors, but the second they see me moving toward them, they scatter like little pussies.

The deep rumble of my engine does little to relax me, and the second I kick the stand, I take off in the direction of some decent beer, a distraction, and if I'm really lucky, a fucking clue as to what's happened to my wife.

The noise levels in the clubhouse are almost unbearable when I step inside. It's always the same on a Friday night.

All the chairs and tables have been shoved aside to create a makeshift ring and Ezra Harris and another junior member are bouncing around each other in the middle.

I can't recognize the other guy with the amount of blood covering his face. Safe to say that the Harrises are about to win another fight.

The crowd roars in encouragement as the scent of sweat, blood and beer fill the air.

I used to live for this as a kid. I thought I had the coolest father in the world and the promise of all this glory in my future.

If only I knew then what I know now.

I'd probably be dead.

I had no other option but to follow in Roger Murray's footsteps.

He and Victor had visions of Reid and me taking over their legacies and ruling over this town.

They wanted us to have all the power. But as it turns

out, Reid wants it all and I want to get as far away from the corruption and bullshit as physically possible.

And something tells me that it might just happen, sooner rather than later. The second I locate my wife, I'm going to suggest that we fuck off somewhere we'll never, ever be found.

Revenge hasn't been the only thing I've been planning over the past five years. Our futures have been high up on my to-do list too.

"Son, I wasn't expecting to see you tonight," my father says from his prime spot beside Victor at the edge of the ring closest to the bar.

"I want in," I state as way of greeting.

"You got it, son," Victor agrees. "And I've got just the man for the job."

He jerks his chin to the other side of the ring, and something explodes inside me.

I don't need to turn around to know who it is.

I already know.

It's been a long time coming. And it couldn't be better.

28

REID

I crack my knuckles just as the crowd roars as Ez finally sends his opponent crashing to the ground.

I've no fucking idea where Victor is finding these fucking pussies from, but they need better training if we stand any chance of them having our backs when shit goes south. And it will go south.

Victor's allies might be powerful, but his enemies are just as dangerous. One day soon, everything is going to blow up in his face, and all those he trusted to have his back will realize that the man they're protecting is me, not him.

An accomplished smirk pulls at my lips as that scene plays out happily in my mind, like it has a hundred times in the past few years.

This plan isn't new. It's been in the works for a long ass time. Since the moment I discovered our father is nothing more than a corrupt, selfish, piece of shit who only cares about himself.

He's meant to be a leader; someone young boys look up to. He has power in this town—hell, he has all the power—

and he abuses it daily by fucking over almost every single resident of Harrow Creek in any way he can.

This place is miserable, and it's only getting worse. But while his greed and wealth are growing, he doesn't give a shit.

The kids are addicts who barely attend school. Our businesses are drowning with each new thief he breeds. The only person truly thriving in this town is the one ruining it.

It's not how it should be. It's not how it used to be, anyway.

Our great-grandfather ran this place with an iron fist. The town was growing, its people were happy. Crime was low because he had the place locked up tight, and families lived normal, fulfilling lives.

Then our grandfather took over, and then Victor. And everything has gone to shit. They'd rather line their own pockets than protect their town.

Well, it stops here.

The cycle of corruption and unnecessary violence, uncontrollable drug use and the disregard for people's lives will be forgotten and a new era is going to start.

All we have to do to make it happen is kill every corrupt cunt in this place.

A humorless laugh tumbles from my lips. As if it's that easy.

The crowd settles and across the ring, a pair of dark eyes find mine.

My lips twitch as a rush of adrenaline shoots through my system.

Oh, fuck yes.

And I'm starting with this motherfucker.

The tension in the huge space changes as more and more Hawks notice what's about to go down.

"You probably shouldn't do this," JD warns quietly.

"I do a lot of things I probably shouldn't." Like watching my best friend fuck my enemy's wife with a knife not so long ago.

I hate to admit it, but it was probably one of the hottest things I've seen. And something tells me just about as enjoyable as the next few minutes are going to be.

"So letting you beat the shit out of me didn't help then?"

Amusement rolls through me, but I don't react.

"Letting me?" I ask, lifting a brow after I've turned to look at him.

"I went easy on you. Felt like you needed it."

"Sure. It had nothing to do with the fact your head was still in the basement, wishing you'd never been stopped."

"I wasn't actually going to do it," he argues.

"Such a fucking liar," I tease, looking back across at Mav, jerking my chin up in acceptance of the challenge.

Reaching behind my head, I drag my hoodie off before handing JD my cell, wallet and keys, and stepping forward.

The excitement ramps up the second I emerge in the ring.

Back in the day, I used to be here every Friday night, beating anyone's ass who was brave enough to try me. But over the last few years, more and more, I've kept my distance. Showing my face here is a big thing, but stepping into the ring. Yeah, this is going to cause a stir. Even more so when my opponent does the same.

"Bro," Ez says with a wide, bloody smile. "Did you fucking see that epicness?" He holds his arms out from his sides and lifts his face to the roof in celebration.

Arrogant motherfucker.

"It was alright. Reckon I can do better."

"Oh, you do, do you?"

"So full of shit, Ez," I mutter, stepping around him as a

group of young Hawks drag the loser's unconscious body into the crowd.

"Who are yo— Oh shit. You serious?" he asks when my opponent drags his hoodie off and steps forward.

"Hell yeah. It's been a long time coming. Catch you later," I say, before moving to the center of the ring.

Mav's eyes lock with mine as he closes the space between us.

My heart pounds to a steady, confident beat as I clench and release my fists.

My knuckles are busted from fighting with JD yesterday, the wounds threatening to open with every movement.

It was good. Needed after what I'd spent the previous hour watching.

But it wasn't enough.

This though. This is going to be everything.

No words are said between us as we stand toe-to-toe.

There's barely an inch difference in our height. But while he has me by the smallest margin there, I have him in muscle.

As a kid, he was always so fucking smug about being taller than me. Little did he know then that height meant fuck all. Not when faced with speed and strength.

Someone blows a whistle and the rumble of the crowd pitters away, right along with their presence.

The only other man here right now is the cunt glaring nothing but pure unfiltered hate into my eyes.

If things were different, we could have held all the power between the two of us. But as it is, I'm going to have it all, this motherfucker is going to have nothing.

No power. No wife. No life.

A sinister smile curls at my lips as I think again about ruining every single thing our fathers have built together.

Their reign of terror is coming to an end, and this motherfucker is going down with them.

Tension crackles as we wait for the signal to start, but fuck that.

I'm Reid motherfucking Harris. I do what I want. When I want. And fuck the motherfucking consequences.

I pull my arm back, and before anyone's registered the move, my fist flies toward his face. It connects with his cheek, making him grunt in shock and stumble back.

It's the distraction I need and as he tries to gather himself, I pounce.

My fists fly, connecting with his face and his ribs as the crowd screams in encouragement.

"You motherfucker," he bellows before catching me off guard with a hard kick to my side, making my movements falter.

It gives him just enough time to get to his feet again.

"You're not going to win, Harris. Not this time."

"Oh yeah?" I taunt. "What have you got to fight for? The one decent thing in your life has gotten up and fucked off, leaving you alone like the loser you really are."

He roars in anger and flies at me, but I'm ready.

I'm always fucking ready.

I block most of his punches, letting him wear himself out, but it's more than obvious he's been training since we last butted heads. He's loads better than I remember, and before long, he's tripped me up and has taken the upper hand.

Blood and sweat cover both our bodies, spittle flies from our parted lips as we try to suck in the air we need as we bounce in front of each other.

"Take him down," JD roars behind me. His is the only voice I can make out. The only one that matters.

With a feral roar, I fly at Mav, more than ready to end this bullshit once and for all.

I know I've won. I've got the girl he's running around town trying to find. It's about time he discovered that no matter how hard he tries, he will never fucking beat me.

Fueled by nothing but hate and anger, I turn it up a notch, and before long, before I'm fucking ready, he collapses into the crowd.

To my disappointment, he's still conscious, and the second he's on his feet again, he comes for me. But he doesn't get very far. Razor's arm darts out, stopping him from closing in on me.

He whispers something in his son's ear that no one else can hear. Whatever it is has the fight draining from him instantly. And with a subtle jerk of his chin in my direction, he admits defeat and disappears into the crowd.

I stand there with the room spinning around me and my ears ringing from the number of hits I took. The high of the win surges through my veins and not a heartbeat later, my little fan club emerges from the crowd, and I'm surrounded by the best men this town has ever produced.

JD, Devin, Ezra, and Ellis all lead me to the bar and grab a bottle of whiskey off the top shelf to celebrate.

"Thought he had you for a moment there," Ellis says with a knowing smirk.

"Fuck off, Bro," Ezra barks. "Reid had that long before they even stepped into the ring. Ain't that right, Boss?"

I nod as I lift the bottle to my lips and swallow mouthful after mouthful. It burns down my throat before warming my belly.

Hell to the fucking yes.

"Looks like you're going to need someone to tend to those wounds," Devin says, his eyes lighting up with excitement before he turns to scan tonight's offerings.

"What do you want? Blonde, obviously. Tall and skinny, short and curvy? You feeling a blowy or anal. That chick over there sucks like a fucking demon. You'd love her."

A blonde, I think. But not one who is here.

"Shut the fuck up, asshole," I grunt.

JD catches my eyes and winks. Motherfucker can practically read my thoughts and I fucking hate it.

"Uh-oh, look out. Seems you're about to get a new one ripped by Daddy before we can find you a girl to kiss it all better."

Victor's shadow falls over us, but I don't look up. Unlike every other cunt in this place, I'm not scared of him.

He wants to take me on, then fucking bring it. I'll take him down without breaking a sweat. He knows it too. He trained me himself.

"You shot your load too early tonight, Son." The way he growls that final word, like it actually means something, makes my spine straighten. "It's going to cost you."

Breaking the rules under his watch costs. But so fucking what? He's already taken enough from all of us. What's a little extra?

"Whatever," I scoff, "it was worth it."

My boys all mutter their agreement as I take another swig of my whiskey and get to my feet. My body protests at the movement, but like fuck am I going to let it show.

"I'm out," I say, finally meeting Victor's eyes.

His narrow suspiciously, but I don't hang around long enough to figure out what he's trying to read. If he wants to know something, he can fucking well ask. Then I'll decide how honest I want to be.

"You fuckers coming?"

"I haven't had a fight yet." Dev argues like a child.

"Stay then. Whatever," I mutter before taking off, not caring who follows.

A few sets of eyes turn to me as I move toward the door, but there's another fight in progress, so most are too focused on that to care about what I'm doing.

Warm air rushes over my skin as I step out in the night, the lingering sweat covering my body instantly cooling.

The second I drop into my car, my adrenaline begins to wane. My fists, my face, and my ribs start to ache. But it's still not enough.

I push the key into the ignition as the rest of the doors open, and familiar voices fill the car.

"What the fuck are you waiting for? Party at the Manor."

"You can fuck right off. If you want to party, you can go to one of your little college gatherings," I bark back at Devin.

"Oh, don't worry, big brother. We've already been, and we'll be heading back later. Letting the minions do some work for a change."

"Fucking prick," I mutter, putting my Charger into reverse before spinning out of the lot and toward home.

29

ALANA

"**H**old her arms above her head," a deep, raspy voice says before the man he's talking to follows orders.

I don't recognize either of them. Not that it matters. The men I know are just as vicious as the ones I don't.

"Tighter," he demands, stretching my body out across the dining table, making my skirt rise up, exposing my panty-covered ass to the room.

My toes no longer touch the floor. I'm floating and totally at their mercy.

The tang of copper fills my mouth from where one backhanded me before they even got started.

I knew they were in the room, they hadn't made a secret of their arrival, but I had no idea what they were doing. I'd been told to close my eyes and lower my head, and that's exactly what I did. I've learned that if I defy them, it only hurts worse in the long run.

"Better to be a good little slut," a deep voice taunts. "You know it only hurts worse if you fight us."

I wanted to fight. I wanted to fight so fucking hard. But I couldn't. I was too small, too weak. Too useless.

At least that's how I felt. My father made sure to remind me of it every day.

I was nothing. Pointless. My only use was as a toy. A plaything for men to use to get their kicks.

I was ugly and stupid. I couldn't do any of the jobs he requested of me properly. The only thing I could do was lie back and open my legs in the hopes of making up for all my misgivings.

I cry out as I do as I'm told, my shoulders smarting, the unforgiving tabletop digging into my hips.

"Your daddy was right, princess. Perfect toy," the man behind me muses before his fingers brush my upper thighs, reminding me just how much of me is on show right now.

I swallow bile as it rushes up my throat. I might think this is bad, but it's only the beginning.

The fabric that's still covering some of my ass is flipped up, letting everyone see my white cotton panties.

"Oh, look at those," the man holding my wrists muses. "Kurt sure understood the assignment with this one."

I bite on the inside of my cheek until more blood fills my mouth.

I want to cry out, scream, demand they stop. But it's pointless. It'll only spur them on.

"You've been a bad girl, haven't you, princess?"

My entire body jolts when a large hot hand lands on my ass cheek, squeezing until tears burn my eyes.

"You know what bad girls get?"

Silence.

"I asked you a question," he roars, his grip on me tightening.

"N-no," I whimper. Although it's a lie. I know exactly what they get, and I know how much it's going to hurt.

The sound of a buckle being undone hits my ears before a leather belt is pulled free.

My mouth runs dry and my body starts trembling violently.

"Aw, she's scared," the one before me taunts.

"Good. She should be." The other grunts before his belt cracks across my ass, the searing pain making me cry out.

I wake sitting up with my screams ringing in my ears and my body trembling.

A sob breaks free as I wrap my arms around myself and close my eyes in the hopes of stemming the tears.

Even after all these years, my nightmares are still so vivid.

Their touch, their voices. All of it is so real.

The image from my dream comes back the second I close my eyes, and bile rushes up my throat.

I scramble from the bed, my tears making my vision blur, not that it's light enough to see anything really.

In seconds, I'm hunched over the toilet bowl throwing up what was left of the cookies I demolished earlier.

I ate them much like I did the first day Mav took me back to his house. Like a ravenous beast who hasn't eaten for a month. To be fair, back then, I almost hadn't. This time, it's been a week, and I've been treated to McDonald's.

A laugh explodes out of me as I repeat my words.

Treated.

What a fucking joke.

I fall back on my ass and rest against the wall, tilting my head to the ceiling.

Sucking in deep calming breaths, I will the image still lingering in my head to vanish.

Whenever I had a nightmare, no matter how many a night, Mav was always there.

In the early days, he even slept in the chair in the corner of my room, hoping that just his presence would help.

It never did.

Nothing ever does.

Night after night, those monsters come for me. Reminding me that I am nothing more than a toy for them to abuse in any way they see fit.

No matter how many times Mav has told me—proven to me—that I'm worth more than those men ever said, one nightmare drags me right back there.

I've no idea how long I sit there, trying to convince myself that that girl is dead. She died the night Mav took me home and gave me a new life. Sometimes, though. She just feels a little too real.

Needing a drink, I climb to my feet and pad toward the sink, but I only take one step when a scream rips from my throat and I jump back in fright, colliding with the solid wall behind me.

"What the fuck are you doing?" I shout breathlessly, glaring at the bloody mess of a man sitting in the chair in the corner of my cell, hiding in the shadows.

He studies me right back, and when he doesn't read the answers to his questions in my eyes, he lets his drop down my body.

I'm wearing the wifebeater JD put on me. It's not as long as I'd like it to be, its arm holes are fucking massive, showing off more than just a little side boob, and the neck is low, exposing even more boobage. Probably the exact reason he chose it.

He leans forward, resting his elbows on his knees, and lifts his gaze.

"What were you dreaming about?" he asks, his deep voice rumbling around the cell.

"You're not likely to get an answer when you've so

blatantly ignored mine," I seethe, crossing my arms under my breasts, making his eyes drop to my cleavage.

He's not as obvious as JD. He doesn't have the same hunger and burning desire in his eyes. But he's interested, there is no doubting that.

Doesn't mean I'll ever be able to flirt or seduce my way out of anything with him though. The man is like a rock.

Ignoring him, I give him my back and continue with what I was going to do. His presence means nothing.

I bend over, sticking my ass right out, aware that my borrowed tank won't cover anything.

His breath catches, but other than that, he doesn't do anything as I drink straight from the faucet.

Once I'm done, I stand and spin around, letting some of the water drip from my chin before I reach out and wipe it with the back of my hand.

"So to what do I owe this pleasure? Did you get bored watching me on a screen upstairs and want a more 3D experience?"

He watches me as I finger comb my hair and I walk back to my bed to sit down.

"What's wrong? Cat got your tongue?" I ask, resting back on my palms and holding his eyes.

His intense stare burns into me, making my skin prickle and my blood heat. It feels wrong sitting here, able to do whatever I want, instead of being bound to a chair while he glares at me.

When the silence and the tension build to the point I can no longer sit still, I slide my feet forward, subtly rubbing my thighs together as I go.

Knowing they've probably had eyes on me ever since they left me hanging before, I haven't finished the job. I'm fucking desperate to, though.

"JD really did a number on you, huh?" I ask.

There's a big part of me that wants to offer to find a first aid kit and help him clean up, but I stuff it deep, deep down.

The cuts and bruises obviously aren't all that fresh. The blood on his face and knuckles is dry, and the bruising already darkening.

"I wouldn't have thought he could overpower you, but I gotta say, you're in a worse state than the last time I saw him."

His lips curl up into a smirk that has one of his cuts splitting open. Fresh blood trickles down his scruff-covered chin and my fingers twitch with my need to wipe and catch it. To see if he tastes different to JD.

I shake my head, irritated with myself.

"What?" he asks, not missing the action.

"Nothing," I spit.

He chuckles but says no more.

"It wasn't JD," he confesses after long silent seconds.

"But he said—"

"A couple of the bruises are from him, sure. But the rest of it. Someone else."

"Okay, and you're down here telling me all about it, why?"

He shrugs and sits back, spreading his legs wide. His shorts pull tight against his thighs, letting me know just how thick and powerful they are.

My mouth waters as I wonder how he might look without them.

"I thought you might be interested to hear about the state I left my opponent in."

"I really don't give a fuck about whatever gangster you left fighting for his life tonight. He probably deserved it."

"I love that you assume I won."

"I'm not stupid, Reid. Your ego is too big to lose."

"Too fucking right. And there's no chance I'll ever let your husband beat me."

It takes a couple of seconds for his words to settle. But when they do, my chin drops and all the air rushes from my lungs.

I'm on my feet and in front of him in a heartbeat.

"You were fighting with Mav?" I demand.

"Bingo, Pet."

"No," I say, shaking my head. "He wouldn't."

"Because he knows he'd lose?" Reid offers.

Mav hasn't fought properly in years. He got a pretty bad concussion and he gave up Friday night fight nights at the clubhouse. Something I was really fucking glad about. I'd seen one too many Hawks get dragged out of that ring and never return.

"You're lying," I spit, convinced that he's just trying to bait me. "Who was it really?"

Reaching his busted hand into his pocket, he pulls his cell free. After unlocking it, he finds a video and hits play, holding it up for me to see.

My eyes widen as they settle on a blurry video of the man before me and my husband in the middle of a crowd.

"No," I gasp, my hand lifting to cover my mouth as the two of them bounce around in front of each other.

The quality of the film might be questionable, but it's obvious that it's been going on for a while from the amount of blood covering them both.

"Keep watching, Pet. You want to experience me claim success, don't you?"

I shake my head as my eyes fill with tears. But as much as I don't want to watch, I can't look away as Reid flies toward Mav, landing a powerful punch into his stomach before an uppercut to the jaw.

My sob echoes around the small cell as I continue

watching the two of them fight before Reid throws one last deadly punch and my husband stumbles back into the crowd. Thankfully, they catch him, but he doesn't get back up.

"NOOO," I scream when the screen goes blank and Reid pockets it again. "No, please. Is he okay?"

Reid watches me cry for a few seconds before he pushes to stand.

His chest brushes mine. My nipples smart, it's not the bad kind of pain, it's the good kind, and I gasp, unable to stop myself.

Reaching out, he threads his fingers through my hair and drags my head back so he can loom over me.

I know I'm not exactly big, but he makes me feel like a little mouse as he gazes down at me. Like he could snap me in two with one quick move.

"Reid, please," I whimper as his grip tightens.

Tears fill my eyes again as I stare at him, silently begging him to tell me that Mav is okay.

'Please,' I mouth.

He smiles and it's pure fucking evil.

"He can't handle pain as well as you can, Pet. You're more of a man than he is."

"Bullshit. Mav is the best man I know."

"Then you really need to get to know some others."

He steps closer, pressing our bodies together and letting his warmth seep into mine.

My nipples pucker and my thighs clench.

"Why did he get into that ring with you?" I demand, focusing on the issue at hand, not my long-lost orgasm.

30

ALANA

The asshole just smirks at me.

Just when I think he's not going to respond, his lips part.

"Poor old Maverick is a little stressed. It seems someone has stolen his favorite toy and he can't find where they've hidden it."

"You're an asshole," I hiss.

He holds my eyes for a beat before the warmth of his hands wrap around my wrists and I'm forced back.

I collide so hard with the wall that all my breath rushes out of me.

He lifts my arms above my head, pinning them to the wall with one of his giant paws before looming over me, trying to scare me with his size.

"Oh, Pet," he muses, as if all of this is nothing but a joke to him. "Haven't you heard, I'm so much worse than that."

"You're all bark and no bite," I accuse.

His free hand lifts and my gasp of shock rips through the room as his thumb brushes my sensitive nipple.

"Is that right?"

I narrow my eyes at him, desperately trying to hide my true reaction to his touch, but I fear it's pointless.

"I think we both know that I've got more than enough bite."

"You're not man enough to take what you want," I taunt. My eyes might be locked on his, but he's so close that I can feel everything he doesn't want me to against my hip. "At least JD owns it."

"You want me to confess that I want to fuck you, Pet?"

Heat floods my veins, making me want to whimper with need. But I hold it in.

So what if the mighty Reid Harris wants to fuck me?

It doesn't mean I'm about to bend over and offer it up like the filthy whore he thinks I am.

He shakes his head, his signature smirk still in place.

"Sure. You're hot. I can see why JD is so determined to break the rules and see if Victor's number-one whore is as good as he thinks she is.

"But unlike him, I care about where my pussy has been. And yours... I've no fucking idea."

"Fuck you," I seethe.

"I think I just covered why that won't be happening." On instinct, my foot lifts from the floor, my knee desperate to make contact with his junk and take him to the ground. But the motherfucker sees it coming a mile off and jumps back.

His eyes darken, his expression cooling even more, making my heart jump into my throat.

"And here I was considering going easy on you," he whispers darkly.

"Please." The word slips from my lips without instruction from my brain. Although I'm not sure what I'm really begging for.

Something tells me it's the opposite of what I should be.

"Oh, Pet," he muses, his eyes darting around my face as if he's committing every inch of me to memory. "You really are my favorite prisoner."

Before I've had a chance to really hear those words, he grips my waist and spins me around, pinning my front to the cold, unforgiving wall.

I cry out as my arms are pulled behind my back, making my nipples rub against the unforgiving wall, sending sparks of desire shooting straight to my clit.

The rattle of metal distracts me before something cold and hard wraps around my wrists.

"Oh, you fucking—" I force myself to stop talking, hating that I'm giving so much away.

"No need to stop on my account," he mutters, leaning in so his breath races over my ear and down my neck. "You know how to end all this, Pet."

"Get fucked," I snap.

"Give me the truth, and I might just let you walk away."

"I don't owe you anything."

"This isn't about what I'm owed, Alana. It's about my future. And if you and your husband are going to get in the way, then I need to know now so I can do something about it."

He pulls me from the wall by my cuffed hands and throws me down onto the cot.

I cry out as my knees hit and my face plummets toward the hard surface. But just before I make contact, his fingers slide into my hair, stopping me.

"I don't give a shit about your future," I confess. "The only one I'm focused on is mine."

"Right now, Pet. You don't have a future outside of these four walls."

"He'll figure out where I am eventually. He'll come for me."

Reid chuckles as he pushes my cheek to the cot, leaving me ass up and totally exposed to him.

"I think I've already proven tonight that I'll win."

"He won't give up," I argue.

"And why is that?"

"Because he won't allow another Harris to ruin my life." I gasp, slamming my lips shut as I realize what I just said.

"Don't you enjoy working for Daddy, Pet?"

I don't say anything.

My chest heaves as my frustration at myself builds.

"I thought a whore like you would love it. A job that gives you all the action you miss out on at home."

Reid sits back on his haunches behind me.

I might not be able to see him, but I know exactly where his eyes are. My skin is burning up.

"Because you need it, don't you? You're nothing but a dirty slut who needs cock. Doesn't even matter whose it is. Can't have your husband's so you'll take any other one you can get."

"Shut the fuck up," I cry, my eyes burning.

It's not true. I didn't want any of those men. But I also can't deny that they gave me something I needed.

"Even now while you're locked down here. You should be scared. Terrified. I know my other inmates are. And yet, all you can think about are our dicks. When you should be cowering to us, you're using your body to manipulate us into getting what you want instead."

"No," I cry, although it's a lie. What he just said is completely true and I hate it.

"Your cunt is dripping, Pet. That's how badly you need it right now."

My sob of shame rips through the air.

I don't realize I'm rocking my hips until there's a woosh

as his arm moves through the air and then his palm cracks against my ass.

"Please," I cry, arching my back as the pain blooms.

More. I need more.

He does it again, making me scream.

"Tell me, Pet. Tell me everything and I might just give you what you need."

I shake my head as my tears soak into the fabric beneath me.

"Just a few of your secrets and I can fill this cunt to the brim, fuck you harder than you've ever been fucked before," he offers. But while my body screams yes, my head knows better.

He's playing me. He's not going to give me anything.

No matter how much he might want it right now, he will walk out of here sometime soon without giving us what we both want.

I know that. I do.

But it still doesn't stop me.

I push my ass back, desperately trying to tempt him as my sobs continue.

Nothing but a shameless, useless, dirty whore, a dark, very familiar voice whispers in my ear.

Suddenly, despite being awake, my nightmare comes back to me in full force.

"No, please. NO," I scream.

Dark laughter bounces off the walls around me as my shoulders continue to smart and my body aches.

"Please, don't touch me."

"It's a little late for that now, don't you think?" I squeeze my eyes closed, trying to grasp Reid's voice and allow it to drag me out of my memory. But it's not enough. *"You love it. You know you do."*

"No," I sob. "Please, just let me go."

"But we've paid a lot of money for this. Be grateful you little bitch."

The sting of Reid's spank brings me back again.

But it's not enough. My past, my fear, my dark and haunting memories have me in a tight hold.

Something presses against my entrance, and I scream.

"No, no, no."

"Don't you want what you're so desperate for, Pet? I know it's not a dick, but it's the next best thing."

I try to crawl away, to escape whatever he's doing, but his hand lands on my hip and I'm anchored in place, giving me little choice but to let it happen.

Story of my life.

Constantly under the control of men.

My body played and manipulated to please them.

I might try and take the upper hand, but ultimately, they always win.

"Please," I whimper.

The words he wants dance on the tip of my tongue. The reason behind all of this bullshit is right there. They would end this.

Could...

But this is never going to end. Reid is never going to let me out of this cell, out of his house and allow me to continue with my life with Mav like nothing happened.

That's a fantasy.

Whether he drags my secrets out of me or not doesn't matter. Not really.

This is it for me now. I'm either going to spend the rest of my life as his prisoner, or he's going to kill me. There is no option here.

"Oh God," I cry when something pushes inside me, stretching me open.

He's right, though. It's not his dick and that realization makes me sob with disappointment.

It doesn't stop my body from sucking whatever it is deeper, though.

"Look at that," he muses. "Such a good little whore."

The fullness inside me makes me sob in relief. But it's nowhere near enough. My hips roll despite this as I fight to get what I need.

"Please," I whimper.

"You need more?" he asks, his voice rough with desire, letting me know that he's not as unaffected by this as I'm sure he wants to be.

"Yes, yes," I beg like the shameless whore he accuses me of being.

I can't help it. I was trained from a very young age to crave everything a man can give me. It's instinctive, so deeply fucking ingrained that I can't stop it.

I scream like a banshee when the thing he's just pushed inside me starts vibrating.

"Oh my God. What the fuck?" I cry.

"Good?" he asks as I push back, desperate for more.

But I never make contact with him and when I rip my eyes open, I find him standing beside me, glaring down at me with a small black remote in his hand.

"You asshole," I hiss as my body begins to climb higher and higher. But I can't enjoy it because I know what's coming. For once, his expression is open, and I can read every wicked thought playing out in his head.

Lifting the remote a little higher in a bullshit show of power, he hits a button, immediately bringing the vibrator lodged deep inside me to a stop.

I collapse on the cot, my limbs trembling and my chest heaving.

"Untie me," I demand, holding his eyes captive.

I'm a mess. My tank is ruched around my waist, my eyes will be red and swollen from crying and I've no doubt got his glowing handprint on my ass.

"Nice try, Pet. I'll see you soon," he says, pocketing the remote and successfully dragging my eyes to his crotch.

His hard dick is straining against the thin fabric of his shorts, leaving very little to the imagination.

I'm not aware I lick my lips until he laughs at me.

"Keep dreaming, Pet. Sleep well."

It takes a few seconds to respond, but I just manage to get the last word out before he slams my cell door.

"Enjoy your right hand, asshole."

His dark laughter is the last thing I hear.

31
—
JD

I march toward Reid's room, blood pumping through my veins.

The second I woke up, I did what I do every day. I check on my little dove.

My eyes widened to the size of saucers the second I found her with her arms bound behind her back and my tank up around her ribs.

But as much as I enjoyed the sight. Fuck me did I. I also knew that she'd been down there for hours like that.

Before I knew what I was doing, I'd pulled on a pair of boxers, and was searching for the asshole who'd done it to her.

Twisting the handle, I throw the door open, although it doesn't crash back against the wall and wake the prick up.

He's in his bed, sleeping like a fucking baby, giving zero fucks about anything he's previously done.

I get halfway across the room before I notice his sixty-inch screen at the end of his bed is on, and it's showing the same image I was just looking at.

Doesn't fucking want her, my ass.

I don't rip my eyes away from her sleeping form until I'm right next to his bed, and when I do, the first thing I find is a small remote that's slipped from his fingers.

What the—

Picking it up, I instantly recognize the logo on the bottom.

"You evil fucking cunt," I mutter, although knowing that doesn't stop me from pressing the on button and turning back to the screen.

To start with, she does nothing. Then I turn it up another notch, and she starts to move, her hips rolling in her sleep as she seeks pleasure.

It's not until I turn it up again that her shriek of shock spills through the speakers, filling the room.

"I fucking hate you," she screams as her hips jolt, forcing her to flip onto her back and spread her thighs.

The view is fucking glorious.

"She doesn't mean it. She loves me really," a rough, sleeping voice says from beside me.

"You been teasing her with this all night?" I ask, not bothering to look at him. Why should I when I've got that beauty putting on a show for us.

"Not all night. Few hours. She was screaming in her sleep so I went down to see if she'd talk."

"Did she?" Seeing as she's still locked down there being tortured with withheld orgasms, I assume not.

"Nearly. I had her right on the edge."

"So I see," I mutter, turning the speed down and making her cry out in frustration.

"You were right," Reid says quietly.

Now that earns him a look.

"I'm sorry. What was that?"

"Fuck off."

"No, no. I think my ears are acting up. Did you just say that I was right?"

"She responds better to desire than fear."

"Well, ho-ly fuck. The almighty Reid Harris can admit when he's wrong."

"You're a cunt," he scoffs, sitting up and resting back against his wrought-iron headboard. Uncomfortable as fuck, but whatever.

"So what's the plan then, Boss? Gonna vibrate the truth out of her."

"Something like that. Got a cell that needs cleaning up first. She wasn't the only one who had a late-night visit."

"What did you do?" I ask.

"Make me coffee and I might let you come watch," he says, throwing his covers off and stalking toward the bathroom in his boxers.

"In a bit, yeah. I wanna enjoy the show a little first."

"You've got five minutes. And if you come on my sheets, you're buying me a whole new bed."

"Jeez," I mutter as he slings the door closed behind him. "Good thing you don't know that it wouldn't be the first time," I say under my breath with a laugh.

I hit the button on the remote twice, turning the speed up and smirk when it makes her practically leap from the bed.

"ARGH," she screams. "Everyone is right about you, you're a sick, twisted, vindictive cunt just like your father."

"True," I agree, watching as she begins to climb toward her release before cutting the vibrator off dead.

"FUUUUUUCK."

Her chest heaves, her hard, pierced nipples pressing against the soft fabric of my tank and her pussy exposed. Fuck me. She's so fucking wet it glistens under the bright spotlights that are shining down on her. What I wouldn't give to get a taste of that.

Knowing that I'm not going to be able to go down there without at least taking the edge off, I tighten my grip on the remote and stalk back toward my room.

I've got my boxers around my ankles as I step over the threshold and kick them toward the laundry basket before falling down on my bed and grabbing my TV remote with my free hand.

I find the right channel for the live feed downstairs and abandon that remote in favor of my dick.

"Oh fuck, yes, little dove," I groan as I squeeze my shaft, while turning her vibrator back on.

"For the love of God, you sadistic motherfucker," she screams, thrashing about on the bed.

"So fucking beautiful, Dove. Open your legs, let me see what you've got," I murmur, wishing she could hear my demands.

I up the speed on the remote, and it has the exact reaction I was hoping for.

"Fucking hell, you're perfect." I groan, working myself to a fast release.

It might be needed, but I already know it won't be enough.

She continues moaning and cursing Reid out as I get closer.

"Yes. Fuck, yes." I grunt, spilling my seed over the carpet, just as she moans like she's about to do the same.

In a rush, I shut off the vibrator, making her curse Reid to hell again.

Too late for that, little dove. He got his one-way ticket down there a long time ago.

There's movement at my door before the smug fuck's head pokes inside.

"I'll get my own coffee then, shall I?"

"As if you didn't just nut in the shower," I bark when he vanishes just as fast as he appeared.

"Just clean the carpet. No one wants to walk on your crusty old cum stains."

"You know, you don't have to watch her every second, right?" Reid teases as I sit at the kitchen island with the live stream on my cell.

"Says the one who fell asleep watching her with the remote in one hand and his co— Ow," I complain when he throws a spoon at my head.

"You can't even admit that doing that got you so hot you had to jerk off about fifty times afterward, can you?"

"Just doing what needs to be done."

"Fuck me. You're pathetic."

"Not what Mav is saying. Bet that motherfucker can barely walk today," he says with an evil grin.

"It was pretty epic," I confess.

"He deserved it. I hope it hurts like fuck," he says before sipping on his nuclear mug of caffeine.

"He really is a mess without her, isn't he?"

"Pathetic."

"He loves her," I say absently, making Reid's eyes jump to mine. "What? You suddenly grow a conscience?"

"Fuck no. I don't give a shit about how he feels about Alana. Just curious as fuck. They've been married for years, and she's that fucking desperate to get laid," he says, gesturing toward the screen where she's rocking back and forth as the vibrator continues on its lowest setting. "How hasn't he caved and fucked her raw?"

"You seem to be doing an okay job holding off. He's obviously got his reasons."

"None of it makes any fucking sense," he complains, rubbing his scruff-covered jaw.

"I believe her, though," I confess somewhat hesitantly.

"What?"

I take a sip of my own coffee as he drills me with eyes that terrify almost everyone in this town. Hell, this state.

"I don't think her and Mav are playing us."

"Fucking hell, J. You haven't even got inside her yet, and she's got you wrapped around her little finger."

My teeth grind and my lips thin at his comment.

"Maybe I'm wrong," I mutter. Although, just like how I knew the best way to crack her, I'm pretty fucking sure I'm right here too.

He's silent for the longest time as he sips his coffee and thinks about my words. I keep my focus on the screen, leaving him to it.

"Say you're not wrong," he says quietly. "Why is she doing all this?"

I shrug. *If I knew the answer to that then we wouldn't be fucking sitting here, would we?*

"She hates Victor."

"Who doesn't," I counter.

"Yet, she's willingly working—"

"Possibly not willingly," I add quickly.

"Well, she's working for him apparently because he has something over Mav and she's trying to protect him," he says, explaining everything we know.

"Right?"

"I dunno, something just seems off. We've all done a lot of bad shit that we could be put down for that Victor knows. Why isn't he threatening us? What does Mav know that we don't? Why is he a risk?"

I place my mug on the counter and turn the vibrator off.

"How about we go down there and find out?"

He studies me for a beat.

"Just remember who's in charge here."

Lifting my hand, I salute him before downing what's left of my coffee and pocketing my cell.

"Wait," I shout when he's at the door. "Shall we make her a coffee?"

He looks back over his shoulder.

"You think that's a good idea?"

"I do. She'll appreciate it."

"Fine. Make her a fucking coffee. She doesn't like it too hot, though."

"Obviously. No one is as big a freak as you, asbestos mouth."

"I'll meet you down there," he says, before taking off and leaving me alone with the coffee machine.

My addiction to the girl in the basement means that I pull my cell back out as I wait. I thought he was going to march straight in there, but to my surprise, her door stays shut.

"Get ready, little dove. Your time for keeping those secrets is over," I warn before finally heading in the direction Reid disappeared a few minutes ago with a perfect latte in my hand for my dove.

The familiar metallic scent of blood hits my nose, reminding me of what Reid said about visiting someone else last night.

I come to a stop at the open door, and my eyes widen in shock.

"Holy hell. You really did need to let off some more steam."

He shrugs as he none too gently throws the cell's

resident onto his cot.

"Is he—"

"Not yet," he confirms. "Not much longer, though."

"When did you decide to end him?" I ask out of interest. He usually tells me when he's decided to open up vacancies down here.

"I didn't. And we're not going to make the decision. She is."

My stomach knots.

"What are you going to make her do?"

He looks up, his signature devilish smirk in place.

"I might have said you were right, but that doesn't mean we're doing things entirely your way," he warns. "But we are getting answers today."

Turning his back on the half-dead guy who's slowly bleeding out on the cot, he unlocks Alana's door and pushes it wide open.

"Good morning, Pet," he announces loudly, like an obnoxious asshole. "Did you sleep well?"

I can't help but laugh as she growls at him like a caged wild animal.

Following him, I step in the doorway to find them glaring at each other, tension crackling loudly.

Oh yeah, when these two finally collide, it's going to be fire.

Obviously, that will have to be after I've had my time with her. That motherfucker might like to win, but not this time.

She's mine.

32

ALANA

Reid fucking asshole Harris stalks into my cell, wearing a shit-eating grin and nothing but a pair of low-hanging sweatpants, looking like he's slept a full eight hours. His cuts and bruises from the night before don't deter from the sheer hotness that is him, if anything, they only add to the dark and dangerous look that makes my mouth water and my thighs clench.

And it only gets worse when JD strolls in behind him wearing the same—only his sweats are black—and he's accessorized it with a mug of steaming coffee.

"Oh, little dove," he muses with a smirk. "This cell smells like pussy and desperation."

Ignoring him and the mug, assuming it's not for me, I focus back on the dickhead standing at the foot of my bed.

"You're a cunt, you know that, right?"

He laughs and JD snorts. "Yeah, Pet. I know. How are you feeling?" he asks. He almost sounds like he cares, but I know better.

"Fuck you," I huff, rolling onto my side, so I can sit up.

My shoulders ache and my hands are numb, but I know better than to complain. If begging doesn't get me anywhere then whining like a little bitch isn't going to work either.

"Oh, Dove. I do love it when you get all feisty."

"Yeah, well, you'd be a little pissy too if someone kept you up all night with a remote-control vibrator shoved up your ass."

"Dude, I thought you put it in her pussy. That's—"

"I did. She's just making a point."

Nodding, JD drops one hand from the mug and pushes it into his pocket. Only a second later, he's pulling it free again and revealing a small black remote.

"You mean this remote?" he asks, his lips twitching with amusement.

"Don't," I warn.

My body is a mess. My muscles are quivering. My pussy is swollen and desperate for a release that fuckhead has kept me on the edge of all night. Although now I watch JD with the remote, I can't help but wonder if he was in on the whole thing.

His thumb moves, hovering over the button.

"JD," I warn, but it doesn't help my cause.

I yelp when the gentle buzzing starts up again.

I'd hoped for a while that I'd get so worked up that even the lowest setting would eventually get me off. But with the constant up and down and one and off, I haven't managed to get there.

I'm beyond desperate for it now. I'm pretty sure my head is going to explode soon if I don't find my release.

I narrow my eyes at him as I fight the need to squirm in the hopes of making the vibrations hit the right spot.

Even if I did, they wouldn't allow it.

"Turn it off," Reid demands, as if he's some kind of white knight coming to rescue me.

Like the good little boy that he is, JD immediately does as he's told and I sag in relief as the buzzing stops.

"Please," I beg, unable to stop myself, "take it out."

"But you really seem to be enjoying it," Reid taunts, making me bare my teeth.

"We brought you a latte," JD says, pocketing the remote and walking closer.

The scent of the coffee floods my nostrils as he moves toward me. My mouth waters and my stomach growls so loudly, they both smirk.

But I'm not that stupid.

"What's the trick? Have you drugged it? Poisoned it?"

"It's not a trick, little dove. Just a latte."

My eyes dart to Reid when he shifts slightly when JD uses his nickname for me.

"What's wrong, Big Man? Don't you like your boy's name for me?"

His lips thin, but he holds back whatever it is he really wants to say.

"You gonna take her cuffs off or what?" JD barks. "I'll happily make her watch while I drink this for her, but it wasn't exactly the idea."

With a huff of irritation, Reid pulls a set of keys from his pocket and disappears behind me.

I guess I don't need to ask whose idea this was.

His warmth hits my back a beat before there is a little pressure on my numb hands and sore wrists then the cuffs release.

"Oh my God." I whimper, my shoulders aching like a motherfucker as I pull my arms around to my front.

I've no idea how long I've been bound, but it's been too freaking long. Especially when I've been desperate for sleep.

"Here you go," JD says, dropping to his haunches in

front of me and holding out the mug like some kind of fucked-up sacrifice.

"Get the fuck up, you moron," Reid snaps, clearly sharing my thoughts.

As much as I want to refuse, the temptation of having my first sip of coffee in Christ knows how many days is too much to deny and I press my lips to the edge of the mug.

So what if I'm about to be poisoned? Maybe it'll be the easier option in the long run.

The moan that rumbles in my chest as the deep, rich liquid gold spills over my tongue is nothing but pure filth.

JD's eyes burn into me, his interest more than obvious, but I refuse to open my eyes as I enjoy the creamy caffeine hit he supplied me with.

Silence fills the room, but I know I haven't lost their attention. My skin tingles with it.

It's not until the mug is empty that I finally look up. I immediately find JD's heated blue eyes.

"Thank you," I whisper, needing him to know just how much I appreciate it. Even if it kills me.

I shriek when a giant hand wraps around my upper arm and hauls me from the cot. "Let's go, Pet." Reid growls, his impatience running out.

He moves faster than my body can cope with and I end up being dragged out of my cell, my feet unable to find purchase on the cold concrete floor.

The scent that fills the air out here makes my lips peel back. But before I get a chance to ask what it is, I'm thrown into another cell, where the eye-watering stench is coming from, landing on my knees in the middle of what can only be described as a murder scene.

I scan the blood staining the walls and floor, but from the smell, I'm sure there are other bodily fluids here too.

The coffee swirls around in my stomach, threatening to make a reappearance.

"What the fuck?" I hiss, keeping my eyes on the small patch of floor in front of me.

"Jonno here isn't doing so good," Reid says, before the scrape of the cot against the concrete makes me wince as he kicks it.

Risking a look up, I gasp as I find a man bound and gagged on his cot.

His face is a wreck, everything swollen and bloody to the point he's unrecognizable. His body is in a similar state to what Tommy looked like a few days ago, only beneath this man is a fast-growing pool of blood. I can't see any obvious signs of injury, but clearly, something is wrong as his blood continues to drip down the small drain beneath him.

I've never been overly squeamish. The sight of blood has never really bothered me. But this is on a whole new level. My stomach contracts and I dry heave as it all becomes too much.

"And he really hates it when his cell is a mess," Reid continues to explain.

He disappears from the doorway, both JD and I staring in confusion at the spot he just left.

He's back before either of us gets to say anything and dumps a bucket of water and a sponge next to me.

"Clean it before he bleeds out and I'll give you the chance to save his life," Reid instructs.

"W-why is he down here?" I ask, my eyes locked on the beaten, half-dead man on the cot.

"That's not your concern right now," Reid says. "If he's still alive by the time you've finished, I'll tell you what he did and allow you to decide whether he lives or dies."

"M-me?" I stutter.

"You," he confirms.

"Why?"

"Why not?"

"Bro, this is—" JD starts, but he's soon cut off by his ringleader.

"The other option is that you do it," Reid snaps, glaring at his best friend, daring him to defy him and let me off.

His eyes find mine and I read everything he doesn't want to say within the bright blue depths.

Accepting my fate, I reach for the sponge and plunge it into the water. At least it's warm.

Climbing to my feet, I navigate the stains on the floor to the farthest wall and begin scrubbing.

My body aches and my muscles burn. My lack of sleep has never been more apparent, or my lack of clothing.

JD's tank brushes against my nipples every time I move, making me more aware of the tiny pieces of jewelry than ever. But that's nothing compared to when I bend over to rinse the sponge.

I still the second cool air washes over my pussy and a loud gasp fills the air.

"Oh, now I'm starting to get it," JD murmurs, while Reid remains mute.

I should predict what's coming next, but my thoughts are too full of them and their reaction to watching me do this to truly understand but no sooner do I stand to my full height again does the vibrating start. And it's not gentle.

"Motherfucker," I bark, slamming the wet soapy sponge against the wall aggressively, spraying myself with water in the process.

Locking all my emotions and disgust down, I continue scrubbing.

I will not let them win. They will not beat me.

After a few minutes, the vibrating slows and my body relaxes. But I don't turn around or acknowledge them in any way.

I shouldn't be grateful for the task of cleaning blood and other unmentionable things from this cell wall, but after days of nothing, having a job feels kinda good. A focus. Something that isn't dwelling on my nightmares or worrying about Mav.

I still as the image of Reid overpowering him at the fight last night comes back to me.

A sob threatens to rip from my throat, but I stuff it down. Deep down.

They want to break me. Beat me down, make me weak and then watch me shatter. But it's going to take more than this.

Whenever Mav used to fight, I was always there to clean up after it. In the first few years we were together, we spent many hours in the bathroom, while I patched him up and even stitched him up a time or two.

I hated it. Hated causing the one man who ever cared for me pain, but I knew I needed to if I wanted him fixed.

Watching him fight terrified me. I used to beg him not to go, not to put himself at risk like that.

The thought of losing him was scarier than anything I'd been through up until that point. He was my hero, my savior, my everything.

All I wanted was to be his in return.

I don't realize I'm crying until a tear hits my arm.

I hang my head, totally defeated. Exhausted and right on the edge of my sanity.

And that's the moment when the vibrating starts up again.

A sob rips from my throat without instruction from my brain.

Stay strong, Alana. You can do this.
You are better than them.

33

MAVERICK

My heart splits in two as I stare down at Alana sitting on her knees before me in my bathroom with silent tears falling from her eyes.

"I'm sorry," I whisper, feeling like the shittiest human on the planet.

She begged me not to fight tonight, but I was a pigheaded, selfish asshole who thought it would be okay.

It was until he stepped into the ring.

Reid fucking Harris.

If I never have to look that prick in the eyes again, it'll be too soon.

Thankfully, our fathers keep us both busy with our own shit that we don't really have to spend any time together.

But every now and then, our worlds collide and usually, it ends up with some kind of explosion.

Tonight was no different.

"Mav," she sniffles, lifting a hand to wipe her wet cheeks.

"I should have listened to you."

"You couldn't have known it would have been him," she *reasons.*

"I should have just stayed home with you."

Her watery eyes meet mine and another piece of my heart seems to fall away.

We both know why I fight. Why I need to burn off some steam. It's an elephant in the room that neither of us has addressed yet.

Alana is still seventeen. A minor. There is no fucking way I'm breaking my promise to her, no matter how hot she might be.

Watching her these past eighteen months has been such an honor. She's growing in confidence, discovering the young woman she was always meant to be.

I refuse point blank to do anything that could hinder her progress.

Every single night without fail, I wake up to her blood-curdling screams. She begs for them to stop, cries, and whimpers. And there is fuck all I can do about it.

I'd hoped at the beginning that they'd lessen with time.

But they haven't.

Night after night, those monsters continue to haunt her.

"It's okay," she says softly.

After soaking a cotton ball in some warm water, she reaches up and gently presses it to the corner of my mouth.

"You don't need to do this," I say, not moving my lips as much as possible.

Every time I speak, the split opens up again.

Her soft eyes find mine.

"Let me look after you," she whispers.

My pulse picks up and my blood heats.

Oh, how I wish you could, Doll.

I fall silent, watching her every move as she cleans up

each cut. She places tape on the deeper ones, but the others she leaves to heal on their own.

"Let me check your ribs," she says, reaching out and pulling my tank up my body.

"They're okay."

She glares at me, raising a brow to silently make me fall in line.

I do. I always fucking do when it involves her.

I help her pull my shirt over my head, leaving it to fall on the floor a blood-soaked mess.

"Jesus, Mav," she breathes, horrified by what she's found.

I don't look. I don't need to. I remember the hits all too vividly.

My entire body jolts when her fingers gently brush my skin. And despite trying to talk myself down with every unsexy thing I can imagine, my dick swells from her innocent touch.

"You should get these X-rayed."

"They're fine. I've broken ribs before. They don't hurt that much."

She gently pokes, making me suck in sharp breaths. I've no idea if she knows what she's feeling for, but it hurts like fuck. If she's trying to prove my previous words wrong, then she's going about it the right way.

She works her way down my ribs, and the lower her hand gets, the more my dick swells until it's obviously pressing against my shorts.

"Doll," I breathe, closing my eyes and tipping my face to the ceiling in the hopes of finding some strength, "I promise you, I'm okay."

"Did you want to try and convince me of that when you're not bleeding all over your bathroom floor?"

Her hand drops from my ribs in favor of resting on my thigh. But it's not just my thigh her fingers land on.

She gasps, and I immediately jump up, forcing her to fall back on her ass, sending all her medical supplies scattering in every direction.

"Fuck. I'm sorry. Shit," I bark, threading my bloody fingers into my hair and pulling until my scalp hurts almost as much as the rest of me.

"It's okay. It's—"

Her eyes drop to my crotch and she swallows, cutting off her words as she continues to stare at the more than obvious bulge in my shorts.

"Leave." I growl, hating how cold and vicious my voice sounds.

"M-Mav," she whispers, scrambling to her feet and coming to stand right in front of me. "It's okay. I want—" Her hand darts forward, and thankfully, I just manage to catch her wrist before she makes contact with me again.

The first innocent graze of her fingers was enough. I'm not strong enough to deal with a more deliberate touch.

"Alana," I snap, my eyes drilling into hers, begging her to stand down. "I-I can't—"

She swallows nervously, her eyes flooding with tears before her bottom lip trembles.

"I'm sorry." She darts around me and flees the room, faster than I thought possible, leaving me standing there with nothing but my regrets and a raging boner.

The loud slam of a door deeper in the house jolts through me and I hang my head in shame.

My eyes fly open. Or at least they want to, but the reality is that they barely move. The swelling is still too bad.

A loud groan spills from my lips as I fall onto my back. My ribs, my face, my everything hurt as memories from the night before come back to me.

What the fuck was I thinking?

The bang of a door and then footsteps force me to lift my head from the pillow. My heart jumps into my throat as hope blooms within me.

Alana.

Something clatters against the kitchen counter and my pulse begins to race.

"Alana," I rasp, but much like the rest of my body, my voice doesn't want to work.

The coffee machine turns on as I fight to sit up and swing my legs from the bed.

My ribs scream in protest. But nothing is going to stop me from getting to her.

Nothing.

My feet barely hit the floor when the footsteps get closer.

Please. *Please.*

A shadow falls over the doorway and I swear I stop breathing.

My hands tremble as I force my eyes open wider. If it's her then I want to see everything.

"Doll?" I say, my voice a little stronger this time.

My visitor finally steps into the doorway and the world falls out from beneath me as my hope shatters and dies right before my eyes.

"Sheila," I mutter, studying the older lady for a beat before giving up and crashing back to the bed in defeat.

"Maverick," she warns, marching toward me with her hands on her hips and a fierce look in her eyes. "Have you even bothered to clean up those cuts?"

I don't respond. What's the point? She knows the answer just from looking at me.

I barely made it home last night. Honestly, I've no idea

how I didn't end up in a ditch, forced to spend the night in my car. The first time I woke up in bed, I was shocked to find the softness of my sheets beneath me.

But while I knew I needed to clean up, I couldn't do it. Physically, I could have probably managed. But emotionally... nope. Not a chance.

When I gave up fighting regularly after I got a concussion so bad Alana thought I'd died, the only thing I really missed were our clean-up sessions. It was the one time I allowed her to get that close. I craved it like a junkie. But I knew it needed to stop.

Every time I came that little bit closer to forgetting my promises, taking her in my arms and slamming her back against the wall.

"Fuck." I groan, throwing my arm over my head as my memories haunt me all over again.

I realize my mistake instantly when pain explodes from my face.

"I thought my ears were deceiving me when I heard the kids talking about Reid Harris stepping into the ring last night with none other than Maverick Murray."

I groan, but it's not enough to stop her.

"What the hell were you thinking? You didn't think you actually stood a chance, did you?"

My arm lands on the bed and I glare at her.

"Thanks for the vote of confidence," I mutter.

"I'm a realist. You know this, boy. You went in there all emotional and hurting. You weren't in the right headspace to take him on. Even if you were in top form and ready. You were always going to lose."

"Ouch," I hiss.

"Truth hurts. Now, shall we see what we can do about this ugly face?" she asks, before spinning around and letting herself into my bathroom, hunting for my first aid kit.

"You don't need to do this," I call after her, pushing myself up and scooting back against the headboard.

"Someone has to," she shouts back. "And correct me if I'm wrong, but I didn't see a queue of women around the block offering up their services."

"Thank fuck for that," I mutter. I can't think of anything worse than some random wannabe gangster wives turning up to tend to my wounds.

I have the only wife I want; I just need to find her.

Sheila returns with an armful of medical supplies and silently begins to clean me up. It's not because she doesn't have plenty to say. She does. I can sense the comments and questions that she's fighting to keep in. She'll only be able to contain them for so long though. Before she leaves, I'll have been forced to listen to all her opinions and worldly advice.

Sheila has been in my life for as long as I can remember. She knows me better than I know myself most days.

Growing up, she was the only real mother figure I had. My mom fucked off before I was old enough to remember her. To be fair, I can't even really blame her. I just wish she was sensible enough to take me with her.

Dad bounced from one woman to the next, knocking up more than a few to ensure this town is littered with my half-siblings, ranging from a couple of years younger than me to toddlers.

But Sheila, from as early as I can remember, she was there taking care of us any way she could.

She's Ivy's grandmother. Hell, she's anyone's grandmother who needs a bit of love and care in this hellhole. But seeing as Ivy and I became inseparable from our first day of kindergarten, Sheila took me under her wing and gave me as much love as she gave Ivy.

She's been a better parent to me than my own. And even after gaining Daisy and losing Ivy, she's still here. Still trying to keep me together and patch me up as if I'm her own.

"You should have called me last night," she chastises as she tries to clean up the dried blood coating my face.

I want to tell her not to bother, but it won't get me anywhere.

Once she's done with my face, muttering her disapproval the entire time, she then makes a start on my knuckles.

"I know you hate this," she finally says. "I know how much you miss her."

"Sheila," I breathe.

It goes without saying that she was the first person Alana and I told about our marriage. She was skeptical at first, rightly so. Everyone in this town thought she'd gone to stay with her mom and Kristie, and then suddenly, there she was holding my hand and wearing my ring.

We knew everyone was going to talk. Plus, the fact I was five years older and she was barely eighteen. Not that that kind of thing was wholly unusual in a place like Harrow Creek. But Sheila saw through us. She knew there was more to it.

We never confessed though. Well, not in so many words. The thing about Sheila is that she knows. She sees deeper than all the others.

Alana's past was too painful for her to talk about more than she had to. She fought against it every single day. There was no way I was going to start telling others her secrets, or my reasons for keeping her safe and then making her mine.

That was our story, our truth.

It isn't for anyone else to understand or even agree with.

The five years I had with her were the best of my life. Yes, I have regrets. Ivy being the most painful of them all. But ultimately, I wouldn't have changed it for the world.

All I can do is hope that we get a chance to have more time.

34

ALANA

"ARGH," I cry out, my back arching and my hips grinding as the vibration hits its peak.

The cell is almost clean. Only splashes of blood remain beneath the cot the almost dead man is lying on and I'm really hoping I don't need to get that close.

Since the second I started on the floor, the torture with the vibrator has only gotten worse.

Pretty sure that's partly my fault though, seeing as I've been crawling around on my hands and knees with my ass and pussy on display for them to enjoy.

I'm wrecked. Fucking destroyed.

My muscles quiver violently, my skin is covered in a sheen of sweat, and I'm pretty sure the stench of the room is never going to leave me.

"Please," I cry out when it stops for a few seconds, just long enough to make me lose the very fragile grip I had on a possible release, before starting up again.

"You've done such a good job, little dove," JD praises, while Reid stands there like a statue.

"I'm done, please. I can't do anymore."

Every movement is hard work. Painful and exhausting. My muscles are like stone.

"What do you say, Boss? She completed your task?"

The vibration stops again and I fall back on my ass, the jolt making the vibrator graze my G-spot and I cry out. But it's not enough.

My hair hangs limply around my face as my entire body trembles with need and exhaustion.

Silence falls, allowing me for the first time to hear the rattling breaths of the man in the cot who's only a few feet away from me.

"What did he do?" I ask, unable to keep the words in.

Reid nods once and looks me dead in the eyes.

"The sick fuck has been grooming and abusing his niece and her friends."

His words slam into me like a freight train and my arms give out, sending me crashing back to the floor.

I cry out as my elbow collides with the hard concrete, but I don't have time to focus on that because my need to get to the toilet is stronger.

I dry heave, my stomach muscles screaming in pain as nothing comes up.

"What did you say?" JD barks, rushing to my side as if he cares.

But Reid doesn't answer him.

He knows.

Reid knows.

I heave again as the warmth of JD's palm rubs down my back.

"So, what do you say, Pet? Does this sick fuck get to live or—"

Wiping my mouth with the back of my hand, I push to my feet and stalk over to the man on wobbly legs.

For the first time since I was thrown in here, I really focus on his face.

Sobs wrack my body as recognition flickers in the depths of my mind.

I've tried to forget it all. Shove it all down so deep that I never have to think about any of it again.

But it never goes completely away. Not really. Some faces, names, and voices are clearer than others.

But I know this one.

And the knowledge that he's still doing the same shit to young girls out there makes me sick to my stomach.

"Dove?" JD whispers, sensing that something huge is happening.

"Die," I spit, my voice firm and sure, exactly the opposite of how I feel right now.

Reaching into the pocket of his sweats, Reid produces a flip knife.

Without second-guessing myself, I reach for it, flip the blade out and with a roar that doesn't sound anything like me, I lunge at the man, stabbing him in the chest.

I must hit something important because blood sprays out from the wound, coating me in an instant. The warm liquid seeps into JD's tank and runs down my arms and chest.

With another scream, I repeat my previous actions.

I do it again, and again and again, until I have nothing left. I fall in a heap on the floor, the knife clattering beside me.

My body trembles violently as a sob rips from my throat.

Pain like I've never experienced before slices through me. But it's more than just pain because there is relief too. A lot of it.

I've done it.

I've taken a monster off the streets —kind of—and stopped him from hurting anyone else.

It might only be the first step in everything Mav and I planned. But I've done it.

What I've done. The true reality of it is nowhere in sight. I'm numb. Totally fucking numb.

I don't even realize I'm moving until a warm torrent of water rains down on me.

I blink as reality comes back to me and shake my head in confusion at the set of eyes that are watching me closely.

I squirm but discover exactly what I thought.

I'm in Reid Harris's arms.

"What are you doing?" I whisper, my voice barely audible.

"You did so good, Pet." I blink up at him, trying to remember what just happened.

I look down, watching in fascination as the water washes the red away from my chest and arms.

The vision of the bloodied man in that cell comes back to me and everything begins to crash around me.

"I killed him," I cry. "I killed him."

Shoving my face into Reid's bare chest, I scream as the tears burning my eyes spill free.

I don't even know why I'm crying.

Horror. Relief. Joy.

Or a mix of all three.

"How did you know?" I whisper, as desperate to hear his explanation as I am terrified.

He swallows roughly but doesn't say anything, forcing me to pull my head back and look up at him.

"Reid?"

"Fuck," he mutters. "I didn't."

My lips part to question him, but no words escape.

And then everything changes again.

One second I'm in his arms, and the next I'm on my feet, standing on unsteady legs as he marches straight out of the shower, and then soon after, the room.

"What are you—"

My words falter as he vanishes from sight. My knees buckle without his support and I fall back, colliding with the wall as if the world has just been ripped from beneath me.

I sink, getting closer and closer to what will inevitably be a painful collision. But it never comes.

"I've got you, little dove. It's okay. Everything is going to be okay."

At the sound of his voice, I throw myself at JD. Wrapping my arms tightly around his neck, my legs do the same to his waist and slam my lips down on his without a second thought.

I need this. Him. Like I've never needed anything else in my life. It's either this or I drown. I'm right on the cusp of it. The memories are right there, clawing their way up from the darkness. But I refuse to go down. Not when I've got someone to hold me up.

But he doesn't kiss me back.

"Please," I whimper. The years of rejection I've felt from my husband burn through me.

Mav loves me. I know he does. I see it in his eyes every time he looks at me.

But he can't see beyond my past.

When he looks at me, he might see a young woman. He might even want me. I've seen the evidence of that desire more than a few times. But it's always there stopping him from taking what he wants. And I hate it.

I hate that I'm tainted. Broken. Tarnished. Ruined by men who never should have looked at me twice, let alone touched me.

"Dove," he warns, his grip on my ass tightening as he tries to maintain control.

"I need you. Please. I-I can't—"

I've no idea what I was about to say or confess to, and thankfully, I don't get to find out because his lips move and only a second later, his tongue sneaks out to find mine.

Every single muscle in my body sags with relief as he gives me exactly what I need.

My fingers sink into his wet hair as I try to get closer, needing everything he can give me to get out of my head. To forget about that cell and what I did in there, but more importantly, the broken, beaten down girl that Mav, and now Reid, it seems, are unable to look at.

A part of me disgusts them, and I get it. I disgust me too. But there is very little I can do about it.

"More," I beg, tugging his hair harder.

"Hold on." He groans, forcing me to tighten my grip.

Releasing my ass, he drags my—his—tank up my body, before pressing me back against the cold tiled wall and pinning me there with his hips.

Lifting my arms, I help him rid me of the bloodstained fabric.

The second it passes my face, I dive for him again.

"Need to clean you up," he mumbles into our kiss.

He continues licking deep into my mouth as the familiar scent of cherries fills the air. And then his hands are back on me.

"Oh God," I complain, abruptly ending our kiss as my head falls back against the wall in pleasure. "JD, please."

"Fuck," he barks, his attention making my skin burn. "You're addictive, little dove."

His hands work over every inch of me, ensuring that the blood and dirt are gone.

"Please," I whimper like a needy little bitch as my hips rock against his.

He's hard. So fucking hard and I need it more than I need my next breath.

They've been mercilessly teasing me for hours, bringing me to the edge but never letting me fall.

I can't take it anymore, I can't—

His fingers slide into my hair, massaging my locks as the bubbles explode.

"I'm going to take care of you, Alana," he murmurs, his electric blue eyes locked on mine.

"Please," the word is barely a whisper and it quickly gets swallowed up by the sound of the water.

But I want it. I want to so fucking badly. To be wrapped in a strong pair of arms, surrounded by his scent, letting me know that I'm safe, that they can't hurt me anymore.

He makes quick work of washing the shampoo out before working in the conditioner. And the second we're done, he lifts me from the wall and walks us both across the bathroom.

"Here," he says, passing me a toothbrush and toothpaste the second my ass hits the counter.

The moment the fresh mintiness hits my tongue, I wince at how disgusting my mouth must have been to kiss.

But his movements never faltered. Not for one second did I think he was disgusted by me. By any part of me.

That's because he doesn't know.

"Yeah, that's enough," he mutters, ripping the toothbrush from my mouth, it clatters into the sink as I'm dragged from the counter.

The moment I'm in his arms, my lips descend on his neck.

He might not be the only one who's becoming addicted.

He kicks the door closed behind us as he marches me back into my cell. I barely register that it's where we are. I'm sure the disappointment will come later that he didn't decide to break all the rules for this and carry me up into the main house. Right now, all I can think is more. Give me more and give it to me now.

"Julian." I moan when he effortlessly lowers me to the cot. His lips find mine and he kisses me breathless, before licking and nipping along my jaw and then down my throat, ensuring he leaves more than a few marks behind.

The thought of him doing it for Reid to see later sends another wave of heat between my thighs.

Oh fuck. Is he up there watching this now?

"More. Please. More," I whimper, raking my nails across his back in encouragement.

But despite the deep rumble in his chest as I hurt him, he doesn't do what I want.

I cry out when he pushes up from my body and stands at the end of my cot.

"Look at you," he muses, rubbing his thumb along his bottom lip as his eyes feast on my naked body.

"I'd rather you touch, not look."

A smirk spreads across his lips as he pushes his hand into the pocket of his soaked sweats. The sodden fabric does very little to hide what's going on beneath. My mouth waters and my muscles ache to get on my hands and knees and crawl to him.

When my eyes roll back up his body and find his, they're dark with need, as if he can read every single one of my thoughts.

"Do you think it still works?" he asks, making my brows pinch.

"Wha— Oh." Everything inside me sinks in disappointment when he holds the little remote up.

"What's wrong?" he asks, concern marring his brow.

I shake my head. "I can't—I-I don't—please."

I startle when the plastic remote collides with the wall. It splits in two and falls to the floor as JD shoves his sweats down his thighs, letting his dick spring free.

He fights with the wet fabric to get it down his legs, while my impatience becomes difficult to ignore.

Spreading my legs wider, my hand descends for my swollen clit. The weight of still having something inside me is a constant reminder of the last few torturous hours and everything they haven't allowed me to have.

"Don't."

His deep voice bounces around the room and my hand pauses instantly.

"Hands behind your head," he demands.

I hesitate. The last time he put them there, he cuffed me to the cot.

"Trust me?" he implores.

My eyes widen in shock that he's even asked, making him laugh.

"Fair enough. You should though, just so you know."

His knees hit the end of my cot as my arms comply with his demand.

The second my fingers wrap around the metal bar behind my head, his scorching touch lands on my inner thighs.

"Can't stop thinking about this," he says absently, his eyes locked on my pussy.

35

ALANA

My hips lift in the hope that, this time, I can entice him in.

My breath catches when his palms begin to slide down my trembling thighs.

Oh God.

My body is burning up, the need I've been battling since Reid pushed that vibrator inside me is even more all-consuming.

JD's hand leaves me and I gasp when he tugs on what must be a string connected to the toy.

He pulls it, making me cry out. It's good. But it's nowhere near enough.

"Admit it. You loved this. You loved knowing that we had control. That we were upstairs watching you."

My head thrashes from side to side as he continues to tease me.

"It makes you feel powerful, doesn't it? Knowing that we're both up there hard as fuck because of this.

"Julian," I scream when he presses his thumb against my clit.

But it's gone as soon as it appears, leaving me gasping for air.

"Please, I need—"

"Shhh, little dove. I know exactly what you need."

He tugs harder, and this time, the toy slides out, leaving me empty and desperate.

"I swear to God, if you don't—"

My threat is cut off when the heat of his breath rushes over my sensitive skin.

And then he's right there. My eyes roll back in my head as his tongue licks up the length of my pussy to my clit before he zeros in on that little bundle of nerves as if he needs it to survive.

Forgetting about his orders, my fingers sink into his hair, desperately trying to get him closer.

"Arms above your head, Dove. Or I stop," he warns darkly, his deep voice vibrating through me.

Doing as I'm told, I grip the bar again, arching my back and shamelessly offering myself up to him.

"So fucking hot." He groans, as he presses my thighs wider and returns to my pussy.

"Holy fuck," I scream when he sucks on me.

There is nothing gentle about the way he eats me. And. I. Am. Fucking. Here. For. It.

He's tongue and teeth, licking, sucking, biting. It's everything.

Every-fucking-thing.

And only goes to prove that the rumors I've heard are true.

Julian Dempsey knows how to eat pussy.

My grip on the bar behind my head tightens, my fingers cramping as he works me toward the release I'm so desperate for.

"OH MY GOD," I scream when he plunges two fingers

inside me, stretching me open and finding the spot the vibrator only managed a couple of times. "Yes. Yes. Yes. Right there. Right fucking th— NOOOOOOO."

I kick my legs like a petulant toddler when he removes all contact and sits up.

"Ow, what the fuck, Dove?" He grunts when my foot collides with the side of his head.

"Don't stop. Please. I'm gonna die if you don't finish me," I warn.

His amused chuckle does little for my irritation.

"It's not fucking funny," I snap, more than ready to cause him more bodily harm if necessary.

"As if I could stop now even if I wanted to," he confesses, his eyes locked on mine, so I can see the seriousness behind those words. His mouth is glistening with my juices and his lips are swollen from my kisses. He's never looked hotter.

"JD," I breathe when he reaches for his sweats and pulls something else from the pocket.

My eyes widen when he holds the silver packet between us.

"Oh," I breathe, my core clenching, desperate to have him inside me.

"Did you plan this or was it wishful thinking?" I whisper as he rips the packet open with his teeth.

"Always be prepared, Dove. Always be prepared."

I watch enthralled as he rolls the rubber down his shaft, covering all his piercings.

My mouth waters, wishing I got a chance to explore them with my tongue.

"Next time." He groans as if he's in physical pain reading my wicked thoughts.

"That better be a promise," I mutter.

"You have no idea, little dove," he whispers as he crawls up the bed between my thighs with his dick in his hand.

My tongue sneaks out to wet my lips as I watch him, and his eyes darken.

"Fuck, you'll look so good on your knees with your lips wrapped around my cock."

Any response I have to that flies from my head the second he presses the thickness of his cock against my clit.

"Yes," I cry. "Give it to me."

He drops lower, pressing just the tip inside me, teasing me relentlessly.

"JD," I warn, my voice low and raspy.

He shifts his position and reaches out.

My breath catches when his giant hand wraps around my throat, his fingers squeezing the perfect spots.

"Should have fucking done this days ago," he confesses, before thrusting forward and filling me in one sharp move.

We both groan loudly, the sound of our pleasure bouncing off the walls in the cell, and I'm sure a speaker or two upstairs, assuming the cameras pointed at us right now have audio allowing Reid to listen in too.

"JULIAN." I gasp for good measure.

"Fuck. You're heaven, Dove. Fucking heaven." He groans, rolling his hips, teasing me while I adjust.

"Fuck me," I beg. "Forget the niceties. Choke and fuck me until I've forgotten everything but your name."

"Damn, Dove. You sure are demanding."

"You love IT," I cry when he does exactly as I said and ruts into me.

"Fuck." He groans again before really picking up the pace.

His fingers tighten on my throat, cutting off just enough of my air supply that my eyes begin to burn and dark spots dance in my vision.

My skin erupts in goose bumps as his hand suddenly slides down my thigh, the roughness of his callouses against my softness, until he hooks my leg around his waist.

Lowering down, he hovers his lips right above mine, allowing him to grind against my clit with every single thrust.

My muscles tense, sucking him deep, desperate for everything he can give me.

Or almost everything.

"I fucking hate you, Julian Dempsey," I scream in frustration when he senses my release approaching and slows down.

"No, you don't," he counters. "You love my cock too much right now to hate me."

"Fuck you," I hiss, desperately sucking in air now that he's eased up on the pressure on my throat.

"Yeah. That's kinda the idea." His eyes flash with wicked intent as his signature cocky smirk spreads across his lips.

Leaning down, he steals my lips in a wet and filthy kiss that I feel all the way down to my toes as he slowly begins to increase his speed again.

Before long, I have to break our kiss to suck in deep lungfuls of air. But he only allows that for a few seconds before his grip on my throat tightens again.

"Oh God," I cry as he presses hard enough to cut off my air supply as he sits back, giving me the most perfect view of his abs tensing as he thrusts into me with abandon.

"You feel so good, Dove. You're squeezing me so tight. So fucking perfect," he praises. "You take my cock like such a good girl."

His words should turn me off. I've heard them so many times in my life, but they don't.

The opposite in fact. They flip some kind of switch in

me that craves the pain, the darkness, the pure filth that I know JD is capable of delivering.

"Harder," I beg, barely able to force the plea past my lips.

He hears it though, and boy, does he deliver.

His skin glistens with sweat as he thrusts into me, hitting me incredibly deep, making my head spin every single time as his fingers tighten around my throat.

Black spots dance in my vision and my eyes water as my release surges forward.

"That's it, little dove. You're doing so good."

A noise that's somewhere between a cry and a whimper spills from my lips as more tears slip from my eyes.

My entire body trembles as a powerful release approaches.

"Fuck, you're so tight. I'm gonna fill you up so good, Dove. You want it?" I've no idea if I nod or agree in any way, I'm too far gone. All I do know is that he doesn't stop.

Sweat covers every inch of my body as I tremble violently. My head spins, the approaching pleasure all-consuming after waiting for it for so long. I might have given myself a few orgasms down here, but they've all been unfulfilling. Especially when I know the two men who live in this house could give me something so much better.

"That's it, little dove. Let go. Come for me." JD's voice sounds a million miles away, despite the fact I know he's right there. I can see him, feel him, but everything seems distant.

Just like in that other cell before Reid scooped me up off the floor. It's like some weird out-of-body experience that I'm watching instead of experiencing.

But then JD presses his thumb against my clit and grinds his hips and... I. Am. Fucking. Gone.

Pleasure like I've never experienced before crashes into

me, swallowing me whole and refusing to release me from its grip.

My body trembles violently as wave after wave assaults me.

Everything goes dark, despite having my eyes open.

JD's roar just hits my ears before blackness comes.

———

I wake up crying. No, sobbing.

Loud, gut-wrenching sobs rip from my throat as tears spill from my lashes.

My body continues to tremble, utterly spent but instead of burning up, I'm freezing.

"JD?"

"I'm right here, little dove," he whispers before I'm rolled onto my side and engulfed by a wall of heat. A strong, inked arm snakes around my waist, his hand between my shoulder blades, holding me tight.

My sobs get louder, my body trembling uncontrollably, so hard my teeth chatter.

I've no idea what's wrong with me, but I also don't have the strength to even try and ask. All I can do is cuddle up to JD's warm body and hold on tight.

By the time my sobs lessen, my throat is raw and my eyes are sore and swollen. I'm still weak, my muscles like jelly. But despite all that, there is a delicious ache between my thighs, reminding me just how good that was, how much it was needed.

With his fingers twisted in my hair, JD gives me little choice but to look up at him.

His huge bright blue eyes stare down into mine, silently asking if I'm okay.

The problem is, I've no idea what the answer to that question is.

Did I get what I wanted?

Yes. And then some, it seems.

I've never come like that before. I've certainly never blacked out. Not through pleasure anyway. There has probably been a time or two that—

I close my eyes, cutting off my connection to him, fearing that he can see my memories playing out in my lighter blue orbs like a movie.

"Hey," he whispers, his hand slipping around to cup my jaw and keep my face tilted to his. "I'm right here. You've nothing to be scared of."

Don't I?

I swallow nervously and let my eyelids open again.

"There you are." Reaching out with his thumb, he brushes away a stray tear, stealing it as his own.

My lips part but no words form for the longest time. And when they do, they rip through me causing tears to fill my eyes all over again.

"I'm sorry."

My heart pounds as her eyes flood with tears and her bottom lip trembles.

I know she came hard. But fuck.

I've never had a woman burst into tears and completely fall apart after I've fucked her. It's... terrifying. But also... kinda nice, in a weird way. She needs me right now in a way I've never experienced with a woman before. And I want her to need me. I fucking crave it.

After the past week, I can't lie and say that lying with her in my arms in post-sex bliss isn't everything I hoped it would be. The crying aside, of course. I'm not a cuddler. Never seen the benefit in it before. But this... this is something I could easily get addicted to.

"Dove," I sigh, hating that on top of whatever she's going through, she feels the need to apologize. "You've nothing to say sorry for." Dipping low, I brush the tip of my nose against hers before tilting her head back and stealing a sweet kiss.

"I-I don't know—"

"Shh," I say, finding her lips again and kissing her concern away.

In only minutes, I'm hard again and ready for round two. Not that I expect it after how roughly I just fucked her. But I can't help it. She's in my arms naked and rubbing herself against me. I dare any red-blooded male not to be affected by her hotness.

We make out like teenagers for the longest time as I try to make up for whatever it was that tipped her over the edge.

At no point is there any noise or movement outside her cell, which surprises me.

There's no fucking way that Reid wasn't upstairs jerking off while he watched all of that. Hell, he's probably up there watching reruns of it right now, wishing that he were me, that it were his hands roaming over her body, that it was his tongue tangling with hers as she mewls in happiness.

Watching her with that vibrator driving her crazy was hot as fuck. I'll admit that Reid was definitely onto something with that brand of torture. But hell, was it hard—pun intended—watching her bend over cleaning that cell. And I swear to God, I almost came in my sweats when she plunged that knife into Jonno's chest.

It was fucking majestic.

I'd wondered why Reid kept him alive as long as he did. Obviously, his subconscious knew something epic was coming. That his end and ultimate committal to hell was going to be a beautiful thing at the hands of a hot as fuck blonde who is way more savage than she looks.

I think Reid might have been onto something that first night I found him watching her. We've underestimated her.

Although, I stand by what I said to him in the kitchen

earlier. I believe that her and Mav aren't planning some big takeover mission.

Whatever she's—they've—been planning, it's more personal. She doesn't want power or control. She wants... escape.

Eventually, her kisses get softer and her body gets heavier in my arms.

"Sleep, little dove. I'll be right here," I whisper.

Gently rolling onto my back, she snuggles into me, wrapping one leg around my waist along with her arm and resting her head right over my heart.

"Promise?" she whispers back.

"Yeah. I promise."

In only seconds, her breathing evens out and her body goes limp.

Finding one of the cameras I know that's hiding, I stare right into it, knowing that my best friend is on the other end right now cursing me out.

Lifting my hand from Alana's arm, I flip him off. Grinning like a fucking psychopath for good measure.

He's going to hurt me so fucking good for this.

I don't give a shit, though. It was totally worth it.

I can only assume it was the epic release and the long-winded foreplay that led up to it, but somehow, I managed to fall asleep with her curled around me like a spider monkey, her soft breaths tickling over my chest.

I can't remember the last time I had a daytime nap, but I really fucking like it. Or it might just be the fact I'm doing it with a hot, naked woman wrapped around me.

Or, at least, I like it until I wake with a start as Alana gasps and suddenly sits up.

"What's wrong?" I ask in a rush, concern for her after the way she broke down before racing through my veins.

She pauses with her arms wrapped around her middle, taking a moment to assess the situation.

"I-I..." she stutters. "Nothing," she finally breathes before turning to look over her shoulder.

"Hey," I say, tucking my hand behind my head and holding her eyes.

Her cheeks heat. It's the cutest fucking thing I've ever seen. Although the dark shadows from whatever she was just dreaming about don't leave.

The woman I choked out while fucking her not so long ago is fucking blushing.

My smirk grows and she dips her head.

"What is it?" I ask, hating that she's hiding from me.

Turning back around, she drops her head into her hands.

"We fucked and I cried," she says into her palms.

"Good thing I know I'm good enough that it wasn't due to poor performance, huh?"

"Fucking hell," she mutters.

"What?" I ask, pushing from the uncomfortable as shit cot to sit beside her. "I'm right and you know it."

Lowering her hands, she shoots me a coy look. "It was alright," she confesses.

"Alright? You're so full of shit, Dove. I'm better than Kane and we both know it."

A humorless laugh falls from her lips.

"Nah, fuck that. There's no fucking way Legend has better moves than I do."

"More metal doesn't equate to better moves. As they say, it's not the size that matters, it's—"

I catch her lips twitch in amusement.

She shrieks when I dig my fingers into her ribs, tickling her until she's laughing and screaming for reprieve.

"Shouldn't have lied to me then, should you?" I tease, lifting her and placing her on my lap.

Her legs wrap around my waist, leaving us almost chest to chest.

"What are we doing?" she asks quietly.

"Bit early for the 'where is this going' conversation, don't you think?"

"Julian," she whispers. "He's going to kill you."

"No, he won't," I assure her. "He'll be jealous as fuck. And he might well hurt me. But he loves me too much to kill me."

Ripping her eyes from mine, she locks her gaze on the wall over my shoulder.

"I'm not—we're not—doing anything to hurt him. We have no grand plan to bring the mighty Reid Harris to his knees. My secrets... what I'm hiding. It's... it's nothing like that.

"I never wanted to hurt Kane, or you, or Reid.

"I know that Mav hates him. But I don't."

"Even after all this?" I ask.

She shrugs. "This..." she repeats before falling silent. I want to interrupt and try and dig some more out of her. "This hasn't been so bad."

I wait for her to laugh, to tell me that she's joking. But she never does.

My chin drops in shock as I think about all the things he's subjected her to. The pretty pink gems in her nipples being the best of those things. In my opinion, anyway.

"You're serious, aren't you?"

"The bed could be more comfortable, and it could be a little warmer. But yeah. I've experienced worse."

She refuses to meet my eyes, but I need to see her. Reaching out, I cup her jaw and turn her to face me.

"Talk to me, little dove. Whatever it is, I'm here."

The darkness of the shadows that haunt her eyes makes my stomach knot and my chest ache.

She shakes her head. It's so subtle that I'd probably miss it if I weren't so close.

Dragging my thumb across her jaw, I capture her bottom lip and tug it down.

"It doesn't matter anyway," I tell her, releasing her lip. "Whatever it is, it doesn't change who you are."

"I'm broken, Julian. Beyond repair," she confesses. "What you saw earlier. It barely scratches the surface of just how fucked up I am."

"Dove," I say, a little harsher than I was anticipating. Her eyes widen, and she rears back a little. "We're all fucked up in one way or another. It's what makes us all so interesting."

She doesn't say anything, but I know my words hit their mark.

"That man in the cell," I start, not using his name. I don't know why but something tells me that she won't want to hear it. "You knew him." It's not a question. It doesn't need to be. I saw the recognition on her face when Reid gave her little choice but to turn her attention on him.

"He knew my dad."

"Right."

"Is he dead?" she asks firmly. There might be a whole host of emotions swimming in her eyes. But guilt or regret over what she did isn't any of them.

"I'd say so, yes. I haven't been back since Reid carried you out."

"Shit," she hisses, dipping her head again. "Why did he do that?"

"Because he cares."

A bitter laugh falls from her lips.

"He does."

"So why did he drop me and run at the first chance he got?" she spits.

My lips part, but I don't have any words to reassure her. I know my best friend better than I know myself some days. He's freaking out because he cares. But I'm not about to tell her that.

"It doesn't matter. It's for the best."

"Whatever it is, Dove. You need to tell him. He won't let you out of here until you do. You know that, right?"

She looks up through her lashes, her legs tightening around my waist, ensuring her burning hot pussy grinds against my hard dick.

"I'm sure you could put in a few good words for me."

I laugh, wishing it's as easy as that.

"No, I didn't think so," she says sadly despite my lack of reply. "I guess we should make the best of what we have then before he gets bored and offs me."

"He won't—"

I don't get any more words out because her lips descend on mine, stealing them along with all my rational thinking.

"I promise not to cry this time," she mumbles into our kiss.

"You take my cock again like a good little whore, and you can do whatever you want, Dove."

I rest back on my palms as she reaches between us, wrapping her delicate fingers around my length.

"Fuck. Don't think a girl's hand has felt that good since eighth grade."

"Eighth grade?" she echoes.

"Hell yeah, what do you think they taught us at Harrow Creek?" I ask with a laugh.

"I don't know. I never went."

"Shit. I'm sorry, I— Fuck. That's good."

"Yeah?" she asks, those shadows finally lifting from her eyes as she expertly works my dick like she's spent her life studying my instruction manual.

"Yeah. Bet this is better," she says before shifting so she can drag the head of my cock through her juices.

"Jesus, you're so wet for me." I groan when she teases both of us, pushing me just inside her.

"You've teased me for days and left me hanging every single time. What did you expect?"

"Fuck. I know. I'm sorry. Delayed gratification?" I suggest with a smirk.

"More like you're dick-whipped by Reid and did what you were told like a good little boy."

I can't help but laugh. "Sorry to burst that little fantasy you've got going on there, Dove. But there has never been, nor will there ever be, any dick-whipping going on under this roof."

"But maybe outside?" she asks, without missing a beat.

"Trouble. You are such trouble."

And to prove me right, she jerks her hips forward and sinks straight down on my length.

"Condom," I blurt as the heat and sensation of her pussy swallowing me whole makes my head spin.

"I'm clean," she says, leaning on her palms, mimicking my position and allowing her to slowly fuck me.

Fuck, if the sight of her taking what she needs from me isn't the hottest thing I've ever seen.

"You can trust me. I swear, I'm not actually that much of a whore."

"I believe you. I just... I don't—" I cut myself off. We don't need to get into my issues right now. Hers are more than enough to deal with.

"I know what I said. About Kane. But it wasn't... I can't—"

"Fuck. It feels too fucking good to argue."

"I've never— Shit." She rolls her hips with me as deep inside her as this position will go and I lose my fucking mind.

"I'll take any first you've got."

"Fuck yeah. I really fucking hope the cameras are still rolling because I'm going to need to watch this back later."

"Dog."

"Loud and proud, baby."

She laughs, but the second I jerk my hips up, grazing her G-spot, her head falls back, and her back arches, thrusting her incredible tits up in the air.

Taking my weight on one palm, I reach out with the other, sliding my hand up her stomach until I cup one of her breasts, squeezing it hard enough to make her moan like the dirty girl that she is.

"Oh, my little dove likes that, doesn't she?" I muse when she strangles my cock. "You take the other one. I want to watch."

She doesn't miss a beat. I'm desperate to take her piercing between my fingers and twist and pull it, making her howl with pleasure. But I know I can't. Not yet, anyway.

One day soon I'm going to go to town on those bad boys and make her come just from them alone. It's a little promise I've made myself.

"Julian," she cries as we both squeeze her breasts again.

"Fuck. I'm pretty sure your pussy was made for me."

Her head falls back again, and I hate it.

"Eyes, Dove. I need your eyes when I make you come."

Slowly, she drags her head up, and her light blue, hungry eyes lock with mine.

A shock of something rushes through me, a wave of possessiveness that I don't think I've ever felt before.

"Mine," I whisper before I'm able to trap the words behind my lips.

I know it's impossible. I know that realistically she belongs to someone else.

She's married to a fucking Hawk, a brother, and here I am balls deep inside her committing the ultimate sin.

I might not know the truth behind her and Mav's relationship, but I do know one thing.

He married her to keep her safe. And something tells me that it's going to fucking kill him when he discovers that he has less of her than he could ever believe.

"I really need to go," I say, rolling Alana onto her back. The warmth of her thighs is too inviting.

"No," she breathes, reaching for me.

"I don't want to. Trust me, I don't."

"Then why are you?"

Good fucking question.

"I need to go find Reid. And contrary to popular belief, we do actually have jobs."

"Oh yeah?" she teases. "I thought you just lived the high life off Victor's blood money."

"Well, there is a little bit of that too," I confess. "I'll come back, I promise."

"Not if Reid kills you on sight." She pouts.

"He won't." He might beat the living shit out of me though.

Ripping my eyes from her sad ones, I drag them down her body.

Her neck and tits are littered with hickeys and bite marks. There's one noticeably darker one on the underside of her breast that I can't resist.

"Julian," she warns, her nipples pebbling at my innocent-ish touch.

"I think you need another tattoo," I muse.

"Oh yeah?"

"Yeah. My bite mark right here. Then anyone who gets the pleasure of seeing your tits will know you're mine."

She swallows nervously, letting me know that she's currently thinking about another man.

The man who really owns her.

Lucky motherfucker.

If I were a better man, I might go and have a word with him about not satisfying her needs and kick him up the ass.

But as it is, I'm a selfish asshole who wants to keep Alana and her incredible pussy to myself.

Her eyes hold mine, begging me to say fuck it to the world outside and stay here with her. But then her stomach growls, reminding us both that she hasn't eaten all fucking day and guilt slams into me.

"I'll come back with something good to eat," I promise, finally extracting myself from between her legs and swiping my still soaking-wet sweats from the puddle they were sitting in.

Deciding against attempting to pull them on, I throw the fabric over my arm.

"I'll bring you clothes too."

Scooting back on the bed, she rests against the wall and wraps her arms around her legs.

"I'm going to need a shower."

My eyes shoot to her pussy where my cum is still leaking out of her.

"We'll see. I like knowing you're down here smelling like me with the evidence of what we've done running down your thighs."

"Caveman."

"Been called worse, Dove. Be good," I warn before I slip through the open door.

I close it behind me and pause, looking down at the locks.

I don't want to do it. I don't want to force her to stay down here. But I know I can't let her out and roam free just because her pussy is fucking spectacular.

"Fuck," I hiss, caving and closing just one of the bolts.

There's no way she'd be able to open it from inside, but I feel better knowing that I leave the rest disengaged.

After grabbing my abandoned cell, I run up the stairs butt-naked with my sweats dripping a trail of water behind me.

I burst through the door with a new sense of energy after getting laid as many times in the last few hours as I have in the last couple of weeks... hell, months.

Shit, my life was boring until my little dove crashed into it.

The first thing I notice is that it's dark outside.

I guess we did fuck like... shit. Three... no, four times?

Holy hell, no wonder I feel good about life right now.

I pause the second I see the state of the living room.

"Yo, bro. You here?" I shout, poking my head into the room to survey the destruction.

It's wrong. So fucking wrong, but I can't help but smile because I know the reason he did this. I shouldn't be smug but fuck... I really fucking am.

"Reid? You here, man?" I call louder, but I'm greeted with nothing but silence.

Traipsing through the kitchen, which thankfully, is untouched, I pull the refrigerator open and grab two bottles of beer before heading upstairs.

Ignoring my door, I continue down the hallway to his room.

"Bro?" I call before pushing the door open. "O-oh someone is pissed," I mutter when I find his room in a similar state to downstairs. "Doesn't fucking want her, my ass."

But despite the destruction, I don't find the man of the house.

"I'll just have to drink both of these myself then," I say as if he's hiding in the closet. Which he's not. He's Reid fucking Harris. And no motherfucking Harris hides from their problems.

They just fuck shit up and disappear, apparently.

Discovering that my cell is dead, I plug it into the charger by my bed while I dump my sweats in the laundry basket and knock the top of my first beer off, downing almost the whole thing in one go.

I moan in delight before wiping my mouth with the back of my hand.

As soon as my cell turns on, messages start pinging through. All from the missing man himself.

Reid: You're a cunt.

I barely smother a laugh. I wonder how long he watched for. Just our first round until we fell asleep, or did he hang around for rounds two, three, and four?

"Sorry, man. I feel for you and your overused right hand, I really do."

Reid: Got a meeting. Don't wait up.

"Sure thing, Dad." I salute my cell before pushing to my feet and heading to the bathroom to shower. Although, really, I don't fucking want to. I'd remain surrounded by her scent every day of the fucking week if I could.

With my cell propped up away from the water, I open the app and find the recorded footage.

Searching for the moment I carried her into her bedroom, I press play and watch it back, for what I know is going to be the first of many viewings.

***

"Shower time," I say, pushing Alana's door open and finding her sitting naked on her bed writing in her notebook.

For the first time since she's been locked up down here, when she looks up, there is real excitement glittering in her eyes and a wide smile on her face.

"Well, well, well, this is quite a sight, little dove."

Closing her book, she rests her pen on top of it, uncurls her legs and pushes to her feet.

We meet halfway between the door and her bed, and the second she's in reaching distance, I wrap my arm around her waist and drag her into my body.

"Mmm, you smell good," she whispers, pressing her nose into my shirt and breathing me in.

"So do you, Dove," I say, threading my fingers into her hair and dragging her head back.

"I smell like sex," she confesses.

"Exactly." I smile down at her, already addicted to the lightness in her eyes.

Something's changed. I'd like to think it's me and my magic cock. But equally, it could have been killing Jonno. She might not want to talk about him or how she really knew him, but it's had an impact. A good one.

I won't lie, I was worried when Reid gave her the ultimatum. I really shouldn't have been though.

I knew she was strong. I've seen that every single day

since she's been down here, but I didn't know she had that in her.

"The shower is running and your clothes are waiting. Come on," I say, taking her hand and tugging her out of her cell.

"You mean your clothes," she points out the second she spots the very small pile of fabric on the counter.

"Hell yeah, you look hot as fuck in my clothes. Why would I give you anything else?"

"I have no idea."

"Go on then," I say, swatting her ass hard enough to make her yelp.

I watch her go, her hips swaying as I imagine what she might look like with my handprint branded on her ass.

"I know you're staring."

"I'm not trying to hide it," I counter.

Lifting my eyes from her ass, I take in the soft curve of her back until I get up to her eyes, where she's looking back at me over her shoulder.

"So I guess you're watching, not joining then?" she says temptingly.

"You've no idea how much I'd love to join you right now," I confess as water sluices down her body. "But I've got jobs to do."

"Ah, Big Man cracking the whip," she says, reaching up and running her hands through her hair, making her back arch and her tits thrust forward.

"I know what you're doing," I warn.

"Showering. What gave me away? Was it the water?"

"Cute."

"So, what did he say? Did you find him with his cock in his hand watching our porno?"

"Nope," I confess. "He went out."

"Oh," she says, turning her back on me and grabbing the bottle of shampoo.

"You sound disappointed, Dove. Did the idea of him up there watching us turn you on?"

"You know it did."

"Bit of an exhibitionist, huh?"

"I guess you'll have to find out if I'm ever allowed out of here."

"We'll make it happen," I promise her.

She shakes her head and steps back under the spray to wash the soap from her hair.

She doesn't call me out on my bullshit, and I don't say anything else.

I want to believe that I'll watch her climb those stairs and rejoin the world, but honestly, I've no idea where Reid's head is at, at the moment or what he really wants from her.

Something tells me that no matter how much he tortures her, he's never going to get the secrets he thinks she's keeping.

Or is what he discovered earlier what he needed?

I've no idea what either of them said to each other earlier but whatever it was affected both of them. And I have a suspicion that it's part of the reason for the mess upstairs and his absence.

"Take your time, yeah? I'm going to be right out there sorting some stuff out."

Slowly, I back out of the room, regretting my decision to leave her but also knowing it's the right thing to do.

"What are you doing?" a soft female voice asks, making my movements falter.

She moves closer, her sweet cherry scent fills my nose, and when I look over, I'm pretty sure my heart skips a beat.

She's dressed in the tank and boxers I left for her, but it's more than that. She looks... relaxed. Happy even.

"Chopping, what does it look like?" I tease, going back to the carrot I'm cutting up.

"Yeah... um... why?"

"Gotta feed the pigs," I laugh.

"The pigs?"

"Your cellmates."

"They get vegetables?" she asks, staring at the piles of multicolored veggies I've already prepared.

"Once a week, yeah. Don't want everyone getting sick and dying too soon."

"A vegetable a week is known to prolong life," she deadpans.

"Who said you needed to go to school to learn," I tease. Although the joke falls flat.

"Can I?" she asks, changing the subject and nodding toward all the food I've prepared.

"Eat your heart out, little dove."

She rushes over and grabs two carrot sticks, stuffing them into her mouth and biting them off almost excitedly.

Guilt floods my veins. I haven't looked after her as well as I should.

Yes, I brought her McDonald's and stole some of Reid's cookies but that's not exactly good enough. I need to do better.

She might be stuck down here for a while yet, but I can at least try and make her stay bearable.

"Come here," I say, abandoning my knife and carrot in favor of wrapping my hands around her waist and lifting her onto the counter beside me.

I work in silence, while she munches her way through everything I've laid out, and after dividing it all up for our inmates, I lay it all on trays with fresh bottles of water and some bread.

"I'm going to deliver these. You okay here?"

"Yeah," she mumbles as she chews on a green pepper.

One by one, I deliver the trays and check in on our guests. All are fucking miserable, exactly as they should be.

None of them are like Alana. They all deserve their place here. And they're ugly motherfuckers.

"You good?" I ask when I return to find her exactly where I left her, still chowing down.

I don't think I was the only one who knew that she could have run the second I turned my back. But for some reason, I was confident she wouldn't.

"Yeah. Could do with some more of those cookies though. They were so good."

"I'll see what I can do. I should warn you though if I've got to try and make them then I'll probably burn the house down."

"Your skills stop at chopping, huh?" she teases.

"Something like that. What about you, can you cook?"

"I'm the perfect housewife."

"Yeah," I muse, letting my eyes drop down her body. "I bet you are. You do know that Mav has been walking around for years with the bluest balls in the world over you, right?"

"He didn't have to. He..."

I study her as if I'll read the rest of that sentence in her eyes.

But as much as I want to ask, I don't. She's been through

enough today already, and despite our nap earlier, she's fading fast.

"Will you do something for me?" she asks once I've put what's left of the vegetables and bread onto a tray and followed her to her room with it.

"If I can, yeah," I agree, expecting her to request a blanket or chocolate or something.

She stops beside her cot and waits while I lower the tray down.

The moment I turn to her, I reach out and cup her cheek. She immediately leans into my touch and it makes me want to scoop her up in my arms and carry her to my bed.

Soon, I promise myself.

I'm going to get her out of here soon.

"Will you go and check on Mav for me? That fight... it looked... brutal," she chokes out, her eyes filling with tears. "I always cleaned him up after and—"

"He hasn't fought for years. You've only been married for three."

She nods.

"Can you? I just need to know he's okay. He's missing his nurse and—"

"Dove," I warn when her voice cracks with emotion. But then she steps closer, wraps her arms around my waist, and rests her cheek against my chest.

Gathering her up in my arms, I hold her tight and drop my nose to her hair, breathing her in.

"Please," she whispers.

My heart fractures before a question I don't want to ask falls from my lips.

"You really love him, don't you?"

"Yeah. I do. I owe him everything. More than you could ever understand."

"One day, Dove. I want to at least try."

"We'll see," she mutters. "So, will you do it?"

I sigh. I knew my answer even before she told me what she wanted.

"Yes." *I'm pretty sure I'd do anything you asked of me right now, little dove.*

38

MAVERICK

The room spins around me when I open my eyes and my stomach rolls.

Oh God.

Glancing to the side, I try to focus on the empty whiskey bottle sitting on the coffee table as the need to vomit becomes more insistent.

I suck in a deep breath and close my eyes again, willing myself to go back to sleep.

But now that I'm awake, all I can think about—aside from just how hard my head pounds—are all the reasons I shouldn't be awake.

Sheila stayed with me for a few hours yesterday. She assured me that Daisy was being well taken care of and she set to work.

The house was a mess, I knew that. Although I don't think I really appreciated how bad it was until she started cleaning.

It just went to prove how much I've been taking Alana for granted. From almost the first day I took her to Dad's house where we stayed to begin with, she became a huge part of my life.

To begin with, she told me that it was because she needed a distraction. But as time went on, she never stopped. Every day the house would be perfect, restaurant-quality meals would be cooked, and all the while, she made it look effortless.

She was only sixteen when I first rescued and hid her. It astounded me how much she knew and was able to do. By the time I bought us this place and we started renovating, I wasn't surprised when she made DIY look easy. Just like everything else she did, it was totally effortless.

She amazed me daily. Made me fall for her harder with every little thing she did.

And now she's gone, all I can think about is how I didn't tell her enough, how I didn't appreciate everything she's given me.

She became my everything. I should have treated her better, told her how I felt, showed her how much she meant to me.

You're a Hawk, Son. That comes above all else. Even pussy.

"ARGH," I scream, grabbing a pillow and smothering my face with it. The second it connects, I realize my mistake and launch it across the room instead, but I fuck that up as well and the bottle topples over and crashes to the tiled floor beneath shattering everywhere.

"Motherfucker."

A pained sigh that's loaded with all my mistakes and regrets passes my lips and fills my—our—empty house. She might not be aware of it, but when I bought this place, I put her name on the deed right alongside mine.

She made sure to tell me that she didn't want anything for free from me. But what she didn't realize is that anything

I could give her pales in comparison to everything she's given me.

A few thousand dollars is nothing when I think of her smile, her laughter, the way she looks when she's lost in her own thoughts, and writing in her beloved diary.

I've no idea how long I lie there, drowning in the whiskey that's still flooding my system, while I remember our time here together.

It's not the end. I know it's not.

Somewhere deep down in my gut, I know. Just like all those years ago I knew she was going to be mine.

She's going to come back to me. She is. I just need to find a way to make it happen.

At some point, I manage to drift off again, and when I come to, the sun is flooding the house, making my eyes water and my head continue to pound.

But that's nothing compared to when there is a succession of loud, obnoxious knocks on my front door.

My pulse picks up as I try to guess who it might be. No one comes here. I made a point of making it off-limits to almost everyone when we moved to allow Alana privacy and to give her the confidence that she's safe. Hell, I'm pretty sure that most don't even know this place exists.

The only other person who has a key and is able to show up unannounced is Sheila. Which is how I know this isn't her.

She'd have barged in already and begun chastising me for getting drunk.

I can hear her words loud and clear, as if she's standing next to me right now.

Since when did drinking solve anyone's problems, young man? Get up, get showered and get out there to fix whatever is fucked up yourself.

I smile as I think of her fierce expression and give-no-shits attitude.

When I don't make a move to answer the door, the knocking starts again.

"All-fucking-right," I bark, swinging my legs off the bed and pushing to stand.

"Ow, fuck," I complain when pain slices through the sole of my foot. "Fucking assholes," I hiss, remembering there's broken glass everywhere.

As if they don't know I'm a hungover mess, now with a bleeding foot, the knocking continues.

"COMING," I bellow before hopping over the rest of the glass, leaving little drops of blood in my wake.

The second I get to the door, I peer through the peephole.

"What the fuck?" I mutter under my breath as my brow wrinkles.

In his impatience, he knocks again, scaring the shit out of me, making my heart skip a beat.

Gripping the handle, I rip the door open and face him.

"What?" I bark, making it clear that his presence here is not welcome.

"Well, good morning to you too, sunshine," JD says, grinning like the cat who got the cream.

"What the fuck are you doing here?" I growl, stepping into the space I created to show him that he's not welcome to even look, let alone step inside our house.

"Been sent to check in," he says absently, his eyes everywhere as he takes in his surroundings. As if he hasn't already done that while he was waiting for me. "Nice place you've got here. Very secluded."

"Which leads me to wonder how you found it."

"I said it was secluded, not invisible." He rolls his eyes, making him look like the irritating asshole that he is.

"Why are you here?"

My grip on the doorframe tightens as my patience wanes. I'm too fucking hungover for this shit.

"Boss's orders. You know what it's like."

"Victor sent you?" I ask, my brows pinched with confusion.

When the fuck has that motherfucker ever cared enough about anyone to insist on a home visit?

"Just doing as I'm told, man. Can I?" he asks, stepping forward, right into my personal space as if I'm giving off 'come in, let's party' vibes.

"The fuck, man?" I bark, forcefully shoving him back.

"Alright," he says, his eyes dropping down my body quickly. "No need to get your panties in a bunch."

I growl.

"You look like you need a coffee. And did you know you're bleeding?"

"I'm fully aware of the situation."

"And you kinda look like you've lost your puppy."

My teeth grind.

"I haven't lost anything; she's been stolen."

"Your wife and a puppy. Dude, you really are having a bad week. I planned for this, you know," he says, finally taking a step back, making me sigh in relief. "And I've got just the thing you need."

I should slam the door behind him and forget he ever graced my doorstep with his annoying presence, but my curiosity gets the better of me.

I watch as he rummages inside the car for something before he emerges with two take-out coffees, a bag of what I'm assuming are pastries, and a big ass, irritating fucking grin.

"Best motherfucking pastries in town, and fresh from the oven." He holds the bag up, waving it in my face, letting the scent wash through my nostrils. "Perfect hangover cure."

"I'm not hungover."

"You're a shitty liar, Maverick Murray. Now move aside, we've got a date with some delicious buttery pastries."

I've no idea why I do it. I blame the sweet scent of the fresh pastry and the mouthwatering rich coffee, but the second he steps forward, I immediately move back, inviting him in.

Goddamn it.

"You've got ten minutes." I growl, closing the door and following him down the hallway and into the open-plan living area.

"Dude, this place is insane," he says, his eyes glued to the wall of windows that look out over our yard, pool, and then nothing but woodland. "No wonder you don't want to share."

Ignoring him, I take one of the coffees from the take-out tray and steal the bag of pastries.

"Hey, who said I was sharing?" he whines like a little bitch as I hop up onto a kitchen stool at the island and take a sip.

Fuck, I needed that.

I continue drinking, letting the caffeine rush through my system as JD takes himself on a tour of our living space.

I tense when he pauses to look at photographs of me and Alana over the years, the ones she put up like a collage on the wall.

My teeth grind and my grip on the coffee makes the cup crumple in on itself as he continues staring.

"JD," I bark, hating that he has his eyes on my wife.

"She's really quite beautiful. Such a shame to keep her locked up here."

"I don't." I spit. It's true. Before we got married, yes, she was under some kind of house arrest, but it wasn't enforced by me. She knew that if any other Hawk saw her that they'd report it to her father and she'd be dragged straight back to hell. But since we said our vows, she's been free to roam wherever she pleases. She just chooses not to most of the time. And I can't say I blame her. I'd rather be here than in our shithole of a town any day. "She's free to do whatever she wants."

"Bet you're regretting that now, huh?" he says, finally ripping his eyes from the photos and walking toward me.

He takes a sip of his coffee before stealing one of the pastries and resting his ass on the other stool.

"Gotta be honest, man. You've looked better."

Irritation rolls through me. Even more so because he's also rocking a black eye and split lip.

"Could say the same to you," I mutter.

"Sometimes you've just got to take one for the team, and help your bro burn off some steam."

If he wants me to ask about Reid, then he's got another thing coming because the less I have to think or talk about that prick, the better.

"So no broken bones or anything then?" he asks when I don't respond.

"Sorry to disappoint. He'll have to try harder next time."

"You know, I don't think you two are all that different, really. You have a lot of things in common. The same kinds of taste."

"JD," I snap. "Why are you here?"

"Following orders," he repeats from earlier.

I study him, suspicious as fuck.

"Well, you can report back that I'm fine."

"Aside from the hangover, the battered body, and the bleeding foot?"

"Why the fuck do you care? Wouldn't you prefer if he'd ended me on Friday night?"

He shrugs. "Jury's still out. Just because Reid and I are tight, it doesn't mean I have to have the same opinion as him."

"What are you suggesting here? That you want to be friends or some shit?"

He takes a long drink of coffee, his eyes locked on mine.

"Just concerned about a brother's well-being. Is that so bad? Did you want me to patch that up for you, seeing as you're missing your nurse?"

39

ALANA

Dear Diary,

It wasn't long ago that I refused to think about tomorrow or dare dream about having any kind of future.

The reality was that one day, the men were going to kill me. They'd choke me too hard or make me do something that my body just wouldn't cope with.

It happened once. I literally thought I was dying with the amount of blood I lost.

I was in agony long before they left me curled up in the corner sobbing. I didn't know what they did, still don't to this day, but it was bad. Really fucking bad.

I was barely conscious when Dad returned to the house and found me. He didn't care that

I was in pain, his biggest concern was the stain I was going to leave on the floor. Which was a fucking joke because we basically lived in squalor. I did what I could to keep the place clean and tidy but the place was already too far gone when I started. I was fighting a losing battle.

I remember begging him for help, for a doctor, for him to take me to the hospital. Anything. But he refused. Told me to go to bed and stop acting like a baby.

I did. What else was I supposed to do? Try and escape and get help. I would be dead if I did that.

The only saving grace was that Kristie and I didn't share a room. The thought of her seeing me in that state was horrifying.

All night I laid there, curled up in a ball, praying that I'd die from the blood loss.

My bed was soaked through.

At some point, I thankfully passed out. And the next time I came to, I had a cannula in the back of my hand, but was still alone in my bloodstained bed, although thankfully in less pain. Those were the lowest days of my life. I had no idea what happened, what had been done to me. Dad appeared every now and then with food, water, and painkillers, but only when he could be bothered. All I could think was, why didn't you just let me die? But I knew the answer. And I was proven right once I'd recovered. It was business as usual, as if they didn't almost kill me.

Thankfully, there was never a repeat of that experience, but its side effects will live with me forever.

I didn't find out the dire consequences of that horrific experience until I was with Mav and he had a decent doctor check me over. Then the true extent of what my body went through that night and in the following days was revealed.

Being with Mav gave me hope. It allowed me to think that I could have a future. That my life might be more than a slave to my father and his sick and twisted friends.

Even when I was locked up in Mav's house, I'd never felt so free. It was incredible.

Which is why I know I should hate it down here. I'm locked in a single room with only a few basic necessities that JD supplied me with on his final visit last night.

I'd hoped he might spend the night with me. It was naïve and foolish of me to think things had really changed just because we had sex, he let me have a shower and some decent food.

But I couldn't help myself.

I'd felt a connection with him the first time he visited me, and every time since, it's only grown. Our chemistry crackles like wildfire when we're close. Or at least I think it does. Maybe it's all one-sided and he's just playing a very good game. After all, they seem to think I'm playing one too so why not, right?

But he said he believed me. That he'd do anything to prove it to Reid and get me out of here.

But what would my life outside of here even look like now? I've no doubt that Mav will pull me into his arms and hold me together like he's always done.

I could go back home with him and continue with our lives as if this never happened.

But do I want that?

I know it's stupid, but just thinking about walking away from JD, from all of this, feels wrong.

Is that Stockholm Syndrome?

The clank of the lock on my door disengaging startles me and I quickly close my notebook and wait to see who's going to appear.

Is it wrong that my heart picks up speed as I think about seeing Reid after suspecting he watched?

"Hey, Dove," JD says as he pokes his healing face into my cell.

"Hey," I say with a smile, trying to ignore the wave of disappointment that washes through me that it's not Reid. "How is he?" I ask, fully aware that he was fulfilling my request this morning to go and find out how Mav is after the fight.

"His usual miserable self," he says with a smirk.

"He's not miserable," I argue, immediately jumping to my husband's defense.

"No, I know. I trust your judgment, and if you say he's decent, then I've got to believe you."

"You'd believe me over his and Reid's lifetime rivalry?" I ask, shocked.

He shrugs.

"I'm willing to give him the benefit of the doubt and judge for myself. I've never had a reason to before."

"Fair enough."

"Here," he says, holding up a bag I didn't see him carrying. "I got you some goodies."

The second he places the bag on the end of the cot, I dive for it.

"Oh my God, donuts," I practically scream as I throw the box open and stuff one into my mouth. "Heywhatareyoudoing?" I mumble around a huge bite when he also picks one up and lifts it to his lips like he's going to devour it.

"I bought them for us. But it's good to know your stance

on sharing food," he teases before making a show of eating almost half in just one bite.

"You're not locked up in a cell," I point out. "You can eat donuts whenever you want," I sulk.

"The guilt trip won't work," he warns me, before throwing the rest of the sugary treat into his mouth.

"You've got a little..." I reach out to wipe the icing from his lip, but at the last minute, he grips the back of my head and drags me close so I can lick it off instead.

"Missed you," he murmurs, making the butterflies in my stomach flutter happily.

"Is he really okay?" I ask, unable to latch onto that comment. I want so badly to believe it, but I know it would be too dangerous to do so.

"Yeah. His face isn't pretty, but that's not new. Hey," he complains when I slap his shoulder. "He was suffering with a killer hangover though."

"I bet your sparkling personality really helped with that," I tease, more than aware of what Mav is like with a hangover.

"He'd smashed a bottle of whiskey and walked over the glass."

"Oh, shit." My heart aches hearing that he's hurt again and I'm still not there to help.

"Fucking prude wouldn't even let me help."

"I'm not sure that's the definition of a prude, Julian."

"Whatever. I offered to be his nurse and fix him up, but he wasn't having any of it."

"Can't say I'm surprised."

"See miserable."

"You're insufferable."

I glance up just in time to see his eyes darken. "Not the first time I've heard that, Dove."

My lips part to question him, but he sees it coming.

Swiping the bag and its contents to the floor, he wraps his hand around my throat and forces me back.

"Julian," I gasp a second before his lips descend on mine.

He licks deep into my mouth, the sweetness on his tongue mixing with mine.

A deep moan of desire rumbles in his chest as he settles between my spread thighs, the kiss getting wetter and filthier by the second.

I should care that he's come here from seeing my husband. Hell, I do care. I really fucking care. But I also can't stop.

When he touches me, kisses me, it's like the world tilts on its axis.

I've only ever experienced it once before. Only this time, it doesn't end before it's even started. This time, I get to indulge.

Sparking the lighter, I bring the flame to the candle and watch the small amount of wax melt away from the wick.

My wish didn't come true on my birthday. I might have been proposed to and soon after listened to the man I love say his vows and promise himself to me. He might have given himself to me, but not all of him, and it's killing me.

Happy with the flame, I look down at the tiny fire-engine red bikini I'm wearing. And after ensuring the girls are as good as they can be, I lift the plate and carry it outside.

"Happy birthday," I sing as I emerge, finding him exactly where I expected, under the shade and relaxing back on our outdoor couch in a fitted t-shirt and shorts.

He sits up and lifts his Ray-Bans, placing them on the top of his head so he can focus on me.

For the briefest of moments, his eyes drop to my body.

Good. They should. I ordered this bikini with one

intention in mind. Gaining his interest and shattering his resolve.

I hoped that he might have gotten over whatever has been holding him back on our wedding day. I knew he was going to have to kiss me to seal the deal, and I was praying for something porn worthy. But it didn't happen. He kissed me but it was something like a grandparent would give their grandchild. Not that I have any experience with that, but I've seen things on TV.

But today. Today, I'm going to do it and give him a birthday present he'll never forget.

"I told you not to do anything."

"And I ignored you."

"Doesn't sound like you," he teases.

Poking my tongue out, I drop down beside him and hold the cake between us so he can blow out the candle.

Our eyes hold for a few seconds before he leans forward and purses his lips. I'm pretty sure time and my heart stop in those few moments.

"Don't forget to make a wish," I force out.

He looks down at the candle and then up at me again.

My heart jumps into my throat and my hands tremble.

I want him. I want him so bad that I'm pretty sure my bikini bottoms are ruined.

He's been nothing but the perfect gentleman since he saved my life, and gave his to protect me. And as much as I appreciated that at the beginning. I need more now. So much more.

The warmth of his breath rushes over my breasts as he blows, making my nipples pebble and obviously press against the thin fabric that is barely containing them.

He moves, sliding the plate onto the coffee table and I jump before I talk myself out of it.

Our lips collide and I throw myself into his lap,

*straddling his waist and grinding down on him as my tongue
sneaks out to deepen the kiss.*

*I almost cry out in relief when his hands slide up my
thighs, his length hardening beneath me. Every single muscle
in my body quivers in excitement, my core clenching,
desperate to feel him inside me.*

*The heat of his hands burn through me as our kiss
continues. He gives as good as he gets. All my daydreams and
fantasies over the past couple of years are shattered.*

*It's everything. Everything and more. And I utterly
drown in it.*

Until it ends.

*His grip on my waist tightens before my back hits the
couch cushion.*

"Mav," *I gasp, trying to catch my breath.*

"I'm sorry, Doll. I'm really fucking sorry."

My eyes burn with tears, that memory, the rejection is
still so real, so raw, despite the fact Julian is kissing me,
touching me as if I'm the most beautiful and desirable
woman on the planet.

JD senses it, his kiss falters ready to pull away.

My grip on him tightens, desperate to stop him from
breaking our connection.

But then a shadow falls over us before someone clears
their throat and reality comes crashing down.

40

REID

My teeth grind and my chest heaves as I stand there, anger vibrating through me like a live current.

Together, they work in sync. She rolls her hips and arches her back as he grinds into her and moves his hand beneath her shirt.

Her moans of pleasure rock through me, threatening my resolve to appear unaffected by this.

I told him that she was off-limits, but I never really expected him to take me seriously. JD never does. He sees a woman he likes, he goes chasing after her like a dog with two dicks before he realizes that she wasn't all that, gets bored and turns his attention to another one.

It'll happen this time. And it'll happen a hundred times over in the few years to come, I'm sure. Alana isn't special. He just wants her because I told him he couldn't have her, and because he has easy access. There is no chasing her. She has nowhere to run.

With my blood boiling through my veins, I take a step closer, letting my body cast them in shadow to give them a hint that they've got company. Not that I really think it'll stop them.

The second I clear my throat, they both pause like two naughty little school kids.

Her nails dig into his shoulders, adding to the more than obvious scratch marks that are already there in her desperation to keep going.

"JD." I growl, my voice dark and deadly.

Finally, he pulls away from her lips and dips his head with a pained sigh.

"Can't you see I'm busy, bro?" he groans.

"I can see perfectly well. Unfortunately, I need you more than she does."

"Doubtful. She's so fucking wet right now. You've soaked through my boxers, haven't you, little dove?"

He rolls his hips and she moans like a whore when he hits the right spot.

"Get your horny ass upstairs. We need to discuss something."

"If you want to shout at me for buying her donuts, go right ahead," he offers, pushing up onto his knees and holding his arms out from his sides. "I'll take it like a man."

"I'd rather you took me," Alana confesses, her voice rough with desire. I don't want to look at her, but when her glare begins to burn the side of my face, my body takes on a life of its own.

My breath catches at the darkness in her eyes. She's horny, sure. But I'm pretty sure there's something else there too.

"Stay and watch if you really want. I'm sure real life is better than watching through a screen," she taunts.

I hold her stare, refusing to react to her offer as I replay the events of yesterday in my mind.

I had my suspicions about what her past entailed. She'd

alluded to a couple of things in her time down here, but I didn't want to believe it. It opens up the possibility of things happening around me that I should have seen. That I should have been aware of. That I should have done something about. But watching her maim Jonno yesterday. It was so fucking poetic yet haunting at the same time.

Before our eyes, she morphed into an entirely different person. Each roar of anger as she stabbed my knife into his body confirmed what I suspected.

It doesn't answer all my questions, or my suspicions. But it sure connected a few dots.

But it was nothing compared to the moment she confirmed it in the shower. In that moment, she was no longer a hot, young woman but a girl. A broken, little girl who'd lost everything to men who shouldn't have had access to her.

And right now, I can see it again within those dark shadows in her eyes.

Refusing to focus on how everything I've learned about her in the last twenty-four hours makes me feel, I return my stare to my horny best friend.

"Two minutes, JD," I bark before turning to leave.

"Two minutes?" he echoes. "I'm good, man. But I'm not that fucking good. Give me twenty."

"Two minutes," I repeat before slipping out of the room to the sound of my best friend shouting, "miserable motherfucker needs to get laid."

I march up the stairs and make a pit stop in the kitchen for an energy drink before making my way to my office.

Part of me expects him to defy orders and make me wait. But much to my delight, only a few seconds later, his footsteps grow louder before his angry form darkens my doorway.

"Ah good, you are capable of putting her down." I scoff.

"The fuck, man?"

"I told you not to touch her." It's a weak argument at best, but I fall back on it nonetheless.

He moves closer, his smug grin getting wider before he drops into his unofficial chair on the other side of my desk.

"You're just pissed she wants me and not you."

I don't react.

"Oh dude, don't pull that impassive, 'I don't give a fuck' bullshit with me," he says, sitting forward and resting his elbows on his knees. "I know you care. I can see it in those haunted eyes of yours."

"Fuck off." I bark.

"Jealousy isn't a good look on you, man."

I bark out a laugh. It's bitter and full of hate, and he sees right fucking through it. "I sincerely hope you wrapped it. Pretty sure she's fucked half the germ-ridden dicks in this town."

"You really need to get to know her better," he counters, resting back once more.

"And you need to stop being so blinded by that pretty little gem in her cunt."

"Oh, man. You should hear the way she howls when you tug it with your teeth. Fucking gold. Oh, wait... You know, don't you? You watched every fucking second of us together yesterday. How many times did you nut? As many as her?"

I neither confirm nor deny his words. Instead, I get down to business.

"I've been given some new contacts," I state flatly.

"Oh?" JD asks, scooting forward.

"Yeah. And not only that, apparently, they're willing to talk."

"Ohhh," he says, his eyes lighting up in excitement as he

rubs his hands together. "That motherfucker is going down."

Something fizzles inside me. I've been so focused on bringing my father and his reign of terror down that I haven't really taken a step back to appreciate just how far we've come.

But right now, we're closer than ever.

"You know that woman in the basement would be more than happy to help in any way that she can," he says, figuratively dousing my excitement with an ice-cold bucket of water.

"Does everything have to lead back to her?" I bark.

"No. But I figure that she could be an asset. She hates that cunt as much as we do. The shit he's made her do, man." JD scrubs his hand down his face, looking more concerned than ever about his piece of ass in the basement.

But how he's feeling now is going to be obliterated if what I'm suspecting is true.

And I hate to admit it, but I think he might be right. Alana could be the missing piece we need on our side to finally put everything I've been working toward into action.

But before I can even consider that, I need the truth and nothing but the truth about all of it right from her lips.

I can't risk being wrong and giving her and Mav the ammo she needs to bring me down right alongside Victor.

"Where did you go earlier?" I ask, doing a three-sixty on our conversation.

"Out," he says, his stupid, smug grin returning.

"What was in the bag aside from donuts?"

"So you were watching," he teases. When I do nothing but glare, he continues, "Just a few things to make her stay a little more pleasant. Nothing exciting."

"It's not meant to be pleasant."

"She doesn't deserve to be down there."

"She still hasn't told me everything," I shoot back.

"Why does she have to? She's explained what's important about working for Victor and being made to lie to Kane."

"We still don't know why. And until I have everything and am confident she's not going to fuck us over, she's not leaving that cell. I don't care how good her fucking pussy is," I state, pushing my chair back and standing to my full height. "Do what you've got to do to get the truth. One way or another, I'm getting every secret in that pretty little head of hers."

"Ah-ha, so you can admit that she's pretty," he calls after me as I storm out of my office in favor of the kitchen.

Just like I expected, footsteps follow me.

"If you can be bothered to check your cell, there are shipment details on it for the guys. Can you speak to Dev and get them set up for the week."

"A please would be nice, Boss," he teases.

"I'm making dinner. Go and do your fucking job."

With a salute, he disappears from the room and thunders up the stairs.

Leaning forward, I rest my hands on the edge of the counter and hang my head.

Squeezing my eyes closed, I try to forget about everything for just a couple of seconds. We've been moving toward the checkered flag with all this for a while, but all of a sudden, it seems like we've taken the last corner and are hurtling down the final straightaway faster than I can control.

Dread sits heavy in my stomach, and it's not just because of what I'm about to uncover. I might be horrified, but honestly, I can't say I'm surprised. Victor Harris and his inner circle are some twisted cunts with no morals and even fewer ethics. They're only after two things: power and money. And it seems they really will stop at nothing to get it. Fuck the lives they ruin in the process. People don't matter, not when you're almighty Harrow Creek Hawks royalty.

"FUCK," I bellow, my deep voice echoing around my silent home.

The end might be in sight, but something tells me that it isn't going to be pretty. This is all about to blow up in our faces and we need to be ready.

"**Y**ou've sure made a lot for two people," JD points out almost an hour later after he's loaded his plate with my homemade chilli.

I shrug, refusing to take the bait. "You don't need to eat the leftovers tomorrow if you don't want."

"I ain't refusing food. I'm just pointing out a fact." He eyes me suspiciously over the table.

"Whatever," I mutter, making him smirk and his eyes twinkle with mirth.

"You care."

"I don't fucking care. I just want all this bullshit over with."

"You're a liar too."

I purse my lips and push my fork into my food.

"Maybe you should take this down there yourself after we've finished."

I want to. Fuck me, do I want to. But as much as I hate to admit, even to myself. I'm scared. Terrified of the darkness and the truth she's hiding.

For the first time since I locked her up down there, I'm starting to understand what JD has seen. She's not hiding a wicked scheme that will end in my demise. What she's holding back is much, much worse than that.

Something tells me that having to talk will break her even more than she already is. And for the first time in my life, I care. I care about how she'll cope with diving fully back into the past as she lays all the horrors on the table for us to absorb.

"I've got to go out. I've got another meeting, and then I'm heading to Maddison to check in on the guys. You're in charge."

His grin widens. "Oh hell, yes. It's party time, baby."

"Just... do not let her out of the fucking basement. No matter how good she sucks your cock."

He shovels a forkful of chilli into his mouth before looking up at me.

"Yeah, we'll see," he teases.

41

ALANA

"Oh my God, what is that smell?" I say in a rush when the door opens and the waft of something mouthwatering hits my nose.

My stomach instantly growls as JD emerges carrying a tray full of goodies.

"Is that wine? Holy shit, I think I love you."

His eyes lock with mine as my words register in my brain.

Shit.

"Careful, little dove. I'm not sure your husband would like that."

Guilt twists up my stomach.

I think we've already done plenty that my husband wouldn't like.

"But yes, it's wine. Chilli, garlic bread, and something special for dessert."

"And a candle." I laugh when he lowers the whole thing to the cot. "Aw, is this a prison cell date?"

"Sure. It can be anything you want if it makes you smile like that," he says, reaching out to cup my jaw. His thumb brushes over my bottom lip and his tongue sneaks out to wet his as if he's imagining us kissing.

Unfortunately, my stomach growls loudly again stopping him from doing anything.

"Eat," he says, lifting the plate from the tray and passing it over.

I stare down at it, letting the scent of the tomatoes and rich spices fill my nose.

It's the first time I've looked at a proper meal in over a week. I'm not sure I know what to do with it.

"What's wrong? I already know you're not a vegan."

"Nothing. It's just... after a week of basically nothing, it's a bit overwhelming," I confess, feeling like an idiot. "Thank you," I whisper.

"You're welcome, little dove," he says, grabbing the fork and loading it with a small mouthful. "But it probably shouldn't really be me you're thanking."

"Reid made this? For me?" I blurt before JD's able to push the fork past my lips.

"Well, he probably wouldn't even confess to that on his deathbed, but he doesn't usually make the size portions he did today, and I can confirm that we didn't just have a dinner party upstairs."

I shake my head, trying to make sense of what he's saying.

"He didn't hurt you?"

"No, Dove. He didn't."

"But—"

"No buts. Just eat, yeah."

I nod as he brings the fork back to my lips, giving me little choice but to part them and let him feed me.

It's bizarre but also... nice. I have very few and very hazy memories of ever being looked after. We lost Mom when I was still too young to really remember much about her, and until Mav took me in, it was every man for themselves in that hellhole of a house.

Lifting my hand, I try to take control of the fork, but JD isn't having any of it.

"Let me, Dove. I like looking after you."

"You're too good for this kind of life, Julian," I whisper.

He shakes his head. "If only that were true. You've only seen one side of me. But trust me when I say there is another you probably wouldn't like very much."

"I doubt that. You couldn't possibly be a bigger asshole than Reid."

He chuckles as he holds out the garlic bread for me to take a bite of.

"Ohmygod." I moan in delight.

"I really hope you make those kinds of noises when you thank me later," JD teases.

"I guess that all depends on what you have in mind."

"Everything, Dove. I'm thinking about everything."

"So what did Reid say? I find it hard to believe he ignored what we did and just cooked us dinner."

"He still wants your secrets. Told me that I wasn't allowed to let you out of here, no matter how much I might want to. But..." he trails off.

"But what?"

"I dunno. Something was different. He was different."

I focus on the wall ahead of me and sigh.

"It's because of what you said in the shower, isn't it?"

"Yeah, probably," I confess. His curious stare burns the side of my face, but I refuse to give him the answers he's desperate for.

How can I? It'll change everything between us. He won't look at me with the barely-restrained heat burning bright in his eyes.

"I think I'm done," I say, pushing his next forkful away.

"Shit, Dove. I'm sorry, I shouldn't have said that. You should eat this. You need it."

"I'm full. Honestly. Maybe I'll have some more later."

Thankfully, he believes me and lifts the plate from my lap.

"Something tells me that you're not going to turn this down," he says, lifting the wine glass and passing it over.

"Absolutely not." I take a sip and moan the second it hits my tongue.

It has to be a fluke, but I'm pretty sure it's my favorite.

My eyes shoot to his, and I quickly discover it's no fluke.

"How did you know?"

"Dove," he teases. "A man never reveals his secrets."

"I hope you know that this is going to go straight to my head."

His smile is sheer wickedness. "Oh, I know. I'm banking on it."

"What's he doing now? Is he watching us?" I ask, curious as to what the miserable fucker does in his spare time when he's not torturing people.

"He's gone out. Doesn't mean he isn't watching, though."

"That's really creepy, you know that, right?"

"We don't usually have anyone we want to watch. It's more to see if they're still alive."

"Right."

"You sure have made things more entertaining for us."

"I would say you're welcome, but I'm not sure I'd mean it."

"What are you talking about? You seem more than happy down here."

I shrug. "I like my own company."

"Is that your way of telling me to leave now that I've fed you?"

"Never. I'm hoping you can provide me with some entertainment."

He reaches out and steals my wine glass to take a sip for himself.

"Mmm," he says, licking his bottom lip. "You have good taste."

"Mav helped introduce me to a few of the finer things in life."

"Well," he murmurs, placing the glass on the tray and giving me little choice but to lie back when he looms over me. "Let me allow you to indulge in some more."

He spreads my legs, settling between my thighs, resuming from where we were rudely interrupted earlier.

His nose gently brushes mine, making me whimper with need and my lips purse, searching for his.

"Julian." I moan when he kisses the corner of my mouth, refusing to give me what I need.

"I love it when you're all needy, Dove. Gets me hard as fuck."

Reaching out, I grab him through his sweats, needing evidence to prove his filthy words.

"Oh fuck." He grunts when I squeeze him.

My mouth waters, and my core clenches.

"Kiss me," I demand.

"Fuck. You drive me crazy." He groans before finally giving me what I need and plunging his tongue into my mouth.

He swallows my moan as I tuck my fingers under the waistband of his sweats and find him going commando beneath.

His shaft is like velvet as I wrap my fingers around him

and slowly work him, my thumb bumping over every piercing.

"Jesus," he mutters into our kiss, his hips jerking forward in search of more.

His hand that's not holding him up slips under my tank and squeezes my breast, making me arch for him.

His kisses and teasing touch make my head spin.

"More. I need more." I moan before I'm suddenly moving as he flips us, forcing my hand to slip from his sweats. "Hey," I complain, "I was playing with that."

"I thought you wanted to thank me for the food."

Sitting up, I stare down at him.

"I thought I had Reid to thank," I tease, grinding over the impressive bulge in his pants, making his jaw pop.

"Trouble is, Dove. He's not here, and I am. It sucks, but someone has to accept your gratitude, and I guess it'll have to be me."

"Such a hardship, I'm sure," I say, sliding my hands under his tank, exposing his abs. "Off."

He complies happily, lifting from the cot and dragging the fabric over his head.

I take a second to appreciate the pure piece of art laid out before me. Muscles, ink, a cock that makes me see stars. JD really is the whole package. And I am more than happy to unwrap him and indulge while I can.

I've no idea how long I'm going to be stuck here. I'm not going to give Reid everything he wants willingly. I don't want to think about the darkest days of my past, let alone talk about them.

Dipping low, I circle one of his nipples with my tongue as my hands explore, loving the way his muscles bunch under my touch.

"Dove." He moans, his fingers threading into my hair. I

expect him to push me lower, to take control, but he never does.

Instead, with his eyes locked on mine, he watches as I take my time, licking every single ridge and indent of his chest and stomach before I get to his sweats.

"Went for easy access, huh?" I tease, tucking my fingers under his waistband, ready to tug them down his thighs and expose the part of him I really want.

"What can I say? I was feeling lucky."

"Such a cocky asshole," I mutter as he lifts his hips to help me out.

Crawling down his legs, I pull his sweats down, letting his hard, pierced dick spring free.

My gaze locks on it as I lick my lips.

It jerks, as desperate for me as I am for it.

"Dove, you should have warned me if you just wanted to stare at it."

Clambering to my feet, I tug his sweats from his body and abandon them on the floor in favor of taking in the god of a man waiting for me.

"Get naked. Right the fuck now." He growls, making my nipples pebble and my pussy flutter.

I do as I'm told, while his eyes eat me up. His attention on my body makes my temperature soar. I crawl back onto the cot between his thighs the second I'm bare.

Lowering my head, I lick all the way up his length, my tongue bumping over every single piercing as I go.

"Oh fuck," he groans as his cock jerks in excitement, "so good."

With my hands on either side of his hips, I continue teasing him, circling each ball until I get to the tip.

His fingers sink into my hair, and this time, he's not so patient as he pushes my head down. Taking the hint, I wrap my fingers around him, and suck him into my mouth.

"Holy motherfucking yes," he bellows as I sink down lower, taking him as deep as I can in this position. "You look so fucking hot right now, Dove. Where have you been all my life?"

I smirk around his shaft as I bob up and down on him, giving him all my best moves, hoping that I'll blow his mind. Hands down, he's given me the best orgasms of my life, and I fully intend to give him the same in return.

Sooner than I was expecting, he thickens, stretching my lips wider as his grip on my hair tightens to the point of pain.

"Fuck. Dove. Fuck. I'm gonna— Fuuuck." He groans before his cock twitches violently, and his hot salty cum spills down my throat. The moan he emits when he falls makes my thighs slick with desire and my impatience unbearable.

"Get up here and sit on my face. I need to taste that pussy."

Not needing to be asked twice, I easily crawl up his body and straddle his head.

"Best sight in the fucking world," he mutters, before wrapping his hands around my thighs and dragging me down.

My scream of pleasure echoes around the soundproof cell as he devours my pussy like a starving man.

"Julian," I cry when he spears his tongue inside me.

His fingers dig into my hips with a bruising grip. My skin is already tender from our first time together, but the thought of having more of his marks on me only has me racing toward my release faster.

"Oh my God." He sucks on my clit until it starts to hurt. I shouldn't like it, but I crave the pain.

His hands slide over my waist before he grips my breasts and squeezes, his thumbs brushing over my nipples.

"Yes. Yes. Yes."

He growls, sending the vibrations from his deep voice rocketing through me, and I shatter, coming all over his face. He stares up at me with happiness shining bright in his eyes.

When I begin to come down from my high, he pushes me down his body, setting me over his waist.

He's hard and ready for round two, and despite the fact that my limbs are still quivering from my first orgasm, I'm more than eager to dive into what comes next.

"I want to watch you ride me. Use me, Dove. Take everything you need."

Thankfully, I didn't end up a sobbing, broken mess after any of the orgasms JD gave me during our little fuck fest. Instead, we stumbled on unsteady legs to the shower and made the most of our continued privacy.

I didn't think I could go again, but JD happily proved me wrong when he wrapped my legs around his waist and fucked me into the wall.

Hands down, one of the best evenings I've had in quite a long time.

I was expecting him to deliver me back to my cell and disappear upstairs to go and do whatever it is he does with Reid up there.

But he didn't, instead, he grabbed the blanket he brought down for me yesterday and crawled onto my bed naked, slipping under it and waiting for me to join him.

"I don't think I've ever done this before," he muses after long, silent minutes.

My back is to his front, his arm locked around my waist

and our legs entwined. I'm so relaxed, so comfortable with him. I don't feel like this thing between us is new. It's like it's always been this way. It's as amazing as it is unnerving.

It's one of the things I always wished Mav would do more often. He climbed into bed with me a handful of times over the years when I had a really bad night, my nightmares leaving me inconsolable.

Every night after it happened, I prayed he'd just slip in behind me and hold me close again. But he never did. If I was lucky, he'd set up home on the chair and watch over me.

"Being in a bed with a woman? Funnily enough, I don't believe you."

"Not cuddling," he confesses. "It's nice."

I wiggle my ass, making him groan.

"It is nice. I agree. But why do I feel like a feral beast is going to burst through the door."

"He can if he wants. I'm not going anywhere tonight."

"Don't you want to go and get into your big, comfy bed?" I ask, barely holding back the grin his words cause.

"Nope. Not unless I can take you with me."

"Aw, such a smooth talker," I tease.

"I mean it, Dove. I want you in my bed, exactly like we are now."

As much as I love that thought, tears fill my eyes, and my heart fractures. As much as I might want it, the moment I'm allowed out of here, I'm running through the front door and away from this place as fast as I can. Even if it means leaving a piece of me behind.

42

MAVERICK

My cell buzzes on the counter as I drink my coffee, praying that this week is going to be more successful in finding my wife than the previous one.

It can't get any fucking worse, that's for sure.

I stare at it. At the name of the man lighting up the screen.

I want to ignore it. To ignore everything. But I know I can't.

Ever since I learned the truth, the last thing I've wanted to do is toe the line and do as I'm told.

But what's the alternative?

We don't have everything we need to bring them down for their crimes. And until we do, there's fuck all I can do.

It'll happen though. I made Alana a promise to wipe every filthy cunt who ever touched her from the face of this earth. And no matter what, I will fucking succeed.

I'm going to show her that not all men, not all Hawks are corrupt fucks who take whatever they want without any care about the consequences or who they hurt.

I will lay her demons to rest and allow her to live the rest of her life without the fear that they're hiding around the corner. Even if I don't get to experience it with her. Even if avenging her is the last thing I do. At least I'll die knowing I didn't break my promise.

"Razor," I bark a second after answering the call and pressing it to my ear.

"Clubhouse," is the only word growled back before the line cuts.

"Morning, Dad. How's it going? Yeah, I'd love to come and hang out with you and your scumbag friends, while they ruin this town one square foot at a time," I mock before downing what's left of my coffee and climbing to my feet. "Ouch," I hiss as I put my weight on my sliced-up foot.

My face might look better, my cuts healing and the swelling reducing, but that still hurts like fuck. I'm pretty sure I got all the shards of glass out, but I'm not one-hundred percent.

Like a pathetic asshole, I hobble through to my bedroom and get dressed.

In only thirty minutes, I'm looking somewhat presentable and dressed in a black pair of slacks and a dark gray button-down. I wince as I push my foot into my shoe, but I have little choice but to grit my teeth and bare it.

"Stop being such a pussy over a cut fucking foot," I mutter as I drop into my truck and spin out of the driveway.

Dread sits heavy in my stomach as I close in on the clubhouse. There's a small bit of hope that I'm driving toward my wife. But my rational side is too strong. If Dad and Victor had found her, I highly doubt they'd call me to immediately come and pick her up.

It's more likely that they've got her and somehow managed to get the truth about what we're planning to spill from her lips.

The dread gets heavier, and my foot presses the gas a little harder to get me there faster.

The second I pull in and park, I throw the door open and march inside the building.

It's busy for a Monday afternoon; there are guys littered throughout the main space, drinking, playing pool, and trying to chat up the girls who are roaming around hoping to snag a Hawk.

Many look over as I race through, but I don't return their attention. I couldn't give a fuck about any of them.

I don't bother knocking on Victor's office door; instead, I just throw it open, harnessing Reid's arrogance.

"Ah, look," Dad muses from his spot beside his boss, "you took your time."

"You called me less than an hour ago."

"Exactly."

"What's going on?"

"We picked up a little rat this morning."

I narrow my eyes in suspicion.

"Thought you might want to give him a visit?"

"Who is it?" I ask, suspicious as fuck.

"Kane Legend."

"Why the fuck would I want to visit him?"

Kane is one of Reid's boys. And just like Reid, I try to stay as far away from all of them as possible.

"And anyway, I thought he was done and starting his life over at MKU."

"Yes, well," Victor muses. "Things aren't always that cut and dry."

"And this all involves me, why, exactly? I don't have anything to say to him."

"Oh, he's not talking. He isn't capable of that right now."

Scrubbing my hand down my face, I try to read between the lines.

"Why have you pulled him in?" I ask, despite the fact I really don't care.

I need to remember that this role that I've been born into is meant to be everything I always dreamed of. If I drop the façade, then there's every chance I'll be the one unconscious in one of their holding cells.

"He's been causing me shit and needs to be taught a lesson."

"And you're up here talking to me about it because..."

"You haven't been yourself recently, Son," Dad says, almost sounding concerned for my well-being. "Thought you might appreciate the stress relief."

"At least he can't fight back," Victor says, his pride for his eldest son glowing brightly in his eyes.

Lifting my hands, I crack my healing knuckles.

"What cell is he in?"

Dad rubs his hands together. "That's what we like to hear."

"Go have your fun," Victor instructs. "We'll join you shortly and make a decision about what to do with the cunt."

Pushing my chair out, I walk toward the door, but my steps falter when Dad's voice fills the air.

"It's always the same. They think one whore is worth giving it up for and everything goes to shit. No single pussy is that fucking good. I should know, I've tried enough."

My fists curl at my sides.

"Don't you agree, Mav?"

Ripping the door open, I march through it, leaving it to slam in my wake.

I don't head straight toward the holding cells; instead, I make a detour to the bar. I've no idea what's coming, but I know it's going to be bad. The dread that was confined to my stomach is starting to seep through my veins.

I nod at the Hawk manning the bar and point to the whiskey lined up along the back wall.

He pours me a large measure and I throw it back.

"Surprised to see you here again so soon," he says, having clearly watched the fight on Friday night.

"We all have to lose every now and then," I mutter, before rapping my knuckles on the bar top and taking off with the alcohol warming my belly.

The second the two Hawks guarding the cell Victor has thrown Kane in spot me, they guess where I'm heading and stand aside.

"Afternoon, Mav," one of them greets. In return, I barely spare him a glance.

I'm not known around here for my friendly attitude. Or at least, I'm not anymore.

When I was young and naïve about what was happening to the unlucky girls of this town, I was the life of the party. I'd spent all my time here, wishing I could grow up faster to become a Hawk. Back then, all I wanted was to initiate, claim my title and fuck as many girls as I could get my hands on.

Oh, how times have changed.

No words are exchanged as I let myself into the room and find Kane slumped in the corner.

His face is even more fucked up than mine, and he's got blood running from his hairline, his shirt soaked through.

The only other thing in the room is a bright spotlight that is shining straight down on him as if he's a one-man show on stage.

"Seems like you've made an enemy of the wrong man," I mutter, pacing back and forth in front of his unconscious body.

I've stayed well out of the deal Kane made with Victor to get out of this life. I think all of us who knew anything about it believed that Kane was playing with fire.

You don't just leave the Hawks and turn your back on Victor. That isn't how this fucked-up life works.

I can only assume that Kane has something up his sleeve to make it happen.

Honestly, I really fucking hope he does. It'll be nice to see that there is a life outside of all this. It'll help to restore my faith that there is more for me and Alana. More than suffering the horrors of her past and holding back on what I want.

A man can dream, right?

Kane groans, but he doesn't come to. Whatever they've given him, it was clearly a decent dose because he's not a small guy. He's a wide receiver for the Maddison Kings Panthers for fuck's sake. Something else that a normal Hawk doesn't get to achieve.

"What is it about you, huh? Why are you defying all the odds?"

The door behind me opens before the deep rumbling voices of my father and Victor make the hairs on the back of my neck stand up.

I've never hated anyone like I hate them, and I really hope that after I've put them both in the ground, I never have to feel it for anyone again.

They come to stand in front of me just as Kane stirs again. And only a few seconds later, he opens his eyes. Confusion floods them as he tries to figure out where the hell he is.

"Ah, you're finally going to join us," Victor taunts.

"What have you given me, you asshole?" Kane slurs, proving that I was right about the dose they administered.

"Just a little something to help make you a little more... agreeable."

"It's going to take more than what you've given me to make that happen," he snaps back, refusing to back down even in his position.

"Oh, I don't know," Victor says, stepping forward into Kane's space, "I seemed to get you here fairly easily."

"What do you want?" Kane spits.

Victor chuckles, but it quickly becomes clear that no man in this cell is scared of him.

"What do I want? You really are fucking stupider than you look, boy."

"We're done, Victor. I told you, take away everything. I want nothing more to do with you or this bullshit life. I am done."

My eyes widen at his words.

He's been given the promise of the most incredible future, and yet he's throwing it all away for love.

It's the first time I've really considered that we might have something in common because I'd do exactly the same for Alana.

"You're a fucking idiot. You don't get to give this up because of a girl. A fucking Hunter girl at that. Have those girls got diamond-encrusted cunts or something?"

"The only cunt around here is you, Victor. Let me go and I'll walk away and never look back."

"It's almost sweet that you think I'll allow that to happen," Victor mocks, smoothing down his obnoxious tie and turning to look at Dad and then me, expecting us to back him.

I do because I have to. But honestly, I'm with Kane here.

"I think you'll do exactly that, Victor," Kane states confidently.

"Oh yeah, and why is that? Why would I let someone who knows so much about me and my business just walk away scot-free?"

"Because I know things you don't."

"Oh?" Victor asks, although he barely sounds interested.

Kane sits there silently for a few moments before pushing his hair back off his brow. It's slick with blood, but it doesn't seem to bother him.

But then he averts his gaze from Victor in favor of my dad, and then he turns his eyes on me.

He stares at me like he knows me. Like he knows my secrets.

My brows pinch in confusion. What the hell could he have to say to me?

"You missing something that belongs to you, Mav?"

My chin almost drops, but I quickly remember where I am and the role I should be playing.

He sees it though and he smirks.

"Yeah, you are, aren't you?"

"You're lying." I growl, causing Victor to turn and glare at me.

"Am I?" Kane shakes his head. "I think you might be missing some information when it comes to your pretty little *wife*."

"Oh yeah?" The effort it takes to sound nonchalant is harder than I ever thought possible.

"Victor, why don't you tell him?"

Immediately, my eyes find Victor. If this motherfucker is hiding shit from me then I'll—

"He's talking shit to get out of this," Victor counters, trying to brush Kane's words aside.

"If you want to see her again, I highly suggest you ignore him, Mav."

My lips part to respond, but no words come out. Instead, my heart pounds, and my hands begin to tremble.

He knows something.

Victor knows something and he's been sitting in front of me playing the innocent.

Red-hot fury burns through my veins.

"You're fucking delusional if you think I'm going to let you go because of that whore," Victor snaps, not helping me to keep my lid on my anger.

"Did you know that she's a whore, Mav? That Victor pimps her out to make men do as he so desires?"

No.

No. My wife is not a whore.

She's... she's mine and perfect and everything I—

"Oh, you didn't? So you didn't know that he's had me fucking her for over a year, hoping I'd fall in love with her?"

I swear to God, my entire world falls from beneath me with just those few words.

"You fucking asshole," I bellow before my body takes a life of its own and flies toward Kane. My fist connects with his cheekbone, making his head ricochet off the wall behind him. But it doesn't help. Not even a little bit.

"I'll take that as a no," he mutters like a smug asshole, rubbing his face as hands grip my upper arms, and I'm hauled back by my father.

Silence ripples around the room as I glare at Kane, more than ready to continue what I just started. Meanwhile, Victor stands between us with a smug as fuck smirk on his face.

"I don't give a shit about that slut, so threaten her all you like. It's not going to help your cause," he spits, making me growl like a feral beast.

How can he say that about my wife?

She's my fucking wife. Alana Murray. She's meant to be untouchable.

Wives aren't allowed to be shared without explicit consent from their husbands, and I sure as shit didn't agree to anything.

"You might not care, but he does," Kane says, tipping his chin in my direction. "And I know that you have very, very limited alliances in this world, but Razor and Maverick are two of them."

Unfuckinglikely. I'd rather side with Reid than his cunt of a father.

"There's one other though, isn't there, Victor? The outside world might think that all your sons are equally as important as each other to you, but they're not, are they?"

He takes a warning step forward, but Kane doesn't so much as flinch.

"I guess people might assume that Reid is your favorite. He is your underboss. The one who will continue this legacy because it's his birthright. But he's not the one you've been grooming to be your little bitch, is he? He's not the one who's been going around doing your dirtiest, most evil tasks, is he?"

Victor pales, but I don't give a shit.

Grayson Harris can burn in hell for all I care. He was being groomed to be as corrupt as Victor. As far as I'm concerned, we're all better off without him here.

"You put so much effort into looking like you don't care, but we know the truth, don't we, Victor?"

"You don't know fuck-all about it."

"Don't I?" Kane taunts.

"So I wouldn't know that you've sent men to London to infiltrate the Cirillo family because you think they have your youngest son?" Kane raises a brow as Victor's face begins to turn beet red. Kane's smug as fuck that he knows all this and Victor has no idea. If I weren't so fucking livid over what he just explained about Alana then I might be laughing right along with him.

It's about time that someone took that cunt down a peg or two.

They continue bickering back and forth as my head continues to spin.

Kane has to be lying. He has to be.

I'd know if Alana was being pimped out by Victor. Wouldn't I?

I hang my head as realization hits. This was my fault.

If I were giving her what she needed at home then maybe...

Fuck.

FUCK.

I don't come back to reality until the safety being removed from a gun makes my vision clear.

"Go on shoot me," Kane taunts as Victor aims the gun directly at his head. "But I can assure you that you'll never find him if you do."

"Vic," I plead.

"I don't give a shit about you or your business, Victor. I want to be as far away from you and everything you stand for as possible. I'll keep your fucking secrets, how sick and twisted you are. It'll be like I was never here."

"And Alana and Gray?" Victor asks, as if he's considering his offer.

"In time, I'll make sure they're delivered back to you safely."

"In time?" he asks like it's the most absurd thing he's ever heard.

"Yeah. Forgive me, Victor, but you're an untrustworthy cunt so I won't be handing them over the second you let me walk out of this room. You'll get Alana first, because I actually feel a little sorry for Maverick. He's clearly in love with a woman he shouldn't be for whatever fucked-up reason. Then Gray will follow if, and only if, you keep to your end of the deal and let me get on with my life."

They'll be delivered back to you safely.

I fucking knew she never ran. I knew deep down in my gut that she wouldn't walk away and leave me and all the plans we made.

You'll get Alana first...

Not if I find her before then.

There is no fucking way I'm sitting around waiting for her to be returned to me when I know she's being held against her will somewhere.

It's just not going to fucking happen.

43

REID

My chest heaves as I stare at the two people beneath my feet on the small screen of my cell phone.

They're not doing anything other than sitting on Alana's cot talking, but it doesn't matter. My reaction would be the same if they were fucking again.

She has no idea, but she's sparked something. Something potentially huge that could significantly help us move forward.

But somehow, I still need to hear the words. I need to know that I'm right, no matter how horrific the truth is.

I startle when my front door swings open and soon after slams closed. I put my cell to sleep and pocket it before I get caught being a creep.

JD is downstairs and there are only a handful of people who can get into this house uninvited. Five to be exact.

"Yo, Bro. Where you at?" A voice booms down the hallway, letting me know who it is.

"Kitchen," I shout back before I take a second to school

my features and pull on the mask he'll expect me to be wearing.

Footsteps pad toward me, but they're not Devin's thumping boots, there's another set. And they're lighter.

Not ten seconds later, I get my answer as my eldest little brother emerges with none other than Scarlett Hunter, nervously trailing him.

My eyes widen in shock. It's no secret that Devin doesn't like her very much.

Jealousy at its finest. Devin and Kane have been tight for years, and Scarlett has been right in the middle, causing a rift for most of them.

"Letty, this is a surprise," I say, studying her as she moves close.

"Do you know where he is?" she asks in desperation. She doesn't say his name, but she doesn't need to.

"N-no. Why?"

What the fuck has happened here that I don't know about?

Fuck.

I've been helping Kane over the past few months, so he can finally cut ties with the Hawks and embark on the life he should have at MKU with his girl. But things aren't that fucking easy.

Victor isn't that fucking easy.

She gives me the CliffNotes of what's happened, while Devin bristles beside her.

"I know you know something, so can you fucking spit it out?" Devin spits.

It's no secret that I'm meddling in shit he doesn't want me to be. But it's for all our benefit. I have to believe that.

"No, I can't. You just need to trust me."

"You know, that's getting harder and harder right now. I

know you're the one behind our supply issue. Care to explain that one?"

"No. What's going on is bigger than your fucking supply."

"Well, did you want to tell Victor that because he's been riding our asses? If we don't do what he wants, then he won't initiate us."

"Of course he will. You're his fucking blood."

"You sure about that? He doesn't seem to give a fuck about Gray."

My teeth grind as I glare at him. I get it. That prick is our little brother. But he's better off where he is right now. As far away from Victor as fucking possible.

"Enough, okay. I just need you to trust that I have all our futures—Kane's included—as my first priority right now. So will you just do as I say and shut the fuck up."

"Jesus, who got your panties in a twist? You need to get fucking laid or something, Bro." Letty startles when a feral growl rips from my lips.

"Let's fucking go," I bark unwilling to stand here listening to this any longer when Kane is in trouble. Pushing from the counter, I physically shove Devin in the direction of the front door.

"Where are we going?" Letty asks quietly.

"The clubhouse. If Victor's got him, that's where he'll be."

She freezes the second our location rolls off my tongue. I know why. She's been there before. She knows the kind of shit that goes down.

She also knows that Kane isn't there for a friendly drink with his old boss.

Fuck. This is a fucking mess.

Walking around her, I lower down so I can look right into her eyes.

If she's coming with us, then she needs to get with the fucking program. If she can't, she can stay here and wait.

"Letty, Letty. Scarlett," I repeat, dragging her back to reality. "Everything is going to be okay. I got both of you out of there, almost unharmed," I say, referring to the day both her and her father ended up tied to chairs in one of Victor's cells. "I'll do the same for Kane. Victor just wants to issue his warning, but he won't win. Not against me."

"W-what are you playing at?" she whispers, searching my eyes as if she'll find the answer.

"That's for me to know, Princess."

A sob erupts from her throat at my use of Kane's nickname for her.

"If he's not okay, Reid. I-I don't k-know—"

"He'll be fine. We're one step ahead of that cunt. You have nothing to worry about."

"You're kinda scary, you know that?" she asks as I wrap my arm around her shoulders and guide her toward the door that Devin's already disappeared through.

"I've been told a time or two, yeah." I chuckle.

Devin is already in my passenger seat waiting when we get there. So much for being a fucking gentleman. Not that Letty cares as she jumps into the back.

"What?" he barks when I just glare at him.

"You're a fucking prick, Bro."

"Me?" he asks, pointing at himself.

"Yeah, you."

"Just fucking drive, asshole," he sulks, turning to look out the windshield.

Letty grew up in the Creek, so nothing we pass on the way to the clubhouse is new to her. But that doesn't stop her from staring out the window with wide eyes.

"Don't tell me you miss the place," I tease.

"Not one bit," she mutters before falling silent again.

The second we pull up to the clubhouse and find everyone's cars here, we jump out and march toward the door.

Eyes turn to me before one of our senior members stalks over.

I guess I could call him a friend. We went through school together and did all our initiation shit to become fully-fledged Hawks together. But I don't. Outside of JD, my brothers and Kane, I don't trust anyone. He is an ally though, and when the shit hits the fan, I'm confident he'll be standing behind me. Not Victor.

"They're down at the cells," he says quietly, ensuring no one but me can hear him. "They were dragging Kane into number three a few hours ago."

Clapping him on the shoulder, I jerk my chin in that direction, silently instructing Devin to move.

"Thanks, man. Appreciate it."

"Call me if you need anything."

With a nod of agreement, I take off, stepping beside Letty, so she's protected by both of us.

I'm pretty sure her previous visit here was her first, and I'd imagine she'd hoped that would be her last too.

We just hit the long dark hallway that leads to our cells when the crack of a gunshot rips through the air.

My heart jumps into my throat as Letty whimpers beside me.

Wrapping my arm around her in support, we approach the door Cash told me they were hiding behind. Reaching out, I swing it open before demanding Letty stay where she is and step inside to assess the situation.

My stomach knots when my eyes land on Kane on the floor, blood rushing from a bullet wound in his shoulder.

Unsurprisingly, Letty defies my order and flies into the cell, immediately dropping to her knees beside him.

Turning away from them, I find exactly what I was expecting: Victor fucking Harris watching the scene play out before him with an accomplished smirk playing on his lips. And right beside him, Razor Murray. Also looking like a smug asshole. But what I'm not expecting is to lock eyes with Mav.

He looks like shit, but then I didn't really expect anything else after fucking up his face on Friday night. But it's the darkness in his eyes that makes me question what's really happened here.

"What the fuck is this?" I bark, directing it straight at my father.

It's no secret that my loyalties are with Kane.

"That's between me and Legend."

"Not when he's bleeding out from the bullet you fired," I spit, glancing down at his gun that's hanging limply at his side.

"My soldier, not yours," he taunts, pulling rank over me.

"Let him go. You made your agreement with him, fucking honor it."

His smirk grows before he slowly begins shaking his head patronizingly.

He lifts his disappointed gaze from me when Letty's rough, emotional voice fills the air. "We're going to get you out of here. You're going to be okay."

"Why did you bring that whore here?" Victor's viciousness cuts through the air and before I know what's happening, Letty is on her feet and marching toward him.

"What did you call me?" she barks, proving that despite leaving this place, she's still a Creek girl at heart.

"Letty," I warn. Her going up against Victor is a bad fucking idea.

"A whore. Just like your mother. Tsk," he taunts, looking

at her as if she's nothing but a piece of shit on his shoe. It's nothing new, it's how Victor treats all women. Chauvinistic asshole. "Coming in here and trying to save that cunt. He's just as fucking useless as you."

"Let him fucking go," she screams, flying toward him. I move, but Kane is faster. Fuck knows how. He hauls her back before she does something really fucking stupid.

"Enough, Princess." Kane growls in her ear, forcing her to stand down.

She spins in his arms, desperately trying to keep him up as he sways.

"I'm leaving," Kane informs Victor. "I'll assume you accept my terms and will leave me the fuck alone. You've left your mark." He points to his shoulder. "If you keep up the rest, you'll get what I promised."

My brows pinch as I pretend not to know what his terms were. Of course the reality is that I was the one to give him the terms, should this situation occur.

Kane knows plenty of things that he shouldn't. But right now, there are only a couple of things that could make Victor—or Mav—bend to his wishes.

My chest constricts that he's used Alana as a bargaining chip. It shouldn't matter. She was the one who put herself in the middle of this bullshit.

But it does matter. And not just because of what I suspect she knows. But because of how JD smiles brighter with her in his life. That motherfucker might be a joker and the life of the party, but that is only one side of him. The other... I'd happily never see again. And since Alana, those shadows seem farther away than ever.

Set her free and send her back to a life that's controlled by Victor... back to her husband who clearly loves her but doesn't treat her right and destroy my boy in the process.

Yeah... that's not going to be happening any time soon.

Helping Letty out, I wrap my arm around Kane's waist and take most of his weight as we head for the door.

But unsurprisingly, Victor's cold voice rips through the room as he has the final say.

"You go back on this and you're all fucking dead. All of you."

I know he doesn't mean me. He's threatening Kane and Letty, but still, my blood turns to ice.

Over my dead fucking body, old man.

I take the stairs from the basement two at a time. I'm flying so fucking high after my time with Alana that nothing could bring me down.

Or at least, I think that's the case until I push through the hidden door and come face-to-face with Doc, his white shirt covered in blood.

"JD," he greets as I stand there shell-shocked.

Movement behind him forces me to look over his shoulder and thankfully, I find Reid standing behind him. He's also covered in blood. But at least he's alive.

"Thank you," Reid says when they get to the door.

"Anytime," Doc says before disappearing out the front door.

Reid closes it behind him before resting his forearm against the dark wood and dropping his head to it.

"What's happened?" I ask, my impatience getting the better of me. "Whose blood is that?"

"Kane's," he says after a few seconds before he pushes from the door and turns to face me. "He told Victor that he was done for good. Gave up everything. Victor pulled him in and shot him."

"Victor shot him?" I gasp. I know he's a sick motherfucker, but Kane's been one of his most loyal soldiers over the years.

Shit.

"Shoulder," Reid says simply. "He'll be fine. He's upstairs with Letty and Devin."

"You've left the two of them in the same room?" I ask, aware that they're not the best of friends.

Reid shakes his head.

"Mav was with them," he states. "I think Kane said something about Alana. He looked wrecked."

"Shit. You think he knows?"

"No. Kane would never have done that. But I did tell him that he could use her for leverage if something were to go wrong with this shit with Victor."

"WHAT?" I roar. "Why the fuck would you do that?"

"Because Kane needs everything he can get right now. And really, we have no idea how disposable Alana is to Victor. She could just be another one of his whores or—"

I act before I think, throwing my fist into his stomach.

All the air rushes out of his lungs as he bends over, bracing his hands on his knees.

I swallow nervously as I wait for him to return the blow. But when he lifts his head and his eyes find mine, all I find is my patient, mostly compassionate best friend staring back at me.

He's the only one in the world who really understands me, and it's moments like this I'm reminded of that.

"I won't let anything happen to her," he says, shocking the shit out of me.

"How can you prom—"

"Because I can. Trust me, yeah?"

He holds my eyes, begging for me to do just that.

I've no reason not to. All my life, Reid has been solid and followed through on every promise he's ever made me. He's been there through my darkest moments, and done everything he can to drag me back into the light.

"Yeah. Okay," I agree.

"I need to—" He thumbs over his shoulder. "We'll talk, yeah. I just need to—"

"Go. Go and make sure everyone is okay. The most important thing right now is Kane."

He nods before disappearing up the stairs.

"Fuck," I breathe, threading my fingers through my hair and pulling until it hurts.

I guess it's inevitable that they find out where she is eventually, but we really don't fucking need that happening now.

If Victor finds out that Reid is going against him, then we're all royally fucked.

Voices rumble from upstairs as I make my way to the kitchen to make coffee. Something tells me that everyone is going to need some.

I make mine and Reid's before footsteps get closer.

Glancing over my shoulder, I find a barely-restrained Devin storming toward me.

"You okay, man."

"I fucking told him that she'd be the death of him," he seethes. "He's throwing everything away because of her."

"He loves her, Dev. Always has."

"It's fucking bullshit, that's what it is." He scoffs. "Most of what Victor spits is shit, but the stuff about pussy ruining your life. That's fucking true. We're literally witnessing it."

"You're wrong," I state, resting my ass against the counter.

"Kane's starting a new life. He's got the world at his feet.

There's nothing wrong with having his girl beside him while he does it."

"He just got shot, JD. Because of her."

"No," I argue, refusing to believe this is Letty's fault. "He embarked on all of this long before they got together. He couldn't have known."

"It's always been fucking her. She's always been in the background slowly poisoning him."

"You really have a poor opinion of women, huh? Thank fuck I don't have any sisters."

"Women are fucking great. I love women. I just don't appreciate them trying to fuck with my brothers' lives."

I keep my mouth shut. What else is there to say? Not long ago, I possibly would have agreed with him. But even in my short time with Alana downstairs, I'm starting to understand the other side of the argument.

Finding someone you can't stop thinking about and having them agree to stand by your side, no matter what life throws at you? Yeah... the prospect of that doesn't sound as scary as it has previously.

"Letty wants a coffee," he says, stealing the one I made for Reid for himself. "White, one sugar."

"Aw, look at you trying to make friends," I tease.

All I get in response is a glare.

"How's the new inmate?" he asks, changing the subject as the machine works its magic.

"She's..."

"You fucked her," he blurts.

"The fuck, Dev?"

"Well, that explains a lot."

"The fuck are you talking about?"

Lifting his free hand, he points at my face and circles his finger. "You've got a post-sex high going on. Plus, there are hickeys. Those bad boys give themselves away, while my big brother is walking around like a bear with a pair of sore testicles.

"So you got in there first and he's pissed, huh?"

My lips open and close like a fish. How has he spoken to me for all of ten minutes and have all this figured out.

"Well, it looks good on you, man. Just a shame it's a vindictive, toxic bitch like her who's done it."

Before I get to argue his statement, he's abandoned his empty mug and taken the one I made for Letty.

With the weight of everything that's going on around us right now, I pull the refrigerator open and search for something to make for Alana.

I promised I'd return with food, but I wasn't lying when I told her I couldn't cook, so my options are limited.

I'm still staring aimlessly when footsteps approach again, only this time, it's someone who can help.

"Step away from the fridge, J," Reid instructs. "I don't have the energy to deal with a house fire right now."

"Hey, I'm not that bad," I argue.

He shoots me a look that screams, 'Yes, you are,' but he doesn't say the words.

"Barbecue chicken wings?" he asks.

"Uh... yeah, I guess," I mutter, suddenly aware that I have no idea what she likes or doesn't like. But I figure that after a week down there with mostly rations, she's probably not feeling overly fussy.

"I told Letty that she could talk to Alana."

I pause, my ass hovering over the stool I was about to sit on.

"Seriously?" I ask, finally sitting down.

"Yeah. I think Letty will feel better if she hears the truth from Alana. And it's not like she has anything else to do."

"I can think of a few things."

He shakes his head as he places everything he's going to need to make dinner on the counter.

"You're an asshole."

"And you're—"

"Really?" he spits.

Rolling my eyes, I watch him as he embarks on making his own barbecue sauce to coat the chicken in.

"What are we going to do when Victor figures all this out?"

Reid's shoulders tense, but he doesn't respond right away.

"We need to get our army ready," he finally confesses.

"You ready for that?"

"Could do with a few more weeks."

"That doesn't fill me with hope."

"He won't win, J. I'll make fucking sure of that."

"What can I do?"

"Get her talking. Anything she can give us that can help. Allies, enemies, anything."

"Nothing too hard then," I mutter.

"Tell her about Kane. Be honest. If she cares about him. About you," he says, making my chest constrict, "then she might be more willing to help."

"Don't you think that maybe you need to give her a little honesty too?" I suggest.

"All in good time. I'm not giving intel to anyone until I know I can trust them one hundred percent."

"Fair enough. But promise me something."

He shoots me a look. "Don't hurt her."

His eyes hold mine for long silent seconds before they drop to the floor.

"I can't promise you that."

"**W**hat is on the menu tonight?" Alana asks the second I let myself into her cell, once again, with a tray in my hands.

"Reid's special barbecue chicken wings, sweet potato fries, and coleslaw," I announce happily, lowering the plate to her lap.

"Wow. He really is full of surprises, huh?"

"You've no idea," I mutter, stealing one of her fries despite the fact I've already eaten mine.

"Hey," she complains, swatting my hand.

She eats in silence, savoring every bite, and I can't do anything but watch. She's mesmerizing. Completely and utterly enthralling.

Sensing my attention, she glances over. I've no idea what she can see on my face, but it's enough to clue her in that everything isn't hunky-dory above our heads.

"What's going on?" she asks curiously.

I pause and it doesn't do anything to alleviate her suspicions.

"Victor shot Kane."

"What?" She gasps, shooting up from the cot so fast, I almost don't catch the plate before it crashes to the floor.

She begins pacing back and forth. Every time she moves, I get a nice shot of her body through the gaping armholes of my tank.

Fuck. She's delicious.

"Is he... is he—"

"He's okay. He's upstairs. Been patched up by Doc. It was a clean shoulder wound. Few weeks of rest and he'll be fine."

"Fuck. I know he wants out, but he's been one of Victor's best men and he just shot him."

"He walked away over the weekend. Told Victor to pull all his favors, everything."

"Shit. Why would he do that? College? Football?" she asks with genuine concern.

"Gone. All he's got is Letty."

The second I say her name, Alana pauses and stares at me. "They're okay?"

"Seems that way. She's up there right now being his nurse."

"Fuck, Julian." She gasps, sinking her fingers into her hair and looking up at the ceiling. "I never wanted any of this. I just wanted a simple, happy life. All this gang bullshit, it—"

"I know," I say, getting to my feet and closing in on her.

"He should have let me run. He should have just let me go and none of this would have happened." Tears spill over her lashes, racing down her cheeks.

"What? Who should have let you go where?" I ask, confused.

"M-Mav, he should have just let me run."

Cupping her cheeks, I wipe under her eyes with my thumbs.

"Where were you running, little dove?" I whisper, terrified that I'm going to scare her off from talking.

"Anywhere. I'd have gone anywhere they couldn't find me. I was done. So fucking done with all the pain and the bullshit. They took everything from me. Every fucking thing."

"Who did? Who hurt you, baby?"

I rest my brow against hers and stare into her eyes, pleading with her to tell me her secrets.

Her lips part, ready to say more, but then her eyes widen in horror as she realizes what she just said and she slams the door closed.

"You need to go," she says, stepping back and putting some space between us. "They probably need you more than I do right now."

"No, Dove. They don't," I argue, watching as she crawls onto her bed and curls up in a ball. "I'm exactly where I need to be. Talk to me, please. Let me help."

"You can't. No one can. It's too late. Too late for me, and too late for all the other lives they've ruined."

45

ALANA

I didn't think he was going to leave, but I was determined to hold strong.

I knew that if I looked into his eyes again, then I'd break.

Hearing that Victor raised a gun to Kane shook me. If he could do that to Kane then I've no doubt he'd do the same to any of his men. No matter how close or loyal.

JD tried to get me to talk. Begging me to open up. But I couldn't.

Everything the last few days has been so good. Spending time with him, getting to know him has been everything.

While we're having fun, it's easy to ignore the elephant in the room. But it's harder to when you're staring it right in the eyes.

I shouldn't have said what I did. But the words just spilled from my lips. I regretted them before I even heard them, but it was too late.

The second he admitted defeat and locked me in my cell alone again, I breathed out a sigh of relief before the tears I was holding back erupted, leaving me sobbing. What made it worse was that half of those tears were for the fact I ruined my dinner.

I was so excited to discover what it was going to be. I should have been enjoying it, not once again drowning so deep in my past that I couldn't even think about eating it.

A big part of me expected him to return. To have a second-go at making me talk and to let me spend the night in his strong, protective arms.

But he never came back.

I'm sure there was a reason.

One of his closest friends had just been shot for fuck's sake. But still, I was a selfish, little bitch who craved his attention. I was quickly becoming a JD junkie.

It was hours after he left when I finally returned to my dinner. The fries were cold and soggy, but the chicken was still mouthwatering and I decided I'd risk food poisoning and demolished them all, followed by the chocolate brownie and the massive glass of wine.

I spent the rest of my night with the one companion that's never let me down over the years. My diary.

It occurred to me while I was busy scrawling out my thoughts that the best way for Reid to learn the truth about everything I've been through would be to hand over my collection.

When I ran from home that day, I only took my current one with me. But I'd planned ahead, and I'd hid the rest of them in the old abandoned shed at the bottom of the yard that Dad used to lock me in when I misbehaved.

I had no idea if I'd ever get the chance to get back to them, but I needed to know that I could access them if I did.

My plan was to get as far away as I possibly could and never look back, but I knew it was wishful thinking.

A few weeks after moving in with Mav, he asked me if I needed anything before he went to work one day, and without thinking, I told him about my diaries.

It was a risk. A huge fucking risk, but I figured that Mav wasn't stupid. And thanks to his position as a high-ranking Hawk, he had good intel on when Dad would be gone and a safe time to access my beloved books.

I was a nervous wreck all day as I waited for him to return.

I knew that if he got caught that I'd probably never see him again and that the next person to turn up at this house would be my father to drag me home.

I wouldn't go willingly though. I would fight with everything I had to stop him. I promised myself that.

Thankfully, it wasn't necessary and when the front door opened a few hours later, it was Mav who called for me. I ran full speed to him and found him in the hallway toeing off his shoes with a whole stack of notebooks in his arms.

I cried. Full, whole body wracking sobs at the sight of them. They held every single thing about my life and I knew that one day, they'd be the evidence we'd need to take my dad and his friends down. I had to believe it was possible. What was the point in my life if it wasn't to put a stop to the way they treated me and no doubt many others.

I slam my diary closed the second the lock disengages to my cell. It hasn't passed me by that only one seems to be locked these days. I'm not sure how I feel about it.

I'm safe when I'm locked up down here. Victor, my father, or any of the others can't get to me. But also, the thought of a nice, soft comfortable bed makes me want to cry. A nice hot bubble bath...

I'm expecting a sheepish-looking JD to poke his head around the corner, so when I look up to see the face of a man who seems to have been avoiding me since the incident in the shower, I have to give him a double take.

"So you are still alive," I tease.

"You think anyone out there could take me down? I'm disappointed in you, Pet," he counters.

All it takes is one sentence to tell me that something has changed.

Was it what he discovered when I maimed Jonno and then freaked the fuck out on him? Or what happened with Kane?

Honestly, it could be either. Or even both. But there is definitely a shift in the air.

"I brought you coffee," he says, holding out the mug in his hand.

"Uh..."

"It's not too hot. No poison."

"Thank you," I say, taking it from him as he sits his ass on the other end of my bed, keeping as much space between us as physically possible.

Still disgusted then. Good to know.

Trying to force down the lump that's crawling up my throat and the hurt that's wrapping around me like barbed wire, I take a sip of my coffee.

The rich, creamy goodness floods my mouth and I close my eyes for a beat to savor it.

"It pains me to admit it, but you have very good taste when it comes to food and drink," I confess, without looking at him.

"I'm glad you appreciate it."

"Who taught you to cook?" I ask, risking a personal question.

If it were JD sitting with me, he'd have no problem telling me the truth. But I've no idea how to take this usually terrifying man that I'm discovering all new things about.

"No one," he says quietly.

"You just figured it out by yourself?"

"Pretty much. It was either that or the five of us would have lived on frozen pizza. Or starved."

"Didn't Hannah cook for you?" I ask. I know things were tenuous with the Harris kids and their stepmom growing up, but I wasn't aware she neglected them.

"She burned everything she touched. Assuming she was home or sober enough to do anything."

"Oh."

"Life as Victor Harris's other half isn't a fun one. I can't even blame her for it, really."

"How many women do you think are only in this town because they don't have a choice?" I muse.

"Far more than we could ever predict," he responds sadly. "Anyway," he says, putting a little more excitement into his voice as he stands. "I came down here to let you know that you're going to be having a visitor in fifteen minutes, so I thought I'd give you a chance to freshen up."

"I'm sorry, what?"

He shrugs. "Thought you might want to brush your teeth or shower or something."

With my mug still in my hands, I push from the bed.

"Who are you and what have you done with Reid Harris?"

"You're cute, Pet. I can retract the offer if you prefer."

"No, no. I'll take anything you've got."

Before he can change his mind, I'm out the door and heading toward the bathroom.

I don't need to look back to know he's hot on my trail. His stare burns into my back, making my blood heat.

He stands in the doorway, resting his shoulder against the frame as I brush my teeth.

"Have the two of you always been voyeurs or is this a new hobby, especially for me?" I ask, leaning into the shower to turn it on.

He chuckles but doesn't say anything. He also doesn't show any sign that he's about to move either.

Unfazed by his attention, I turn my back on him and peel JD's tank from my body before shoving his boxers down my legs.

I don't miss the sharp intake of breath from the man behind me, and I'm sure as shit smirking as I step into the shower, knowing he can't look anywhere else but my ass.

"So do you watch porn together or..."

"Pet." He growls as I reach for the shower gel.

"What? It's a serious question."

I glance over my shoulder in time to see him comb his hair back, his eyes raking up my body.

"You could join me, you know. I bet JD would get a kick out of that."

"I'm good. Thanks," he mutters, but from the roughness of his voice, I'm not sure he really means it.

"You know, he helped me out by shaving my legs a few days ago. You could—"

"I'm sure you're more than capable, Pet. Just do what you need to do. You're on the clock."

"Ah, yes. This must be an important visitor if you want me smelling fresh for them."

"I don't give a shit how you smell, Pet."

"I forgot this was for my benefit. Silly me for thinking you were getting something out of it."

With soap bubbles running down my body, I spin around.

Credit where credit's due, his eyes hold mine.

"You have five minutes. If you're not showered and dressed, I'll drag you out wet and naked."

"Oh, you'd love that, wouldn't you?"

"Five minutes," he repeats before disappearing from my sight, although not before his eyes drop to my body.

I finish up with a smile playing on my lips.

Men are so fucking easy. Even the ones who think they're untouchable.

The second I pick up the tank that's been left for me to put on, I notice the difference.

It isn't JD's.

Lifting it to my nose, I suck in a deep breath, allowing my senses to be flooded with nothing but pure Reid.

Before I get caught, I quickly pull it all on, and after brushing my wet hair, I walk out of the bathroom miraculously within my allotted time.

He's waiting for me with a mug in his hands, his ass resting back against the counter.

"I'm impressed," he muses.

"I assume that isn't something you say to many people," I counter, making his brows shoot up.

"You'd be right there. Take a seat."

Following orders, my ass hits the chair a beat before the door at the top of the stairs opens and footsteps float down to us.

Reid hasn't given any names, and despite my irrational fears that he could have invited any of the monsters he spends time with down here. Realistically, I know he hasn't. This place is sacred. He wants it kept secret. So whoever is heading this way is in his inner circle. And I'd put money on exactly who.

Not thirty seconds later, a familiar, albeit pale, face appears in the doorway.

"How are you feeling?" I ask in a rush.

"Like I got shot by the devil," Kane mutters as someone else follows him into the room and tucks herself into his side.

"Scarlett," I greet.

"Umm... hi," she squeaks, too busy looking around Reid's basement with wide, horrified eyes to pay much attention to me.

"Could you both give us a minute?" I ask, unsure as to whether the big man will allow it.

Letty's shocked eyes finally find mine.

"Uh..." Kane hesitates.

"Behave," Reid warns, shocking the shit out of me before he walks over to where Kane and Letty both just emerged. "Come on, bro," he says, gesturing for Kane to go first.

"Is this a good idea?" Kane asks.

Reid mumbles some kind of reply, but it's too quiet to hear.

46

MAVERICK

"Tell me he was fucking lying," I roar the second the door closes and Kane and his little posse have vanished from our sight.

My entire body is vibrating with barely-restrained anger as I glare at Victor.

"Tell me he was fucking lying. Tell me that you haven't been whoring my wife out." Spittle flies from my face, with every word I spew.

But it doesn't matter. None of it does.

Victor fucking Harris doesn't give a shit.

His cocky 'you can't touch me' smirk is firmly in place as he stares back at me, not giving a single fuck that he's broken the one sacred rule we live by.

You don't fucking touch brothers' wives without explicit consent.

I shake my head, a bitter laugh spilling from my lips.

Of course Victor fucking Harris doesn't follow his own rules.

He is the most untrustworthy and corrupt cunt I have ever met.

Why did I ever think marrying her would be enough?

We should have run. We should have said fuck it to revenge and let the residents of this town wipe themselves out.

It's going to happen one way or another.

All Victor cares about is power and money. He couldn't give a shit about the people. About the lives he's meant to be protecting, nurturing, and supporting.

I take a step forward, my fingers curling at my sides, desperate to reach for the gun that's tucked into the back of my slacks and finally do what I've spent almost a decade dreaming about.

"Son," Dad warns, reminding me that he's also in the room.

Fuck. I could have taken them both out at the same time. It would have only left Alana's cunt of a father and I'd have wiped out the three main culprits.

"I'm done," I seethe, my voice barely audible. "I am fucking done. I'm going to find my wife and we are leaving this shithole of a town and we are never looking back."

Victor grins. He fucking grins. It is nothing but pure malice and spite.

"You can try," he taunts. "But I can assure you that you won't get very far. And even if you do, you'll never satisfy her. A whore like Alana needs more than you could ever offer her. But you already know that, don't you? It's why you've never tried."

The roar that rips from my throat doesn't sound like me.

I fly at him, but both Victor and my father see it coming. One moment I'm a heartbeat away from taking him down and the next my body is colliding with the wall, pain shooting through my shoulder as they both laugh like hyenas.

"Try and take us on, boy. I fucking dare you," are Victor's final words before the door slams, leaving me alone to drown in my own misery in a cell designed for our enemies.

———

"**D**id you want me to patch that up for you, seeing as you're missing your nurse?"
JD's words from the morning he came to visit me cycle around and around in my head.

I didn't think anything of it at the time.

Alana was missing, and I was alone with my wounds.

But it wasn't until I was lying in bed last night, replaying the events of the day over and over in my mind, desperately trying to make sense of it all, that those words came back to me.

She always used to call herself my nurse. Even joked about dressing up a time or two, hoping it would hurt me less.

Obviously, I quickly diverted away from that line of conversation. The last thing I fucking needed when she had her hands all over me patching me up was her in a tiny nurse's outfit that left very little to the imagination.

How would JD know that?

Because him and Reid have her. That's fucking how.

The second the idea hits me, it grows legs fast.

That's why JD randomly turned up that day.

He told me that he was following orders and allowed me to believe—weakly—that Victor had sent him.

But that was bullshit.

I was right. Victor didn't give a shit about my well-being after that fight.

Alana did though.

JD was following Alana's orders.

But why?

"Did you know that she's a whore, Mav? That Victor pimps her out to make men do as he so desires?"

No.

I refuse to believe that's the reason she's with them.

Reid and JD don't have issues getting women.

There's something else.

Something bigger.

What if they know?

What if they've discovered the reason I hid her all those years ago, the reason I married her?

No. It can't be that either.

If they knew, they'd want me too.

"FUCK," I bellow, slamming my palms down on the handlebars of my bike as I wait in the undergrowth on the other side of the road to the hidden gates that lead to Reid's manor.

It's no secret that he owns the place. The mystery is how to get in. If you didn't know better, you'd go to the main gates at the front. But those are locked up like Fort Knox.

This place though. This is the spot. It's where I followed Ezra and Ellis to earlier.

I fucking knew he'd call in a favor from them. All it took was a little patience outside their place in Maddison County and I was golden.

They brought two cars here and then left in one. And only a few hours later, my assumptions were correct when Letty drove the other car out with Kane in the passenger seat.

That should have been my cue to enter, but I was too fucking slow.

Now I'm stuck here waiting for someone else to come

visit the asshole who looks down on the rest of us like he's the fucking king of the world so that I can get inside.

The fences are too high. And even if they weren't, I know he's got the place covered with security. The second I even attempt to climb it, I'd trigger some kind of alarm that would have me discovered in seconds.

Night falls, leaving me in darkness. The only good thing is that I'll see headlights and be able to get into position long before a car approaches.

Assuming one ever comes.

She's in there though. I'm sure of it.

I don't care how fucking long it takes. I will get inside, and I will discover the truth.

Watching Alana suffer with her nightmares, her fears over the past five years has left me feeling utterly helpless.

I didn't think it could get any worse.

But this past week... fuck. It's been a whole new kind of hell.

I knew that wherever she was that she'd be suffering her nightmares alone. But to know that she's been there with him.

Fuck.

It's taken me too long to figure this out.

I've been running around town like a headless fucking chicken, trying to sniff out clues, and all the while she's been up here on this hill. Right under my nose.

Keep your friends close and your enemies closer...

That has never been truer.

I should have known.

I should have fucking known.

I've long stopped watching the clock when headlights finally illuminate the deserted track ahead.

My heart jumps into my throat as I hop up from my hiding spot in favor of another right next to the gate.

It's not as hidden. I just need to hope that whoever this is isn't on high alert.

My palms are sweating by the time the car pulls up to the gates.

I recognize it instantly and my concern for what's happening inside that house only quadruples.

Kane has left, so Doc isn't here to check on him. Which means he's here for someone else.

And my gut tells me exactly who that is.

No sooner has he driven through the gates, do I slip in right behind, praying the darkness covers me.

With my heart racing, I lock my eyes on the dark and sinister old manor house ahead and I close in on it.

One way or another, I'm getting my wife back tonight.

I don't care what it takes.

Reaching back, I pull my gun from my pants and undo the safety.

Tonight, I'm taking back what's mine, and together, we're going to vanish. I don't care what kind of carnage I leave in our wake.

This bullshit is done.

It is over.

"**W**ell, that went well," I muse after Kane and Letty left.

Thankfully, she didn't lunge for Alana the second Reid and Kane left the room.

Part of me expected Letty to try and gouge Alana's eyes out for the shit she pulled.

But instead, they actually had a decent, honest, and what Letty probably thought was a private conversation.

In truth, the three of us sat and watched it on the sixty-inch TV in the living room that, thankfully, Reid had put back together after his little temper tantrum the other night.

Neither of us has mentioned it. What's the point in doing so? The issue is more than obvious. He wants her and I got her first.

It must be a real shock for Reid Harris not to come first, but I refuse to feel bad for him.

Yes, there might be plenty of shit in his life, but it wasn't so long ago that all I could see was that he had everything and I had nothing. I might have learned the truth since, but I'll still grab onto any kind of win I can get.

"I'm not sure they'll ever be best friends but yeah. It could have been worse," Reid agrees as he stirs one of his signature dishes.

I swear, in another life, the man could have been a famous chef. He is that fucking good.

The rich spices of his curry fill the air and make my stomach growl.

"I don't think either are in the market for a new BFF anyway. Letty never belonged here, and Alana... I dunno. I don't see her as the kind of woman who has a lot of girlfriends."

"Does she have any friends?" he asks seriously.

My lips part to respond, but I quickly find that I don't have any answers.

"No, I didn't think so. Her sole person in life is Mav, isn't it?"

My heart aches for her. What was her life like before she found herself here if she only has one person in her corner?

"Yeah, I think so. Do you remember when they got married?" I ask, trying to think back.

"Not really."

"One day she didn't exist and the next she was his wife."

"Yeah," he agrees.

"But didn't she leave to go and live with her mom and sister?"

"That was the story," he mutters.

"The story? You mean, you don't believe it?"

"Back then, sure. I didn't have a reason to question it. But now? No, I don't believe a fucking word of it."

No. Neither do I.

My stomach growls loudly as Reid adds something else to his curry and then grabs some plates. Thankfully, he still has enough left after Letty's butter fingers last night that left more than a few shattered plates all over the floor.

"Go and get her," he suddenly says, shocking the shit out of me.

"W-what?" I stutter, barely able to believe what I'm hearing.

"Get her up here, get her out of her comfort zone, and let's see what we can find out."

"You want her to eat with us?"

"Yeah."

I hesitate, not believing him.

It's stupid. Reid never says anything he doesn't mean. If he says he wants her up here, then he wants her up here.

"O-okay. I'll go get her then."

He nods, too focused on his curry to reply.

As I descend the stairs to the basement, a weird mix of excitement, anticipation, and dread swirl about in my stomach.

This could be good. It could be the start of him giving her the freedom she deserves.

Or... or it could be a game.

Reid might hate his father for how manipulative he can be. But the apple hasn't fallen all that far from the tree. When he wants something, he usually gets it. One way or another. Quite often that will involve someone getting hurt or dying.

Just look at Jonno. Reid clearly had a game plan there. Not that Jonno didn't deserve to die. He did. He was the scum of the earth. But still.

I slide the one secure lock on Alana's door back and push the door open.

"Is it your birthday, little dove?" I ask as I step into the room. I find her as I usually do, with her beloved notebook before her, pen in hand.

I've no idea what she writes in it. She could be a master songwriter for all I know. Poems maybe, about a brutal captor and his hot as fuck best friend.

I smirk to myself. Oh yeah. She's totally written about me in there, whatever it is she's doing.

"No, why?"

"Reid would like to extend an invitation for you to join us for dinner."

She stares at me blankly.

"Dove?" I say softly when she doesn't do anything.

Moving closer, I drop to my haunches beside her cot.

"He... he wants me to come up?" she whispers, sounding unsure of herself.

"Yeah. He's made chicken curry."

"Why?" she asks, finally turning to look at me as if she'll read the answers on my face.

"He's softening, Dove. Just make the most of it," I say. Unable to tell her that he wants her out of her comfort zone in the hopes of getting more secrets.

"Bullshit," she snaps, suddenly finding her fire. "Reid Harris doesn't soften for anyone."

"Everyone's got a weak spot," I counter.

"If you're trying to tell me that Reid's weak spot is me, then I know you're lying. My husband, sure. But not Reid."

"Whatever you say," I mutter. Pushing to my feet again, I hold my hand out. "Will you join us?"

It takes her a second but finally, her hand slides into mine, allowing me to pull her to her feet.

"But what will I wear," she mocks.

I glance down at her body, my teeth grinding when I take in Reid's tank hanging from her shoulders.

Possessive motherfucker.

"Aside from the fact this isn't mine," I say, resting my finger on the neck. Slowly, I drag it down until I'm circling her nipple and making her whimper. "I think you look pretty damn perfect."

"I guess I'll just have to take your word for it."

"You will. Hungry?"

"Starving."

Unable to stop myself, I cup her cheek and lower my lips to hers, stealing a quick yet filthy kiss.

My cell buzzes in my pocket and I laugh, forcing her to pull back.

"What's so funny?" she sulks.

Pulling my cell out, I light it up and hold it between us, already predicting what I'm going to find.

"If you needed any more evidence that he's always watching, then there it is."

> Reid: I said bring her up for dinner, not eat her for dinner.

"Now there's an idea. Maybe I should lay you out on the dining table and have you for my main course. What do you think, Boss?" I ask, looking up at the camera. "You wanna share her with me?"

Alana whimpers, letting me know that she'd be totally onboard with that plan.

"Filthy little dove," I tease before my cell buzzes again.

> Reid: Do as you're told, you irritating prick.

"Uh-oh, someone's in trouble."

"Standard. He'd be bored if I toed the line all the time. Come on."

With her hand clasped in mine, I tug her from her cell and toward the stairs.

It's not until we're halfway up, I realize she's trembling.

"Dove," I say, looking back. "Are you scared?"

Her large blue eyes meet mine and it's all the answer I need.

"It's just us and a curry dish. It's not really that scary, is it?"

Whatever thoughts are spinning around her head don't leave her mouth. I want to push her, but I also know that it's probably not the best idea.

I do know what is though.

Moving faster, we emerge through the hidden door, and no sooner have I closed it behind us do I slam her back against it.

"Julian, what are you—"

I claim her lips as I hook her thigh up around my waist.

She melts for me almost instantly. Her body relaxes and her muscles turn to jelly as she kisses me back just as passionately as I do her.

Sliding my hand down her thigh, I palm her ass. Squeezing until she yelps in pain.

"Are you wet for me, little dove?" I murmur into our kiss.

She doesn't answer me. She doesn't need to. The way her hips are desperately grinding against me, searching for more is all I need.

Lifting my hand from the wall beside her head, I slip it between our bodies and straight between her legs.

"Oh shit." I grunt when I find her dripping wet.

Fuck. This girl is everything.

She's fucking terrified, and yet she's horny as fuck.

"Please," she whimpers when I tease her entrance, pushing just the tips of my fingers inside.

"Dirty. Little. Whore," I breathe, ripping my lips from hers and kissing across her jaw. I suck on the sensitive skin beneath her ear at the same time I thrust two fingers deep inside her.

She howls, ensuring that the man of the house is fully aware of what's happening.

Footsteps stomp our way and I smirk against the sweet skin of her throat.

The second his eyes land on us, I'm pretty sure his gasp sucks all the air clean from the room.

"Julian," Alana cries when I rub her G-spot, my thumb finding her clit to really drive her crazy.

"What the fuck are you doing?" Reid booms, making Alana still in my arms. Although, it doesn't escape my notice that she doesn't so much as attempt to push me away.

"Stress relief, Boss," I tease. "Alana was feeling a little apprehensive about this. Want to help?" I offer.

"Dinner's ready," he sulks.

"And we'll be right there. Won't we, Dove?"

"Oh God," she whimpers.

"Look at him," I demand, shifting slightly so she can see over my shoulder. "Open those pretty blue eyes and let Reid see how beautiful you are when you fall."

"JD," he grunts, although he doesn't move.

Stupid fuck. As if he isn't as desperate as she is. If only he were a little less pigheaded about it, he might get the result he craves.

"Come for me, Dove. I want you squeezing down on my fingers while you stare into his eyes. Show him exactly what he's missing."

Her body starts to tremble as her release surges forward.

"She's so fucking wet right now, man," I tell Reid. "So fucking desperate for cock."

"Please, please," she whimpers.

"Later, Dove. After we've eaten, I'll do whatever you want. I'll eat this pussy all fucking night if you tell me to. Fuck you over and over until you're screaming for mercy."

"Please, please," she begs as she gushes all over my hand.

"You love being watched, don't you? You love knowing that Reid is watching, experiencing what a filthy whore you are."

"Oh my God. JULIAN," she screams as she falls.

"Eyes on Reid," I bark when her heavy lids begin to fall closed.

"That's it, Dove," I praise as her body convulses, her pussy trying to suck my fingers deeper. "Such a good girl for us."

I keep working her until she's spent.

He's still watching; I can feel his presence behind me.

"I bet he's so fucking hard for you right now," I murmur in her ear.

She whimpers.

"You want it, don't you? If I asked you to, you'd get on your hands and knees right now and crawl to him, beg him for his cock."

She swallows, but she doesn't give me a verbal answer.

I don't need one. Her juices running down my hand is enough.

"One day, you're going to do it," I tell her.

Her breathing is erratic, her nipples hard against the fabric of her tank and her eyes dilated with desire.

She cries out when I finally pull my fingers from inside her and lift them between us.

"Look at me," I demand, releasing Reid from her stare.

She does as she's told.

"Good girl," I praise, before opening my mouth and sucking on my fingers, letting her sweet taste flood my lips.

"You're missing out, man. She tastes so fucking good." I groan around the digits.

A beat of silence passes. My cock aches, desperate to sink inside her, but I'm pretty sure doing so might just tip him over the edge.

That's an activity for another time. Just like watching her beg for his dick.

Shit. Why does the idea of watching her with him get me so fucking hot?

By the time I release Alana and turn around, he's gone.

Fucking pussy.

Shoving my hand into my sweats, I squeeze my aching dick as I turn my eyes back on Alana.

"Fuck, you look sinful right now, Dove."

Her lips are swollen from my kisses, her neck is red with hickeys, her chest is still heaving, and I know that if I were to rip those boxers from her body that her thighs would be slick.

"Come on," I say, taking her hand and leading her to the bathroom. "Let's do as we're told for once."

Her eyes are everywhere as we move through the house.

"Not what you were expecting?" I ask.

There's no doubting Reid's favorite color when checking out his house, but it's way homier than most people expect.

"I don't know what I was expecting," she confesses as I open the bathroom door and gesture for her to enter.

"Oh wow," she gasps, taking in the black suite.

"In a former life, Reid was a chef and interior designer."

"He's full of surprises, huh?"

"You've no idea, little dove," I say, making a beeline for the sink to wash my hands while she pees. She doesn't even question the fact I'm in the room. And I like that she's that comfortable around me more than I should.

"That smells amazing," she whispers when we finally walk into the large kitchen to find Reid sitting at the table with our dinner already plated up and waiting for us. Somehow I managed to refrain from demanding she sucked my dick while we were alone. It was hard—pun intended—but I managed it. "And this room is incredible."

Ignoring the table, she walks straight over to the wall of floor-to-ceiling windows that showcase the view of the valley in the distance.

"It looks better from up here," she muses.

No one replies, but it's not because we don't agree.

"Come and sit, Pet. It's already cold," Reid sulks.

"Dude, stop pouting," I tease. "It doesn't suit you."

Flipping me off, he spears a piece of chicken with his fork and stuffs it in his mouth.

Pulling the chair out next to mine, Alana drops into it while Reid sits at the head of the table like the king he wants to be.

"Why am I up here?" she blurts before even picking up her fork.

"Thought it might be nice," Reid responds before grabbing his wine and taking a sip.

"Really," she mutters, not believing a word of it.

"I can send you back down to eat this on your lap if you like," he offers.

"No. This is good. Just... surprising."

"Well, enjoy," he says with a smile before following it up with an ominous, "Who knows when it might happen again."

Alana doesn't react to that, instead, she reaches for her

knife and fork and picks up a little sauce-covered rice, lifting it to her lips.

"Oh my God." She moans, making me semi-hard again. "So good."

Reid doesn't say anything, but I don't miss the way his chest puffs out. Arrogant fucker knows he's a good cook but he fucking loves hearing it.

There's no hesitation before her next mouthful. She eats with the gusto of someone who's been locked away from the world for over a week.

Reid's hands drop to the table, his dinner forgotten as he watches her with dark curiosity dancing in his eyes.

I get it. I've probably had the exact same look on my face every time I've taken her down something to eat.

With a smirk, I leave him to it. Devouring my own dinner like I also haven't eaten in a week, instead of only a few hours.

All thoughts of my food are forgotten as my eyes lock on Alana.

I love watching people enjoy my food.

And by people, I mean JD, my brothers, and Kane. That is about as many people as I can cope with.

But watching Alana devour my curry like it's the best thing she's ever put in her mouth is something else.

JD is busy eating too, but I know he's clocked me.

While this whole thing might be a game to put Alana out of her comfort zone to get her talking, I can't help but feel like JD has his own agenda.

Starting with that little show he put on out in the hallway.

I should have fucking known that sending him down there to get her wouldn't have been as simple as it should have.

Abandoning my fork on the side of my plate, I attempt to rearrange myself beneath the table discreetly.

I've been hard as fucking steel since the second I heard her cry out. And then when her eyes locked on mine as JD finger-fucked her into oblivion. Fuck. Me. It was everything.

Although not quite enough for me to take up his offer of helping.

From where I was standing, he certainly didn't need any.

There was a part of me that wanted to pull out my gun and take his fucking head off. But the other, more insistent part, begged me just to watch.

Watching him drive her crazy was something fucking else.

And the moment he threw her over the edge.

Fuck.

I haven't come that close to coming in my pants since I was a fucking preteen.

Fucking pathetic.

I just had to remind myself that this is what she does. It's why Victor made her his whore.

She holds this magical power to reel men in with her sexuality and make them do what she wants.

Or she's just so broken that she doesn't know anything else, a little voice starts up.

"When did you first move in with Maverick?" I ask, needing a distraction from reliving the moment she fell with her eyes locked on mine over and over in my head.

She looks up, her loaded fork lowering as she tries to figure out why I'm asking.

"You disappeared at sixteen from what I remember. Then you suddenly turned up married to Mav at eighteen. How did that happen exactly?"

"Bro, just let her enjoy her dinner," JD says.

Alana swallows nervously as she reaches for her wine.

I can't say that I'm a red wine fan. Nor is JD. So imagine my shock when I found multiple bottles of a certain wine in my cupboard after his little shopping trip the other day.

I assumed that she told him her favorite. But I can't find any evidence of that on the footage from the live stream.

"We were always friends. We reconnected."

"Bullshit," I spit.

"Reid," JD barks, while Alana practically downs her wine, her face growing hot.

"You never left, did you?"

Her eyes lift to mine, and I find nothing but pure fear staring back at me. Her chest heaves as if she can't drag in the air she needs.

Usually, I feed off that fear, use it to fuel me to dig out the information I really want.

So why does that look in her eyes make my chest constrict?

Suddenly, the glass that was in her hand falls, shattering on the tiled floor at her feet, sending red wine splashing everywhere.

"Dove, what's wrong?" JD gasps as Alana reaches up and grips her throat, her face now red and patchy.

"W-what was in th-th-that?" she rasps, staring at the curry.

"Chicken and—"

My words are cut off as her eyes roll back and she collapses, sending her plate and everything in front of her flying as she goes down.

"ALANA," JD cries, but I'm faster.

I have her in my arms in seconds.

Her skin is flushed as she fights to suck in any air, her body trembling violently.

"Prawns," I blurt, already marching toward the couch behind me.

"Call Doc. Call him right now," I bellow.

"It's okay, Pet. It's going to be okay," I say as softly as I can, all the while trying not to panic like fuck.

I'm almost to the couch when she vomits all over both of us.

"We're going to get you help, okay? Doc's coming. He'll know what to do."

"EpiPen," she wheezes out.

JD's panicked voice rings out behind me as he barks at Doc, trying to explain what's happening.

"She needs an EpiPen. Tell him she need—"

"He's got it," JD says, rushing over and stopping right beside us.

"Get her a clean shirt," I bark when he does nothing but stare at her, all the blood drained from his face.

"He said to lay her down on her back, keep her warm. And if... if she stops breathing—"

"She won't," I assure him. "It's going to be fine." It has to be fine.

We need her.

I need her.

And not just to help me take Victor down.

JD's footsteps echo around the silent house as he runs for a clean shirt while Alana continues to fight for breath.

"Fuck," I hiss, sitting her on the edge of the couch and pulling her vomit-covered tank from her body. I drop it to the floor beside me as JD emerges and tugs another over her head.

"You still with us, little dove," he asks, dropping to his knees beside her and gently cupping her jaw.

Ripping my own sodden shirt off, I let it drop on top of hers.

She doesn't move or say anything.

"She breathing?" I whisper.

He holds his hand over her nose and lips, and I swear to

God that my heart fucking stops as he waits to feel something.

"It's shallow. She needs Doc now."

"He'll be here. Why didn't she tell us?" I ask. It's pointless, but I need something to focus on other than what is happening right now.

"Why the fuck would she need to? Maybe you should make up medical questionnaires for future inmates," he snaps.

Alana suddenly sucks in a loud wheezing breath that makes us both freeze.

"I'm right here. It's going to be okay. We've got you, Dove. We've got you, okay?"

When she does nothing, he looks up at me. I fucking hate the broken, panicked look in his eyes.

It fucking kills me.

JD doesn't let anyone get close to him.

But for whatever reason, Alana has slipped in through a couple of tiny cracks in his armor.

He can't lose her. He just fucking can't.

I can't.

"I'm going to let Doc in. Keep talking to her. Keep—"

"Go," he says in a rush, giving me little choice but to run out of the room and down the hallway.

The second I have the front door in my sights, I rush toward it and pull it open.

I've no idea where Doc was before JD called him, but he must have been close because, by some miracle, he's pulling up in front of my house.

He's out in a flash and rushing toward me with his trusty bag in his hand.

He's like a male, medical version of Mary Poppins or some shit with the array of things I've seen him pull out of that bag over the years.

No matter what the medical emergency, he's always prepared.

"She's in the kitchen," I say, the second he's close enough to hear me.

He rushes past me and I swing the door closed, taking off behind him.

It's not until I get to the kitchen doorway it occurs to me that I should have warned him who it is.

He gives the pale, ghostly still woman on the couch a double take before he lowers his bag to the floor and flips the top open.

"She's barely breathing, Doc," JD says.

"I've got just the thing. Give us some space, please?"

Reluctantly, JD stands and comes to stand beside me as Doc administers the EpiPen.

"She's going to be okay," I whisper, watching Doc's every move as he checks her over.

I swear time stands still, but eventually, her breathing begins to get easier and thankfully, a little bit of color comes back to her cheeks.

"Thank fuck for that," JD mutters.

Neither of us says anymore as Doc continues to work. My cell buzzes in my pocket, but I don't give a shit about anyone who wants me right now.

No one is as important as the woman on my couch.

Once Doc's happy with her condition, he turns to face us both.

"Alana Murray?" he asks, his brows lifted in curiosity.

It's no secret she's missing. Maverick running all over town looking for her has ensured that anyone who cares to listen knows she's vanished.

"Don't know what you're talking about, Doc," I say innocently.

He shakes his head at me.

I'm not worried about him knowing. I'm pretty sure there isn't a more trustworthy man in this town than Doc. He might be under Victor's control like everyone else, but there is no love lost between them.

"It's been a while since I treated this one," he says cryptically. "The obvious aside, it's a relief to see her safe. I always worried about her."

ALANA

Voices float around me, but I can't get a grasp on who is talking or what is going on.

I'm floating. Soaring high.

I've no idea how I got here. But it's nice.

And I'm not alone. That's the best bit.

Or is it?

What if it's them?

My heart begins to race, my breathing increasing as I picture them.

Have they come for me?

Is that why everything is dark?

I thought I was safe in Reid's basement.

But it was all a trick. He was just holding me. Biding his time before handing me back over to those sick monsters.

I won't survive them this time. I barely did the last time.

Tears burn my eyes as I fight to keep control.

My breathing is erratic, the breaths I'm taking aren't going to my lungs. Nothing is working.

If I can't even breathe, how am I going to be able to fight them off?

You're not.

This time, they are going to kill you.

"No," I scream, and everything only gets worse a few seconds later when hot hands land on my arm. "Get off me. No. Please. Don't touch me."

"Little dove, it's just me. It's okay. You're okay."

That voice. I know that voice.

A hot, firm hand holds mine.

"Reid and I won't let anything happen to you, okay. You're safe."

"JD?" I blurt, something familiar triggering in my head.

"I'm right here. Are you allergic to seafood, baby?" he asks.

Seafood.

Am I...

"There were prawns in the curry," another deep voice says before the heat of a second body burns my side. "I didn't know, Pet. If I did then—"

"What the fuck is going on?" JD barks.

It takes everything I have, but I manage to crack my eyes open, just enough to see him pull his cell from his pocket.

I have no idea where I am. Nothing about my surroundings is familiar. But he's here. So is Reid.

I'm safe. I'm—

"Security breach," he says, a little calmer than he probably should.

"Shit," Reid hisses.

No sooner have they said those words there's a crash somewhere in the distance.

The warmth of Reid's body is gone in a flash and I watch as he pulls his gun from the back of his pants. Aiming it right at the door.

I'm still dreaming, right?

This isn't real.

None of this is—

"Mav," I cry, seeing him like a vision in the doorway.

His eyes find me for the briefest of seconds and everything in my world slots into place.

He's here. He came for me. He found me.

Only, it isn't a dream because he's also holding a gun and he has it pointed right at Reid.

"No, please. Don't do this. Don't—"

Bang.

"NOOOOOO," I scream, but before I get to discover what just happened, the darkness flicking in my vision takes hold and I fall down and down in the pits of darkness, where only the worst monsters live.

"Please, no. Someone help me."

Want to find out what happens next? One-Click your copy of **Relentless**, book #2 in the Harrow Creek Hawks series.

THE REVENGE YOU SEEK
SNEAK PEEK

Chapter One

Letty

I sit on my bed, staring down at the fabric in my hands.

This wasn't how it was supposed to happen.

This wasn't part of my plan.

I let out a sigh, squeezing my eyes tight, willing the tears away.

I've cried enough. I thought I'd have run out by now.

A commotion on the other side of the door has me looking up in a panic, but just like yesterday, no one comes knocking.

I think I proved that I don't want to hang with my new roommates the first time someone knocked and asked if I wanted to go for breakfast with them.

I don't.

I don't even want to be here.

I just want to hide.

And that thought makes it all a million times worse.

I'm not a hider. I'm a fighter. I'm a fucking Hunter.

But this is what I've been reduced to.

This pathetic, weak mess.

And all because of *him*.

He shouldn't have this power over me. But even now, he does.

The dorm falls silent once again, and I pray that they've all headed off for their first class of the semester so I can slip out unnoticed.

I know it's ridiculous. I know I should just go out there with my head held high and dig up the confidence I know I do possess.

But I can't.

I figure that I'll just get through today—my first day—and everything will be alright.

I can somewhat pick up where I left off, almost as if the last eighteen months never happened.

Wishful thinking.

I glance down at the hoodie in my hands once more.

Mom bought them for Zayn, my younger brother, and me.

The navy fabric is soft between my fingers, but the text staring back at me doesn't feel right.

Maddison Kings University.

A knot twists my stomach and I swear my whole body sags with my new reality.

I was at my dream school. I beat the odds and I got into Columbia. And everything was good. No, everything was fucking fantastic.

Until it wasn't.

Now here I am. Sitting in a dorm at what was always my backup plan school having to start over.

Throwing the hoodie onto my bed, I angrily push to my feet.

I'm fed up with myself.

I should be better than this, stronger than this.

But I'm just... I'm broken.

And as much as I want to see the positives in this situation. I'm struggling.

Shoving my feet into my Vans, I swing my purse over my shoulder and scoop up the couple of books on my desk for the two classes I have today.

My heart drops when I step out into the communal kitchen and find a slim blonde-haired girl hunched over a mug and a textbook.

The scent of coffee fills my nose and my mouth waters.

My shoes squeak against the floor and she immediately looks up.

"Sorry, I didn't mean to disrupt you."

"Are you kidding?" she says excitedly, her southern accent making a smile twitch at my lips.

Her smile lights up her pretty face and for some reason, something settles inside me.

I knew hiding was wrong. It's just been my coping method for... quite a while.

"We wondered when our new roommate was going to show her face. The guys have been having bets on you being an alien or something."

A laugh falls from my lips. "No, no alien. Just..." I sigh, not really knowing what to say.

"You transferred in, right? From Columbia?"

"Ugh... yeah. How'd you know—"

"Girl, I know everything." She winks at me, but it doesn't make me feel any better. "West and Brax are on the team, they spent the summer with your brother."

A rush of air passes my lips in relief. Although I'm not

overly thrilled that my brother has been gossiping about me.

"So, what classes do you have today?" she asks when I stand there gaping at her.

"Umm... American lit and psychology."

"I've got psych later too. Professor Collins?"

"Uh..." I drag my schedule from my purse and stare down at it. "Y-yes."

"Awesome. We can sit together."

"S-sure," I stutter, sounding unsure, but the smile I give her is totally genuine. "I'm Letty, by the way." Although I'm pretty sure she already knows that.

"Ella."

"Okay, I'll... uh... see you later."

"Sure. Have a great morning."

She smiles at me and I wonder why I was so scared to come out and meet my new roommates.

I'd wanted Mom to organize an apartment for me so that I could be alone, but—probably wisely—she refused. She knew that I'd use it to hide in and the point of me restarting college is to try to put everything behind me and start fresh.

After swiping an apple from the bowl in the middle of the table, I hug my books tighter to my chest and head out, ready to embark on my new life.

The morning sun burns my eyes and the scent of freshly cut grass fills my nose as I step out of our building. The summer heat hits my skin, and it makes everything feel that little bit better.

So what if I'm starting over. I managed to transfer the credits I earned from Columbia, and MKU is a good school. I'll still get a good degree and be able to make something of my life.

Things could be worse.

It could be this time last year...

I shake the thought from my head and force my feet to keep moving.

I pass students meeting up with their friends for the start of the new semester as they excitedly tell them all about their summers and the incredible things they did, or they compare schedules.

My lungs grow tight as I drag in the air I need. I think of the friends I left behind in Columbia. We didn't have all that much time together, but we'd bonded before my life imploded on me.

Glancing around, I find myself searching for familiar faces. I know there are plenty of people here who know me. A couple of my closest friends came here after high school.

Mom tried to convince me to reach out over the summer, but my anxiety kept me from doing so. I don't want anyone to look at me like I'm a failure. That I got into one of the best schools in the country, fucked it up and ended up crawling back to Rosewood. I'm not sure what's worse, them assuming I couldn't cope or the truth.

Focusing on where I'm going, I put my head down and ignore the excited chatter around me as I head for the coffee shop, desperately in need of my daily fix before I even consider walking into a lecture.

I find the Westerfield Building where my first class of the day is and thank the girl who holds the heavy door open for me before following her toward the elevator.

"Holy fucking shit," a voice booms as I turn the corner, following the signs to the room on my schedule.

Before I know what's happening, my coffee is falling from my hand and my feet are leaving the floor.

"What the—" The second I get a look at the guy standing behind the one who has me in his arms, I know exactly who I've just walked into.

Forgetting about the coffee that's now a puddle on the floor, I release my books and wrap my arms around my old friend.

His familiar woodsy scent flows through me, and suddenly, I feel like me again. Like the past two years haven't existed.

"What the hell are you doing here?" Luca asks, a huge smile on his face when he pulls back and studies me.

His brows draw together when he runs his eyes down my body, and I know why. I've been working on it over the summer, but I know I'm still way skinnier than I ever have been in my life.

"I transferred," I admit, forcing the words out past the lump in my throat.

His smile widens more before he pulls me into his body again.

"It's so good to see you."

I relax into his hold, squeezing him tight, absorbing his strength. And that's one thing that Luca Dunn has in spades. He's a rock, always has been and I didn't realize how much I needed that right now.

Mom was right. I should have reached out.

"You too," I whisper honestly, trying to keep the tears at bay that are threatening just from seeing him—them.

"Hey, it's good to see you," Leon says, slightly more subdued than his twin brother as he hands me my discarded books.

"Thank you."

I look between the two of them, noticing all the things that have changed since I last saw them in person. I keep up with them on Instagram and TikTok, sure, but nothing is quite like standing before the two of them.

Both of them are bigger than I ever remember, showing just how hard their coach is working them now they're both first string for the Panthers. And if it's possible, they're both hotter than they were in high school, which is really saying something because they'd turn even the most confident of girls into quivering wrecks with one look back then. I can only imagine the kind of rep they have around here.

The sound of a door opening behind us and the shuffling of feet cuts off our little reunion.

"You in Professor Whitman's American lit class?" Luca asks, his eyes dropping from mine to the book in my hands.

"Yeah. Are you?"

"We are. Walk you to class?" A smirk appears on his lips that I remember all too well. A flutter of the butterflies he used to give me threaten to take flight as he watches me intently.

Luca was one of my best friends in high school, and I spent almost all our time together with the biggest crush on him. It seems that maybe the teenage girl inside me still thinks that he could be it for me.

"I'd love you to."

"Come on then, Princess," Leon says and my entire body jolts at hearing that pet name for me. He's never called me that before and I really hope he's not about to start now.

Clearly not noticing my reaction, he once again takes my books from me and threads his arm through mine as the pair of them lead me into the lecture hall.

I glance at both of them, a smile pulling at my lips and hope building inside me.

Maybe this was where I was meant to be this whole time.

Maybe Columbia and I were never meant to be.

More than a few heads turn our way as we climb the stairs to find some free seats. Mostly it's the females in the huge space and I can't help but inwardly laugh at their reaction.

I get it.

The Dunn twins are two of the Kings around here and I'm currently sandwiched between them. It's a place that nearly every female in this college, hell, this state, would kill to be in.

"Dude, shift the fuck over," Luca barks at another guy when he pulls to a stop a few rows from the back.

The guy who's got dark hair and even darker eyes immediately picks up his bag, books, and pen and moves over a space.

"This is Colt," Luca explains, nodding to the guy who's studying me with interest.

"Hey," I squeak, feeling a little intimidated.

"Hey." His low, deep voice licks over me. "Ow, what the fuck, man?" he barks, rubbing at the back of his head where Luca just slapped him.

"Letty's off-limits. Get your fucking eyes off her."

"Dude, I was just saying hi."

"Yeah, and we all know what that usually leads to," Leon growls behind me.

The three of us take our seats and just about manage to pull our books out before our professor begins explaining the syllabus for the semester.

"Sorry about the coffee," Luca whispers after a few minutes. "Here." He places a bottle of water on my desk. "I know it's not exactly a replacement, but it's the best I can do."

The reminder of the mess I left out in the hallway hits me.

"I should go and—"

"Chill," he says, placing his hand on my thigh. His touch instantly relaxes me as much as it sends a shock through my body. "I'll get you a replacement after class. Might even treat you to a cupcake."

I smile up at him, swooning at the fact he remembers my favorite treat.

Why did I ever think coming here was a bad idea?

Chapter Two
Letty

My hand aches by the time Professor Whitman finishes talking. It feels like a lifetime ago that I spent this long taking notes.

"You okay?" Luca asks me with a laugh as I stretch out my fingers.

"Yeah, it's been a while."

"I'm sure these boys can assist you with that, beautiful," bursts from Colt's lips, earning him another slap to the head.

"Ignore him. He's been hit in the head with a ball one too many times," Leon says from beside me but I'm too enthralled with the way Luca is looking at me right now to reply.

Our friendship wasn't a conventional one back in high school. He was the star quarterback, and I wasn't a cheerleader or ever really that sporty. But we were paired up as lab partners during my first week at Rosewood High and we kinda never separated.

I watched as he took the team to new heights, as he met with college scouts, I even went to a few places with him so he didn't have to go alone.

He was the one who allowed me to cry on his shoulder as I struggled to come to terms with the loss of another who left a huge hole in my heart and he never, not once, overstepped the mark while I clung to him and soaked up his support.

I was also there while he hooked up with every member of the cheer squad along with any other girl who looked at him just so. Each one stung a little more than the last as my poor teenage heart was getting battered left, right, and center.

With each day, week, month that passed, I craved him more but he never, not once, looked at me that way.

I was even his prom date, yet he ended up spending the night with someone else.

It hurt, of course it did. But it wasn't his fault and I refuse to hold it against him.

Maybe I should have told him. Been honest with him about my feelings and what I wanted. But I was so terrified I'd lose my best friend that I never confessed, and I took that secret all the way to Columbia with me.

As I stare at him now, those familiar butterflies still set flight in my belly, but they're not as strong as I remember. I'm not sure if that's because my feelings for him have lessened over time, or if I'm just so numb and broken right now that I don't feel anything but pain.

It really could go either way.

I smile at him, so grateful to have run into him this morning.

He always knew when I needed him and even without knowing of my presence here, there he was like some guardian fucking angel.

If guardian angels had sexy dark bed hair, mesmerizing green eyes and a body built for sin then yeah, that's what he is.

I laugh to myself, yeah, maybe that irritating crush has gone nowhere.

"What have you got next?" Leon asks, dragging my attention away from his twin.

Leon has always been the quieter, broodier one of the duo. He's as devastatingly handsome and as popular with the female population but he doesn't wear his heart on his sleeve like Luca. Leon takes a little time to warm to people, to let them in. It was hard work getting there, but I soon realized that once he dropped his walls a little for me, it was hella worth it.

He's more serious, more contemplative, he's deeper. I always suspected that there was a reason they were so different. I know twins don't have to be the same and like the same things, but there was always something niggling at me that there was a very good reason that Leon closed himself down. From listening to their mom talk over the years, they were so identical in their mannerisms, likes, and dislikes when they were growing up, that it seems hard to believe they became so different.

"Psychology but not for an hour. I'm—"

"I'm taking her for coffee," Luca butts in. A flicker of anger passes through Leon's eyes but it's gone so fast that I begin to wonder if I imagined it.

"I could use another coffee before econ," Leon chips in.

"Great. Let's go," Luca forces out through clenched teeth.

He wanted me alone. Interesting.

The reason I never told him about my mega crush is the fact he friend-zoned me in our first few weeks of friendship by telling me how refreshing it was to have a girl wanting to be his friend and not using it as a ploy to get more.

We were only sophomores at the time but even then, Luca was up to all sorts and the girls around us were all more than willing to bend to his needs.

From that moment on, I couldn't tell him how I really

felt. It was bad enough I even felt it when he thought our friendship was just that.

I smile at both of them, hoping to shatter the sudden tension between the twins.

"Be careful with these two," Colt announces from behind us as we make our way out of the lecture hall with all the others. "The stories I've heard."

"Colt," Luca warns, turning to face him and walking backward for a few steps.

"Don't worry," I shoot over my shoulder. "I know how to handle the Dunn twins." I wink at him as he howls with laughter.

"You two are in so much trouble," he muses as he turns left out of the room and we go right.

Leon takes my books from me once more and Luca threads his fingers through mine. I still for a beat. While the move isn't unusual, Luca has always been very affectionate. It only takes a second for his warmth to race up my arm and to settle the last bit of unease that's still knotting my stomach.

"Two Americanos and a skinny vanilla latte with an extra shot. Three cupcakes with the sprinkles on top."

I swoon at the fact Luca remembers my order. "How'd you—"

He turns to me, his wide smile and the sparkle in his eyes making my words trail off. The familiarity of his face, the feeling of comfort and safety he brings me causes a lump to form in my throat.

"I didn't forget anything about my best girl." He throws his arm around my shoulder and pulls me close.

Burying my nose in his hard chest, I breathe him in. His woodsy scent mixes with his laundry detergent and it settles me in a way I didn't know I needed.

Leon's stare burns into my back as I snuggle with his

brother and I force myself to pull away so he doesn't feel like the third wheel.

"Dunn," the server calls, and Leon rushes ahead to grab our order while Luca leads me to a booth at the back of the coffee shop.

As we walk past each table, I become more and more aware of the attention on the twins. I know their reps, they've had their football god status since before I moved to Rosewood and met them in high school, but I had forgotten just how hero-worshiped they were, and this right now is off the charts.

Girls openly stare, their eyes shamelessly dropping down the guys' bodies as they mentally strip them naked. Guys jealousy shines through their expressions, especially those who are here with their girlfriends who are now paying them zero attention. Then there are the girls whose attention is firmly on me. I can almost read their thoughts—hell, I heard enough of them back in high school.

What do they see in her?

She's not even that pretty.

They're too good for her.

The only difference here from high school is that no one knows I'm just trailer park trash seeing as I moved from the hellhole that is Harrow Creek before meeting the boys.

Tipping my chin up, I straighten my spine and plaster on as much confidence as I can find.

They can all think what they like about me, they can come up with whatever bitchy comments they want. It's no skin off my back.

"Good to see you've lost your appeal," I mutter, dropping into the bench opposite both of them and wrapping my hands around my warm mug when Leon passes it over.

"We walk around practically unnoticed," Luca deadpans.

"You thought high school was bad," Leon mutters, he was always the one who hated the attention whereas Luca used it to his advantage to get whatever he wanted. "It was nothing."

"So I see. So, how's things? Catch me up on everything," I say, needing to dive into their celebrity status lifestyles rather than thinking about my train wreck of a life.

"Really?" Luca asks, raising a brow and causing my stomach to drop into my feet. "I think the bigger question is how come you're here and why we had no idea about it?"

Releasing my mug, I wrap my arms around myself and drop my eyes to the table.

"T-things just didn't work out at Columbia," I mutter, really not wanting to talk about it.

"The last time we talked, you said it was everything you expected it to be and more. What happened?"

Kane fucking Legend happened.

I shake that thought from my head like I do every time he pops up.

He's had his time ruining my life. It's over.

"I just..." I sigh. "I lost my way a bit, ended up dropping out and finally had to fess up and come clean to Mom."

Leon laughs sadly. "I bet that went down well."

The Dunn twins are well aware of what it's like to live with a pushy parent. One of the things that bonded the three of us over the years.

"Like a lead balloon. Even worse because I dropped out months before I finally showed my face."

"Why hide?" Leon's brows draw together as Luca stares at me with concern darkening his eyes.

"I had some health issues. It's nothing."

"Shit, are you okay?"

Fucking hell, Letty. Stop making this worse for yourself.

"Yeah, yeah. Everything is good. Honestly. I'm here and I'm ready to start over and make the best of it."

They both smile at me, and I reach for my coffee once more, bringing the mug to my lips and taking a sip.

"Enough about me, tell me all about the lives of two of the hottest Kings of Maddison."

"**O**kay... how'd you do that?" Ella whispers after both Luca and Leon walk me to my psych class after our coffee break.

"Do what?" I ask, following her into the room and finding ourselves seats about halfway back.

"It's your first day and the Dunn twins just walked you to class. You got a diamond-encrusted vag or something?"

I snort a laugh as a few others pause on their way to their seats at her words.

"Shush," I chastise.

"Girl, if it's true, you know all these guys need to know about it."

I pull out my books and a couple of pens as Professor Collins sets up at the front before turning to her.

"No, I don't have diamonds anywhere but my necklace. I've been friends with them for years."

"Girl, I knew there was a reason we should be friends." She winks at me. "I've been trying to get West and Brax to hook me up but they're useless."

"You want to be friends so I can set you up with one of the Dunns?"

"Or both." She shrugs, her face deadly serious before she leans in. "I've heard that they tag team sometimes. Can you imagine? Both of their undivided attention." She fans herself as she obviously pictures herself in the middle of a Dunn sandwich. "Oh and, I think you're pretty cool too."

"Of course you do." I laugh.

It's weird, I might have only met her very briefly this morning but that was enough.

"We're all going out for dinner tonight to welcome you to the dorm. The others are dying to meet you." She smiles at me, proving that there's no bitterness behind her words.

"I'm sorry for ignoring you all."

"Girl, don't sweat it. We got ya back, don't worry."

"Thank you," I mouth as the professor demands everyone's attention to begin the class.

The time flies as I scribble my notes down as fast as I can, my hand aching all over again and before I know it, he's finished explaining our first assignment and bringing his class to a close.

"Jesus, this semester is going to be hard," Ella muses as we both pack up.

"At least we've got each other."

"I like the way you think. You done for the day?"

"Yep, I'm gonna head to the store, grab some supplies then get started on this assignment, I think."

"I've got a couple of hours. You want company?"

After dumping our stuff in our rooms, Ella takes me to her favorite store, and I stock up on everything I'm going to need before we head back so she can go to class.

I make myself some lunch before being brave and setting up my laptop at the kitchen table to get started on my assignments. My time for hiding is over, it's time to get back to life and once again become a fully immersed college student.

"Holy shit, she is alive. I thought Zayn was lying about his beautiful older sister," a deep rumbling voice says, dragging me from my research a few hours later.

I spin and look at the two guys who have joined me.

"Zayn would never have called me beautiful," I say as a greeting.

"That's true. I think his actual words were: messy, pain in the ass, and my personal favorite, I'm glad I don't have to live with her again," he says, mimicking my brother's voice.

"Now that is more like it. Hey, I'm Letty. Sorry about—"

"You're all good. We're just glad you emerged. I'm West, this ugly motherfucker is Braxton—"

"Brax, please," he begs. "Only my mother calls me by my full name and you are way too hot to be her."

My cheeks heat as he runs his eyes over my curves.

"T-thanks, I think."

"Ignore him. He hasn't gotten laid for weeeeks."

"Okay, do we really need to go there right now?"

"Always, bro. Our girl here needs to know you get pissy when you don't get the pussy."

I laugh at their easy banter, closing down my laptop and resting forward on my elbows as they move toward the fridge.

"Ella says we're going out," Brax says, pulling out two bottles of water and throwing one to West.

"Apparently so."

"She'll be here in a bit. Violet and Micah too. They were all in the same class."

"So," West says, sliding into the chair next to me. "What do we need to know that your brother hasn't already told us about you?"

My heart races at all the things that not even my brother would share about my life before I drag my thoughts away from my past.

"Uhhh..."

"How about the Dunns love her," Ella announces as she

appears in the doorway flanked by two others. Violet and Micah, I assume.

"Um... how didn't we know this?" Brax asks.

"Because you're not cool enough to spend any time with them, asshole," Violet barks, walking around Ella. "Ignore these assholes, they think they're something special because they're on the team but what they don't tell you is that they have no chance of making first string or talking to the likes of the Dunns."

"Vi, girl. That stings," West says, holding his hand over his heart.

"Yeah, get over it. Truth hurts." She smiles up at him as he pulls her into his chest and kisses the top of her head.

"Whatever, Titch."

"Right, well. Are we ready to go? I need tacos like... yesterday."

"Yes. Let's go."

"You've never had tacos like these, Letty. You are in for a world of pleasure," Brax says excitedly.

"More than she would be if she were in your bed, that's for sure," West deadpans.

"Lies and we all know it."

"Whatever." Violet pushes him toward the door.

"Hey, I'm Micah," the third guy says when I catch up to him.

"Hey, Letty."

"You need a sensible conversation, I'm your boy."

"Good to know."

Micah and I trail behind the others and with each step I take, my smile gets wider.

Things really are going to be okay.

DOWNLOAD NOW TO KEEP READING

ABOUT THE AUTHOR

Tracy Lorraine is a *USA Today* and *Wall Street Journal* bestselling new adult and contemporary romance author. Tracy has recently turned thirty and lives in a cute Cotswold village in England with her husband, baby girl and lovable but slightly crazy dog. Having always been a bookaholic with her head stuck in her Kindle, Tracy decided to try her hand at a story idea she dreamt up and hasn't looked back since.

Be the first to find out about new releases and offers. Sign up to my newsletter here.

If you want to know what I'm up to and see teasers and snippets of what I'm working on, then you need to be in my Facebook group. Join Tracy's Angels here.

Keep up to date with Tracy's books at
www.tracylorraine.com

ALSO BY TRACY LORRAINE

Falling Series

Falling for Ryan: Part One #1

Falling for Ryan: Part Two #2

Falling for Jax #3

Falling for Daniel (A Falling Series Novella)

Falling for Ruben #4

Falling for Fin #5

Falling for Lucas #6

Falling for Caleb #7

Falling for Declan #8

Falling For Liam #9

Forbidden Series

Falling for the Forbidden #1

Losing the Forbidden #2

Fighting for the Forbidden #3

Craving Redemption #4

Demanding Redemption #5

Avoiding Temptation #6

Chasing Temptation #7

Rebel Ink Series

Hate You #1

Trick You #2

Defy You #3

Play You #4

Inked (A Rebel Ink/Driven Crossover)

Rosewood High Series

Thorn #1

Paine #2

Savage #3

Fierce #4

Hunter #5

Faze (#6 Prequel)

Fury #6

Legend #7

Maddison Kings University Series

TMYM: Prequel

TRYS #1

TDYW #2

TBYS #3

TVYC #4

TDYD #5

TDYR #6

TRYD #7

Knight's Ridge Empire Series

Wicked Summer Knight: Prequel (Stella & Seb)

Wicked Knight #1 (Stella & Seb)

Wicked Princess #2 (Stella & Seb)

Wicked Empire #3 (Stella & Seb)

Deviant Knight #4 (Emmie & Theo)

Deviant Princess #5 (Emmie & Theo

Deviant Reign #6 (Emmie & Theo)

One Reckless Knight (Jodie & Toby)

Reckless Knight #7 (Jodie & Toby)

Reckless Princess #8 (Jodie & Toby)

Reckless Dynasty #9 (Jodie & Toby)

Dark Halloween Knight (Calli & Batman)

Dark Knight #10 (Calli & Batman)

Dark Princess #11 (Calli & Batman)

Dark Legacy #12 (Calli & Batman)

Corrupt Valentine Knight (Nico & Siren)

Corrupt Knight #13 (Nico & Siren)

Corrupt Princess #14 (Nico & Siren)

Corrupt Union #15 (Nico & Siren)

Sinful Wild Knight (Alex & Vixen)

Sinful Stolen Knight: Prequel (Alex & Vixen)

Sinful Knight #16 (Alex & Vixen)

Sinful Princess #17 (Alex & Vixen)

Sinful Kingdom #18 (Alex & Vixen)

Knight's Ridge Destiny: Epilogue

Harrow Creek Hawks Series

Merciless #1

Relentless #2

Ruined Series

Ruined Plans #1

Ruined by Lies #2

Ruined Promises #3

Never Forget Series

Never Forget Him #1

Never Forget Us #2

Everywhere & Nowhere #3

Chasing Series

Chasing Logan

The Cocktail Girls

His Manhattan

Her Kensington

Made in the USA
Middletown, DE
03 August 2024

58431391R00272